Praise for *Training in Charity*

"Through this gripping, often humorous narrative the progression of professional and social maturity of medical students experiencing their first exposure to actual patients is shared with readers. Those with or without medical backgrounds will enjoy watching the story unfold against the backdrop of one of the most legendary of public hospitals."

—Alex Doolas, M.D., Emeritus Steven Economou Professor of Surgery, Rush University School of Medicine

"Readers of *Training in Charity* will be quickly swept up in the whirlwind of young doctors in training in the 1970s: an organized chaos of fascinating characters—medical students and residents in training caring for patients and doing rounds under the guidance of demanding professors in a New Orleans hospital famous for serving patients from all walks of life. In this novel reminiscent of *The Paper Chase*, readers will experience an insider's view of the life and education of the young protagonist, Adam Sinclair, as he navigates a world of medicine largely unseen to most. This story goes down like a cold Dixie beer served with a delicious Creole gumbo, transporting us into another world with a ringside seat to a pivotal stage in students' medical education. This well-paced tale will make you laugh at times and also bring you to tears. When you finish, you'll want to get a pair of bandage scissors and go on rounds with Dr. Sinclair."

—William Anthony, author of *Farnsy*

"Writing through the eyes of medical students on a surgical rotation at the famous Charity Hospital in New Orleans, the author allows us to see first-hand how life-saving judgments are made on complex cases. It gives insight into both how difficult managing critically ill surgical patients is as well as understanding how students and residents learn under fire. It offers historical perspective from an older era. Students aren't creating notes on computers and surgeons aren't using robots to perform surgery. This story follows in the footsteps of *MASH* in showing surgeons who use considerable expertise to help patients in critical need despite low-tech circumstances. For those with a deep interest in the complexity of medicine and for those who simply want to be entertained by an exciting story, *Training in Charity* is an absorbing and satisfying read."

—Neil J. Stone M.D., Bonow Professor of Medicine, Feinberg School of Medicine, Northwestern University, Suzanne and Milton Davidson Distinguished Physician

"America's large urban hospitals, like the venerable Charity Hospital of New Orleans, are the ideal venue for young doctors not just to learn clinical medicine but how to 'practice' it. Inside Charity's walls, from the field hospital-like setting of its emergency room to the surgical suites, Adam Sinclair moves from student to healer by listening to his mentors and showing compassion to the diverse patients who show up at Charity's doors. The book is set in a city of infinite contradictions—old and new, sacred and profane—and Adam becomes what we should demand from all our healers: a realist with a heart. Allen Saxon's story about a young doctor's life lessons in the wards of Charity is a great read, full of insight and compassion. It should be required reading for medical students embarking on their first clinical experience. And anyone who has trained at the now sadly-closed Charity will relish reliving his stories."

—Mike King, author of *A Spirit of Charity*

TRAINING
in
CHARITY

a novel

Allen Saxon

CHRISTMAS LAKE PRESS

Published by Christmas Lake Press 2025
www.christmaslakecreative.com
Copyright © 2025 by Allen Saxon
ISBN 978-1-980865-38-0

This is a work of fiction. The resemblance of any of the characters to real persons, living or dead, is coincidental. They are fictitious—except for the named New Orleans musicians. They are not fictitious; they are legendary.

Interior layout by Daiana Marchesi

TRAINING
in
CHARITY

To Vicki, David, Hillary, Katie, and the Gang

With gratitude to Sharon and Steve Fiffer and the Wesley Writers

Bill Anthony
Ann Fay
Sally deVincentis
Jean Diamond
Judy Iacuzzi
Sara Marberry
Kendra Morrill
Katy Okrent
Loree Sandler
Rachel Seidman

Acknowledgments

Although writing fiction, every novelist draws from their own experience. For me, choosing the training of medical students in the 1970s as a theme creates its own challenges. The practice of medicine requires a background in technical and scientific concepts but, at its core, centers on the need to appreciate that healthcare is about providing service to those in need. There is a fine balance that must be achieved between understanding and applying the scientific basis of medical practice and communicating with compassion, empathy, and concern for the patient's well-being. This book was written with the intent that it would be entertaining and appeal to an audience of those both with and without formal medical backgrounds.

In accordance with achieving this goal, I have relied on the valuable assistance of many individuals for their input and suggestions. I am grateful for the editorial skills of Mary Loretta Kelly, Kate Sloan Fiffer, Thomas Fiffer of Christmas Lake Press, and the members of the Wesley Writers Group. Input from Kelly Dwyer of the Iowa Writers' Workshop was helpful as well. Their involvement has made this work accessible to the general reader while allowing the energy and excitement of the medical scenes to proceed without confusion.

Many friends have looked at the entire manuscript or parts of it and helped with additional commentary. Dr. Crew and

Phyllis Cleveland, Dr. Ermilo and Sue Barrera, Drs. Mike Hanley and Christine LaRocca, Dr. Neil and Karla Stone, Kathy Ritenour, R.N., and Hank Klibanoff and Laurie Leonard have been of great assistance. I apologize to any others I may have neglected to mention.

Of special note are Steve and Sharon Fiffer, co-leaders of the Wesley Writers Group. who regularly teach the elements of writing while they review the group's work. Their availability, patience, and clarity are invaluable.

The support of my family has been very much appreciated. My wife, Vicki, has read every draft and iteration of this story from the outset.

Finally I am grateful for the opportunity to teach medical students at both Rosalind Franklin University and the Northwestern University Feinberg School of Medicine. I remain inspired by the commitment of their faculties and the dedication and idealism of their students.

NEW ORLEANS

Mid-1970s

Week One

CHAPTER 1

THE LONG TABLE in the hospital's cafeteria had only been designed to seat six. But that morning, students in their short white coats pulled up chairs until fourteen of them crowded together. At first they sat in silence, heads down, each contemplating the past two and a half days of orientation. Adam Sinclair cradled his paper coffee cup, half full of warm, bitter brew that milk and sugar couldn't quite fix, feeling the shared uncertainty of beginning the first hospital rotation of his medical career.

Although seemingly endless lectures and demonstrations had filled the past two days, no one had explained what would be expected of them once they began working in the hospital on their respective surgical services. Adam leaned in when a white coat at the end of the table finally spoke.

"Did anybody actually get the first reading assignment done? How could they give us *a hundred and eighty-five pages* right off the bat?"

Several of his fellow students shook their heads, but that provided little consolation for Adam, who had struggled to complete just thirty pages of the difficult text.

"Each of the chapters in that book is fifty pages or more," said another white coat, "and they assign them with each lecture."

"I hear there's no time to study and the residents can be real assholes," added white coat three. "They want you on the ward really early in the morning and you have to stay all day."

Others spoke up, and the conversation started flowing.

White coat four: "It's the hardest rotation by far. Some guys flame out under the pressure."

White coat five: "If you fail and have to repeat the block, it's pretty much impossible to get a good residency."

White coat six: "Yeah, and there's no quizzes or midterm, only the final exam at the end of the rotation."

White coat seven: "And it covers everything in the whole friggin' book."

White coat eight: "A couple of years ago some guy freaked out, quit school, and joined a Hare Krishna sect."

Adam was picturing a young man in sandals and a flowing robe (exchanged for the short white coat) tapping a tambourine while dancing on a street corner when two doctors approached the table. Their long coats marked them as residents. Their clipped words confirmed it.

"I'm Larry Kochenko. This is Bennett Turk. We're second-year residents. Who's going to rotate on General Surgery Service 1?"

Adam raised his hand, as did two of the others seated at the table.

Kochenko nodded to each of them. "We're going to be in the OR with the rest of the service this morning. You guys be on the ward at one o'clock and we'll meet you there when we're done."

To Adam, both residents, although only a couple of years older than the third-years, possessed the demeanor of accomplished doctors. Kochenko's hair was long in back, his aviator glasses tinted. His gray slacks had a slight bell-bottom flare, and his coat was unbuttoned with his stethoscope casually draped around his neck. Bennett Turk had shorter hair—practically a crew cut—and with his buttoned coat, stethoscope tucked into one pocket, and stainless steel bandage scissors safety-pinned into a buttonhole, he appeared more formal. The residents strode away as briskly as they'd walked up. Adam drained his coffee cup and checked his watch. He had just enough time to take a short walk and try to clear his head.

The other two students were already on the ward when Adam arrived just before one o'clock. They stood huddled together in the middle of the aisle between the two rows of beds. They appeared lost, uncertain, and afraid to approach the patients. Clinging tightly to their notebooks, they watched as the nursing staff ignored them and went about their business. Barnett Styles was tall, with neatly-combed blond hair and black glasses with thick frames. His white coat stretched tight across his shoulders, weighted down by the contents of the side pockets—a small notebook on the left and a wire spiral-bound copy of *Guide to Surgical Therapeutics* on the right. A reflex hammer, stethoscope, otoscope, and tourniquet were stuffed in as well. The pocket protector on his chest was so packed with pens that it caused his name tag to droop towards the floor.

Adam remembered Styles, who'd sat one table away from him in histology lab. They hadn't made much small talk, instead spending most of their time peering into their microscopes. In lecture, Barnett sat on the side of the room opposite Adam. That was the section for the guys with degrees in engineering or from the military academies. Adam chose the other side of the lecture hall, among those designated as the class hippies, though as he was a relatively straight-laced farm boy from the Midwest, the designation didn't quite fit him.

While Barnett had remained quiet and reserved for the first two years of medical school, Shrevi Kumar was well-known to everyone in the class. He was a native New Orleanian. His parents were first-generation immigrants from India who ran a grocery store in Gentilly that served the Indian community, selling assorted foods and spices native to their homeland. They had worked hard to provide their first-born son with every opportunity to grab the American Dream, enrolling him in the finest private schools and giving him the educational foundation to attend the university and enroll in its medical school. Shrevi had responded by leaving his family's heritage behind and completely adopting local culture, indulging in regular helpings of crawfish and beer, daily beignets and café au lait, and evenings in uptown bars dancing to zydeco and trying a variety of unsuccessful pick-up lines on the girls he met. In his first two years at the medical school, it was not uncommon for him to sneak out of lecture and call his bookie if he thought he could pick a winner in the afternoon's races at the Fairgrounds.

Adam joined them, and, after brief introductions, they stood and looked around the ward. "What are we supposed to do now?" asked Barnett.

"I dunno," said Adam. "They told us to meet them here, so I guess we wait."

"Can't do any reading here," said Barnett, whose study habits reflected the discipline and concentration associated with his degree in engineering and his commitment to five years' service in the Navy after they paid for his medical education.

"I don't think I could concentrate on the reading here, either," added Adam.

Barnett sighed. "Well, standing around like this isn't very productive. I have enough trouble trying to study at home with a new baby and all."

"Let's just find a place to sit and wait," said Shrevi.

He pulled a racing form from his book bag and headed towards the nurses' desk at the entrance to the ward.

An hour and a half had passed when one of the house staff finally appeared on the ward. His eyes were intense but barely directed at the students.

"Y'all must be our newbies. M3s or 4s?"

"We're third-years," Adam answered.

"Well, shit!" said the resident. "We were hoping for fourth years—they know so much more. I don't know why we don't get many senior students to take a surgical rotation. It's a requirement for juniors and only an elective for seniors, but they must think they learned it all as juniors. Or maybe they're just lazy asses and it's too hard for them. Anyway, I suppose we should make introductions. I'm Todd Wantz, first-year resident. Who are you?"

"Adam Sinclair."

"Barnett Styles."

"Shrevi Kumar."

"Well, you can call me Dr. Wantz. Let me make sure I got this."

He pointed a stubby finger at each student, intimidating them one by one as he spoke. "Styles, right? And Sinclair... And what was it again?"

"Kumar."

"Yeah, got it. Now, you guys know this is going to be a rotation that requires your attention and hard work for the full six weeks. We expect you to have made rounds every morning *before* us. There's a centrifuge and tubes in the treatment room so you can spin a hematocrit on every patient on the ward and have those results ready when we get here. You'll need to change dressings, write notes, go to the OR, and see patients in the clinic as well as attend your lectures and keep up on your assignments. We're also down one first-year resident on this service, so we'll need even more from you. Tell family and girlfriends you'll see them after the rotation." Wantz paused for half a second. "Now why the fuck are you just standing around? There are patients on the wards to see. The female ward is down the hall and to the right, third one down that corridor. We are on call for the ER tonight, so don't plan on going home... You can start by studying the charts on the wards so you can learn the patients; then come down to the Emergency Room on the first floor." Before anyone could say anything, Wantz added, "And one more thing: this is the department chair's service. Don't get in our way. We run a tight ship."

CHAPTER 2

IN THE DAYLIGHT, Charity Hospital was a mountain. The gray stone exterior towered skyward. Art deco adornments carved at its entrances made it appear from a different time. It was immovable, indestructible, resistant over the years to all nature could throw against it. Its imposing size was exaggerated by its symmetry, which allowed it to house two separate medical schools. Inside was a beehive of activity: people of all colors, sizes, and styles of dress scurrying back and forth, making their way to clinic visits, to find friends or relatives on the wards, or seeking to relieve their suffering by joining the long queues in the Emergency Room.

At night, the wards were quiet, church-like, barely lit transepts flanking the long corridors that, like the nave of a cathedral, led to a crucifix—not a fancy altarpiece but rather an old cross hanging from a rusty wire, barely noticeable in the darkened hallway.

Filled with stale, humid air, tinged with the odor of perspiration, vomit, and human waste barely masked by strong disinfectant, the halls of Charity were peaceful, the quiet only broken by sounds from within the wards: the steady hum of the window air conditioners struggling against the heat and humidity of New Orleans and the shuffle of the night-duty LPNs as they moved from bed to bed, checking temperature, pulse, respirations, and blood pressure and emptying bedpans and urinary catheter bags.

If the wards were as quiet as a chapel during vespers, at 2 a.m. the ER was as explosive as a battlefield. The triage area overflowed with people stepping out of line, crowding the nurses' table in front of the seating area and screaming to be heard while someone's portable radio added to the din, blasting the latest funky music of the Meters at maximum volume. The sea of bodies would only momentarily open and quiet when ambulance drivers opened the double doors and hurried an injured patient to the trauma rooms.

Adam pressed himself against the wall in Trauma Room 1 as chaos unfolded around him. He had followed two of the resident physicians into the room after the ambulance drivers rushed in a patient strapped to a backboard and moved him from their stretcher to a hospital cart.

"Get out of the way!" the ambulance driver had shouted, and Adam had stepped back only to be pushed farther away by the crowd of people that had flooded the room.

Larry Kochenko had immediately stepped to the head of the gurney and taken over, squeezing the bag through which oxygen flowed. A nurse and respiratory therapist stood near him, preparing equipment for placement of an endotracheal tube to allow better control of the patient's airway and ventilation of his lungs. Bennett Turk focused on examining the patient's chest and abdomen while a nurse used a heavy scissors to cut through the patient's clothing. Another nurse inserted a second large-bore intravenous catheter into the patient's opposite arm, drawing several test tubes of blood with different colored rubber stoppers before attaching an additional bag of clear IV fluid.

"Carlos," she barked to the orderly, "get those boots off!"

"Palpable pressure at the wrist," stated one of the nurses.

Adam did not want to be in the way, but he moved closer to see the patient. He was a young Caucasian male, probably mid-twenties, not responding when Turk spoke to him or pinched his left nipple. His extremities were straight, without any obvious deformity to indicate fracture. There were skin abrasions on his chest and legs as well as a large bluish bruise on his mid-forehead. His right eyelid was swollen shut.

"No breath sounds right lower chest," stated Turk as he placed his stethoscope back into his coat pocket.

Adam watched Kochenko insert the silver blade of a laryngoscope into the patient's mouth and slide a breathing tube along it. The nurse attached the oxygen bag to the tube and continued squeezing it while Kochenko wrapped adhesive tape around the tube and secured it to the patient's cheeks and chin.

"We'll need a ventilator," Kochenko said to the respiratory therapist, who nodded in response. Adam stepped back as the therapist hurried past him and left the trauma room.

A blonde nurse placed a pair of latex gloves, a package of lubricating petroleum jelly, and a long clear plastic tube fitted with a syringe on one end into Adam's hands.

"Put in the NG," she said.

Adam stared at the nasogastric tube. Last year in his Clinical Laboratory course, he had to pass a tube into his lab partner's stomach to obtain a sample for acid measurement. Adam could still see his lab partner sitting on a high metal stool, squirming, coughing, and turning purple as he unknowingly continued to direct the tube into his classmate's windpipe rather than the esophagus.

Seeing Adam's reluctance, the nurse grabbed the tube, and after tearing bits of adhesive tape and placing them on the rail of the cart, she deftly lubricated the tube with petroleum jelly and slipped it into the patient's nose.

"Pay attention. You'll have to do it next time," she said as she advanced the tube until gently pulling on the syringe caused a trail of brown liquid to flow back.

"It's easier of course when the patient has a brain injury like this so they don't flinch," she added, disconnecting the syringe and attaching the tube to a suction machine, which continued to drain more of the brown scum. She emptied the syringe into an emesis basin and leaned forward to tape the tube to the patient's nose.

"Listen for the air," she commanded.

Adam placed his stethoscope on the patient's belly, and the nurse pushed his hand up a bit towards the left ribs as she reconnected the syringe full of air and forced it through the nasogastric tube. A loud whoosh echoed through his stethoscope.

"Seems to be in place OK, I think," he said as the nurse reattached the suction machine and the brown liquid resumed its flow.

When Adam looked up he saw a wide-eyed Barnett pressed against the opposite wall, trying to stay out of the way. Shrevi stood alongside the cart. The smaller nurse was standing across from him, wearing gloves and pulling up on the man's penis as she pushed a Foley catheter into the man's bladder. Shrevi winced as the catheter was pushed in and yellow urine began to drain into the plastic bag hanging at the foot of the cart. The respiratory therapist returned, pushing a small ventilator that was now being attached to the endotracheal tube. Kochenko and Turk were both watching the man's chest move through inspiration and expiration. Neither of them gave any indication that they had seen Adam struggle with the NG tube.

"Urine looks clear... No obvious blood in it. Think he needs a chest tube?" Kochenko asked.

Turk looked at the urine collecting in the bag before turning his attention back to the right side of the patient's chest. "Probably no urologic injury, then..."

"Blood pressure is now 100 systolic, pulse 98," said one of the nurses to everyone and no one in particular.

Turk stared down at the patient's chest and placed his left hand so that his middle finger lay in the space exactly between two ribs. His right hand began to tap on his left middle finger as he moved his left hand from space to space between the ribs.

"Let's get our X-ray first before chest tube..." said Turk. "Left lung is clear, but he has a lot of dullness on this right side... No evidence of any pneumothorax, and he's too stable for this to all be blood in his chest."

Adam thought back to his Physical Diagnosis course. A collapsed lung should be a very resonant sound when the chest was percussed. Dullness would indicate something blocking the sound transmission—usually fluid—but Turk's comment meant that if the patient had been bleeding into his chest, it would have taken so much blood to create the dull sound that he should have been in shock, with a very rapid pulse and a very low blood pressure.

"I'll bag him as we go to X-ray..." Kochenko disconnected the ventilator, reattached the bag and tubing from the oxygen tank, and squeezed the oxygen bag. "Be nice if the state of Louisiana would buy us a portable X-ray machine."

"Bloodwork is all cooking," said the blonde nurse as she tucked the patient's arms to his sides and covered him with a blanket.

"His name is Ronald Candy," said the small nurse, who wore deep purple eye makeup. "Card in his wallet looks like he's an apprentice pipefitter. No other medical information."

She tossed the wallet into one of the work boots that had been placed on the floor in the corner of the trauma room, disconnected him from the EKG monitor, and began pulling the cart across the hall to the X-ray room.

"Brewery Breath," Kochenko said as the patient was positioned for the X-rays. "When a car hits a telephone pole head on—the pole always wins."

The X-ray technicians worked efficiently, taking multiple views of Ronald Candy's head, spine, chest, and abdomen before he was maneuvered back across the hall and reattached to the ventilator.

"We'll be across the hall checking the films," Turk told the nurses.

"Keep an eye on his vitals," added Kochenko as he motioned for Adam and Shrevi to follow into the hallway where the X-ray developer was beginning to spit out the completed films.

Turk pulled the films from the machine's tray and placed them on the view box. He switched on the lights, illuminating the films from behind.

"Looks like you either got a whopper pleural effusion or a very unusual hernia through the diaphragm."

Two more residents arrived. Adam sensed they were more senior to the others. The one who spoke was tall, with neatly combed brown hair. He wore a green scrub suit with a stethoscope tucked into his back pocket and a ballpoint pen in the shirt pocket, from which dangled a name tag that read, "Terry Rogers M.D. Dept. of Surgery."

Next to Rogers stood a diminutive Asian man wearing scrubs, a long lab coat that seemed a little too big, and horn-rimmed glasses. He stared intently at the films, nodding in agreement with Rogers' assessment. Adam caught the name "Kittamura" on his tag.

Once back in the trauma room, Rogers put on a pair of sterile gloves after pouring antiseptic solution on the patient's chest, placed some blue towels around the site, and stuck a needle attached to a large syringe between two ribs and into the patient's chest. As he pulled back on the plunger, nothing significant entered the syringe.

"No blood or fluid in the chest," he said. "Kittamura, you think this guy could have herniated his liver through his diaphragm?"

Kittamura nodded in affirmation.

"We'll need to take him to the OR as soon as Holiday and Doyle have reviewed his films." With that, Rogers stepped back into the hallway and Adam followed.

Holiday and Doyle, the two chief residents on Service 1, were looking at the view boxes down the hall. Bobby Doyle was the more colorful of the two, a little overweight, with wisps of unkempt blond hair protruding from under his black cloth scrub hat emblazoned with the fleur-de-lis emblem of the New Orleans Saints and speckled with little red embroidered footballs. On his feet he wore wooden, open-backed clogs with dark leather uppers that showed evidence of having been splattered many times by blood and body fluids.

It was rumored that Tom Holiday had at one time played football for the university and had returned to Charity after his residency was interrupted by a tour of duty as a combat surgeon on a Navy ship off the coast of Vietnam. He wore standard operating shoe covers over sneakers, and a standard light blue bouffant-style paper operating cap was visible in his right coat pocket, leaving his close-cropped hair and receding hairline visible.

Doyle and Holiday spoke softly with Rogers and then followed him back into the trauma room. Adam trailed in along with them and stood by at the foot of the bed as they all looked at the helpless naked figure on the cart.

A commotion rocked the hallway as a parade of paramedics and stretchers rushed by. A tall, thin nurse with stringy brown hair popped into the room.

"Gunshots," she said only once and left.

A rapid exodus ensued as white coats, nursing staff, respiratory therapy, Shrevi, and even Carlos the aide disappeared towards the other trauma rooms. Adam was left standing and staring at the monitors and ventilator.

Terry Rogers stuck his head into the room again. "Take care of this guy until we get him to the OR."

And then he too was gone.

Adam listened to the sound of the ventilator maintaining inspiration and expiration and watched as the IV fluid dripped from the hanging bags into the patient's veins and urine flowed down the catheter into the plastic bag hanging from the railing on the foot of the cart. As he stood amid the clutter of discarded IV casings, plastic wrappers, crumpled gauze, torn tape, and discarded clothing, Adam's pulse quickened. He swallowed hard at the lump in his throat and wiped his sweaty palms on his pant legs as he considered Rogers' instructions: "Take care of this guy." Adam was perplexed.

What do I do now?

He reached down, grabbed the patient's wrist, and took his pulse.

Chapter 3

After a long wait, Adam's anxiety was relieved by the reappearance of the blonde nurse. Now he could see her name tag: "Judy Delormeaux." She took charge—rechecking the vital signs and recording the urine output. She reassured Adam that the patient would remain stable to get to the operating suite.

The respiratory therapist returned to check the ventilator.

"I set his tidal volume at 500 and his rate at 14," he explained. Adam nodded in agreement, not really understanding.

Dr. Lemoyne, the neurosurgery resident, appeared in response to a call from Rogers. He completed the most thorough neurologic exam Adam had ever seen. Lemoyne tested Ronald's reflexes and muscle tone. He pinched Ronald's nipple firmly (with no response to the discomfort) and fully examined his eyes closely, opening the swollen one so that he could use his ophthalmoscope to both shine light on his pupils and look deeper inside his eyes. He looked into Ronald's ears and then was handed a syringe filled with ice water and a small red rubber catheter with which he instilled water into Ronald's ear while observing the response of his eyes.

"I think he's just got a bad contusion—no skull fracture or localizing findings. Tell your residents to do what they need to—we'll recheck him in ICU."

"Got it," said Rogers, suddenly appearing in the doorway. "Let's get him up to the OR." He and Judy exchanged looks that suggested their familiarity went beyond professional communication.

Adam stood at the scrub sink, cleaning his nails with a small plastic pick as they had been taught. Turk stood next to him, re-explaining the basics of scrubbing to Shrevi, who had forgotten the orientation. He now energetically followed instructions, scrubbing his arms and fingers with a rigid plastic brush while he held his arms upright so that the suds drained towards his elbows.

Shrevi excitedly spoke about what he had seen in the other trauma room. "I ain't never seen nothin' like that. Boy had two holes in his chest and one in his right temple. He had nothin'— no pulse, no pressure. Wantz was talkin' about opening his chest for cardiac massage but Rogers came in and said, 'Forget it. He's dead.' Then he sent Wantz to one of the other rooms and told me to come up and see this surgery."

When they had finished scrubbing, they imitated Turk, holding their hands up high as they crossed the hall and backed through the double doors of Room 6. Adam felt like one of three heroic masked men on their way to help save a life.

The scrub nurse handed each of them a sterile towel to dry their hands. Both Adam and Shrevi again emulated Turk as he wiped his hands and arms. Adam looked at Ronald, lying with his arms outstretched as the anesthesia resident checked his monitoring devices and the machine that dispensed a mixture of oxygen and anesthetic gas into Ronald's endotracheal tube.

Holiday had painted Ronald's chest and abdomen with brown antiseptic solution and placed sterile towels and drapes over him to outline and protect the surgical site.

Taking the scalpel from the scrub nurse, Holiday made a long incision from the lower sternum, skirting around the belly button and reaching all the way down to the pubic bone. At first it seemed brutal, but Holiday's smooth, fluid motion mimicked a ballet, which amazed and fascinated Adam as the skin parted down to the muscle and the edges of exposed fat filled the incision with blood.

Adam heard a loud sigh behind him and turned just in time to see Shrevi's eyes roll back as he fell forward and planted his face directly on the OR floor.

CHAPTER 4

"I DON'T CARE how good their middle linebacker is this year! They ain't gonna be worth shit if they don't have a decent offensive line…and hell, they're gonna be playin' two freshmen," Doyle said as he stood across the operating table from Holiday.

"I've got your boy sittin' on a stool in the hallway, sippin' orange juice," said the circulating nurse as she reentered the operating room.

Doyle looked over at Adam. "Don't worry, he's OK. We see one of those every rotation." He looked back at Holiday. "Their quarterback don't seem to be able to scramble too well neither."

Adam couldn't believe they were discussing the prospects for the university's upcoming football season while Holiday examined Ronald Candy's abdominal contents.

Holiday gently pulled the liver back into the abdomen while Doyle continued on about the quarterback's lack of ability to find receivers once he was out of the pocket. Adam pulled tightly on the Mayo retractor he had been handed but couldn't see into the belly where the diaphragm had torn.

"Looks like the cava and hepatic veins are intact," said Holiday. "This boy's one lucky SOB… Quarterback's got a good arm, though… Give me an O Ethibond on a big needle, please."

The scrub nurse handed him a long, thick green suture, its large, curved needle held in a long stainless holder with gold accents on the rings for the thumb and forefinger. Holiday placed a stitch, then another and another. He was repairing the diaphragm, but Adam couldn't see it from where he stood.

Holiday asked the scrub nurse for a number 28 chest tube and a six-inch clamp. He made a small incision between two ribs on the patient's right side, placed the end of the chest tube in the jaws of the clamp, and pushed the clamp through the small incision and into the chest. Reaching through the hole in the diaphragm, he pushed the pink surface of the inflating and deflating lung out of the way, released the clamp, and pushed the chest tube into its position within the chest. He placed a large black suture in the skin and used it to wrap around the tube, tying it tightly to prevent any slippage.

Holiday calmly asked for more of the Ethibond sutures, methodically placing them and tying until he had closed the diaphragm.

"Besides that," Doyle said, returning to football, "they probably only got one really good receiver."

"But that new boy from Jackson is really fast," countered Holiday.

The liver was now in its normal position.

"I suppose we should remove the gallbladder before we close," said Holiday.

"Yeah, I'd hate to have to present this guy having a post-operative gallbladder attack to the Morbidity and Mortality Conference. They'd skin us alive," added Doyle.

"How many gallbladders have you done?" Holiday asked Turk, who was quietly standing across the operating table on Doyle's left and had been holding a retractor similar to the one Adam had been pulling on to allow the surgeons to see the operative field.

"Two," he answered.

"C'mon over here and take this one out. I'll help him," he said towards Doyle, who had already stepped back from the table and was pulling off his gown and gloves.

"That's fine. I'll go check on the other cases and see y'all on the ward for rounds."

Holiday moved to Doyle's side of the table, passing Turk at the foot as he moved into the operator's spot next to Adam, who continued to pull on the retractor while trying to remember what the gallbladder looked like.

Turk's hand shook as he slowly applied a clamp to the end of the gallbladder. Despite Adam tugging on the retractor and Holiday using his large left hand and a moist lap pad to push the colon and duodenum out of the way, Turk's movements remained uncertain and hesitant.

His dissection moved slowly until he separated the gallbladder from its attachments and placed it into a metal basin offered by the scrub nurse. He made a short incision in the skin off to the right side and pushed a clamp through it, opening the jaws as Holiday positioned a latex drain, called a Penrose, into the instrument. Turk closed the clamp and pulled it through the hole to the outside skin, bringing with it half the drain while Holiday positioned the remaining half under the surface of the liver, adjacent to where the gallbladder had been attached. Turk placed a safety pin in the exposed part of the drain and sutured the drain to the skin with a single silk stitch.

Holiday stepped back to the scrub nurse's table and examined the gallbladder in the basin. He took a scissors and cut it open.

"No stones or sludge," he said. "Let's start closing."

Closing the incision took longer than doing the actual surgery. Turk slowly placed sutures into the tight fascia layer that gave strength to the abdominal wall while Holiday sewed more quickly from the other end of the incision.

After the muscle layer of the abdominal wall was closed, Holiday stepped back from the table.

"Mattress the skin with silks," he instructed Turk. "I'll see you in Recovery."

"Pick-ups and a stitch, please," Turk asked the scrub nurse. She handed him a pinching forceps to grasp the skin and a straight needle with a black suture attached to the end. She surprised Adam when she gave him a matching forceps and suture.

"You know how to do a mattress suture?" asked Turk.

"Not really."

"Well, watch as I do this." After placing three stitches, Turk added, "Now you start at the other end."

They began to work simultaneously, but after Adam had placed his first suture, he realized that tying them was another issue.

"Make sure you take a pack of ties home at the end of the case to practice, or get a piece of nylon cord—bedposts or coffee table legs work great for practice. Watch how I do this and try a couple. If you're having too much trouble, just place the stitch and I'll tie them at the end."

Adam watched intently as Turk worked. He copied his suture placement and then Turk slowed down his knot tying.

"Watch carefully," Turk said. "Cross 'em like this...pull your knot down and then square it with this motion."

Adam imitated Turk's movement and watched the skin edges come together. He felt a sense of accomplishment as each knot held the skin edges in place. The incision became smaller until there was no longer room in the middle for both of them to sew at the same time.

When Turk finished the last stitch, he used a sterile moist lap pad to wash the skin and applied a layered gauze dressing. The drapes were removed, and Ronald's arms were brought to his sides. A wheeled cart could be positioned next to the table.

"On the count of three," said the anesthesiologist. The nurses and Turk each grabbed a corner of the sheet under Ronald, and Turk's nod directed Adam to grasp the corner closest to him.

"One, two, three," and they lifted and swung Ronald's limp body onto the cart while anesthesia made sure his breathing tube did not dislodge. The circulating nurse covered the naked body with a blanket while the anesthesiologist attached a bag connected to a portable tank and began pumping oxygen into

Ronald's lungs as they walked the short journey out of the operating room and down the hall to the Recovery Room.

The Recovery Room was filled with people but not frantic like the ER had been. Several patients were on gurneys, some on ventilators, and still others wearing oxygen masks. The smell of disinfectant permeated the room. Three separate air conditioners hummed in their windows, creating a much cooler room than the single, overtaxed units on the wards could provide. Nurses moved back and forth between the patients' carts on one wall and the broad desk that sat in front of the opposite wall of supply cabinets. Their conversation seemed like whispers compared to the regular mechanical whooshing of the ventilators.

Kochenko sat at the desk, writing orders on charts. Barnett stood behind him and looked up as Adam approached.

"Got to see an appendix," he said. "What did you see?"

"Hernia through the diaphragm." Adam tried to sound nonchalant.

Adam looked up at the clock on the wall above the sink. Five in the morning. The night had passed so quickly. He focused on what he had seen—the knot tying, the anatomy, how the patient was handled in the ER. Strangely, he wasn't tired, but now a full day's work lay ahead of him. All he really wanted was a warm shower and to know how long it would take before he'd be comfortable talking about football in the operating room.

CHAPTER 5

RAYS OF EARLY morning sunlight were creeping around the edges of the paper shades on the windows in the men's ward. The sound of heavy footsteps announced Wantz's arrival.

"What the hell are you standing around for? There's a lot of work to get done—and where the hell's the other student?"

He raised his index finger and pointed to Barnett. "You, Styles—get down to the ER. Holiday and Kittamura headed there to see another damn patient—missed the call trade-off by about twenty minutes. You get a good history and physical on the chart. We have to be ready to present all the new admissions to Dr. Theodorakis on afternoon rounds."

Wantz and Barnett hurried out of the ward and Adam stood alone, staring at the patients, uncertain how to care for them before attending lecture and wondering how to prepare for rounds with Dr. Theodorakis, Chairman of the Department of Surgery and the Chief Attending Surgeon on Service 1.

Just as Adam felt overwhelmed, Bennett Turk walked onto the ward.

"Need a little help?" he asked. "First couple days can be pretty overwhelming."

"I'm not sure what all I need to do," said Adam. "Dr. Wantz said we have to present to Dr. Theodorakis today."

"First thing is we gotta make rounds. You know, change the dressings, review the charts, order labs, all that routine stuff. You gotta spin your own hematocrits. We want to know that blood count every morning. Get one of those tablets of progress sheets. You can write a note on each patient, record the important labs, and share them with the other students. We can knock these work rounds out in no time."

Adam followed Turk's lead, and they moved with a rhythm so efficient that they finished their rounds just before the other residents arrived on the floor, accompanied by Barnett, who could not suppress his excitement as he described the case he had seen to Adam.

"It was amazing," he said. "This guy, stabbed just above the clavicle, almost no blood pressure in the ER. Holiday opened the chest, put his hand in, and compressed the subclavian vessels while they moved the guy to the OR. When they got there, Kittamura divided the clavicle so they could fix the vessels. It was amazing, and they acted like it was just another routine case. So calm... I could have sworn the guy was a goner."

"I heard these guys are really good surgeons by the time they're senior residents," said Adam. "I knew you were going to be tied up in surgery, so I stuck everybody's fingertips, filled the capillary tubes, and spun all the hematocrits in the centrifuge in the treatment room." He waved the small notebook in which he had recorded the results. "I still haven't seen Kumar."

"Well, where the hell is he?" It was like Wantz had snuck up on them.

"He'll be here." Adam tried to sound confident, although he actually had no idea where Shrevi was or whether he would even show up when the service was ready to start rounds.

Rogers and Kochenko appeared, each carrying cups of stale, lukewarm coffee. Adam watched them all for a moment, trying to remember who was who. He knew Kochenko and Turk were second-year residents. Wantz was a first-year—an intern. Rogers was the third-year resident, considered the workhorse of the service since he supervised the first- and second-year trainees and bore full responsibility for making sure everything ran smoothly. From a technical perspective, he was expected to be much more advanced than the younger residents. He was allowed to be the operating surgeon on more complicated procedures with the more senior residents, Kittamura or Holiday or Doyle assisting him.

At ten minutes to eight o'clock, Shrevi arrived. He was sipping from a paper cup with the logo of Café Du Monde in the French Quarter. His left hand clutched four white paper bags.

"Where the hell you been?" Wantz demanded. "We start rounds at 5:30. If you are not in the operating room, I expect you to be here getting the work done. Dressings should be changed, notes written, and blood counts checked by spinning hematocrits…"

Before he could continue, Rogers stepped in front of Wantz and took one of the white bags from Shrevi.

"Thanks," he said. "This is a real treat."

Shrevi held up the other bags and flashed a broad smile. "It wouldn't do for anybody to have low blood sugar after such a busy night."

Rogers reached into the bag and pulled out a square of fried dough made almost unrecognizable by the powdered sugar that covered every visible surface.

"They're still warm," he said, passing the bag to Kochenko and gesturing for Turk and the students to join him.

"Better save some for the other guys," he said, "even though in an hour these will be hard as a rock."

Shrevi opened another bag and offered its contents to the still-frowning Wantz, whose demeanor softened as he bit into the beignet and managed a slight smile despite the powdered sugar that leaked out of the corners of his mouth and onto his chin. Soon they were all ravenously devouring the French donuts, spilling powdered sugar onto their white coats, scrub suits, shoes, and the floor.

CHAPTER 6

ADAM ARRIVED ON the female ward at ten minutes to one o'clock. Rounds with Dr. Theodorakis were scheduled to begin at 1 p.m., but no one was there. Adam looked for the charts as he remembered which patients had been assigned to him, hoping they would all be straightforward if he were called upon to present them on rounds. One patient was an elderly Black lady whose varicose veins had caused the skin on the inner surface of her lower legs to erupt into large, raw ulcer craters that had become infected by bacteria that normally lived on her skin. She was receiving intravenous antibiotics, and her raw legs were being treated with special dressings called Unna boots. Turk had explained that the tight wraps on her legs would reduce swelling and the zinc oxide paste contained in the dressings would help the ulcers heal.

"Theo will want to see her legs," Rogers said as he entered the ward and approached Adam at the old lady's bedside. "Get these dressings off and put some new Unnas on her bedside table so we can replace the dressings after rounds. Then we'd better hurry to the male ward to start rounds with the chief."

The top dressing was an elastic Ace bandage that Adam easily unraveled and removed. Beneath this was a layer of white rolled gauze, with the brown edges of the Unna boot visible just below the white wrap.

Adam awkwardly lifted her left heel and tried to unwrap the next layer. Rogers stepped closer.

"You gotta get one of these," he said pulling a large scissors from the right pocket of his coat. "Always gotta have a bandage scissors."

He slipped the lower, blunted, longer blade beneath the white gauze and snipped and clipped up the middle so that he could lay the gauze to the sides, exposing the remaining boot.

"Be careful you don't injure the skin when you cut the last layer." Again, he slipped the lower blade beneath the remaining brown wrap and carefully pulled upwards as he snipped the boot and peeled it off to the sides. The skin of her lower left leg was discolored with a brawny pigment and had a thickened texture that indicated not all the swelling had subsided. Adam recalled the term "pitting edema" as he pushed his thumb deeply against the skin and watched the indentation disappear very slowly.

Rogers handed the scissors to Adam.

"See one, do one, teach one," he said. "You do this side."

Adam unwrapped the Ace bandage and mimicked Rogers' example. Pulling the edges of the boot to the sides exposed a large ulcer crater on the inner surface of her leg, bits of healing bright red tissue visible through a covering of pus and dark, deadened skin.

Rogers looked down at the ulcer. "Got a long ways to go. Leave 'em covered with saline-soaked gauze and we'll rewrap them after rounds with Theo. Don't be late for the start of rounds."

He grabbed his scissors and disappeared out the door.

Adam looked to the front of the ward. Through the open wooden double doors of the treatment room across from the nurses' desk, he spotted a nurse stocking medications in one of the cabinets. A thin woman, she appeared older than most of the ward RNs. She wore the standard heavy white shoes and stockings, a tight long skirt, and a short-sleeved white blouse revealing her skinny arms. Salt and pepper but mostly gray curls protruded from an old-fashioned starched nurse's cap, the kind young nurses received at graduation but most no longer wore while they were on duty. A nursing school pin was visible on the corner of her cap.

"Hi, I'm Adam, one of the new M3s on Service 1."

"Ah'm Sally," she responded. "What kin Ah do for you, hon?"

"I need some Unna boots and saline dressings for the lady with the leg ulcers. Are there any on the ward?"

"Oh, honey… Those are few and far between around here." She moved some of the supplies she had placed in the cabinet while shaking her head. "Nope. You'd better check with the nurse on the male ward. She may have a few, but we are plumb outta 'em. Got a bottle of saline and some gauze, though."

He thanked her, took the bottle of sterile salt water and packages of gauze sponges, and returned to the patient's bed, where he ripped open the paper wrapper containing the gauze and poured saline onto a sponge, repeating the maneuver until he had several pieces of gauze similarly prepared. He pulled the moistened gauze from the packaging and opened the folded pieces, placing them over the exposed ulcers, replacing the cap on the bottle of saline, and leaving the fluid and an unopened gauze pad on her bedside table. He was three steps away when the patient called out, "That's cold, young man!"

As he turned and scurried into the corridor, he said, "It will feel better in a few minutes," then headed to the men's ward, intent on not being late for rounds.

The ward was quiet when Adam entered. Holiday, Kittamura, Rogers, and Kochenko stood with Barnett at the foot of a bed near the far end of the ward. Kochenko thumbed through a chart as they quietly talked among themselves. Adam looked towards the nurses' desk on his right. A young nurse was staring down at the desktop, studying the medication clipboard. Her uniform looked to have been tailored for a perfect fit—unwrinkled slacks and a freshly pressed short-sleeved blouse, her nursing pin neatly secured to the collar. She had strawberry blonde hair tied back in a bun and tortoise-framed reading glasses pushed towards the tip of her nose as she studied the clipboard. With her perfectly proportioned figure and the studious look on her face, Adam thought she exuded competence, intelligence, and sexiness all at once. A surprising combination.

Wantz entered the ward behind him, leaned forward, and whispered, "Forget it, ain't nobody gettin' any of that."

Adam ignored him and approached the nurses' desk.

"Hi, I'm Adam, one of the new M3s. Are there any Unna boots on the ward? Need a couple for a patient on the female side."

"There might be a couple in the cabinet in the treatment room." She gestured to the other side of the ward, barely looking up from the medication list. He noticed the broad gold band and diamond on her left hand but couldn't help being taken by her piercing blue-green eyes.

In the cabinet Adam found an open box and placed two of the rolled boots in his coat pocket, leaving another two in the box. When he stepped out of the treatment room, the attractive nurse was still leaning over the papers on her desk, but when she briefly looked up he thought he detected a faint smile.

"I took two," he said, approaching her desk. "I left another two."

She looked up and nodded. Definitely a faint smile.

Wantz had joined the others at the end of the ward. All the residents on Service 1 were there, except Doyle and Turk. Shrevi must still be with them. The residents continued to speak in hushed tones, an air of anticipation hanging over them.

As Adam approached the group, Rogers spoke to him. "Miss Viola called from the department office. He's running late. Should be here to start in about fifteen to twenty minutes. Make sure you know your patients' histories."

Barnett followed him along the row of beds.

"I thought it would be hard to remember all this stuff, so I summarized each patient on an index card. Here's yours…" he said, handing Adam a small stack of white cards. "I got some for Shrevi too, but I think they're still in the OR."

"Thanks. What's going on?" he asked Barnett.

"That old man is the guy who had a perforated colon… Turk explained about this guy's diverticulitis. Had the perforation resected and has a colostomy. Had to go back to the operating room and have an abscess in his belly drained last week. He's still running a temperature and looks sick… They're wondering if he has another abscess. He's the guy that Doyle said last night should get the SNOW award."

"SNOW award?" repeated Adam. "I didn't hear that. What's that?"

"Every week Doyle gives the designation," Barnett scowled. "Sickest—" he paused but looked knowingly at Adam, "—on the ward."

Adam understood the word left unsaid and cringed. "That's disgusting."

Barnett kept talking but Adam didn't hear him. He was preoccupied with watching the nurse leaning over her desk at the end of the ward.

CHAPTER 7

AN ELECTRICITY THRUMMED through the air, followed by the sound of many footsteps as a crowd gathered in the hallway. The shuffling of feet outside the ward grew louder, and then suddenly, there in the doorway, Dr. Stanislaus Theodorakis quietly stood, calm, tanned, dressed like a model from *Esquire* magazine in an expensive patterned sport coat, gray linen slacks, and mahogany Italian leather loafers—immaculate, confident, in complete contrast to the exhausted, nervous lot that greeted him.

The Service 1 residents stood gathered on one side of the first bed, while Dr. Theodorakis stood on the other. His entrance unleashed a flow of white coats as students and residents from the other services filed into the ward, filling the spaces between the patients' beds, crowding in, each seeking a spot for the chief's rounds. Adam's heart raced as he recognized he might have to present in front of everyone. All the residents and students from the other three surgical services were there.

"Good afternoon, sir," Holiday greeted Theodorakis. "We have new students on the service. This is Barnett Styles and Adam Sinclair, both M3s. There is a third student, but he is still in the OR with Doyle and Turk."

"Any M4s taking the elective block?"

"No, sir."

Barnett and Adam nodded, but Dr. Theodorakis didn't acknowledge the introduction. Adam recognized they were clearly on the ladder's lowest rung.

"Let's get started." Dr. Theodorakis moved towards the patient's bed.

"Which medical student is assigned to this patient?"

Barnett began the presentation of the patient whose appendectomy he had seen. Adam heard all the terms that made Barnett sound like a walking textbook: "...epigastric discomfort...two episodes of emesis...migration to the right lower quadrant...rebound tenderness at McBurney's point."

Although he tried to focus on Barnett's presentation, Adam was distracted by the attractive nurse, who joined the group, pushing the wheeled chart rack along with them. She was as attentive to the discussion as any of the students or residents. Her cool professionalism was as appealing as her looks.

Doyle, Turk, and Shrevi appeared on the ward. The other students and residents parted like a swinging door to allow them to join Service 1 near the chief.

"Turk took forever with that hernia," Shrevi whispered in Adam's ear as he took his place next to him.

At the end of the ward, Wantz began the presentation of the febrile patient with the perforated diverticulitis who had been the center of the residents' attention before the Chief of Surgery's arrival. The students stood in awe as he gave a presentation like none they had ever heard. Staring straight ahead, eyes transfixed somewhere in space, he launched into a rapid recital covering every detail of the patient's history and physical, pausing only now and then to take a short breath.

Dr. Theodorakis did not ask which student had been assigned this patient. He leveled his gaze at Adam and asked, "What is diverticulitis?"

Adam surprised himself by answering without hesitation. "Inflammation of small outpouchings on the wall of the colon… They occur as weaknesses in the wall of the colon, usually corresponding to points where blood vessels enter the wall of the intestine."

That was the extent of what Adam remembered from last year's Pathology course.

Oh shit, what's next?

"What are the indications for surgery?" asked the chief.

Adam looked at Turk and at the sea of faces of the other students all awaiting his answer. He heard himself saying, "Obstruction, perforation, bleeding, or a pattern of intractable disease."

Where the hell did that come from?

Barnett smiled. Turk nodded, giving tacit approval.

Dr. Theodorakis took the patient's pulse and wiped beads of sweat from the man's forehead. "How's he doing now?"

Holiday answered, "He's still running a fever, sir."

"He's sweating and his pulse is 118," Dr. Theodorakis stated. He looked at Kochenko and Wantz. "Please tell the students the likely sources of this man's temperature."

Kochenko answered. "Wind, water, or wound, sir. It could be post-operative fever from his lungs, a urinary tract infection, or he could have a developing wound infection or another intra-abdominal abscess."

"Could also be a reaction to a medication. We've got him coughing and his urinary catheter is still in place," added Wantz. "I didn't see any redness of his incision."

Dr. Theodorakis pulled back the covers and examined the man's incision. "You're right, there's very little erythema, but there is fluctuance to the mid-wound." He gestured towards the abdomen and waited while Barnett, Shrevi, and Adam all felt the sponginess in the area he had pointed out.

"Do we have a suture removal set and some culture tubes?" the chief asked. "I'm certain that he will improve and that cultures will identify enteric bacteria as the cause of his wound infection." Dr. Theodorakis looked at Shrevi. "Do you know why?"

"Well, he had a hole in his gut," Shrevi answered.

"A perforated colon, to be more exact as to the source of the bacteria, Doctor," corrected Dr. Theodorakis as he began to remove sutures in preparation to take cultures.

Somehow, when he said it that way, Shrevi's answer felt wrong, even though it was right.

CHAPTER 8

ON THE FEMALE ward, they ended with Adam's patient. His stomach knotted. He knew nothing about leg ulcers, other than that they were treated with wraps. Thankfully, Dr. Theodorakis did not ask a lot of questions. Instead, he explained to the group that this patient had congestive heart failure. He emphasized that her cardiac condition had caused fluid to accumulate in her legs and the resultant swelling caused the skin of her legs to break down.

"How do we treat these ulcers?"

"Unna boot wraps," Adam answered, thereby demonstrating his entire knowledge of the topic before the group again moved in descending pecking order and took the elevators up to the ICU.

Adam vowed to himself to study leg ulcers in detail. He wondered how Barnett would present the history on the stab wound patient who hadn't been able to give one.

Dr. Theodorakis seemed keenly interested when Adam presented Ronald Candy, who remained unresponsive and on the ventilator. After he described the physical findings and diagnosis, Holiday and Doyle answered questions about the operative findings and how the repair was done. Dr. Theodorakis pointed out to the group that herniating the liver through the diaphragm was a much less common response to blunt abdominal trauma than herniating the more mobile stomach or spleen on the other side of the abdomen.

They approached the stab wound, and Adam imagined Barnett would be chastised and humiliated for not knowing enough detail, but when they reached the patient's bed, Turk spoke up.

"This patient is a male in his late twenties or early thirties. He came in as a 'John Doe' after having been stabbed in the lower neck and supraclavicular region. A single stab wound was present, and he was hemodynamically unstable with a low blood pressure of fifty systolic. No other history could be obtained, and he was taken immediately to the operating room."

Adam realized the valuable lesson Turk had demonstrated— in this case, not being able to obtain a history was the history. Given the circumstances of the patient's condition on admission, there was no rebuke from Dr. Theodorakis. He simply accepted Turk's statement of fact and was much more interested in hearing Holiday describe the patient's intra-operative findings and management. Dr. Theodorakis emphasized to the students the importance of understanding the angle of the blade when a patient is stabbed. Understanding angle, depth, and size of the blade could help predict the extent of underlying injury.

"Why is it important that you come back and do a thorough neurologic exam when he wakes up?" he asked the three Service 1 students. Barnett answered that the patient had suffered a period of low blood pressure and that either that alone or the injury itself could have resulted in reduced blood flow to the brain with subsequent neurologic problems.

Dr. Theodorakis nodded at the answer and asked no more questions. He simply gazed at the patient and said in a soft voice, "Nice case."

With that he turned and disappeared. The other services dispersed, leaving Service 1 as a group standing around the patient's bed. Adam breathed a sigh of relief that he had made it through rounds without revealing his distressing lack of knowledge. The junior residents all looked to Holiday, who, along with Doyle and Kittamura, was slowly starting towards the door.

"Meet for rounds at the usual time tomorrow morning, 5:45. Male ward," said Holiday.

After the senior residents left, Wantz was the first to speak up.

"I don't think anybody else in the program could have saved that guy. That boy Holiday's got ice in his veins."

As the students began to leave the ICU, Rogers stopped them to explain. "'Nice case' is the highest praise Dr. Theodorakis ever gives."

CHAPTER 9

THE THREE STUDENTS trudged back to the male ward to recover the book bags they had left in the cabinet near the nurses' desk. After the preceding night's work, fatigue had caught up with each of them. They moved in slow succession, trying not to strain their tired muscles and unable to focus their foggy brains.

They turned to leave just as Wantz entered the ward.

"Where do you're think you're going? Are you lazy jerks? There's two new consults to be seen—a big fat prostitute on Gyne and some renal patient needs her belly looked at on Medicine. Nobody goes home until they've been seen. Turk's the guy on call and he went to see the case on the Gyne floor. You can meet him there."

He turned to Shrevi and pointed a threatening finger in his face.

"And you! Don't ever be late for rounds with the chief again!"

Kumar stammered back, "But I was in surgery and Turk hadn't finished the hernia…"

"Don't wait for Turk to teach you anything," Wantz declared. "You probably won't learn much from him. Besides, he's going into the lab next year and won't be around after that. Make sure those consults are done and their notes written."

Wantz stomped out of the ward, leaving the three students deflated.

"Does that mean Turk is going to do research?" asked Adam. "He must be really smart."

Barnett shook his head. "It's a euphemism. It means he's getting kicked out of the program."

"I don't understand," said Adam.

"This is a pyramidal program," explained Barnett. "It starts with about twelve interns. The bad ones get weeded out right away. Then some go into other specialties like urology or ortho. Later they thin out the group some more."

"But why?"

"Don't know for sure. As I understand it, the criteria vary and may be pretty subjective. If you seem slow or not proficient in the OR, or are not attentive in your patient care, or even if one of the attendings just doesn't like you, they assign you a lab project—'going into the lab for a year.' Problem is the year never ends—once you're in the lab, they don't take you out."

"That seems pretty arbitrary," said Adam, a bit shaken. "What happens in the lab?"

"Some guys do a successful project, but even so, if they want to finish their clinical training most of those guys have to find another program," said Barnett. "I heard some guys stay for years waiting to come back on the clinical service, but that rarely happens."

"How do you know all this?" asked Shrevi.

"Thought about going into General Surgery," said Barnett, "but it's too demanding."

Adam nodded and glanced at his fellow students. None of them had expected more work after a long night on call. Shrevi looked as though he was about to cry, and Barnett shrugged and sighed.

"I've got a five-month-old daughter at home," he said, "and I haven't seen her awake for three days."

Adam didn't waste any time thinking about Wantz's insistence that everybody had to stay.

"Why don't you guys take off and I'll see the consults," he said. "We'll never get through this rotation if we're all exhausted. I think we'll do better sharing some of this work. I just have a walk through the Quarter to get home and no plans other than trying to do some of this reading tonight. So take off. As long as one of us gets a history and physical on the chart, Wantz won't care."

"Thanks, buddy. I owe you one," Barnett sighed as he hoisted his book bag and headed for the door. "See you tomorrow morning."

"Yeah, thanks," added Shrevi. "Ah gotta git some sleep—nevah been this tired before."

As Adam reached down to pick up his book bag, the attractive nurse from rounds returned to her desk.

"You guys did a nice job with your presentations on rounds," she said. "My name is Jennifer, but my friends call me Jen."

"I'm Adam," he answered, and oddly, he wasn't tired anymore.

CHAPTER 10

TURK WAS STANDING at the foot of one of the beds in the center of the far wall when Adam arrived on the ward. Lying in the bed with a sheet barely covering her was the biggest person Adam had ever seen—easily in the range of 400 pounds.

Turk smiled as the student approached the patient's bed. "So you drew the short straw?"

"I don't mind. What's up?"

"Well," Turk began, "this is Luanne. She's a thirty-one-year-old female who was emergently operated for a tubo-ovarian abscess five days ago. Yesterday her wound started draining and this morning they opened the entire length of her incision and drained an infection. They want us to help with her wound care."

He pulled the sheet down, making eye contact as he stated, "Luanne, this is Dr. Sinclair. He is one of our medical students. He'll be helping with your wound care."

She merely nodded in acknowledgment. Adam shared the skepticism in her eyes. What he knew about wound care could be written on the head of a pin.

Turk pulled the sheet the rest of the way down and removed the abdominal pads held by tape across her entire lower belly, revealing a surgical wound worse than anything Adam could have imagined. A disrupted crater of gaping tissue stretched across her lower abdomen just above her pubis, extending to the prominent pelvic bones on both sides just above her hips. The sides of the wide-open incision were lined with seven or eight inches of discolored subcutaneous fat covered with pus. The depth of the incision was filled with a murky fluid that obscured the bottom of the wound itself.

Adam's eyes widened as he stared at the mess that was the patient's lower abdomen. *Stay professional,* he thought as he regained his composure. *Don't let her know you think it looks bad.* Bad was an understatement. It looked frightening.

He wondered how something that looked so hellish could ever heal.

Turk handed Adam gloves and a culture tube and watched as the student swabbed the base of the wound and prepared the tubes as he had seen done earlier on the male ward. It was a truly good thing that Adam wasn't squeamish. Turk used gauze sponges to clear the fluid from the base of the incision.

He spoke softly as he inspected the wound. "This is called a dehiscence. I can't clearly see the muscle fascia, but it is probably disrupted, so the important part of the wound closure is gone. I don't see any intestine, but with this much wound breakdown there is a chance it may extrude—if it does, that's called an evisceration and that requires an emergency trip back to the operating room."

He turned slightly to address the patient. "Ma'am, if we try to close this incision, it will just get infected again, so we are going to treat you with special dressings and let it heal slowly. That is called 'secondary intention healing.' Although there still is some risk of continued infection and further wound breakdown, we should be able to get it to close completely."

She nodded, but Adam wasn't sure she understood. Turk continued, "If it breaks down too much you might eviscerate, and then we have to go back to the operating room immediately." He paused, sensing she didn't understand the word. "Eviscerate means your guts come out."

Luanne looked shocked and scared, but Turk calmly continued. "As we get the wound clean, you will develop granulation—that's healing tissue. It will take a couple of weeks to replace the lining with that healing tissue, but in a few days, it will be more secure so nothing will pop out. If it heals well enough, we can even put stitches in the skin to speed up the last part of the process."

The patient nodded to indicate she finally understood. Adam was also reassured by Turk's calm explanation, although he couldn't imagine what the healing process would look like.

It took twenty minutes for them to clean the wound. Turk explained each step to Adam as they blotted away the remaining fluid, wiped the pus from the wound, and gently peeled the cellular debris off the surface. They packed the entire wound with gauze dressings soaked in saline. When they were finished, Turk got a clean sheet and wrapped it tightly around the patient. He secured it with safety pins so the sheet became a large bandage holding the dressings in place.

"So you can get out of here, let's go see the other patient," Turk said. "I'll come back and write a note later and you can do a history and physical tomorrow when it's convenient. I'll take the cultures to the lab."

"Why did they ask us to see that patient? The gynecologists are surgeons. Don't they take care of their own complications?"

"It's 'share the wealth,'" Turk answered. "They know how we're going to manage the wound and they could do the same dressing changes... But if something worse happens, they'll get called on the carpet at their department's Morbidity and Mortality conference. This way, they can say that General Surgery was managing the patient and making all the decisions. They think that absolves them of any responsibility if there is a bad result."

"Will a wound like that really heal?"

"Can't be certain," Turk responded. "It's pretty difficult to control for more infection in a place like Charity with open wards and all. If she eviscerates, there is a pretty high associated mortality rate. Ideally, we would stand a better chance of getting the wound to heal if we could change the dressing twice a day. If she does heal, she'll probably be left with an incisional hernia...but at least she'll still be."

CHAPTER 11

IN GENERAL, THE patients on the medical wards were sicker than those on the surgical services. They suffered from heart or lung failure, kidney disease, uncontrolled high blood pressure, or diabetes. Peering into the ward, Adam could tell by the number of oxygen set-ups and heart monitors that many of these patients would remain in the hospital much longer than the surgical patients who were otherwise basically healthy until the moment when they were stabbed or shot, beset by a bad gallbladder or appendix, or injured in an accident.

Adam and Turk stood in the doorway. Two LPNs sat on a wooden bench by the door, and one of them looked up and pointed a shaking finger. "Don't go in there… There's voodoo in there."

Turk shrugged as he and Adam skeptically stepped through the entry and approached the chart rack. Turk thumbed through the charts as the treatment room door opened and a young Black man appeared. He was dressed in sharply creased tan slacks and a white oxford button-down with a red, yellow, and navy striped tie. Despite the severe New Orleans humidity, his shirt remained crisp and clean as though it had just been starched and pressed.

"Hey, Jermaine," Turk greeted him. "Heard you got a consult you wanted us to see."

"Yeah, it's the darndest thing," he replied, handing Turk the chart. "Girl in bed 7…down the row on the right."

As they began walking towards the bed, Turk made introductions. "Adam Sinclair, M3, meet Dr. Jermaine Battiste—internist par excellence."

Battiste smiled. "Nice to meet you—actually, I'm a second-year resident. Got this lady I wanted an opinion on… Nineteen-year-old previously healthy girl came into our clinic three days ago complaining, 'My eyes is puffy and my ankles is swelled.' I dipsticked her urine in clinic and it was loaded with protein, so we admitted her with a diagnosis of nephrotic syndrome. You know what that is, Adam?"

Adam recalled last year's Pathology course. "It's a kidney disease where the body can't hold protein because it leaks into the urine."

"Yeah, that's right. It may eventually result in renal failure, but it is usually a very gradual process—might even be tolerated for years. This patient walks into the hospital clinic looking and sounding otherwise normal. Last night the nurses find this little old lady who was admitted to the ward across the hall with a diagnosis of congestive heart failure standing at the foot of the bed reciting a voodoo prayer at about two in the morning…and now we got this."

They stood at the foot of the bed, right where the old lady had been seen the night before. The young girl's face remained expressionless, eyes open as she stared straight towards the ceiling, neither blinking nor acknowledging her visitors.

"Completely catatonic," stated Battiste, "doesn't respond to words or touch. Her belly is a little distended, and my chief resident thought I should have you guys see her to be sure nothing is going on inside that could account for her mental status change. I don't see any evidence of infection, labs are OK except her kidney function is slightly worse than on admission, white blood cell count is normal… I got an obstructive series of the abdomen, which looks pretty nonspecific to me." He pointed to the X-ray films sitting on her bedside table.

Turk picked up the films and held them towards the ceiling lights as he studied them. He passed the first one to Adam. "I agree, the abdomen looks pretty nonspecific—maybe a bit of a paralytic ileus. See, Adam, there's a little air in the small bowel, which may account for the distension if she has lost peristalsis."

He looked at the second film and Battiste spoke. "We sat her up as much as possible to get the chest X-ray."

"No air under the diaphragm to suggest perforation, no pneumonia," Turk explained as he handed Adam the second film. He took his stethoscope, listened to the patient's chest and belly, and then used his right hand to press on the four quadrants of her abdomen. Throughout the exam she didn't flinch and her expression never changed.

"No obvious tenderness," concluded Turk.

"I got an ultrasound ordered," added Battiste, "but her liver functions are normal and I don't see any signs to suggest sepsis."

"Yeah—I agree," said Turk. "We'll put a note on the chart and follow up after the ultrasound is done."

Battiste looked at Turk. "One more thing, really strange. C'mon across the hall." Together they walked to the nurses' station in the opposite ward, where a chart and X-ray sat on the desk. Battiste handed the X-ray to Turk.

"After they found her chanting the curse, the old lady disappeared, just up and left—but look through her ER record and this chest X-ray... Fulminant congestive heart failure... wouldn't expect her to walk out of the hospital like that."

Turk held the X-ray up to the light and turned so he could share it with Adam.

"See this," he said, "the lung fields are normally dark because they are filled with air. Hers are completely white and the blood vessels are more prominent... All the classic findings indicating the fluid overload of heart failure."

"How was she able to even breathe with all that fluid in her lungs," asked Adam, "let alone walk out of the hospital?"

Turk shook his head. Battiste shrugged and replied, "Powerful juju, people really believe that voodoo stuff here."

As he waited by the elevator, Adam was overcome with fatigue. He was thinking about how comfortable his bed would feel when the elevator arrived and the doors opened. He jumped with a start when he realized he still had to replace the dressings on the old lady's leg ulcers.

CHAPTER 12

"Ah'm Rosalie," she said. "I like to know my doctors' names."

"I'm Adam," he stammered as he wrapped her legs.

"Well, Dr. Adam, if you're my doctor I expect I'll see a lot of you, then."

"It's Adam Sinclair," he said, looking for her full name on the chart.

She waited for him to speak.

"Mrs. Patton, I'm sorry if I was rude before when I removed your dressings. I should have introduced myself then. I'll be sure we change them more comfortably from now on, and I will do my best to get your legs to heal."

She offered a satisfied, knowing smile. "I know you will, Dr. Adam. Now you go home and get a good night's sleep. You look tired as all get out."

Chapter 13

THE WALK HOME to his studio apartment in the French Quarter usually allowed Adam to reflect on the day's lectures and organize his thoughts for the night's studying. The first chaotic night on call had left him unsettled. It wasn't the injuries he'd seen, but rather that he didn't feel he understood all the cases he had encountered in such a short period of time. He found himself unable to decide how to divide his study time, and whether he should read first about leg ulcers, stab wounds, diaphragm injuries, or wound healing. For the previous two years, when all his time was spent in class, the assignments were well-defined and the reading reinforced the same material covered in the lectures. Nothing in the classroom had been unexpected and no one talked of voodoo curses.

He was also bothered by what he had heard in the hospital. The word referring to the sickest patient on the ward brought to mind the racism traditionally associated with the South, which simmered below its polite surface. When he'd been a child living in a town with no Black people, the word was abstract and had no power, but applied to patients in the hospital it became instantly demeaning and hateful. Hearing it in the vocabulary of an educated physician made it cut like a knife.

Depending on his mood, Adam had his choice of routes back to his apartment at the corner of Decatur Street and Esplanade Avenue. He would take Chartres if he was in a hurry to get home to study, as the street was quiet and he could proceed quickly without interruption. Royal Street took a bit longer because he couldn't help but linger past the art galleries, restaurants, and boutiques and appreciate the stark contrast with the little Midwestern farm town where he had grown up. He remembered its one main street—lined by an implement store, two barbershops, two small groceries, a tavern and pool hall, a pharmacy with a soda fountain, and a restaurant that featured a meatloaf special on Tuesdays—as quaint, but its small town charm was no match for Royal Street's vibrant colors, unique architecture, and cuisine.

In the French Quarter, Adam felt he had stepped into an old European city. The uneven streets were made of stone that had been used as ballast in the ships that had carried slaves to the Port of New Orleans. He thought this must be what living in Paris would be like, not realizing Paris was as well known for its wide landscaped boulevards and magnificent gardens as for its old buildings or that New Orleans held a strong Spanish influence. There were also more Spanish influences in the Quarter than Adam had ever realized. The streets had been modeled after towns in Spain, and in many places the original Spanish street names were set in tile on the corners of buildings whose iron railings and tiled roofs reflected their true origins. Still, Adam romanticized his living circumstances as those of a struggling artist along the Left Bank of the Seine.

Across Canal Street, Carondolet became Bourbon Street, by far the most lively and entertaining of his possible routes home. The most notorious street in the French Quarter inherited its reputation as a den of iniquity after the city's infamous red-light district, Storyville, was closed down in the early part of the twentieth century. The musicians and others moved to the clubs on Bourbon from the brothels, and soon the street became a tourist attraction.

It was barely dusk and the sidewalks were already crowded with visitors and partygoers. The Alabama frat boys were easy to spot in their Crimson Tide shirts, and the over-accessorized transvestites were obvious, wearing dangling hoop earrings, long strands of pearls, large rings adorned with fake jewels, oversized wigs, and fancy high heels that made it difficult to navigate the cobblestones.

Adam enjoyed strolling down Bourbon, imagining the backgrounds of the people he saw. He paused to watch a conservative-appearing family walking directly down the middle of the street. They reminded him of the people in the town where he grew up. The father, sporting thick glasses, a flat-top haircut graying at the temples, and a skinny black tie and wrinkled blue suit, furtively glanced from side to side.

Pentecostal minister from Iowa, thought Adam, *probably thinks if he veers off center they'll be sucked into one of the strip clubs and forced to spend eternity in hell.* The man's prim wife reminded Adam of the women who appeared in magazine ads for refrigerators or washing machines. She clung tightly to the hands of her two wide-eyed teenagers, a boy and a girl, trying to discourage them from peering into the clubs, which swung their doors open to reveal a stripper dancing on the bar or around a pole, enticing onlookers to enter.

Adam paused to window shop in one of the countless souvenir stores. He enjoyed studying the displays of Mardi Gras beads and New Orleans cups, banners, and T-shirts emblazoned with stupid or silly slogans. His favorite was the black T-shirt with the image of a red crawfish in the center that read, "Bite the tail, suck the head"—instructions on how to best savor the local delicacy. The native crustaceans were displayed in multiple formats—bottle openers, calendars, mugs, and plates, and even on brightly colored lingerie mounted on busty mannequin torsos. Adam looked across the street to the poster of the busty brunette on the wall of the 809 Club. He broke into a wide grin as he recalled how he and several of his classmates had decided two years before to celebrate the completion of the Gross Anatomy final exam by attending a performance.

A great memory for the fifty-year class reunion...that is, if I make it through the third-year rotations.

He walked towards the corner of St. Peter, looking for the familiar neon sign of the Tasty Kitty Club, where he strained to see who was the barker that night whose job it was to swing the doors open long enough to entice the tourists. He hoped it would be the pretty girl with great legs, large breasts, and those perfect teeth that flashed a devastating smile. On the nights she was working, he would not turn onto St. Peter but continue the extra block just so he could walk past her.

Initially, when Adam walked by, she would open the door and say, "Six girls dancing tonight… C'mon in." Over time, she began to recognize Adam, and he would smile and nod as he passed, softly saying, "Good evening." She would smile back and eventually stopped opening the door, simply returning the greeting in a voice drenched with honey.

Adam longed to stop and talk to her. He wondered what kind of background she must have had to end up working at a seedy strip club. Was she a stripper too? Was she escaping a drunken stepfather or a drug-addicted boyfriend? Had she been sexually or physically abused? Had she grown up so poor and uneducated that this was the only job she could find? He couldn't imagine that she had chosen this occupation. Adam desperately wanted to learn more about her, but he was reluctant to stop. If she came into a clinic at Charity, he would have been perfectly comfortable talking with her about her life history. But here on Bourbon Street there was a social divide he could not cross.

That night, she wasn't at the door. Instead, the other barker was there—a gaunt White man, blond crewcut, uneven yellow teeth, tattered striped blue and white short-sleeve shirt with a pack of Camels in the pocket, faded jeans, and dirty cowboy boots. Adam turned right onto St. Peter.

Heading towards Jackson Square, he passed some of the evening's early revelers as they bought Kool-Aid red drinks in hurricane glasses from the window at Pat O'Brien's. Nearby, a few tourists milled about the entrance to Preservation Hall, although it wouldn't open for a couple of hours.

Worth waiting for, he thought, recalling all the Friday nights he had spent there, sitting on the floor listening to all the greats—Willie and Percy Humphrey, Big Jim Robinson, Narvin Kimball, Bunkie Smith, Cie Frazier, and Sweet Emma Barrett, who continued to play piano even after one hand had been paralyzed by a stroke.

No time for that now, though, gotta study.

Adam passed the Cathedral and entered Jackson Square at the time of day when many of the local artists were packing up for the evening, removing the pictures they had leaned against the fence surrounding the square. A few continued working, completing caricatures of tourists who sat patiently beside their easels.

Adam glanced into the window of the Gumbo Shop. Although he was hungry, he was so eager to get home to study that the saltines and peanut butter in his studio apartment would have to suffice for tonight. He turned left onto Decatur Street, walked past the iron fence that surrounded Jackson Square, and paused at the corner stoplight. Waiting for the light to change, he heard a familiar voice calling from the Café Du Monde across the street, "Docteur! Le Docteur!"

Chapter 14

Teddy Lemieux was Adam's first gay friend. They had met by chance during Adam's first semester in New Orleans when they shared a table on the Café Du Monde's always-crowded patio. Teddy was a fixture in the French Quarter. He couldn't walk down Royal Street without stopping and poking his head into most of the shops just so he could say hello to whomever was behind the counter. He kept an opulent apartment on the upper floor of a frame building just across from the Quarter on Esplanade. His home was filled with beautiful antiques that had been in his family's plantation home upriver "for generations." He was an expert on Louisiana history. He could spend the Saturday afternoons when Adam wasn't studying describing the architecture of the city, reviewing past and present restaurants, or comparing the latest political scandal to those of the past. He loved to keep up with fresh society gossip—both in the city and around the country—particularly when it involved Hollywood celebrities.

Sitting at the Café and listening to Teddy talk about the pot of jambalaya that his ancestors' servants kept on the plantation stove for seventy-five years was quite a bit different from the conversations Adam had heard back home. The rural Midwestern town where he grew up didn't have any outdoor cafés, just an old greasy spoon with a faded linoleum floor that was populated early in the morning by farmers in bib overalls and muddy boots. No fancy café au lait for them, just the dark brew poured from a Pyrex pot that sat on a hot plate behind the counter. Their conversations never involved art or history but were confined to more practical matters like how much the soybean yield per acre would increase if you tiled your field to improve the water run-off. Over time, Teddy's acquaintance made New Orleans seem like home to Adam. He advised him on where to shop, recommended a Chinese laundry, and steered him clear of the bad restaurants that advertised heavily just to attract tourists.

Adam recalled his reticence the first time Teddy had invited him to his home for dinner. Sensing his reluctance, Teddy had responded, "Oh for God's sake, I'm having eight people for dinner. Two of them are women, so stop worrying that I am planning to make a pass at you. And don't think that because I'm gay this will be some kind of orgy... I haven't done that in years, and besides, I'm so old now I can't even recall at those parties who does what to whom ."

The dinner had been a memorable evening. Beginning with the introductions to Teddy's other guests over champagne cocktails served with tiny crab-filled beignets, the conversation fascinated Adam. Over courses of crawfish bisque, shrimp and artichoke casserole, and poached red snapper served with Nantua sauce plated on elegant china from Teddy's family's ancestral plantation, accompanied by side dishes of creole ratatouille and dirty rice washed down by French champagne, Adam listened to discussions of the influence of Greek and Roman architecture on the columns that graced the old Southern mansions, Southern politics, the history of Mardi Gras, and the art and culture unique to New Orleans.

As a freshly made zabaione was served for dessert, Teddy entertained everyone with the story of "the judge." During the preceding Super Bowl weekend, Teddy had decided to rent his apartment at an exorbitant rate to a judge and his wife from Philadelphia. Wanting to keep an eye on his apartment and his antiques, he had informed them that his valet would stop by to make sure their needs were met. Everyone laughed at the irony when he described his surprise, upon showing up as the valet, at discovering the judge and his wife were Black. He laughed heartily when he reported that he ended up cooking, cleaning, and doing laundry for them all weekend as they enjoyed the comforts of his apartment's furnishings, most of which dated back to his family's history of being slaveholders.

"Docteur! Docteur!" Teddy was still calling from under the green awning at one of the small round tables on the café's patio. He stood out in his bright blue beret, colorful Hawaiian shirt, crisp khaki shorts, and leather sandals. His sunglasses hung by a strap around his neck below his well-manicured goatee. "Docteur, Docteur!" he continued. "Come join me, mon ami!"

Adam crossed the street and stood on the sidewalk. Even though they were separated by the low railing around the patio, he was close enough to see the flecks of powdered sugar the beignets had left trapped in Teddy's beard.

"Thanks, Teddy," Adam said, "but I've got to get home to do some studying. I've been up all night on Surgery call."

"That explains why you look so awful, mon ami! Have you eaten anything?"

"No, I was just going to head home and have some crackers and peanut butter while I read."

Teddy looked horrified as he climbed over the patio railing, being careful to bring the last half of his remaining beignet with him.

"I'll not hear of it, Docteur! You cannot learn to save lives on an empty stomach!"

He grabbed Adam by the arm and almost dragged him back up St. Peter, making a sharp left onto Royal Street. He pulled the surprised medical student another two blocks until he turned right on St. Louis and stopped in front of Antoine's Restaurant.

Teddy faced the elegant maître d' who stood stiffly at the restaurant's entrance.

"I need to speak to Laurance."

"Good evening, Teddy," he said, smiling. "You are not attired in a manner befitting our dress code."

"Of course not," Teddy answered. "I am not here to dine, but I must speak to Laurance for a moment."

The maître d' took a few steps into the restaurant. Moments later, he returned, accompanied by a tuxedoed waiter.

"Laurance, my dear friend, this is Doctor Sinclair, a top-notch student of medicine who has spent the night dragging souls from the brink of death. He needs sustenance. Can you help us?"

"Teddy, neither of you are dressed to be served and the dining room is full. We won't have a table for at least two to three hours."

"Nonsense!" Teddy replied. "We do not wish to dine here tonight. I simply want a meal prepared for my friend to take home so that he will be well-fortified before returning to his sacred mission to stomp out disease tomorrow morning."

"Teddy!" the maître d' interjected. "You know we do not do carry-out."

Teddy stared at him eye to eye.

The maître d' looked at Laurance and relented. "Take his order and ask the chef to prepare it as a favor. Make sure he knows it is for Teddy."

"Excellent." Teddy offered a wide smile. "Put it on my tab with the usual gratuity."

Adam stood dumbfounded while Teddy began to order without bothering to ask for a menu.

"He will start with a half dozen oysters Rockefeller and a half dozen Bienville, a salade Antoine…the Pompano Pontchartrain is exquisite…but you may prefer the crab mous amandine, as this season's soft shell are superb."

"The crab sounds delicious," Adam said, "but Teddy, I can't afford to pay you back for this."

"Nonsense, mon ami. It will be on my account. I insist."

Laurance smiled and reentered the restaurant. The maître d' laughed. "Only for you, Teddy."

Teddy turned back to the medical student. "You see, Docteur, that is the advantage of living in a city that appreciates elegance. Laurance has been my personal waiter for fifteen years, since my family's previous waiter retired. He is particularly grateful to me for introducing him to my friend Jeremy. They have lived together for seven years and are like a married couple. Rather an unusual circumstance usually denied to men of our persuasion, n'est-ce pas? Most of us find ourselves doomed to one-night stands or flitting between short-lived affairs."

Laurance soon returned with two shopping bags. Adam noted that for a place that didn't do carry-out, the kitchen staff certainly knew how to package a meal. He carried one of the bags and Teddy the other as they walked back towards the Café Du Monde and then continued on Decatur Street.

When they arrived at his apartment near the corner of Decatur and Esplanade, Adam opened the iron gate to the walkway that led to the building's entrance and the courtyard. Teddy handed him the second bag and patted him on the shoulder.

"Goodnight, mon ami. Study hard and be refreshed to pursue your calling in the morning. I will probably be at the Café Du Monde on Saturday afternoon observing the passing humanity. If you are free, come by and we will share some beignets."

The gate swung shut. Teddy rounded the corner and headed up Esplanade. Adam balanced the shopping bags and his book bag as he took a deep breath, salivating over the aroma from the bags, and made his way upstairs to his apartment.

CHAPTER 15

ADAM WAS AWAKENED by the loud buzzing of his alarm clock. His fingers stumbled over the surface to turn it off even though the apartment remained fully lit. On the coffee table, the heavy blue surgery textbook remained open to the chapter on wound healing. A yellow marker lay in the crease between the open pages, still uncapped from highlighting text on traumatic diaphragmatic hernias and leg ulcers. The dinner from Antoine's was scattered around the book. One plate was covered by the empty shells of the oysters Bienville, while next to it another plate contained four empty shells and two uneaten oysters Rockefeller. On the other side of the book, the largest plate was uncovered, but only a forkful of the soft-shell crab had been tasted. Next to that, the salad hadn't even been opened, and the French bread remained wrapped in aluminum foil.

Adam grabbed the small fork and scooped up the remaining two oysters. Even at room temperature, the flavored spinach was still delicious. He made his way across the room to the small kitchenette, where he placed the crab and the salad in the refrigerator. He undressed on his way to the bathroom, leaving his dirty clothes in a pile by the bathroom door.

The quick shave, warm shower, and fresh clothes revived him. He pulled a necktie from the pile of dirty clothes on the floor and stuffed the rest into the white linen laundry bag in the corner. He lifted his white coat from the back of the chair and packed his textbook and notebook into his canvas book bag. Then he turned out the lights and stepped into the hall, closing and locking the apartment door behind him.

Decatur Street was not a friendly or welcoming place before sunrise. The cobblestones smelled of piss and beer. Two people who were either drunk, homeless, or both were sleeping in doorways. Near the corner a dimly lit bar was still open. As he passed by, Adam looked through the open doors and could see a few shadowy figures still leaning on the bar.

Three more blocks and Adam reached Jackson Square. The patio of the Café Du Monde remained dark and empty, but two servers were wiping tables in the small, well-lit interior. The carry-out window was open for ordering from the patio, but Adam preferred to go inside to greet the servers and order a bag of beignets and a café au lait directly from the staff in their short-sleeved white shirts, linen caps, and dark aprons.

Before leaving, Adam stopped at a table, opened the bag, picked up a shaker, and sprinkled in an abundance of powdered sugar. He pinched the bag closed and shook it vigorously to make sure the beignets were well-coated.

Although it was said that the French Quarter became safer the closer one got to Canal Street, the last part of Adam's journey to the bus stop always unnerved him more than walking the three blocks from his apartment to the Café. He tried to avoid the string of seedy bars that remained open and the stragglers spilling out onto the street. The rough-looking bikers, rednecks, and disheveled hippies seemed as though they were looking for a fight, some still drinking from Styrofoam cups or accompanied by tough-looking women with tattoos and smeared eyeliner.

Adam always felt relief when he finally boarded the bus, took a seat, and tasted his first warm beignet. It was a short ride up Canal Street, and the brief walk to Charity gave him time to finish his coffee and French donuts. He stuffed the empty cup and bag in the trash receptacle on the corner across from the hospital and crossed the street, thinking about how the day would be organized. There was lecture in the morning and rounds to do, but he had no idea what else would be required by the residents, particularly Wantz.

Adam headed straight for the male ward when he stepped off the elevator. The morning light was beginning to make its way around the window shades. In the dim light, he recognized Shrevi standing near one of the beds in the middle of the row.

"Wantz says we've got to run the blood counts, change the dressings, and write a chart note on every patient before lecture. And if a patient we're following goes to surgery, we're expected to be in the OR, even if we have to miss lecture. Plus he wants us to write a history and physical on every patient on the ward. Some of these post-ops are ready to go home, so what's the point of doing another write-up?"

A short while later, a tired-looking Barnett joined them. "Sorry, guys… up all night. My baby's got colic. I went to the female ward first and did all the hematocrits. I got them recorded right here."

He pulled a folded sheet of yellow paper from his pocket. "You can have the results on your patients."

Adam smiled. "Thanks, that's great that you ran all of them." He saw Barnett as a complete straight arrow, so damn dependable, smart, and well-organized. He couldn't even imagine him loosening up and just having fun. *Probably was an Eagle Scout. Bet he never smoked a joint in college.*

Shrevi chimed in, "Wantz says we got to get all the dressings done and our notes written before lecture, but he told me we gotta make senior resident rounds with Holiday and Doyle about 6:30."

Barnett looked at his wrist. "It's ten to six. Let's get as much done as we can before they get here… I got running the hematocrits down cold, so why don't I do the ward while you guys change the dressings and write the notes… We'll have to do the histories after lecture."

Each student had only finished one or two patients when Wantz returned.

"Don't you guys know that the sickest patients are the ones in ICU? They're the ones you should see first every day!"

The three students finished writing their notes and placed the charts back in the rack.

While the other two left for the ICU, Adam pushed the cart back to the nurses' desk just as Jen entered the ward.

"Good morning," said Adam, thinking ahead to what he should say next.

"Hi," Jen answered.

Flustered, Adam couldn't think of anything worthwhile or clever to say, so he just smiled and watched as she plopped her large floral print bag onto the desk. Next to her Tupperware lunch container and thermos, a copy of *Watership Down* was just visible at the top of the bag.

When they reached ICU, Adam went straight to Ronald Candy. He found Ronald's chart on a clipboard hanging on the foot of the bed. The notes from the night nurses suggested that there had been no change in his condition since he arrived after surgery.

"Ronald," he said, shaking him slightly, but there was no response. Adam pulled his stethoscope from his coat pocket and listened to Ronald's heart and lungs. The ventilator maintained a constant rhythm to his respiration. Adam thought the sounds of Ronald's breathing were loud and coarse. He didn't have much ground for comparison but assumed that was fairly normal for someone on a ventilator who had a tube in his chest. The chest tube appeared secure, and the nurses' notes did not indicate anything unusual about the tube's drainage. Before he removed the dressing on the abdominal incision, Adam noticed some pink fluid staining the gauze around the drain. He knew pink was preferable to the green of bile leaking from the liver.

Before Adam could write a progress note on the chart, Holiday and Doyle arrived on the unit. They were followed in short order by the rest of the service—Kittamura, Rogers, Kochenko, and Turk. Wantz arrived shortly after. They congregated around Ronald's bed, and the other students interrupted what they were doing with their patients to join them.

After rounds, Holiday addressed the students. "We've got a couple of elective cases to do in the OR. Since you don't know these patients, you can finish your notes and dressings. After today, plan to go to the OR with the patients you follow. We need one of you to drop off a chart and X-rays at the Surgery Department's office for this week's Bullpen. We can catch up later when you finish rounds. We don't expect any rounds with Theo today, we're not on call for the ER, and we don't have clinic today, so maybe you can get out early, like about 6:00 or 7:00."

Holiday walked towards the elevators, leaving Wantz the only remaining resident with the students. Wantz thrust a large manila folder and an even bigger X-ray folder into Adam's hands. "Give these to Miss Viola in the Surgery Department office. Don't fuck it up...and remember I want those histories and physicals done on all the patients."

Wantz left the three students staring at each other. No one spoke, but they were all thinking that 6 p.m. didn't seem early or even realistic if they had to complete all those histories and physicals.

Chapter 16

THE MEDICAL SCHOOL elevator squeaked and groaned until the doors opened and Adam stepped across the hall and entered the department office. He was greeted by a thin, proper Black lady in a conservative blue dress with a string of pearls around her neck. Behind her was a credenza filled with pictures, notebooks, and a small awards plaque. On either side of the credenza stood multiple file cabinets. To her right, above the narrow table that extended her desk space, four framed composite pictures identifying the students in each class were arranged in order on the wall.

Miss Viola was a medical school legend. It was said that she began her career working in the Housekeeping Department at Charity and had risen from that position until she had become the most essential employee in the Department of Surgery. The residents said that Dr. Theodorakis relied on her completely to keep the department running smoothly and often sought her advice regarding administrative matters and scheduling. She was the liaison for any student who had concerns about his or her rotation.

"I was told to drop this off for Bullpen tomorrow." Adam placed the X-ray folder and chart on the corner of her desk.

"I'll be sure he gets it." She turned away and surveyed the class pictures on the adjacent wall. "But now, Dr. Sinclair, I think you had better get to lecture."

"Yes, ma'am," Adam replied and scurried for the door.

In contrast to the large lecture halls for the first- and second-year classes, the room for the surgical lectures only held about twenty students. Adam made his way towards the back row, where he found a seat between Barnett and Shrevi. Before he sat down, he noticed an abandoned copy of the morning's *Times-Picayune* on the seat in front of him with the headline, "GOVERNOR INDICTED AGAIN."

Dr. Brewster, the head surgeon on Service 4, stood at the lectern. He had a stern frown and a reputation for taking pleasure in humiliating residents and students by asking difficult questions on rounds and embarrassing them when they didn't know the answer.

His topic for the morning was inguinal hernias. Without any introduction, he gave a brief review of historical perspectives, then flashed his first slide on the screen. There were no labels on the picture of inguinal anatomy being projected.

"Can anyone name the important anatomical landmarks relevant to hernia surgery?" Dr. Brewster asked. "How about a volunteer coming down here and using the pointer?"

No one spoke up. Dr. Brewster did not hide his scorn when he used the wooden pointer aggressively to explain the anatomical landmarks.

Adam was surprised when he glanced at Shrevi's notebook and discovered that his classmate had made a drawing of the inguinal area and labeled everything before Brewster began explaining the anatomy.

Seeing the astonishment on Adam's face, Shrevi leaned towards him and whispered, "Turk taught me all the anatomy when I watched him do that hernia."

When Brewster finished the lecture, Shrevi said, "Let's get some lunch in the cafeteria. They got jambalaya today."

"I'll meet you there after I call my wife," said Barnett.

"I got an errand to run, so I'll just meet you on the wards in time for rounds with the residents," added Adam.

When he returned to the first floor, Adam rounded the corner and proceeded down a hallway to the campus bookstore. He entered and turned to the left, away from the textbooks and towards the wall where the stethoscopes, reflex hammers, blood pressure cuffs, and other supplies were displayed. After searching with no luck, he approached the thin young man who stood behind the cash register, chewing gum and leaning forward on his elbows while reading a paperback by Mickey Spillane.

"Got any bandage scissors?"

"Naw," replied the young man, not looking up from the page. "Ah think we been out of them for a while. Might be some on back order."

"Any idea when they'll be coming in?"

"Don't rightly know… Might be next week…or next month. Mebbe not comin' at all."

Adam nodded and turned to leave, thinking, *No wonder it's called the City that Care Forgot.*

Walking onto the female ward, Adam found Doyle talking to a tall, thin Black man at the foot of Mrs. Patton's bed. Adam stepped towards the head of the bed.

"Good afternoon, Mrs. Patton," he said before looking towards Doyle.

"Hello, Doctor," she replied gesturing towards the young man standing with Doyle. "This is my son, Cyril."

Adam reached to shake his hand, a little surprised as she continued the introduction. "This is another of my doctors, Adam Sinclair. He works with Dr. Doyle." Adam hadn't known he was anybody's doctor, but he liked being referred to that way.

Doyle turned to Adam. "Her dressings are OK. I plan to let her go home tomorrow after one of the internists adjusts her medications. Head up to ICU. We're going to meet there for rounds. I'll be along shortly."

Adam made it a point to turn towards Mrs. Patton. "Excuse me, then, ma'am. I'll try to get here early tomorrow to do your dressings."

She acknowledged him with a satisfied smile.

Barnett, Shrevi, Kochenko, Turk, Kittamura, Rogers, and Wantz were already on the unit when Adam arrived. While they were waiting, Adam picked up the chart of the man who had been stabbed in the neck. The name 'John Doe' had been crossed out and replaced by a handwritten 'Demarcus Foster.' Adam turned to the nurses' notes but had no time to read them since Holiday stepped onto the ward along with Doyle.

The group crowded around Foster's bed. Holiday took the dressing down so that everyone could see the incision. He asked Mr. Foster to squeeze his fingers, offering the index and third finger of each hand to the patient.

"Left is maybe a little weaker than the right, but pretty good. Can you tell me your name?"

"Demarcus."

Adam watched Holiday's brief neurologic exam intently and thought about how to interpret the findings like a doctor: *Soft voice but not hoarse—no injury to the laryngeal nerve and ability to speak intact. No damage to the brain's language center.*

When they reached Ronald's bed, Adam chose his words carefully as he described his observations. He was pleased and relieved when Rogers confirmed his findings and stated that now they just needed to watch for any developing infection and await any neurologic recovery.

On the wards, rounds with the residents were much more relaxed than those with Dr. Theodorakis. Most of the residents seemed to enjoy taking the time to answer the students' questions or to explain the details of a patient's illness. Even Wantz lost his perpetual scowl while explaining the differential diagnosis of blood in the stool.

The group returned to the Medicine female ward, where Dr. Battiste, the medical resident, was looking at Mrs. Patton's chart. Turk leaned towards Adam's ear and softly said, "Glad Battiste is caring for her. Managing her heart failure as an outpatient is going to be a challenge. Doyle likes to get him involved when we need an internist."

"The way he talks, I didn't think Doyle likes Black people," Adam whispered to Kochenko and Turk.

"Likes good doctors," said Kochenko.

On the Medicine ward, the Voodoo Lady remained catatonic. Adam summarized her status: "Ultrasound of the gallbladder is normal, and her abdomen is now soft to touch without any grimacing…but there has been further worsening of her kidney function as reflected in the continued elevation of her BUN and creatinine."

Adam told the story of the voodoo curse and the disappearance of the little old lady from across the hall. Doyle rolled his eyes. "I suppose Marie Laveau is in the next bed." Adam understood the reference to the nineteenth-century voodoo queen from his walks past the museum in the Quarter, but Barnett stepped to the foot of the next bed and looked at the clipboard that hung from the bed frame.

"No, sir… This is Betsy Crawford."

They rode the elevator down to the Gynecology floor, and Adam removed Luanne's dressing as he explained the history of her pelvic infection and emergency surgery. Luanne didn't seem to mind having the young doctors crowding around her bed, staring at her huge gaping wound. She didn't speak but watched their faces closely for their reactions.

"Be nice if we could use some streptokinase on the superficial stuff," said Rogers.

"You guys know what that is?" Doyle addressed the three students, all of whom strained to remember that term from Pharmacology class. "It's an enzyme that loosens and digests unhealthy tissue or blood clots. Some people recommend it for wound debridement; using it to remove the nonviable surface tissue might get the wound to heal faster…but good luck finding any around here… I doubt the pharmacy has any. It would be a big surprise if the State of Louisiana would pay to stock any here."

He poured some saline onto the gauze that sat on her bedside table and placed the moist gauze on top of her wound.

"Sinclair, you know how to debride this and redress it?"

"Yes, sir," Adam answered.

"Good. You finish up here and you guys make sure you've got all the dressings changed and progress notes written. We'll meet at 6 a.m. in ICU for rounds. The department has Grand Rounds at 9 a.m., and Bullpen starts at 11 a.m. Everybody else can take off… Kochenko's on call to stay in house tonight."

CHAPTER 17

ADAM HAD COMPLETED the history and physical exam on both the consults. He found Barnett on the male ward preparing to examine the man with the perforated colon. Barnett had positioned the bedside tray table at the foot of the bed. The tabletop was crowded with a reflex hammer, tuning fork, stethoscope, blood pressure cuff, and an otoscope. Next to the instruments he had placed a pad of yellow Charity Hospital notes, his copy of *DeGowin's Bedside Diagnostic Examination,* and the mimeographed outline of the history and physical that had been distributed in last year's Physical Diagnosis course.

Barnett, reading from the opening question on his outline, turned to Adam and said,

"It doesn't seem appropriate to just ask, 'What brings you into the hospital today?'"

"No, it seems pretty obvious," agreed Adam.

Adam stood by, watching as Barnett methodically worked his way through the history and physical, examining every anatomical structure and orifice, writing his notes as he proceeded.

Shrevi joined them, holding several loose yellow sheets in his hand.

"This is going to take us forever to do each of these," said Barnett. "I've only done those consults, still gotta do the wards. How many have you done?" he asked Shrevi.

"Got all mine done." He waved the sheaf of papers.

"How did you ever do them all?" asked Adam as they watched Barnett complete his notes on the yellow pad.

Before Shrevi could answer, Wantz and Kittamura entered the ward.

"How are those histories?" demanded Wantz.

Barnett handed him the fifteen pages he had recorded in his best handwriting. Wantz thumbed through the papers.

"Jesus Christ! Who the fuck do you think is going to read anything this damn long? Do it again so we can make sense of it."

He tossed Barnett's work into the metal waste basket next to the desk. Barnett's face dropped.

"What about you?" he asked Shrevi.

"I did four of 'em." He held up seven of the progress note sheets.

"Let me see one." Wantz took the first two pages from Shrevi. Adam and Barnett could see that he had written one and a half pages on one side only.

Wantz concentrated on reading, remaining silent like a tea kettle that hadn't yet begun to boil.

"Now this is what I'm talkin' about, for Chrissakes! This is good… It's complete, it's thorough, and it's short."

He handed the papers back to Shrevi. "You need to teach these guys how to do this." As he left the ward, Wantz almost bumped into Kittamura, who had been quietly watching them.

Adam and Barnett crowded around Shrevi while Kittamura retrieved Barnett's history from the trash, sat down at the desk, and began reading.

"How'd you condense these?" asked Adam.

"And how did you get so many done?" added Barnett.

Shrevi grinned. "Oh hell, I figured he wasn't going to read everything on the chart, so I just copied the ones that were already on there into my handwriting. Turk had originally done the one I handed him."

"Brilliant," said Adam, but Barnett looked skeptical.

"I think we're supposed to do them ourselves…even if it is a pain in the ass." *Eagle Scout, for sure.*

As Barnett returned to the bedside table and began to rewrite his history on the yellow progress sheets, Kittamura stood up, holding Barnett's papers. Adam watched as Kittamura walked up to Barnett and said quietly, "May I keep? Good English."

Barnett and Kittamura spoke briefly before the resident left the ward while studying the discarded notes.

Barnett looked down at the now empty yellow notepad and sighed. "My wife's going crazy with a crying baby. I've still got to change the dressings on my other patients and the one in ICU."

"I'll do the dressing changes for you. Just go home to help your wife," said Adam. "Besides, this will be good practice for me before I tackle the dressing on the fat lady on the OB-GYNE floor."

Shrevi was anxious to leave too, but he followed Adam's example.

"I've got nothing cooking tonight, so I'll write the progress note on this guy and then do the dressing in ICU while you do the GYNE one."

After Barnett thanked them and departed, Shrevi retrieved the chart while Adam carried dressings from the treatment room to the bed at the end of the ward. He began to awkwardly pull the tape off the old dressings when Jen approached.

"Do you know how to do wet to dries?"

"Sort of," Adam made a poor attempt to hide his ignorance.

"Let me show you a better way," she said.

She took a bandage scissors from her pocket, used it to loosen the rest of the dressings, and after putting on a pair of gloves, pulled the remaining dressings off and tossed them into the small waste basket beside the bed.

"The theory is that if a moist dressing dries in contact with the wound, any dead tissue will stick to it and be removed when you peel off the gauze." She opened some gauze pads and reached for the bottle of sterile saline on the patient's nightstand, then saturated the gauze. Adam watched carefully but looked up long enough to see Shrevi peering over the chart. He smiled and winked. She continued, "If you unfold the gauze, you can place a smooth layer flat against the wound and its edges. Try not to leave the moist part of the dressing on the surrounding healthy skin because it will macerate it."

Jen positioned the first piece of gauze and watched as Adam completed the coverage of the wound. She then instructed him to apply a layer of dry gauze and larger abdominal pads that covered the whole wound. A generous amount of wide adhesive tape was used to hold the dressings in place.

"Tomorrow I'll have some Montgomery straps to hold the dressings. They'll be less irritating than all this tape on the skin."

"Thanks." Adam stared after her as she walked back to her desk while he wondered what Montgomery straps were.

Shrevi stepped closer to him. "Nice job," he said, not referring to the dressing.

CHAPTER 18

JEN'S INSTRUCTIONS MADE Adam more comfortable beginning the dressing change on Luanne, whose body overflowed the bed as she lay with her back propped up on pillows. She didn't seem to mind being exposed as he readied his supplies on the bedside table. A dingy bedsheet was draped across her knees and lower legs. Her gown was pulled up to her chest, exposing her huge abdomen and the dressings across her lower belly. Her breasts filled the folded gown, but a giant nipple stared at Adam from under the crumpled edge. She was comfortably situated as Adam carefully removed her dressings and tossed them aside.

"We'll probably need to trim away some of that stuff on the surface."

Adam turned to find Bennett Turk standing behind him, opening a small disposable instrument set containing a pointed scissors and tweezers.

"Go ahead and cut some of that stuff before you replace the dressing," Turk said.

Adam took the instruments and tentatively clipped at the loose, pus-like strands covering the wound edges. "You've got to get rid of that gray fatty stuff lining the edges," Turk continued. "You have to cut it back until it bleeds." He looked at Luanne and added, "Let us know if it hurts."

"Don't be worryin'. You'll be the first to know if it hurts!" she answered. Reassured by Turk's presence, Adam cut more boldly and soon the edges were oozing.

"It will usually stop with gentle pressure from the gauze, or you can use one of these on the bleeding points," Turk added, drawing a little wooden stick from his chest pocket. He pointed to the tiny, dark bulb where it looked like the end of the stick had been dipped in something. "Silver nitrate," he said as he touched the end of the stick to a bleeding point on the edge of Luanne's wound. The tip of the stick turned gray as it left a dark scab on the wound edge, and the oozing stopped.

"Where can I get that streptokinase stuff that Rogers mentioned?" asked Adam.

"I doubt there's any available…but you can check with Doc Augustin down in the pharmacy."

"Anything else I need to do before I leave?" Adam hoped his eagerness counted for something.

"I got nothing," said Turk as he turned to leave the ward, "but check with the other guys."

Adam applied the last pieces of tape to the dressings. "How was that?" he asked. "Not too uncomfortable, I hope." He pulled the sheet up and the gown down.

"No, not too bad," she said. She even smiled when he told her he'd be in early the next day to change her dressing again.

$\backsim$

Adam rode the elevator up to the floor where the resident call rooms were located. He walked down the hall and got a whiff of incense when he stopped in front of a door that was slightly ajar. He knocked gently and pushed the door open just enough to see into the darkened room. Kochenko was sitting cross-legged in the shadows on the end of the bed. His palms were outstretched, resting on his knees, and he was humming softly. His eyes were closed until he opened first one and then the other as he heard Adam enter the room.

"Meditation," he said. "Great for mind and body, just like the Maharishi says... Rejuvenates everything."

"I finished the dressings," said Adam. "Anything else you want me to do?"

"I don't have anything." He paused and gave a sly grin. "Don't look for Wantz... I'm sure he'd find something for you to do. I think everyone has pretty much scattered. Doyle and Holiday may have left the hospital. Rogers is down in the ER, but he's just hangin' out to talk with his girlfriend." He closed his eyes and began humming again as Adam pulled the door closed behind him.

$\backsim$

Adam rang the bell at the pharmacy pickup station. A young woman in a short white coat greeted him.

"Is Dr. Augustin around?" he asked.

"I'll check if he's still here," she replied and disappeared among the rows of metal shelves stocked with plastic bins filled with bags of intravenous fluids, vials of medication, and jars of pills.

Adam waited nervously. Secretly, he was anxious to meet the director—he'd heard the rumor his first year that the pharmacy was run by a man whose son was a guitarist for Parliament-Funkadelic, and that every time they played in New Orleans he was besieged by hospital employees wanting free tickets.

A tall, distinguished Black man approached the door. "I am Dr. Augustin," he said. "Were you looking for me?"

"Yes, sir, I'm Adam Sinclair...an M3 on the General Surgery rotation. I was wondering if you had any streptokinase."

"What do you want it for?"

"I've got a patient upstairs with a really bad open wound, and my residents thought it might help to clean it."

"You know the State of Louisiana doesn't want to pay for any of those fancy medicines," he stated.

"Yes, sir, I suppose not...but I thought it couldn't hurt to ask."

"Come back midweek," he said, turning away and disappearing among the stocked metal shelves.

CHAPTER 19

As he walked down Canal Street, Adam thought for a fleeting moment that he'd like to listen to music at Preservation Hall, but there was so much material to cover he felt he had to discipline himself to study on Friday nights. He paused at the corner of Canal and St. Charles. Directly across Canal was the French Quarter, where St. Charles became Royal Street. Before crossing the street, he looked up at the glaring purple and white "K and B" sign that marked the entrance to the corner drugstore.

Good time to pick up a few necessities, he thought.

He strolled through the aisles, grabbing a navy blue canvas gym bag, a tube of toothpaste, a can of shaving cream, a travel toothbrush, and a plastic razor. He added a bar of soap and a plastic soap dish to his cart, then stopped at the first aid supplies. The rolls of adhesive tape, elastic bandages, band-aids, tweezers, and other implements almost obscured the empty hook with the sign reading "bandage scissors."

On his way to the cashier, Adam passed through the section containing school supplies. Among the crayons and colored pens he spotted a small, blunt scissors, the kind first graders used on construction paper. He tossed it into his cart.

At the checkout counter, he placed his purchases into the gym bag so he didn't have too much to carry. After paying, he crossed Canal, and after walking a block on Royal he turned right for a block and then made a left turn onto Chartres. The gym bag in one hand and his book bag in the other were a bit heavy, but he still paused to look into the expansive windows of Hurwitz-Mintz Furniture. Each window display represented a complete room decorated with thick Oriental rugs and a mix of antiques and formal furniture. The center of the living room display was a massive, tufted leather sofa surrounded by delicate wooden end tables. Ming vases, overstuffed chairs, and a cut-crystal bar set completed the inviting scene. The bedroom display contained classic upholstered seating, beautiful wooden chests, dressers, and armoires along with a big, soft four-poster bed unlike anything Adam had ever seen. The air of sophistication and elegance suggested the genteel richness of life in an old plantation home, much like the one Teddy's ancestors had owned, he supposed.

After a moment he moved along the street, heading straight home, anticipating the pleasure of finishing the soft-shell crab and salad still resting in his refrigerator.

CHAPTER 20

ADAM ARRIVED AT Charity before sunrise on Saturday. By 5:15, all the hematocrits had been done and rounds were continuing smoothly. Shrevi did the male ward, Barnett the female, with Adam starting in ICU and then moving on to the consults on the other floors. The first vestiges of daylight were peeking around the window shades when Adam stood at the foot of the bed reading Demarcus Foster's chart.

He flipped through the pages, noting that Barnett's history was only two pages.

He asked, "Who stabbed you?"

"Mah wife."

"Your wife? Why?"

"That woman's got a powerful temper."

Adam had so many more questions, but he felt rushed because he had to make rounds again with the residents before the morning conferences. He completed his ICU work and moved on to the other floors.

The Voodoo Lady continued to stare into space, and her belly remained soft. The only change Adam noted was a worsening of her kidney function. Both the BUN and creatinine had substantially elevated, and her recorded urine output had dropped well below normal.

Adam joined his classmates and the residents on the male ward.

"We're going to need to get to the amphitheater for Grand Rounds," said Holiday. He looked at Rogers. "Terry, you and Wantz had better go downstairs to meet the students who have Bullpen today and give them their assignments. You students join us when you've finished."

Shrevi hurried after the residents as they left the ward and headed for the elevators. At the end of the ward, Barnett watched Jen finish redressing his patient's wound infection. As he approached the bed, Adam could see that the gauze pads were no longer being held in place by multiple pieces of adhesive tape stretched across the patient's skin. Instead, individual strips of tape were stuck to the side along the length of the incision. The part of the tape that covered the dressings had been folded on itself so that no adhesive surface was in contact with the dressings directly over the incision. She had made a small hole in each piece and was tying a long white shoelace that she had threaded through the holes to create a secure lattice holding the gauze in place. Barnett's attention was focused on what the nurse was doing.

"Montgomery straps," announced Adam.

Jen looked up at him. Adam thought she was even prettier when she smiled that way.

"These won't irritate his skin like pulling the tape off every time the dressing is changed. Just leave the side straps in place, untie the laces, put a new dressing on, and then re-thread and tie the shoelaces."

Barnett nodded his understanding. "Thanks," he said, still studying the dressing.

CHAPTER 21

ADAM FELT HE was stepping into another century when he entered the surgical amphitheater located on the operating room floor. The Delgado Auditorium was a large room lined by a semi-circle of tiled tiers and wooden benches that had been built in the time when notable surgeons of the day demonstrated their skills and new techniques to visiting colleagues, before sterile technique was a rigorous practice.

The students sat high up near the rear of the hall. The front rows were occupied by residents, surgeons from the neighboring community hospitals, and academic faculty. Grand Rounds began promptly at 9 a.m., when one of the residents on Service 4 presented a case of portal hypertension with gastrointestinal bleeding in a patient with cirrhosis of the liver. Adam remembered the appearance of a slide of a similar liver from Pathology, but the complexity of the discussion of surgical treatment was difficult for him to follow. Dr. Brewster of Service 4 was arguing aspects of surgical technique with the head of Service 2. Adam understood that they were saying something about reducing the pressure in the veins leading to the liver while maintaining adequate blood flow to nourish the liver, but the rest of the argument was lost on him. They argued back and forth until Dr. Theodorakis ended the conversation by simply stating to a red-faced Dr. Brewster, "The studies done in my laboratory have not borne out those assertions."

With the discussion ended, Adam opened the spiral notebook that he carried in his book bag, turned to the first empty page, and wrote in big block letters: READ SECTION ON LIVER DISEASE.

CHAPTER 22

AT THE END of the conference, the amphitheater momentarily resembled the seventh inning stretch at a baseball game when the home team was losing. Like fair-weather season ticket holders, the community surgeons and teaching attendings filed out. The students who were standing up and talking or stretching used the opportunity to move down into the closer seats.

The premise of Bullpen was simple. Throughout the course of the year, members of the senior class would be selected to perform a history and physical exam on a patient and then present their findings to the amphitheater and be grilled by faculty. As a teaching exercise it was entertaining and informative, but for the underclassmen there was an undercurrent of dread knowing that someday it would be their turn to present.

Kochenko had joined Wantz on a wooden bench at the front of the room. Wantz held an X-ray folder that Adam realized was the same one he had delivered to Miss Viola. Dr. Theodorakis moved over to chat with them until all the students had taken their seats and two nervous senior students entered and sat on another wooden bench facing the residents' bench. They were accompanied by their patients, both wearing Charity Hospital gowns, faded linen robes, and cardboard sandals.

There was an immediate hush when Dr. Theodorakis turned to face the audience.

"Let's begin," he stated. "Dr. Johnson, you are first."

The fourth-year student approached and stood at the lectern, fiercely gripping it to keep the room from seeing his hands shake. Staring at his notes before him, he gave himself away as his voice cracked before he had completely uttered his first sentence.

"Mr. R.G. is a forty-two-year-old Black male who presented to the Charity ER five days ago after vomiting bright red blood. At the time he presented he had vomited three times, each time approximately one cup. He also reported sharp, fairly constant epigastric discomfort for the week preceding the vomiting. He has no significant surgical or past medical history. He has no allergies and denies use of any medications including any aspirin products. He smokes a pack of cigarettes per day and drinks a six-pack of beer daily. His family history and review of systems are completely negative. On physical exam his blood pressure is 110/70, pulse 84 and regular, respirations 12, and he is afebrile. HEENT exam is negative, the neck is supple without mass or bruit, chest is clear, heart tones are regular without murmur, his abdomen is scaphoid, nontender, no masses. Rectal exam reveals dark stool that is guaiac positive. Musculoskeletal, GU, neuro, and psychiatric exams are normal."

Johnson paused. Anticipation filled the room until Dr. Theodorakis broke the silence.

"Impression?"

The medical student took a deep breath. "I believe the patient has gastrointestinal bleeding, probably from the upper GI tract."

"You've made the obvious deduction," said Dr. Theodorakis, "but can you tell us the differential diagnosis that may lead to that presentation?"

Johnson responded, "Gastritis, esophageal varices, gastric ulcer, duodenal ulcer..."

As the student continued his answer, Dr. Theodorakis stepped to the chalkboard and began a numbered list, writing the diagnoses as Johnson recited them.

"Gastric cancer, duodenal cancer, gastric adenoma, duodenal adenoma, pancreatic carcinoma, tumor of the ampulla of Vater..."

Dr. Theodorakis continued with his list, but after number nine he stopped writing the diagnoses and only continued numbering: ten, eleven, twelve, thirteen...

By the time the chairman had reached number nineteen, Johnson was wide-eyed and beads of sweat visibly glistened on his forehead. He continued, "Aorto-duodenal fistula, trauma following instrumentation, local invasion of the stomach by adjacent colon cancer..."

Dr. Theodorakis stopped numbering at thirty-four and addressed him. "Okay, Doctor, you've mentioned many diagnoses, but let's take a careful look at your list."

He turned to the audience. "As you can see, Dr. Johnson has only mentioned problems of a surgical nature. As thoughtful physicians, it behooves us to remember when we evaluate a patient with GI bleeding that not all causes of bleeding require a surgical solution."

He followed this with a discussion of a variety of medical problems—hemophilia, coagulation factor deficiencies, platelet abnormalities, including Von Willebrand's disease, and rare vascular abnormalities such as Osler-Weber-Rendu syndrome, which (if that wasn't hard enough to remember) was also known as hereditary hemorrhagic telangiectasia. He emphasized that all these must be considered when evaluating a GI bleeder.

"Dr. Johnson," the chief continued, "at this point what is your working diagnosis and what confirmatory studies would you request?"

"I believe this represents a bleeding ulcer, and I would want either an endoscopic examination or the performance of an upper GI X-ray."

Wantz stood up and pulled the X-ray films from the manila folder. He mounted them in a row on the view boxes at the front of the room and switched on the lights behind the films.

"There's the upper GI," said Theodorakis. "Please read it for us."

Johnson approached the view box as though it was going to bite him and spent an intense moment studying the films.

"I believe this irregularity on the edge of the duodenum represents an ulcer crater filled with contrast," he said, pointing to an area on one of the films.

"That is correct," stated the chief. "Those of you who cannot appreciate this from where you are sitting, please come down for a closer look when you leave today. Next case."

The next student approached the lectern as tentatively as Johnson had. His presentation was surprisingly similar to the first case.

"Well, Doctor, everyone in the room knows the differential diagnosis of upper gastrointestinal bleeding. Let's cut to the chase. What is the diagnosis in your particular patient?"

The student straightened up, confidently answering, "I believe this patient has a bleeding peptic ulcer."

"Why, Doctor, are you certain? What do you think of that blue lesion on his lower lip that I can see even from across the room?"

The patient automatically stood up as Dr. Theodorakis approached him. The chairman pulled a gauze sponge from his suit coat pocket and used it to pull down the patient's lower lip before asking the man to hold the gauze pad himself.

"This is the classic vascular lesion of Osler-Weber-Rendu syndrome—hereditary hemorrhagic telangiectasia. Please note it on your way out today."

As they began to leave the amphitheater that morning, a few students, including Adam, Barnett, and Shrevi, stopped to take a closer look at the ulcer on the X-ray films, but all two hundred students paused to remember the lesion prominently displayed as they filed out past the man who stood by the doorway tugging his lip down with a folded piece of gauze.

CHAPTER 23

ADAM HEADED STRAIGHT for the female ward after Bullpen. A new box of Unna boots had been placed on the cabinet shelf in the treatment room. He helped himself to a couple, along with rolled gauze and Ace wraps.

When he approached Rosalie Patton's bed, she was eating from the lunch tray that had been placed on the roller table in front of her.

"Hi," he said. "Ma'am, would you prefer I come back after you've finished lunch?"

She smiled. "That's polite, but no, Doctor. I am just going to sip my coffee, so you do what you need to—besides, my son is going to come for me in a little while."

"Yes, ma'am," Adam replied. "If you don't mind my saying so, I was a bit surprised to hear that you are going home. Your legs aren't healed."

"No," she said. "That's the truth of it, but my heart's bad… Fact is, it's worse than it was… I get short of breath easier and more often. Dr. Battiste says I keep getting short of breath because my heart don't pump so good anymore. You know, Doctor, nobody lasts forever. So I figure if my heart is going to quit on me I'd rather be home with my children and grandchildren. Dr. Battiste and Dr. Doyle say they can take care of me in clinic."

For the first time it struck Adam that not everyone stayed in the hospital until they were completely healed. *Wise choice, be with your family.*

He was still thinking about seeing her in clinic when he realized how much trouble he was having trying to remove her dressings with his first-grade scissors. He shifted his attention to the scissors and took smaller bites of the old gauze, gradually snipping away at it. He gently pulled it apart so that he didn't hurt her, then carefully applied fresh dressings to both legs.

He placed the last layer with the Ace wraps, hoping the dressings would be secure and would last once she got home.

"I hope it doesn't take too long for your legs to heal," he said, "but honestly, I'll be glad to be seeing you in clinic."

He was standing by the elevators when he recalled Turk's comment about Luanne, the fat lady with the open wound. "Be nice if we could change her dressing twice a day." *Why not?* Adam asked himself.

She was much more awake than she had been in the early morning. She must have had some memory that he had been there, because she seemed surprised to see him.

"Best try to do this twice a day," he said, trying to sound like an experienced physician.

She seemed pleased as Adam worked on removing the morning dressings. Without prompting, she began telling Adam about her childhood.

"Lived in the Ninth Ward with my mama. We got by, but things were tough. Mama worked as a seamstress, cleaned hotel rooms for a while… I didn't care much for school, but I always went to church. By the time I was twelve I was singin' in the choir with all the adults. I guess I had a good voice. On special days we'd go to the lake for seafood. We never sat in the dining room, but they'd sell us a carry-out, and Mama and me, we'd sit on a bench near the pier and watch the sky over the lake as we ate our shrimps and catfish. We'd sit there as the sun moved in the sky and watch the colors change on the water. Mama made sure I had plenty of those moist wipes to clean my fingers so I wouldn't get grease on my nice dress. Those are my best memories of Mama."

Adam had finished changing the dressing and was anxious to go home, but he couldn't bring himself to interrupt her. He didn't leave until after he had heard the stories about how she used to catch beads as a child at Mardi Gras and once got a Zulu coconut in the parade a few months before her mama died.

Adam found Rogers and Turk in ICU. Turk had just finished inserting a special IV line under Ronald's clavicle.

"I changed my patient's dressings and thought I'd better see if there is anything else I need to do," interrupted Adam.

"I can't think of anything," said Rogers. "You go enjoy the day. We'll see you tomorrow."

In the city of Dixieland and zydeco, that was music to Adam's ears.

CHAPTER 24

ADAM NOTICED HOW hungry he was as he walked home through the French Quarter, tempted by the smells coming from the many restaurants he passed, several of which had filled their windows with pictures of plates piled high with beans and sausage or seafood and large bowls of gumbo. He was debating whether he should stop at Central Grocery for a muffuletta, or even take the streetcar uptown for oysters at Casamento's, when he saw Teddy sitting at his familiar corner table in the Café.

Adam stepped past the line of tourists waiting for tables and approached. Teddy was carefully studying a letter and didn't notice Adam until he pulled a chair away from the table.

"Docteur!" he exclaimed, looking up and flashing a big grin through the flecks of powdered sugar that dotted his goatee.

"Garcon!" he cried, waving his hand so all the servers noticed. "More beignets and a café au lait for the good doctor!"

"You were pretty intent on that letter," Adam said as he sat down.

"It's from the judge," Teddy answered.

"You mean the guy you rented to for the Super Bowl?"

"Exactly," he said. "His Honor from Philadelphia. It seems he wants to rent my apartment again next September so that he and his wife can celebrate their wedding anniversary in the Crescent City. He specifically mentioned how comfortable they were and asked if I can make my wonderful valet available to them again."

"Are you going to do it? You didn't seem to relish the idea of waiting on a Black couple while they enjoyed the luxury of your family's antiques," Adam said as the order of beignets was placed on the table.

"On the contrary, of course I'm going to do it," said Teddy, waving a beignet in a little snowstorm of powdered sugar and looking quite serious. "After all, the judge is a very generous tipper!"

Week Two

CHAPTER 25

THE THREE ARRIVED on the male ward at about the same time. Shrevi looked at the clock and yawned. Barnett looked like he had shaved, but Shrevi looked like he hadn't shaved and smelled like he hadn't showered.

"Five o'clock on a Sunday morning. Y'know, last night I planned to go to Bruno's uptown—they had a Cajun band. I sat down on my couch, closed my eyes, and woke up around midnight."

"I fell asleep while reading," said Adam. "Never felt like I had to study on Saturday night before."

"I was up with the baby for a bit—tried to do some reading—but once I lay down, I didn't hear a thing until my alarm went off," added Barnett. "I haven't had time to finish that first reading assignment."

In the dim light, Adam could see that the residents must have discharged several patients late yesterday. Empty beds were freshly made.

Barnett stayed on the male ward while Shrevi made his way down the hall to the female patients. A quick elevator ride brought Adam to the ICU.

He approached Demarcus Foster's bed. Adam changed his dressing and pricked his finger for a blood count without awakening him from his deep slumber. He quietly wrote a progress note, placed the chart at the end of the bed, and moved on towards Ronald.

Adam didn't anticipate any change in Ronald's status, so he routinely cleaned Ronald's fingertip with an alcohol swab and stuck him with a needle. He was startled when Ronald jerked forcefully, tightening all the muscles in his arm, and pulled his hand away. Then Ronald opened his eyes and stared, not so much at Adam but all around the room and into space.

"Ronald?" Adam stammered. But there was no reply, only a far-off look and the back and forth shaking of Ronald's head.

Service 1 gathered in ICU to begin rounds at 9 a.m. Without Dr. Theodorakis or the pressure of ER call, the residents could be relaxed and unhurried. They stood around Demarcus Foster's bed. Adam reviewed what he had learned about each of the residents who had been strangers to him a few days ago. Holiday and Doyle, the fifth-year and most senior residents, were accomplished surgeons. Both seemed to have seen it all and couldn't be upset by anything that came through the ER doors. Kittamura, the fourth-year, had actually been a practicing surgeon in Japan. His residency training in the

U.S. was required for licensing and provided a much-needed opportunity for him to master the English language. Adam had been surprised to learn that he lived in his call room, sending what money he made overseas to his wife and children, who waited for the opportunity to join him. Rogers, the third-year, was an affable guy whose surgical skills seemed to approach those of the more senior residents. As for the junior residents, Kochenko had a zen-like calmness, Turk was quiet and gentle, and Wantz was an asshole who liked to order students around.

When they reached Ronald's bed, Adam carefully described what had happened when he tried to obtain blood earlier. Kochenko immediately dropped the folded newspaper he had been carrying on the foot of the bed and stepped forward. He made a fist and firmly twisted his knuckles against Ronald's sternum. Ronald opened his eyes, squirmed to avoid the pressure, and kicked the newspaper to the floor.

Adam reached down to pick up the paper, noticing the headline: "INVESTIGATION OF GOVERNOR WIDENS."

Doyle said, "Looks like our boy is gonna wake up…guess his brain is less swollen!"

Adam handed Kochenko his paper. Holiday addressed Turk: "Come back and write his IV fluids. You know how tricky those hyperal solutions can be."

Before leaving the unit, Wantz watched Adam replace the dressing on Demarcus that Holiday had removed during rounds. With the new dressing in place, Adam tried to tear adhesive tape to secure the fresh gauze. Despite his attempts, he could not tear the tape.

Wantz impatiently grabbed the roll of tape and unrolled a long piece. In one motion he placed it on the dressing and ripped it from the roll. He repeated the maneuver rapidly until the entire stack of gauze was sealed securely to the patient's chest, dropped the roll on the bed, and walked away.

Adam quietly slipped the roll of tape into his coat pocket. *That'll give me something to practice during my study breaks*, he thought.

Adam found Barnett and Shrevi standing in the middle of the male ward. They looked just as lost as they had been their first day on the service.

"We got anything else to do?" asked Adam.

"We've been waiting here since we finished rounds," answered Barnett.

"Waitin' around is a killer," said Shrevi. "It's a damn waste of time."

Kochenko and Turk paused at the doorway as they entered the ward.

"What are you still doin' here?" Kochenko asked.

"Didn't know if there's more for us to do," said Barnett.

"It's Sunday," said Kochenko. "Rounds are done. Go home."

CHAPTER 26

SHREVI AND BARNETT left the floor immediately, but Adam remained by the elevator, considering his options. It was a bit early to do the second dressing change for the fat lady on the Gynecology ward, but if he did it now he could avoid returning to the hospital later that day and would have the remainder of the afternoon to catch up on the endless assigned reading.

When he arrived on the ward, Luanne was awake. He approached her bed after collecting the necessary dressings. As he came closer, he saw she had an awkward look on her face.

"I'm sorry, Doctor. They didn't get me no bedpan and I can't get up to the bathroom by myself."

After she spoke, Adam recognized the smell of urine. He pulled back the top sheet to find that her wound dressing was damp and she was lying on a soaked sheet. "That's OK," he said. "We'll just change the bed, too."

He placed the dressings on her bedside table and walked back to the treatment room for new linens, a new bed pad, and a clean pillowcase.

He paused as he considered the logistics of changing the bed linens for someone this obese. Her wound was so precarious that moving her too much could cause her to eviscerate.

"Whatcha gonna do?" said the LPN, who had watched him emerge from the treatment room.

"I need to change her linens. They're wet."

If the LPN resented his intrusion into the ward, she didn't show it.

"Roll to your side, honey," she instructed Luanne. "Much as you can."

Adam worried she would fall out of bed as she turned onto her left side. The LPN pulled up the moist sheets and pad and rolled them against Luanne's back.

"Now you roll back far as you can to the other side." She pulled the linens out from under Luanne. The nurse took the fresh linens from Adam and stretched the pad and downsheet into position, rolling the rest of the linens against Luanne's back. "Now you roll back to the other side," instructed the LPN.

"That's clever—I'd never think to change her sheets like that," Adam said.

"Mm-hm," the LPN responded.

Adam stepped around the bed and helped the LPN unroll the clean pad and sheet and tuck the edges under the mattress. When Luanne returned to lying on her back, he quickly changed her wound dressing before covering her with a clean sheet. He looked around for the LPN to thank her, but she was nowhere to be found.

Luanne seemed to be embarrassed and only managed a quiet, "Thank you, Doctor."

"See you tomorrow," answered Adam, thinking about how the lesson the LPN had just given him couldn't be found in a textbook but was probably just as valuable as those that could.

$\sim$

After he arrived back in his apartment, Adam placed his notebook, pens, markers, and the big blue Surgery textbook on his coffee table. By the end of the week, the lecturers had added an additional sixty pages to the 188 assigned at the orientation. Adam knew he could never read all of it by that evening, but he was determined to make as big a dent as he could. He opened the textbook to the preface page. The top of the page contained a quote that seemed to be more of a threat than a historical statement:

"It is astonishing with how little reading a doctor can practice medicine, but it is not astonishing how badly he may do it. "

—Sir William Osler

Later, sitting on the grassy levee near the Café Du Monde, he thought about the past week in the hospital as he spooned the last of his carry-out gumbo. Living in the South wasn't anything like he had imagined growing up with the grainy TV footage of violence accompanying civil rights demonstrations, voter registration drives, or attempts at school desegregation. The patients he had met, although poor and uneducated, were probably no different than those who could be found in the ER of Cook County Hospital in Chicago, Bellevue in New York, or LA County on the West Coast. They had in common that they all needed medical care—a need that did not recognize income level, background, or skin color. He had watched the residents work so hard to provide that care to all who required it. He returned to his apartment to continue his reading, more determined than ever to acquire the knowledge and skills a physician needed.

CHAPTER 27

SURGERY CLINIC DIDN'T begin until 1 p.m., but the students arrived at 12:30. Plenty of patients were already waiting. The male surgery space reminded Adam of his old junior high school gymnasium. There were no bleachers, but the wooden benches, scuffed old floorboards, and three walls of exposed brick were reminiscent of a gym. Long windows embedded with wire mesh allowed natural light to enter. Each window was further protected by a black metal grate jutting out a few inches from the wall. Lining the walls were the patient examination areas. Each consisted of curtains hung from wire frames to create a bit of privacy around a small exam table.

Only three nurses were assigned to staff the clinic, which provided post-operative visits and evaluations for new patients referred from other departments or the Emergency Room. Kittamura, Wantz, and Barnett were assigned to the female clinic, a similar room located further down the long hallway.

Shrevi and Adam joined the rest of the Service at the long tables in front of the exam rooms.

The first few patients they saw were straightforward post-operative visits, but they were hampered by a lack of information, as none of the patients' charts had been brought up from Medical Records. In each instance, Turk instructed Adam to take a quick but thorough history and write a note on a clinic pad including all of the patient's identifying information.

There was a steady stream of patients to be seen throughout the afternoon. It didn't take long before Shrevi and Adam were allowed to see patients by themselves and call on the residents to confirm their findings. This way, they could keep all the exam rooms filled and the flow of patients moving. The patients who required elective surgery were more carefully evaluated by the residents.

The afternoon wore on. The changing light began to cast shadows through the long windows. Adam was waiting for the next patient when Doyle approached the nurses' table.

"Sinclair," he said, "come with me."

They walked down the hallway and took the elevator to another floor, where they entered the Internal Medicine Clinic. Battiste, the medical resident, was standing by an exam room and greeted them with a smile.

"Thanks for coming," he said. "She's in here."

Rosalie Patton was seated in a wheelchair in the examination area. Adam was struck by the fact that she seemed even more frail than she had been on the ward. An oxygen tank was attached to the back of her wheelchair with green plastic tubing looped over her ears and resting in her nostrils. She breathed in little gasps, still short of breath despite the extra oxygen.

"Mrs. Patton," Adam began, "I'm—"

"Dr. Sinclair," she said, "nice to see you again."

Doyle and Adam examined her legs together. The open sores were drier, smaller, and much cleaner.

"How are you?" asked Adam.

"Oh, Ah'm dying," she spoke in small gasps, "but Ah'm better since Dr. Doyle and Dr. Battiste got me this oxygen tank for home… Cain't hardly walk anymore, though. My son had real trouble getting me and my chair on the bus to get here."

Doyle reached into the pocket of his lab coat, pulled out two tan, rolled Unna boots, and handed one to Adam. They removed the cellophane wrappers and began redressing her legs. Adam watched closely as Doyle began to wrap her right leg. He tried to appear confident as he placed the dressing on the left but secretly hoped no one would notice that he was trying to mimic Doyle's every move.

"They says my kidneys aren't doing too well," she said. "Seems like every time Dr. Battiste gives me more water pills my kidneys try to stop working, but when he stops the pills, I have more breathing troubles. At least I am going to die with good-looking legs… It can be a little tighter, Dr. Sinclair."

"Your legs will be looking like Betty Grable's," said Doyle.

"Just a little darker," she smiled faintly as they finished wrapping.

Adam added a layer of white gauze and an Ace bandage around each leg while Doyle wrote a note on the chart and stepped out into the waiting area to talk with her son.

Adam joined them in time to see Doyle pull a ten-dollar bill from his wallet and, to Adam's surprise, hand it to her son.

"Cab fare home," Doyle said.

By the time they returned to the Surgery Clinic, only a few patients remained waiting to be seen.

This will probably be my last patient today, thought Adam as the skinny Caucasian man approached the table and uncomfortably sat on the chair across from him. Even to Adam's inexperienced eye, the man appeared chronically ill. He was rail thin with an ashen complexion, sunken eyes with dark circles under them, and salt-and-pepper stubble across his chin.

"I been having fevers for a month," he said, "got a painful lump on my thigh, and past few days my low back's been hurtin' somethin' fierce."

After the nurse recorded a temperature of 101 degrees, the patient entered the exam cubicle with Adam, who asked him to remove his shirt first. Adam was able to localize the man's pain to the area of the first lumbar vertebrae, but he couldn't see or feel any abnormality in that area. He then examined the man's chest with his stethoscope. The lung sounds were clear, but he heard the "whoosh" of a murmur when he listened to the heart.

The man was slowly removing his slacks when Turk joined them in the exam room. A swollen and reddened mass was obvious on the anterior surface of the left thigh.

Turk stepped forward, grabbing the man's forearms and twisting them as he examined them.

"You been skin-poppin'?" he asked.

"Yeh," came the reply as the patient looked down at the floor.

"What're you using?"

"H."

"How long?"

"Couple of years but really hit heavy past three months after my woman left."

"Adam, look at this," Turk said, holding out the patient's forearms. "These are called 'track marks,'" he said, indicating the scabbed cords that were once healthy veins.

"Sir," he said to the patient, but also using the moment to explain to the student, "you've got an abscess on your thigh from injecting. We need to drain that."

He listened to the patient's chest with his stethoscope and examined his back. "You have a heart murmur that could mean bacteria have gotten onto your heart valve, and the back pain could be that your bloodstream carried infection into your bone. We'll get an X-ray to look at your spine. You'll need to be admitted to the hospital, and it may be for a while."

"Sure, Doc," replied the patient, still staring at the floor. He didn't seem upset at the prospect of a hospital stay.

Turk and Adam accompanied the patient to the X-ray exam room. As they approached the room and Adam walked alongside the patient's cart, he suddenly thought of Rosalie Patton.

"I'm Dr. Sinclair," he said. "I'm the third-year medical student who will be helping to take care of you."

The man looked up at him. "I'm Danny… Danny Frer."

Moments later, Adam stood with Turk outside the exam room. They reviewed the films of the man's chest and lumbar spine. Turk carefully explained the images, but even with his inexperience, Adam didn't need much explanation to recognize the obvious destruction of the first lumbar vertebrae.

"Osteomyelitis," said Turk.

The clinic nurse had stayed late while they were in X-ray. She had a minor surgery tray ready when Turk and Adam returned. Once Danny was positioned back on the exam table, Turk prepped the skin of his thigh with antiseptic paint and handed Adam a pair of sterile gloves. They both put gloves on, and Turk placed sterile towels around the abscess. He prepared a syringe with local anesthetic.

"Take the scalpel and cut about two inches long in the center," Turk said as he handed Adam the blade. "Go all the way through the skin and then use a hemostat to spread the edges."

Adam held the blade and slowly moved it across the skin, leaving a mark but not going all the way through.

"Press a little firmer," instructed Turk.

Adam applied more pressure and the blade popped through the skin. Immediately, pungent green pus poured out of the patient's thigh.

Turk swabbed the material and placed the swabs in culture tubes. He handed the tubes to the nurse and began packing the wound with a yellow gauze.

"Iodoform," he said to Adam. "Gauze is impregnated with iodine to kill bacteria. Gonna need an IV," he added.

The nurse left and returned with the necessary supplies. Turk placed a tourniquet on the patient's arm and prepped the skin with an alcohol swab. He searched for a few moments until he found a site, threaded a small catheter into a vein and attached the tubing, then began infusing the plastic bag of fluid.

"I was lucky to start it," he said. "These are really rotten veins."

The patient nodded in agreement. "I done used most of them up."

CHAPTER 28

EVEN THOUGH IT was only a little past eight o'clock on Wednesday morning, the Emergency Room was crowded and noisy. People who had decided that early morning was the best time to seek care for their chronic medical problems were lined up with those suffering the ill effects of a long night carousing on Bourbon Street. As Adam approached Trauma Room 4, a gurney was pushed into the hallway. Guiding the cart, Wantz spied Adam.

"Thirty-four weeks pregnant, blunt trauma against steering wheel. Shock from blood loss. Come to the OR with me now!" he commanded.

They began pushing the cart towards the OR when the other elevator opened and Doyle and the senior OB resident joined them. Adam dropped his bag by the OR door and went to scrub. No one joined him at the sink. When he returned to the OR, he was surprised to see the others in gowns and the patient draped.

Rogers addressed the two senior residents. "Motor vehicle accident. Seat-belted driver, no passengers. Hit head on by a drunk driver in the wrong lane. He was ejected from his vehicle and dead at the scene. Looks like she had blunt trauma to her belly from the steering wheel. Front of her car pretty badly smashed in. Was conscious at the scene… First baby and she's thirty-four weeks."

As soon as he was gowned and gloved, Adam approached the table and was handed a suction. His first view into the abdomen startled him. The baby floated freely in the blood being suctioned from the belly. The child was perfectly formed but blue and motionless. Adam couldn't recognize the ruptured uterus, but he did see that the umbilical cord disappeared into a cavernous pool of blood.

Carlos entered the room with more blood for the patient along with Holiday and a pediatric resident. The limp infant was placed in a towel and handed to the pediatrician.

After a brief examination, he said, "Nothing I can do."

The circulating nurse handed him a blanket and he covered the baby.

"Sorry," he murmured before leaving the room.

Holiday stepped up towards the table.

"How's the bleeding, Bobby?"

"Pretty bad. I oversewed the edges of the uterus, but it doesn't seem to have slowed anything."

"Pressure is about 60," said the anesthetist. "I'm having trouble keeping up with the blood loss."

"We should close the uterus and give Pitocin," said the OB resident.

"They're sending a Pitocin drip from the pharmacy," said the anesthetist. "I'll hang it as soon as it arrives."

"Mind if I take your place?" Holiday asked Rogers, who was serving as the first assistant.

Rogers deferred to the more senior resident.

Sweat had formed on Adam's forehead as he watched Holiday and Doyle try to stop the bleeding. He felt his knees weaken and closed his eyes as his heart pounded. He stiffened his legs and kept his eyes closed as he listened to the conversation at the table.

"I got the Pitocin running as fast as it's safe to give. Any effect?" asked the anesthetist.

"Not that I can see," answered Doyle. "She's oozing from all around the uterus and it's not contracting with the Pitocin."

Adam opened his eyes and saw that the pelvis was still accumulating blood despite the fact that both Wantz and the OB resident also held suctions in the field.

"We're going to have to tie off her internal iliac arteries to slow the blood flow into the pelvis," said Doyle.

"Could you page Dr. Kittamura and have him join us?" Holiday asked the circulating nurse.

"I'll get the right iliac if you can retract the uterus for me," said Doyle. "Give me an O-silk on a Mixter clamp, please."

The need to suction the area had not abated when Kittamura scrubbed in and Adam was told to step back from the table. Although Holiday and Doyle were senior by ranking, they deferred to the older, more experienced resident.

"Ruptured uterus from blunt trauma in pregnancy," Holiday explained. "We tied off both internal iliacs, but trying to reduce the blood flow hasn't curtailed the bleeding."

"Can't seem to get her systolic pressure above 70...66 now," added the voice from the head of the table.

"You got any other suggestions, Kitty?" asked Doyle. "Closest I've been to this situation was a bad pelvic fracture and that patient died."

Kittamura surveyed the situation. He placed a couple of additional sutures without much impact.

"Only option is hysterectomy," he said.

There was a pause at the table.

"Better to have a live mother even if she can't get pregnant again, but it's your call," Holiday said, looking directly at the OB resident.

"I'll have to do it," he said. "Can y'all get me some Heaney clamps?"

Adam was struck by how dispassionate the surgeons seemed as they quickly worked to remove the patient's womb and pass the bloody mess into the bucket that sat on the nurse's table. Despite Kittamura's call that it was the only option, Adam couldn't help but feel they were compounding one tragedy on top of another.

Finally, Doyle's voice broke the silence. "Well, it looks like that massive bleeding has turned into barely a trickle."

"Blood pressure is up to 90," said the anesthetist. "Gonna top her off with another unit."

Kittamura and Holiday stepped back, removed their gowns and gloves, and left the room.

"Would you mind keeping her on your service?" asked the OB resident. "She probably won't be comfortable on an OB floor."

"Probably won't be comfortable anywhere," said Doyle, "but we'll admit her."

They were only a few feet out of the room when Adam felt a shaking chill overtake him. He shuddered when the cramps and nausea began. They had barely passed the next operating room when he stepped into the nearby alcove, dropped his bag, bent over the scrub sink, and vomited. He wiped his mouth with a paper towel and put his head back as he leaned against the wall between the scrub sinks. He let himself slide downwards to the floor and, with his arms folded over his knees, began to cry uncontrollably.

CHAPTER 29

ADAM WAS SURPRISED to see Turk and Kochenko standing over him when he looked up. Turk handed him some paper towels. Adam wiped his eyes and mouth.

"That kind of case is hard on everyone," said Kochenko, "but you have to get past it. If you dwell on it, you won't be able to treat the next patient who comes in. All we can do is our best, and sometimes the outcomes aren't what we want. Take a moment to get yourself together and then go back down to the ER. Wantz went to see a bellyache down there."

Wantz was in an exam room with an uncomfortable-looking young man lying on a cart. A bag of intravenous fluid was hanging, and Wantz was examining the man's abdomen. Without acknowledging Adam, he continued his examination, pushing on the right lower part of the belly and eliciting a grimace from the patient when he quickly let go.

"When did you eat last? Got any allergies?" he asked, barely waiting for the answers. He flipped through the patient's chart and stated without looking up at the patient, "You've got appendicitis. Need to get it out now. Soon as an OR's available."

Wantz left the room, and Adam picked up the chart from the foot of the bed. The young man looked as though his discomfort was mixed with a bit of bewilderment tempered by resignation.

"My name is Dr. Sinclair. I'm the third-year medical student who will be following your case. When did your pain begin and can you describe it?"

Adam carefully asked all the questions he could remember from the Physical Diagnosis course. The young man's history was standard for appendicitis—pain started around the navel, then he threw up, then the pain moved to the right lower abdomen. By the time Adam performed his own examination and confirmed the tenderness that Wantz had elicited, the patient was more relaxed, even offering more information and asking questions on his own.

"I ain't never been in no hospital before. Never felt nothin' like this. Y'all sure I gotta be cut? Cain't ya jes gimmee some pills?"

"I'm pretty certain that diagnosis is correct," said Adam. "It would be different if you were a girl and we had to wonder if your pain was from your tubes or ovaries, but I just examined you and I can be certain you aren't a girl."

The patient weakly smiled. "I guess you all gotta do what you gotta do, then."

"I'm going to step out in the hallway to finish my paperwork. It shouldn't be too long before we get you feeling better."

As he stepped out of the exam room to write his findings on a tablet of progress notes, Adam felt like an accomplished physician. The history he had taken flowed easily onto the yellow sheets, and he was pleased both with the completeness of it and with how quickly he had been able to obtain it. While he waited for Wantz to return for the appendectomy, he saw his classmate Phil Sheridan and two orthopedic residents looking at the X-ray view box on the wall near the door to the X-ray room.

"Hey, Adam," Phil called. "C'mere, you oughta lookit this."

Adam joined them and looked at the pictures showing the upper part of a leg.

"Right femur," explained Phil.

Adam could see that the obvious fractures in the bone were lined up and held together by a metal plate and screws.

"C'mon," Phil said, "you gotta meet Admiral Franklin. This guy is really something else. Had him in the hospital in traction, but he wouldn't stay still enough to let the bone set so he got operated. Just released him yesterday and now he shows up with his cast off and pain and a swollen knee. C'mon, you gotta meet him."

Lying on the table in the X-ray room was a thin young Black man. His pants were off, there was a recent incision on his right thigh, and his right knee was markedly swollen. Over a light blue denim work shirt, he was wearing a short, dark jacket elaborately decorated with gold braid and epaulettes. Sitting slightly askew on his head was a dingy white yachting cap with a wrinkled black visor and an embroidered anchor.

"Admiral Franklin," said Phil, "this here's our consultant, Dr. Sinclair. Gonna review your case. Tell him how you originally broke your leg."

The Admiral looked straight at Adam with his right eye, but his left eye deviated almost ninety degrees away and looked across the room.

"Broke my leg jumpin' from a second story window," he said.

"Why'd you jump?" asked Phil.

"Her husband come home."

"When you left the hospital yesterday you were wearing that special cast we put on your leg. Where'd it go?"

"Had to cut it off... Got in the way when I went to visit my girlfriend."

"What happened that you had to come back here?"

"Runnin' fo' mah life... Ah was running fo' mah life. Went out the back door when her man got home. Started down the alley and this big Doberman started chasin' me. Got a block away and tripped in a pothole, hurtin' mah laig."

"And the dog?"

"Come up and licked mah face."

"At least you didn't have to leap from the second floor again."

"Second floor... Naw! Naw... Different house."

CHAPTER 30

ADAM TRIED TO appear comfortable after scrubbing in for the appendectomy, but the image of the dead baby came up like a wave of nausea, giving him pause. He forced himself to approach the table and rested his folded hands on the patient's thigh as he watched Wantz make the classic McBurney incision in the lower abdomen. Kittamura retracted the skin edges and Wantz opened the last layer of the abdominal wall, probed the belly with his index finger, pulled up the cecum, and flipped a rigid, reddened appendix into the operative field. While Kittamura held the exposed portion of large intestine, Wantz divided and tied the blood vessels to the appendix, clamped and removed the inflamed organ, tied a suture around the stump, and placed a stitch to invert the bowel wall where the appendix had been attached.

Adam was so intent on remembering the anatomy and the steps to remove the appendix that the baby was soon forgotten.

CHAPTER 31

AFTER STOPPING ON the Gyne floor to change Luanne's dressing, Adam returned to the ER, but it was difficult to find the other students and residents of Service 1. The Emergency Room even more crowded than it had been earlier in the day. All the seats in the waiting area were filled. The walls were lined with people waiting to be seen, and two long rows of people still registering nearly reached the entrance.

Adam found Turk in one of the treatment rooms, helping a shaky Barnett close his first laceration.

"If you're looking for everybody, I think they're all scattered around," Turk said. "Try some of the other treatment rooms or the trauma area. I think the other student went with Rogers and Kittamura to see a GI bleeder. Kochenko is in one of the trauma rooms with a guy who was robbed and beaten. Wantz went to the Medicine side to see a guy with abdominal pain and vomiting. I'm not sure where Holiday is. We've only got a couple more stitches here."

As he turned to leave the room, Adam noted that the patient was wearing handcuffs that kept him attached to the cart. Doyle was around the corner, talking with two police officers. They both wore the uniform of the NOLA police department, but one of the officers was tall with broad shoulders and a military bearing while the other was short, his uniform rumpled. His shoulders were not as broad as his waistline.

"Officer Beaudry, Officer Guidry," Doyle nodded. "I trust you did not have too long a wait to get your prisoner treated."

Beaudry smiled. "Since we made sure no more parking tickets were left on the windshields of the doctors' and nurses' cars parked along Poydras, we have had nothing but prompt and efficient service."

"Good," said Doyle. "I know how tedious those four-hour waits were. I'm glad these issues are resolved. If you'll excuse us, my medical student and I have to see a GI bleeder in Room Three."

With a nod, he indicated for Adam to follow, and Adam scurried down the hall two steps behind. When they entered the treatment room, Shrevi, Rogers, and Kittamura were evaluating a middle-aged man on the cart.

"Upper GI bleed," said Rogers. "Endoscopy Room is ready for us to bring up as soon as we get another IV in him. Either of you students ever start an IV?"

Both shook their heads and answered "No" simultaneously.

"Kitty, wanna show these fellas how to do an IV while I call the Blood Bank?" asked Rogers.

Kittamura reached into the chest pocket of his white coat and pulled out an IV catheter still in its sterile packaging. He took a tourniquet out of his right pocket and applied it to the patient's upper arm while the nurse set up a bag of IV fluid and tubing. From his other coat pocket he pulled a roll of plastic tape and tore a long piece into strips that he hung from the side of the cart. He then cleaned the skin of the patient's forearm with an alcohol swab. Inserting the IV cannula into a visible vein, he smoothly advanced the catheter as he withdrew the central needle. A rush of blood occurred, and he placed his thumb on the skin overlying the catheter. Pressure with his thumb stopped the back flow of blood while he attached a small syringe and withdrew five milliliters of blood. Kittamura handed the syringe to the nurse, who placed a needle on it and filled a test tube topped with a red rubber cork while he attached the IV tubing. He opened the stopcock, began running in the IV fluid, and secured the exposed catheter hub by winding pieces of tape around it.

He smiled at the students. "See…easy. You do the next."

Chapter 32

Adam stood at the operating table and swallowed hard, willing himself not to think about the baby. He had only seen a field of crimson in the endoscopy when the residents diagnosed a bleeding ulcer and now was finally barely able to focus on what the residents were doing even as he remembered the differential diagnosis from Bullpen.

Rogers was the operating surgeon, with Doyle as first assistant and Adam and Shrevi tugging on retractors. They worked quickly, and soon the bleeding was controlled and the last steps of the operation completed, including cutting the nerves that stimulated further acid secretion in the stomach. They began to close the abdomen. Kittamura appeared in the doorway.

"Wantz closing laparotomy for bowel obstruction," he said.

"I've done about thirty cases where I've had to resect the stomach for bleeding," Rogers told the students. "You know, in Japan they do a lot more resections because they have more stomach cancer."

"Yeh," said Doyle. "I've done about a hundred and fifty resections. Kittamura, about how many gastric resections have you done?"

"'Bout five hundred," he said softy.

Adam was sure there was a satisfied grin under Kittamura's mask.

Chapter 33

WANTZ AND BARNETT were wheeling the bowel obstruction patient into Recovery. Adam stepped back to make way for them to pass when he noticed Barnett had a look of consternation on his face. Before Adam could ask if everything was all right, he overheard Doyle and Kittamura having an animated discussion in the hallway.

"Jesus, Kitty," said a displeased Doyle, his voice carrying although he tried to whisper. "You gotta know he should've checked the potassium before the old man went into the OR! Dammit, the guy probably didn't need an operation!"

Doyle turned towards Adam.

"Sinclair, do you know what an 'ileus' is? Somebody on this service better!"

Without waiting for an answer, he continued, "They took a guy with a potassium of 2.2 into the OR and didn't find a bowel obstruction... The damn intestine was just paralyzed from the low potassium caused by his diuretics!"

Kittamura hung his head. "Did not see lab slip myself... only listen to intern."

Adam let Doyle pass and then found Barnett sipping a cup of coffee in the nurses' break room.

"What's the deal?" Adam asked. "Doyle is not happy about your case."

"Wantz was pretty hot to get this guy into the OR," said Barnett. "We opened him up, and although the small bowel was dilated, we couldn't find any point where it was obstructed. During the case the Anesthesia resident asked us if we knew the potassium was only 2.2. Kittamura said the bowel was only paralyzed by the hypokalemia, so we closed. Turns out this little old man has heart disease and takes a hefty dose of diuretic to avoid fluid build-up... Causes his kidneys to lose potassium and that affects intestinal motility."

Before Adam could respond, a commotion occurred across the Recovery Room. Two nurses were staring at the old man's cardiac monitor mounted on the wall just above Barnett's patient's cart. Doyle joined them quickly and Wantz got up from where he had been sitting at the nurses' station when one of the nurses called out, "PVCs!"

"Low potassium likely the cause," said Doyle. "Get some lidocaine and the crash cart."

Barnett dropped his coffee cup into the sink and followed Adam towards the gurney. It was easy to see the irregular pattern of spikes on the EKG monitor. When they reached the foot of the bed, the deep spikes became rapid, wide, and regular.

"Shit," exclaimed Doyle. "V-tach... Give the lidocaine and check his pressure!"

Adam and Barnett were watching the patient's monitor when the pattern suddenly changed into an undulating wave.

"V. Fib—he's coding!" announced the nurse.

The pandemonium that ensued rivaled that of the busy ER as more nursing staff quickly congregated around the patient's cart. The patient's original nurse continued to administer the medication in the syringe while the other nurse who had been with her stood with a clipboard, recording the events and medications taken from the crash cart. Another nurse flipped a switch on the monitor and watched as a white strip of paper emerged from the machine recording the electrical rhythms of the patient's heart. Two additional nurses lifted the patient's shoulders and slid a smoothly varnished piece of plywood under the patient's back.

Soon Adam and Barnett were taking turns pumping on the patient's chest while Doyle gave orders for more medications and the Anesthesia resident returned to check the ventilator settings and connection to the patient's breathing tube.

"Prepare to shock him," said Doyle.

Wantz moved to the side of the bed carrying the defibrillator paddles.

"Everybody back from the cart," ordered Doyle. "Clear."

Wantz placed the paddles on the patient's chest and delivered an electric shock that caused the patient's entire body to jerk in spasm.

All eyes were on the EKG monitor, where the tracing was now a flat line which remained inanimate after the shock with no resumption of any of the heart's electrical activity.

"Go again," said Doyle, "and give some epinephrine and an amp of bicarb."

"Clear," said Wantz before he sent another electric current running through the paddles.

"Resume CPR," said Doyle.

Barnett stepped aside and Adam pushed along the patient's breastbone, pumping the chest in a steady rhythm against the supporting backboard until his own arms and shoulders ached.

When Barnett again took over, Adam saw that Holiday and Turk were standing behind the crash cart. They watched the proceedings with concern. Holiday was scowling and shaking his head. Kittamura stood to their right with his head hung down. Wantz remained near the side of the cart, staring at the monitor and still clutching the defibrillator paddles as his arms dangled beside him.

Adam stared so hard at the cardiac monitor's screen that he began to imagine that the little metal box had swallowed up the patient's heartbeat and was now obstinately refusing to release it.

The resuscitation had become a mechanical routine when Doyle said, "It's been thirty-five minutes. I'm calling it."

The activity stopped, and the nurses rolled away the crash cart and began quietly cleaning up. Anesthesia removed the tubes from the patient's mouth and nose and used a towel to wipe away the remaining saliva and snot.

Doyle spoke to Kittamura and Wantz. "Let's go talk to the family."

Adam wondered what they could possibly say to the old man's relatives and how often other mistakes were made. Would they explain the low potassium that made the intestine appear obstructed and then caused the change in heart rhythm? Doyle and the others seemed to share the mistake, although Wantz had actually made the error. How would Doyle approach the family? Despite his concern, Adam couldn't bring himself to follow them.

Chapter 34

Shrevi joined Adam on the men's ward late in the afternoon. They found a frustrated Barnett at the bedside of the patient with the perforated diverticulum. Normally calm and placid, Barnett was hunched over the patient with a look of absolute exasperation on his face. He held the patient's left arm while intensely studying its surface. A tourniquet was placed above the elbow and pieces of tape were attached to the patient's bed frame. Discarded IV catheters and their packaging littered the patient's bed.

"Kittamura told me he needed a new IV catheter. I've stuck him a bunch…got into a vein a couple of times but can't maintain it. They keep infiltrating," Barnett said, indicating the swollen areas near the needle punctures where fluid had leaked under the skin.

"I guess I could use some help. One of you guys want to try?" he asked.

Shrevi didn't respond, but Adam uttered a confident, "Sure," just before a wave of nervousness shot through him as he remembered his inexperience.

"Be my guest," Barnett said as he handed his classmate an alcohol swab.

Adam switched the tourniquet to the upper portion of the patient's right arm and prepped the back of his hand. As he rubbed the alcohol swab on the area, two veins dilated. Barnett handed Adam an IV catheter and watched as Adam stretched the overlying skin, punctured the vein, and advanced the plastic sheath forward while withdrawing the center needle.

There was a good blood return. Not much dripped out before Barnett attached the IV line and snapped off the tourniquet. They taped the catheter in place and watched the IV fluid drip into the tubing chamber and flow into the vein. Adam held his breath as he watched the IV site closely. After it didn't infiltrate, he waited another full minute to be sure it continued to work properly.

His chest swelled with pride when Barnett thanked him and muttered, "Smooth."

Adam couldn't wait to practice his newfound skill again. After they cleaned up around the bed and tossed the leftover debris and needles into the proper containers, they left the ward together. Adam looked back and smiled, realizing that sometimes, it's the little victories that make one's day.

CHAPTER 35

ADAM LEFT THE others and stopped on the Gyne ward, where he changed Luanne's dressing. She seemed glad to see him and recounted a story from her childhood about how scared she was when she saw her first alligator in the Audubon Park Zoo. In those days a lot of Black people didn't feel welcome uptown, and she feared that an old White man who kept staring at her might pick her up and throw her off the bridge into the alligator pond.

Adam listened politely as he worked quickly on her dressing change. He excused himself, saying that he had to return to the ER, but before he left he replied in a voice that unconsciously resembled a Southern drawl and brought a smile to Luanne's face, "Well, I'm sure glad you didn't get 'et by no alligator."

The residents' dining area was spartan—a few long, dark wooden picnic tables with attached benches set in an out-of-the-way room painted in a faded and chipped light blue. Despite the austerity, the room provided a welcome relief from the noise and activity in the rest of the hospital.

Service 1 had already claimed one of the tables. Doyle and Holiday sat next to each other, their backs leaning against the wall. Doyle had an empty plate in front of him and an angry look on his face left over from the Recovery Room. Holiday sat next to him, slowly spooning gumbo from a Styrofoam cup. Barnett and Kochenko sat across from them, and Wantz was finishing a plate of jambalaya at the other end of the bench.

Shrevi joined Turk in helping themselves to bowls of gumbo and French bread from the steam table on the other side of the room. Adam avoided the gumbo, helping himself only to bread, a couple of pats of butter, and a glass of iced tea. The ice for the tea had long since melted, but nevertheless the tea was cool, refreshing, and thirst-quenching. Adam filled his cup a second time before moving to the nearby table.

Barnett was speaking when they sat down.

"Is there a chance we'll be able to get out early again on Sunday?" he asked. "My wife could sure use some help with the baby."

"Doubt it," Wantz began.

Holiday cut him off. "Have to wait and see when all the work's done. Probably get out after we finish rounds."

"That would be good," Shrevi said. "I should probably head over and visit my parents."

"Why? You got a lot of laundry for your mom to do?" asked Kochenko.

"Well, yes I do, but I should visit them anyway, you know. I mean, heck, they're paying my tuition. Twelve hundred dollars a year is a lot of money. I oughta at least come by."

"Goes up every year," said Kochenko, shaking his head. "Mine was only eight fifty. How about you, Ben?"

"'Bout the same," Turk answered.

Doyle was still leaning back against the wall with his eyes closed while Holiday looked as though he had only been half-listening to the conversation. He stared into his Styrofoam cup, concentrating on its contents. The plastic spoon stirred the remaining rice and gumbo, but the question stirred old memories.

"Hey, Tom, how about you?" asked Kochenko. "I mean, back in the day, what did it cost you to become a doctor?"

Holiday jammed the plastic spoon into the half-eaten cup of gumbo as one by one the residents' beepers started going off.

"My twenties," he replied, looking directly at them as they all checked their pagers and collectively stood up to return to the ER.

CHAPTER 36

ALTHOUGH AT TIMES the quick pace of the ER seemed to border on chaos, there seemed to be a rhythm to the residents' work. Adam sensed that their efficiency was guided by some unspoken sense of direction as to which resident would treat which patient and what operation was suitable for each doctor's level of training. Holiday and Doyle supervised everything, standing in the hallway and leaning against the tiled wall sipping coffee. Their conversation was only interrupted when a new patient was brought to one of the trauma rooms, when there were new X-rays to review, or when they needed to go to the operating room.

Adam walked down the hallway, checking each trauma room for activity. Barnett was with a patient in the third room he passed and motioned for his classmate to join him.

"Ten-year-old boy… Was standing in his front yard when a car jumped the curb, knocked him down, and ran over him."

Adam looked down at the cart. The child trembled with fright and was crying. His mother sat on a folding chair next to him and held his hand. Despite his being upset, he appeared to be breathing well and the monitor revealed a normal blood pressure and heart rate of 110.

"Examine him," said Barnett.

Adam stepped up to the right side of the cart, introduced himself, and pulled down the sheet covering the boy's upper body and abdomen. A tread mark extending from his lower right chest all the way across his left clavicle was clearly visible despite his dark skin. The boy's chest moved regularly and symmetrically with each respiration. Adam placed his stethoscope on the child's chest and moved it from side to side as he carefully listened to the sound of air moving in and out of the lungs normally. The boy's heart sounded normal although it was beating quickly. Each valve closed with a crisp sound, and Adam heard no murmurs. He pressed on the ribs but determined no tenderness or abnormal movement indicating fracture. Finally, he placed his stethoscope on the abdomen and listened carefully in several spots to the sound of normal peristalsis. He felt for any tenderness, particularly in the areas of the liver and spleen. When he found none, he completed his exam by tapping on the outstretched fingers of his left hand, listening to the sounds that defined the liver as being normal in size. Barnett acknowledged the mother with a nod while he and Adam stepped back to whisper between themselves.

"I don't find anything abnormal," Adam said.

"Me neither," said Barnett. "He seems fine."

"But how could he not have crushed his liver, lungs, or heart?" puzzled Adam.

"His labs are OK and his chest X-ray doesn't even show any rib fractures," said Barnett.

"What are we gonna do?"

"Doyle says we're just going to put him in bed and watch him closely. He told me to check his blood count every four hours to make sure there's no internal bleeding."

"That's all?"

"That's it."

~

The evening continued with a regular stream of patients. Some, such as an abdominal stab wound or a case of appendicitis, required the students to follow the resident staff to the operating room, while others were admitted to the wards for later diagnostic tests and still others were evaluated, treated, and sent home.

Around midnight, Adam joined Shrevi as he accompanied a cart heading for the operating room.

"Auto accident," said Shrevi. "Slammed her car into the side of another car that ran a red light. Kochenko stuck a long blunt needle into her belly and filled a syringe with blood. Says she's bleeding internally."

The image of the blood-filled abdomen of the pregnant woman returned to Adam momentarily but disappeared when they got to the operating room and he scrubbed in to hold a retractor while Holiday assisted Kochenko in removing the lady's ruptured spleen.

Returning to the ER, Adam found Barnett in the hallway with Doyle and Rogers. He hoped they were ready to get some rest since it was nearly three in the morning. Before he could ask, the double doors from the ambulance ramp swung open and two ambulance drivers frantically pushed a cart towards them and the trauma rooms. Sitting bolt upright on the cart was a thin Black man wearing blue jeans, dirty, torn canvas sneakers, and a dark T-shirt.

His shoulder was elevated away from his body, but his blood-stained right arm dangled from the outstretched elbow. As the attendants rolled the wild-eyed man past the residents, he stared in their direction and exclaimed, "Ah tol' him if he was gonna shoot her he'd hafta shoot me fuhst…and he did!"

Chapter 37

"**Her daddy must** not be much of a marksman if he had to use a shotgun."

Doyle's voice stood out above the din of the trauma room as he leaned against the doorway, sipping from another Styrofoam cup of lukewarm coffee. On the cart in the center of the room lay a still figure: short, squat, her blood-stained clothes cut off and left in a heap on the floor. Rogers stood at the head of the table, taping the endotracheal tube in place while the respiratory therapist squeezed the bag and checked to be sure the oxygen was connected properly. A nasogastric tube drained reddish-brown stomach fluid into the suction canister on the wall. Kochenko stood on the patient's right, Turk on her left, securing the tubes each had placed in her chest.

"I was going to go to the OR with Ortho," Doyle said to Holiday, who stood in the corner of the room. "That guy needs an arteriogram when they fix his arm…maybe a vascular repair."

"Go ahead," said Holiday, "we're fine here."

Adam's heart was racing.

"Fine here?" he whispered to Barnett. "Her blood pressure is running about 50 systolic and her belly is studded with little pellet holes."

"Gonna need another IV in the other arm," the nurse said as she tossed a tourniquet to Adam.

While the ER routine was set in motion, a urinary catheter and nasogastric tube inserted, Adam applied a tourniquet, prepped the arm, and punctured the skin with an intravenous catheter... Nothing... No flash of blood back through the catheter; only a bulging welt forming at the site where he thought the vein was. Suddenly his confidence ticked away like the second hand on the clock mounted on the wall of the trauma room.

Panic and embarrassment surged through him. He heard Judy speak softly behind him.

"Looks like you're having a little trouble, Doc. Let me try."

Leaving the tourniquet in place, the nurse flexed the patient's wrist, wiped an alcohol swab across the skin, and smoothly inserted a large bore IV into one of the veins on the back of the patient's hand. She advanced the catheter, withdrew the central needle, and attached the IV. The fluid dripped through the tubing without difficulty. She adjusted the rate of flow while one of the other nurses hung a unit of universal type O blood. Her ease in starting the IV only compounded Adam's feeling of failure.

As soon as the first two units of type O blood were hung, the patient was covered with a sheet, her IV tubes were readied, and the group began moving the cart towards the elevators.

They raced to the operating room. The requested blood arrived shortly after the surgical team wheeled the patient into the room.

"Blood pressure is about 80," said the Anesthesia resident as he hung the first of the units.

Holiday stood in the position of the operating surgeon to the patient's right. Rogers was the first assistant across the table. He was flanked by Kochenko, who was holding a retractor while Barnett stood beside Holiday, pulling on another. The abdomen was pulled open to create as much exposure of the injured organs as possible. Standing on a platform behind Kochenko, Adam could barely see into the belly.

"I don't think there's an organ without a pellet in it," said Rogers. "Got the spleen out, but there's still some bleeding behind the liver and we can't see the source, so we've got that packed tightly with lap pads. No other bleeding, but it's gonna take a while to fix all of this. She's even got a pellet through her gallbladder and one through the head of the pancreas. Hey, look at this... Do you know what this is?"

As he spoke, he inserted a hemostat into a hole in the small intestine. He closed the instrument and withdrew a long white structure from inside the intestine.

"It's a worm," said Barnett.

"Ascaris, to be exact," answered Kochenko. "A parasite."

"We learned about them in Tropical Diseases," said Barnett. "The professor said we would probably never see one."

"He was wrong," said Holiday.

The parasite was placed in an emesis basin and quickly removed from the operative field. Adam looked over Rogers' shoulder as Holiday removed the gallbladder and then methodically approached each of the other injuries.

They continued to work through sun-up. The gradually lighter sky filtered through the windows, brightening the room but not the mood as they focused on the figure lying on the table.

"Pretty stable at 90 systolic," the anesthesiologist finally announced. "Making some urine too. How are things down there?"

"Pretty much got the bowel injuries repaired. No blood is leaking through all the pads we placed behind the liver, but I'm going to have to take them out soon and deal with what's behind there. Try to get her pressure to 100 before I remove the packing."

Adam stepped down to stretch his legs. He glanced at the clock on the wall—a quarter after eight. The night had passed and with it a portion of the morning. He had lost track of time. His world had seemed to stand still as he focused on the efforts to save the wounded patient. He also had not been aware of the quiet figure in scrubs who had entered the OR and stood at the foot of the table.

"I heard you got a bad one," Dr. Theodorakis said. "What's the extent of the injuries?"

"Multiple perforations from shotgun pellets. Got everything fixed except I had to pack an area bleeding from behind the liver—probably an injury to the vena cava, but I wasn't able to get adequate exposure before."

"Mind if I scrub in?"

"No, sir, of course not."

Theodorakis stepped into the anteroom where the scrub sinks were located. Adam concentrated, trying to recall what he had read about injuries to the large abdominal vein behind the liver.

Rogers spoke up. "Very hard to expose and control…That's why there is such an extremely high mortality rate associated with them. If you haven't read the textbook chapter on trauma yet, you guys should read it as soon as you can. Dr. Theodorakis wrote it."

∾

The Chief of Service reentered the room, bringing with him an expectant hush. He held his arms up as water dripped from his elbows. He displayed no sense of urgency as he accepted a towel from the scrub nurse, dried his hands and arms, and was assisted into a gown and gloves. When he approached the table, Holiday stepped to the side so Theodorakis could occupy the operating surgeon's spot.

"Suction, please."

His left hand began to remove the lap pads and hand them to the nurse as he held the suction ready in his right. When he removed the last pad and lifted the edge of the liver, the suction tubing wiggled as the flow of dark blood welled up in the belly to obscure his line of vision. He re-applied pressure with a single pad in his hand while he calmly requested, "Scissors to me."

"Blood pressure has dropped to 70," said Anesthesia.

There was no wasted motion as Theodorakis cut the ligament holding the top of the liver, allowing Rogers to pull the liver's edge away from the injured big vein beneath it. He handed Holiday the suction and placed a pad over the injured vessel.

"Gentle pressure," he said as Holiday pressed down on the gauze pad. "Side-biter clamp and a 4.0 prolene suture, please," he continued, opening his right hand in the direction of the scrub nurse to receive a small angled vascular clamp.

Adam couldn't see the actual site of injury, but he watched as the clamp was applied, and then the suture mounted on a needle holder was passed into Theodorakis' waiting hand.

Working in the depths of the belly, the chief placed three sutures with smooth and deliberate motion, tying each in sequence. He removed the clamp and waited while Holiday stood ready with the suction.

"That should do it. We'll make rounds as usual in the afternoon."

His gown and gloves were handed to the circulating nurse and he was gone. The tension and stress evaporated.

"Blood pressure 110," said the anesthesiologist. "She's actually making a fair amount of urine despite the blood loss."

They took their time again inspecting the abdomen to make sure there were no missed pellet wounds or any oozing. Rubber drains were brought through the skin and placed near the loop of intestine Holiday had sewn to drain the injury to the pancreas—the Roux-en-Y loop. Rogers again emphasized how dangerous and life-threatening the leakage of pancreatic fluid could be if the loop didn't heal and digestive enzymes from the pancreas drained into the belly.

"The drains may protect by allowing a leak to drain to the outside, but even so, if the loop breaks down the leak can wreak havoc on the adjacent organs. You guys should be sure to read the section on pancreatic injuries, and always remember the first rule of internship: 'Eat when you can, sleep when you can, and don't screw around with the pancreas.'"

Adam hurried before rounds. He stopped at the campus bookstore to grab a candy bar for lunch and noted the scissors rack still empty. He then returned to the hospital, hoping to get as much of his work rounds done as possible before attending the chairman's teaching rounds. He hoped he could at least have time to change the dressing on Luanne. As he crossed the street to the hospital, he remembered that Doc Augustin had told him to stop by the Pharmacy again.

When he rang the bell at the window, he was greeted by a young woman in a white coat. He introduced himself and she replied, "Wait here."

A few minutes later, Doc Augustin appeared from an unseen office far back in the Pharmacy. He handed Adam a brown paper bag, then turned and disappeared back to where he had been.

Adam walked away and opened the bag to find three tubes of streptokinase.

Luanne was in good spirits when Adam arrived. She told him how they used to fish for catfish when she was a child and how her mother would serve them fried and breaded with collard greens on Sundays after church. Adam smiled as he listened while noting how simple it was to apply a thin layer of streptokinase with a tongue blade to her wound. He smeared a thin layer onto all of her wound's surfaces and replaced her dressings.

"This is special medication that will help heal your wound faster," he said with so much confidence that no one would have believed he had never seen a tube of streptokinase before that morning. She smiled at his reassurance and smiled even more when he said he would be looking forward to their next visit even as he stifled a yawn.

CHAPTER 38

DANNY FRER SURPRISED Adam. The medical student had thought addicts were sociopaths, criminals to be feared. Danny was harmless; he was just sad and withdrawn. An air of melancholy hung heavily about him. When they had admitted him from clinic, Turk had explained how difficult it was to treat pain in a junkie. On the one hand, the patient clearly needed medications to control the pain from his infected thigh and collapsed vertebrae. On the other hand, Turk had said that they didn't want to feed his habit since some addicts would take advantage of the situation to demand higher and more frequent doses of drugs.

Danny had been satisfied with the medications Turk had prescribed, but the tiny intravenous that had been established when he was admitted had only lasted overnight. He clearly needed his IV restarted so that he could receive both his pain medication and antibiotics. Adam recalled how skilled Judy was when she helped him in the ER. His confidence had evaporated after he failed to place that patient's IV. There was no nurse available to help him now.

Wantz was the only other member of Service 1 who was on the male ward at the moment, and he was preoccupied with reading a chart near the nurses' station. Adam hesitated as he approached him.

"Dr. Wantz, I've got a patient we admitted from clinic who needs a new IV catheter. He's a drug user with a thigh abscess and an infected vertebrae."

"You've been down in the ER and seen IVs started. You should know how to do it. It's a student procedure, you know. Just put a tourniquet on his arm, prep the area with alcohol, slide in the catheter, and hook up the IV, for Pete's sake!"

With that, Wantz placed the chart in the rack, turned his back to Adam, and marched out of the ward. Adam was left with no alternative but to try to start a new intravenous for Danny before he could leave for lecture. Although he could feel his heart pounding in his chest, he tried to appear calm when he organized the alcohol pad, tape, and four catheters of different sizes on Danny's bedside table.

He placed a tourniquet on Danny's right arm and felt for any easily accessible vein. Instead of the soft, compressible tube he was hoping to find, Danny's arm contained scars and cords of firm tissue. Adam wasn't certain which if any represented a usable vein.

Sensing his dilemma, Danny offered encouragement. "Don't feel bad, Doc. I done this to myself. Go ahead and try… Do your best. It's my fault."

Adam wiped the alcohol pad over Danny's forearm and judged where he thought there might be a vein. He punctured the skin with the IV catheter, but as he advanced the catheter he didn't see a return flash of blood to indicate he had entered a vessel.

"Try again, Doc," said Danny. "I know I needs those medicines."

Adam tried, five times in fact, both arms. Danny never flinched when Adam stuck him.

"I done it to myself," he repeated after Adam's fifth try.

Adam was now feeling exasperated and completely inept. Failure was unacceptable. Perhaps he wasn't cut out for medical school after all. If he tried to find a resident, they would see he was incompetent, and besides, he would be late for lecture. He held Danny's outstretched arm, still searching intently for a vein. Finally, he looked up.

"Think you can find a vein?"

"I'll try."

Adam cleaned Danny's arm again with alcohol and checked that the tourniquet had remained in place. He made sure the IV line and tape were ready and then handed the plastic intravenous cannula to the patient.

Danny's movement was experienced and smooth as he inserted the catheter into a spot on his forearm that Adam had examined but hadn't recognized. A good blood return occurred after he had advanced the cannula and only ceased when Adam attached the IV, secured the site with tape, and started the fluid infusing.

"Thanks," Adam said softly, feeling some embarrassment but a lot of relief that an IV would now be in place when Theodorakis arrived for rounds.

"Thank *you*, Doctor," Danny said.

Chapter 39

ON AWAKENING IN the Recovery Room, the girl who had suffered the shotgun blast became unruly. Almost immediately after she had forcibly pulled out her breathing tube, her hands and feet were tied with restraints while she screamed profanities.

"You fucking cocksucker sonsabitches! Get this fuckin' tube outta mah nose!"

Barnett stood wide-eyed at the nurses' desk, afraid to approach her. Doyle calmly sidled up next to him.

"Don't have to worry about her not being able to breathe with the endotracheal tube out. Can hear her screaming all the way at the elevators. Who's following this patient?"

"Her name is Leticia Powell," stated Barnett. "She's a thirty-year-old female who sustained a shotgun blast to her lower chest and abdomen…"

Doyle cut him off. "We know all that. Did you scrub on her surgery?"

"Yes, I did," answered Barnett.

"Good. She's your patient, then. You talk to her and take care of her drains and dressings. Ask one of us if you got any questions. I ain't wasting my junior residents' time on her until she shuts up. Congratulations, you've got your first private patient."

Her scream shook the room.

"MOTHERRRRFFFFFUCKERS!"

Doyle shook his head as he left. "No wonder her daddy shot her."

Chapter 40

ADAM THOUGHT THAT Billy, the appendectomy he had scrubbed on, was doing well, but he was complaining of shortness of breath and that the right side of his chest hurt. Wantz had ordered a chest X-ray and now motioned for Adam to join him at the foot of the bed.

"You need to snog him," said Wantz. "Lubricate a red rubber catheter and stick it down his nose to tickle his trachea. That'll make him cough. All these patients close up some airways after anesthesia, and coughing re-opens them... Make sure he's coughed well before we start rounds with Theo."

After Wantz left the ward, Adam was still collecting the necessary supplies in the treatment room when Turk approached him.

"What are you doing?"

"Wantz told me to snog that appendectomy patient. I was just getting the catheter and some gloves and lubricant ready."

Turk left the treatment room and took a few steps to the patient's bedside. Adam added a gauze sponge to his stock and followed him.

Turk looked at his watch while he felt the pulse in Bobby's wrist.

"He's tachycardic. Got a heart rate of 140. That's too fast. Did you check his legs for blood clots? We need an arterial blood gas."

"Blood clots?" Bobby asked. "What you mean? My momma died of blood clots at thirty-eight after her his-toe-wrectomee."

"We want to be sure you don't have one up in your lungs," said Turk. "We'll need to draw a blood sample."

The arterial blood was a deep red as it pumped into the glass syringe that Turk held firmly at the patient's wrist. When the syringe was completely filled, he withdrew the needle from the radial artery, placed a rubber stopper on it, and dropped the syringe onto a pile of ice in an emesis basin.

"I'll take this to the lab... Be back before rounds with the chief. Be sure you know your patients," he said.

Adam was shuffling his patients' cards, still trying to commit them to memory. Shrevi and Barnett joined in at the nurses' desk. Jen had the day off, and Adam would have much preferred chatting with her than trying to remember his patient's last hemoglobin level.

Turk returned with Holiday. They all gathered at Billy's bedside.

"His pCO2 is 26," said Turk, "and his pO2 is only 62. You guys know what that means?"

"He's breathing too fast and not maintaining his oxygen level." Adam felt proud that he remembered his Physiology course.

"Pulmonary embolus," Barnett added the diagnosis.

In the next moment, Holiday and Turk had Bobby on a cart, an oxygen tank and cannula supplementing his breathing. Once situated, they wheeled him out of the ward.

"We're going to X-ray so I can do a pulmonary angiogram," said Holiday. "You guys wait here and do rounds with Theo. Let the others know where we are."

CHAPTER 41

ADAM, SHREVI, AND Barnett were at the nurses' desk with their textbooks open when they heard the ding of the elevator doors and the parade of approaching footsteps. They placed the books in their canvas bags and held tightly to their index cards.

Dr. Theodorakis entered the ward, followed by the residents and students from the other surgical services. Adam knew his patients' histories and their lab work. He hoped he wouldn't be embarrassed in front of his fellow students by any difficult questions from the chief.

He needn't have been concerned. Dr. Theodorakis's focus that morning was not to ask much of the students. He accepted a brief summary of each patient's history and then spent his time addressing the group. After a short update on the condition of Barnett's patient with diverticulitis, he discussed the difficulties in differentiating a superficial wound infection from an intra-abdominal infection. At the bedside of the man with the bleeding ulcer, he re-emphasized the diagnostic points that had been made in Bullpen.

Theodorakis frowned when informed that the appendectomy patient had been taken downstairs for a pulmonary angiogram. He listened patiently to the story of Danny Frer but didn't provide any further academic discussion. Adam wondered if perhaps some doctors felt junkies' problems didn't merit more attention.

On the female ward, Dr. Theodorakis listened carefully to the reports on all the patients. He didn't offer anything that might serve as consolation for the woman who had lost the baby and her child-bearing ability.

Adam was among the first to crowd into the elevator that would take the group up to the ICU. He was crammed into a corner by those who followed, all hoping for an advantageous position when the group reached the first patient's bedside. Just before the doors closed, leaving the remaining students and house staff waiting for the next elevator, in the quiet of the ride Theodorakis explained to Doyle the technique he had used to visualize and repair the vena caval injury.

When the elevator doors opened, Dr. Theodorakis's description of the lifesaving technique he had performed was greeted by the screams of its beneficiary. A cascade of curse words echoed through the halls. Doyle and Theodorakis remained for a moment in the hallway, continuing their discussion until the other elevators arrived and Barnett and Shrevi joined Adam and the other students and residents in filing into the unit.

Leticia Powell turned her head from the nurses towards the three medical students and continued her tirade.

"You mutha-fuckers is tryin' to kill me," she screamed. "I want these tubes out and I want a plate of red beans and rice, damn you! Get these fuckin' straps off my hands!"

Faded heavy cloth straps encircled her wrists and were tied to the bed frame, keeping her hands held close to her sides. Her diatribe continued as the group approached her bed, some of the students keeping a safe distance two or three steps back. She suddenly became silent when Theodorakis entered the ward and took his place at the head of the bed. When he began discussing her case, she stared at him with an exaggeration of the same awe in which he was held by the students and residents. She remained calm and quiet, still focusing on Theodorakis when the group moved on to complete rounds.

"Let's go see that pulmonary angiogram," said Theodorakis, and the group shifted like a herd of sheep into the hallway. Adam gestured towards Leticia and gave Barnett a questioning look as they approached the doorway, but Barnett just shrugged. For once, it seemed, he didn't have an answer.

"You can see the clots right here where the contrast in the pulmonary arteries abruptly ends, Westermark's sign," Dr. Theodorakis pointed out as everyone crowded around the X-ray view box. The main pulmonary arteries extended from the edges of the heart and were rendered white by the injection of contrast. The image on the right contained a darkened area.

"Clot," whispered Wantz as Dr. Theodorakis pointed to the area and then to the smaller branches on the left, extending from the main artery like Medusa's hair across the lung field.

Adam tried to step closer to study how the small vessels on the left extended all the way to the chest wall while on the right many of them did not fill with contrast and ended abruptly in the mid-lung field.

"Can anyone explain Virchow's triad for us?" Theodorakis's tone indicated that he expected the answer from one of the students.

Yesterday's lecture was still fresh in his mind, and Adam found himself answering before anyone else.

"Virchow's triad is named for Rudolf Virchow, the pathologist who, between 1846 and 1856, established that the three primary factors that result in deep vein thrombosis and subsequent pulmonary embolism include stasis or reduction of blood flow in the veins, injury to the intima or lining of the veins either by blunt, penetrating, or surgical trauma, and a state of hypercoagulability."

Theodorakis acknowledged his answer by stating, "I have long been interested in whether a state of hypercoagulability exists and, if so, whether that could have any genetic or inheritable properties."

"Sir," Adam felt a sense of immediacy as he replied, "this patient's mother died of a blood clot when she was thirty-eight years old after having a hysterectomy."

Theodorakis pondered Adam's revelation for a moment and then turned towards Shrevi.

"How do we test for hypercoagulability and determine its genetic nature?"

Shrevi turned pale, wrinkled his brow, pursed his lips, paused, and thought as hard as he could. He was becoming so visibly anxious that Adam glanced over to Barnett, worried that their classmate might faint again.

Finally, Shrevi let out an exasperated sigh. He cast his eyes towards the floor and answered quietly, "I don't know, sir."

"Neither do I," said Theodorakis, "neither do I."

CHAPTER 42

"**I**T'S SCARY TO think we're going to have to take that final exam in a couple of weeks," said Barnett when they sat down in the cafeteria after the morning lecture. "My daughter is asleep when I leave in the morning and asleep when I get home. I read every night until 12:30 or 1:00 in the morning and only get to see her when she wakes up with colic…and then I don't get to sleep or study."

"This shit's really hard," said Shrevi as he stirred cream into his coffee. "No kiddin' about the sleepin'… They expect us to know everything on the wards and we're only finishing the second week of the rotation."

"This is sure different from studying for a regular course," said Adam. "No way to think we can get all the reading done, let alone review for a test. None of us has probably ever gone into an exam unprepared—it's scary."

As they rose to return to the hospital, Adam recognized the long braid of one of their classmates sitting alone across the cafeteria with her head down and her back towards him.

"I'll catch up to you guys on the ward," he said, veering off towards her.

When Adam approached, she turned her head and tried to hide her face.

"Hey, Melissa, what're you doing by yourself? Is something wrong?"

She wiped her hand across her cheek as she turned back towards him.

"No, I'm fine," she sniffed. "I'm just so…so…frustrated."

Adam flipped a chair around and sat facing her with his arms resting on the back of the chair.

"About what?"

"No…no… I'm fine… It's fine."

"Melissa, you don't look like it's fine. What's up?"

He hated to see her so upset and holding back. Melissa was a friend from freshman year Anatomy Lab. She was from a small town in Nebraska. Her parents had been quite religious and her father a surgeon. Moving to New Orleans was quite a departure for her, the first time she had been out of her home state for any prolonged time, with the exception of the medical missionary trips she had gone on with her parents.

In a short time working together, the four male students in Adam's group and the three in Melissa's all developed a profound respect for her. She had long, thin fingers and wielded a scalpel with unusual precision, no matter how leathery and distorted the fixative had made the cadavers' tissues. The professors even commented on how clean her dissections were. Adam and his partners would often crowd around her table so she could demonstrate the structures that had been difficult to identify in their cadaver.

"I'm having a bad time on Service 4," she said. "Dr. Brewster and the residents make me feel like I can't do anything right. They never ask any questions on rounds of the two male students on the service with me, but I get grilled over and over. They keep asking me questions until I can't answer. In the operating room, when it's my turn to cut sutures, I cut them the same as anybody else but they always insist they're either too long or too short. It just seems unfair."

"Like they have a different standard because you're a woman?"

"I didn't say that."

Adam ran his hand through his hair. "Don't have to—everybody knows doctors have been mostly male and Surgery is the ultimate old boys' club, but things are changing."

"Are they now?"

"Sure, look at our class—six girls. But the class behind us—twenty-five, and the first-year class has thirty-five. Every specialty is going to have to be more accepting of women before too long."

"Tell that to the men who make me feel so stupid. The next group of women isn't going to have it any easier."

"You, stupid? Remember freshman year when everybody was struggling to learn the muscles of the lower extremity because we had a Histology test the day before the Anatomy exam? You stayed in the lab after hours and helped me learn all those muscles and nerves. I only got a good grade because you made it so clear. Just hang in there and don't let those guys get you down."

"Thanks, Adam," she smiled. "I'll try."

"Good," he said as he stood to leave, "but do me a favor."

"What's that?"

"Don't set the curve too high on the Surgery final."

CHAPTER 43

SEEING DAYLIGHT WHEN he left the hospital was a treat for Adam. All the frustration and fears of the week evaporated when he stepped into the French Quarter. He walked along Royal Street, where the tourists were less rowdy than those on Bourbon and he could take his time browsing in the antique shop windows. He heard music, at first in the distance but growing louder as he approached the corner where the Royal Street Grocery was located.

In front of the store, a group of street musicians were playing zydeco—a hippie girl in a long caftan playing fiddle, a couple of guitarists, a very animated accordion player, an older man in a porkpie hat playing a beat-up old stand-up bass, and two percussionists—one playing a snare drum mounted on a tiny bass drum while the other played a washboard with a couple of spoons.

Adam entered the grocery store and bought a cold soda. He stepped out of the door and dropped his book bag onto the wooden bench along the storefront. Sitting down, he leaned his head back against the wall, closed his eyes, and let the first swig of root beer cool the back of his throat.

His mind wandered back to his first impressions on moving to New Orleans. The culture was so exotic and different from where he had grown up. He thought of his journey from the sleepy little farm town, his first girlfriend, and his buddies from school, many of whom either went into the service or attended college close by before returning to their hometown. He still felt the trauma of the loss of friends that made him want to become a doctor—a person who saved lives. He recalled sharing crayons with the boy who sat next to him in second grade and drowned shortly after school let out for the summer. He remembered being sick to his stomach for days when a high school friend was hit by a car while riding his bicycle on a country road, and again a year later when a tractor flipped over on a classmate who had taken a summer job mowing along the highway. Those friends remained in his thoughts. He hadn't expected pre-med courses in college to be so hard or trying to get into medical school to be so competitive. Nothing before, though, had left him feeling so unmoored and adrift as the challenges he saw in actually caring for patients. He felt that he had entered a new world of critically important demands, ones that he worried he might not be able to meet. No amount of classroom work had prepared him for Ronald Candy, Leticia Powell, or Luanne's wound.

His ears perked up and his eyes opened to watch when the washboard player began his solo. He was older than the other musicians, but his youth seemed restored as he swayed while the spoons danced over the metal ridges.

Adam's foot was still tapping when the other musicians joined back in. As they played, he studied each one. They were of different racial backgrounds and ages but completely in sync as they played the lively music that was said to have originated in the early part of the century in the rural areas of Southwest Louisiana, where the population was mostly people with a mix of French, Spanish, African, and Native American ancestry.

Living in New Orleans had familiarized Adam with the role that the city's music history had played in American culture. Congo Square, the area where slaves once gathered to socialize, play African music, and dance, was considered the birthplace of jazz. From those origins the music mutated and was carried into the streets by European-style brass bands and into social clubs and bars, as well as the whorehouses of Storyville. Musicians like Louis Armstrong had brought the music to Chicago and other parts of the country.

Musical creativity was baked into the soul of the city. Adam felt fortunate that he had been able to attend the city's Jazz and Heritage Festival twice since he had moved there. He had witnessed performances by dynamic gospel groups and seen pioneers of rock and roll and rhythm and blues, as well as masters such as Professor Longhair, Fats Domino, and the Meters.

It was not only the musicians and the variety of their styles that had awakened Adam to the uniqueness of the city. He also felt a sense of community from the men who waited on him early in the morning at the Café Du Monde, from Teddy, from the artists who displayed their work in Jackson Square, from the lady in the Chinese laundry on Chartres Street who inspected every shirt carefully and replaced buttons he didn't even know were missing. Adam felt particularly welcomed by the waitress at Felix's who knew his habits so well that she would hand him a menu, laugh, and say, "The oyster stew is exceptionally good tonight." Regularly on his walks home, Adam saw a guy whizzing by on a yellow bicycle wearing his Mardi Gras magician's costume, his face painted white with a green handlebar mustache and his head covered by a huge top hat festooned with Mardi Gras beads.

He finished his soda, placed a dollar in the bucket the musicians had set in the street, and began his walk home, anticipating that if he could quickly read the chapter on hernias, there might still be time to go see who was playing that night at Preservation Hall.

CHAPTER 44

EARLY MORNING ROUNDS went quickly. Kochenko and Turk offered to help the students so they could get to Grand Rounds on time. Adam moved efficiently but hesitated at the entrance to the female ward. The woman whose pregnancy was ended by the car crash would be discharged soon, and he'd felt awkward and speechless while he changed her dressing over the past few days. From the doorway he saw Turk sitting on the bed, speaking softly and holding the woman's hand. When Turk stood to leave, the patient grasped his hand and smiled weakly. Whatever Turk had said must have brought her the comfort that Adam couldn't express.

After Grand Rounds, when the department surgeons had exited the auditorium, the white-coated students filtered down to the front seats and prepared for Bullpen. The first student presenter stepped to the lectern and, mustering a fair amount of conviction, introduced his patient.

The case was that of a thirty-seven-year-old man from Algiers who worked in a local oyster bar. He had come to the Emergency Room after two days of abdominal pain associated with nausea, vomiting, and severe constipation. His history was only remarkable for an appendectomy ten years before. The student ran through all the other sections of the history and physical, noting the absence of any drinking history or family illness. The patient had no allergies, and the lengthy Review of Systems failed to identify any symptoms that might suggest any unidentified problems.

Only after he completed his presentation did the student's hands begin to tremble. He waited for Dr. Theodorakis to attack him with a string of difficult questions but regained his composure when Wantz mounted the patient's X-rays on a view box and Dr. Theodorakis asked him to interpret the films and provide the audience with his diagnosis.

"The small intestine is markedly dilated," he said.

"And your diagnosis?"

"I believe the patient had a small bowel obstruction."

"On what basis?"

"He's had previous surgery, so he may have scar tissue, that is, adhesions, blocking the bowel."

"Do the X-rays support this diagnosis?"

The student paused as he stared at the patient's films.

Before the student could answer, Dr. Theodorakis turned towards the audience.

"Ninety-five percent of small bowel obstructions are due to either adhesions and scarring from previous surgery or incarcerated hernias. The history of previous surgery therefore is extremely important…and the presence or absence of an incarcerated hernia should be easy to determine on physical exam. The X-rays clearly support this diagnosis, showing, in addition to bowel dilated above the point of obstruction, the findings of air fluid levels and a paucity of air in the colon."

He used a penlight to point to the features on the X-ray.

"When you consider the diagnosis of a bowel obstruction, you should remember to always ask yourself four questions: Is the small or large intestine involved? Is the obstruction partial or complete? Is this really a mechanical blockage or is the intestine merely temporarily paralyzed—a condition called an 'ileus'? And finally, is the circulation to the intestine compromised or not—that is, is the bowel strangulated or not?"

Adam and Barnett looked at each other without speaking, but both wishing they had known to ask those questions a few days ago before Wantz had rushed the old man who died into surgery.

The senior was notably relieved when he stepped away from the lectern and sat down. The second student did not even feign an air of confidence. She approached the lectern while her patient, an older woman, was wheeled on a cart to the front of the amphitheater. Although covered by a sheet, her large belly was obvious.

The student's hair was frizzing in the New Orleans humidity, adding to her nervous appearance. She straightened her large glasses as she began her presentation. Her voice didn't carry well over the lectern, but it was clear to those leaning in to hear that this patient had had no previous surgery or any hernias. Still, her presenting symptoms were similar to those of the previous patient.

"Before we consider less common causes of bowel obstruction, please finish reporting your physical exam," requested Dr. Theodorakis.

The student read from her notes, beginning with the patient's vital signs, general inspection, and head and neck exam. Her voice softened with uncertainty through the cardiopulmonary exam and was barely audible by the time she finished.

Dr. Theodorakis's jaw was set when he leveled a stern gaze at her and asked, "What about her internal pelvic exam?"

The student paused, searching for an answer before her response echoed through the assemblage like a mortal sin for which no number of novenas or Hail Marys could compensate— "I didn't do one…"

A hush followed the collective deep breath that filled the auditorium.

She's screwed, thought Adam.

Without gloating, Dr. Theodorakis simply stated, "Had an internal exam been performed, you likely would have been able to discern that the enlargement of her abdomen was not just distended intestine. You would have been able to identify a large pelvic mass representing an advanced ovarian carcinoma that has created this patient's bowel obstruction… We should all remember that a pelvic exam on a woman can often provide further information about abdominal symptoms… Can you tell me any reason you deferred this exam in this particular patient?"

For a few moments the student fumbled with her notes. She looked up as if for help from her classmates, but all they did was move forward in their seats, heads cocked as they waited for her answer to finally come.

She let her head hang and whispered to the floor, "But I'm going into psychiatry..."

Week Three

Chapter 45

MONDAY MORNING WORK rounds were completed before seven. Barnett and Shrevi headed to the cafeteria to grab breakfast before lecture, but Adam lagged behind on the male ward.

Jen arrived at seven. Adam stood midway down the row of beds, thumbing through the chart in his hands, hoping she wouldn't notice when he glanced up at her. He tried to look busy with the patient in the fifth bed while she placed the big canvas bag she carried on her desk and stored her purse in the lower desk drawer.

Adam approached her desk. He set his chart down on the corner and noticed that the large book peeking out of the top of her bag was *Burr* by Gore Vidal.

"Hi… Good morning," he said. "Weren't you carrying a different book last week?"

"Yes, I was. I read a lot."

"I don't expect you get to read much here."

"No, I don't, but I read a lot at home in the evening. My husband often goes out for drinks after work and comes home late. Sometimes I take the St. Charles streetcar to work and read on the way."

"Wasn't Burr the guy in that duel with…uh…somebody else in government?"

"Yes, he was Vice President when he killed Alexander Hamilton."

"That's why they put him on the ten-dollar bill." Adam tried to sound confident, unwilling to let his ignorance of history keep him from imagining them sitting together over a glass of wine and discussing the Continental Congress.

"Hamilton's on the bill, not Burr," she said.

She picked up the chart he had left on the desk. Before replacing it in the rack, she remarked, "I saw you with this at Bed 5 when I came in… You do know this is the chart for the patient in Bed 1?"

"Oh…uh…yeah…sure… I was checking on both of them. Good seeing you this morning," he said. "I've…uh…got to get to lecture."

After walking to the elevator, Adam realized the lecture wouldn't start for over an hour. He would have time to change Luanne's dressing. This early she might still be sleepy and he could avoid any small talk.

After lecture, Adam walked across the street to the hospital, feeling that he was beginning to discern a rhythm to the surgical rotation. Morning work rounds were the time for the students to change dressings, write progress notes, spin the hematocrits, and draw blood for other tests or check completed lab results. At some point during the day they would make rounds with the residents, though this varied depending on the operating schedule. A couple of times a week, Dr. Theodorakis met them for teaching rounds. Sandwiched into the morning schedule were the lectures presented at the medical school. Often the lectures conflicted with the elective surgical schedule or an emergency operation. Wantz said that the students should scrub in on all the patients they followed, but Kochenko suggested they could choose to scrub or attend lecture. Turk recommended at least one of them attend the morning lecture and then share their notes. They were expected to study the notes and read the corresponding textbook material in the evenings, but each lecture condensed a textbook chapter of fifty to seventy-five pages. It was impossible to keep up.

Adam stepped onto the opposite curb and made his way up the ambulance ramp to enter the hospital. It seemed that there were three types of time associated with the rotation on Surgery. One was "not enough." There was never enough time to study either the textbook and lectures, or a specific patient's problem, or complete the work on the wards. The second was "wasted." The time waiting for the residents, for lab or X-ray or an operating room was unproductive and occurred no matter how one hoped to avoid it. And finally, there was a third dimension of time—"complete suspension." Adam didn't quite understand it, but he had experienced it with Ronald Candy's surgery. In the operating room he lost all awareness of time as Holiday and Doyle worked while conversing about football. They had moved so smoothly and efficiently that Adam had been surprised to discover the night had passed and it was 5 a.m. when they arrived in the Recovery Room.

∽

Adam arrived in the clinic ahead of Barnett and Shrevi. The waiting area for the male clinic was filled. There was standing room only, with the line of patients extending into the hallway.

"Sinclair," Rogers said as he and Turk started down the hallway, "c'mon with us. We're going to meet Doyle in the female clinic. Your buddies can help out here."

As soon as they arrived, Doyle directed Adam to the first cubicle. "You work in there. We'll be seeing patients in the other exam rooms if you have any questions. Turk or Rogers can check on any of the people you see."

Adam pulled the curtain aside, arranged the folding chairs so they faced each other across the desk, and sat down. He straightened his tie, pulled a ballpoint pen from his pocket, and slid the pad of progress notes in front of him. He worried that he might not be able to handle whatever problem entered his cubicle. He took a deep breath when the nurse opened the curtain and ushered in the first patient.

She was a pleasant, heavyset Black lady wearing a faded yellow blouse and a gray skirt.

"I'm Dr. Sinclair," said Adam. "What brings you in today?"

"I've been having pains in my stomach."

"When did they start?"

"Don't rightly know… Been goin' on for a few weeks."

"What are the pains like?"

"Hurts."

"Where are they located? Do they move around?"

"Starts here," she indicated her upper abdomen. "Bothers my back."

"Is the pain related to what you eat?"

"Don't know… Usually get them at night."

"After dinner?"

"Hour or so."

"Any specific foods bother it?"

"Lately french fries," she said. "Twice with french fries I vomited."

Adam looked at the chart the nurse had given him—just a manila folder containing one page with her identifying information and vital signs written down by the nurse.

He began to write on the yellow pad in front of him:

Chief Complaint: pains in the stomach for a few weeks.

History of Present Illlness: Ardella Wright is a 42 yr old female who presents to the Charity Hospital Surgery Clinic with complaints of abdominal pain over the past few weeks. The pains occur an hour after eating and radiate to her back. She has vomited after eating french fries…

"Have you ever been jaundiced?" he asked.

"What's that?"

"Have your eyes ever turned yellow? Has your urine got dark like Coca-Cola or have your stools ever been white?" He asked all the questions that might indicate that a gallstone had blocked her bile duct.

"No," she said. "No yellow, didn't see no Coca-Cola."

Adam completed each section of the history, noting her past history of no surgery, no tobacco use, little alcohol, no allergies or medications, and four childbirths.

The pages of his yellow pad were neat and well-organized when he put down his pen and stated, "I'll need to examine you now."

He helped her onto the exam table and pulled out the footrest. She lifted her blouse from her skirt, unbuttoned it, and lay back. Adam felt the pulsations in her neck, listened with his stethoscope for any abnormal sounds in the blood vessels, and listened to her heart and lungs. She pulled up her bra and he made sure there were no lumps in her breasts. Finally, he examined her abdomen. He was surprised that her belly was soft. There was no tenderness anywhere, particularly in the right upper quadrant where the gallbladder rested under the edge of the liver.

"I'm going to step out for a minute to talk to my resident physician. Excuse me for a moment. I'll be back shortly," he said.

Turk was holding a chart outside the next cubicle.

"Can you check this lady for me?" Adam asked. "I think she's got a bad gallbladder, but she's not tender now. Probably needs an oral cholecystogram or an ultrasound for diagnosis."

"Sure." Turk placed his chart into the cart and followed Adam back into the exam room.

"This is Dr. Turk," said Adam.

"How do you do, ma'am?" said Turk.

He picked up Adam's notes and quickly scanned them. Then he stepped to the patient and pushed on her upper belly.

"Not tender now?" he asked.

"No, sir…not now."

"I agree with Dr. Sinclair. I think your gallbladder is bothering you. We should probably do a test of it."

"What kind of test?" she asked.

"An ultrasound would be a good one," said Turk.

"Is that what the doctor in the Medicine Clinic done?" she asked. "Let me have my purse."

Adam handed her the handbag she had left on the table. She sat up and opened it, pulled out a sheet of paper, and handed it to Turk.

"The Black doctor in the clinic give me this," she said.

Turk read the ultrasound report from the Charity Hospital Department of Radiology. Most telling was the impression at the bottom of the page: "Thick-walled gallbladder containing multiple stones with shadowing. Impression: Cholelithiasis."

Stapled to the report was a sheet from a prescription pad. Written on the smaller sheet was "To Surgery Clinic—Symptomatic Gallstones.—Battiste."

When Adam finished with the second patient and stepped out of the exam cubicle, Rogers approached him. "Hey, c'mon, I got a patient you should examine."

Rogers led him into another exam cubicle, where a young woman in a faded sundress that looked as though its floral print had bloomed long ago sat in the chair next to the exam table, her hands folded in her lap.

"Stand behind her," said Rogers, "and feel her neck."

Adam stepped in front of the patient.

"I'm Dr. Sinclair," he said as he made eye contact with her. "I'm one of the third-year students on the Surgical Service, and Dr. Rogers would like me to examine your neck."

She nodded her approval, and Adam stepped behind her and placed his fingertips alongside her trachea. The left side of her neck felt normal, but on the right, an ovoid spongy mass abutted against her windpipe.

"Could you swallow, please?" Rogers instructed the patient.

Adam felt her trachea rise and descend. The lump stayed between his fingertips.

"So it's not fixed to the trachea, right?"

"Correct," Adam said, remembering from Physical Diagnosis class that adherence to underlying structures could be a sign of malignancy.

"Ma'am, we should admit you and remove that lump. I think it's a tumor of the thyroid gland," said Rogers.

Both the resident and the student could see that the word "tumor" brought fear to her eyes.

"Of course, it could just be a benign thyroid nodule," said Rogers. "Either way, it should be removed."

"That's what I come in for," said the patient, not seeming reassured.

The waiting room was empty when Rogers and Adam stepped from behind the curtain to finish the admitting paperwork for the patient. Doyle and Turk were standing next to the folding table used by the nurses.

"We're done," said Doyle. "We should go over to the male side and see if they need any help finishing up."

"Just saw a thyroid tumor I'm going to admit. Be nice to do it while my daddy's visiting. He'd probably like to see me operate," said Rogers.

"He comin' in?" asked Doyle.

"Yeah, he finally found someone to cover his practice in Abbeville for the weekend. He's been invited to speak at Grand Rounds. If you guys want to go ahead, I'll finish here and meet you in the other clinic."

Before leaving, Adam tore a sheet off the yellow tablet, wrote a note, and stuffed it in his pocket: READ THYROID TUMORS.

Chapter 46

MID-WEEK, WHEN ADAM pulled the morning's dressing off Luanne's wound, he realized how different it appeared. The dirty yellow subcutaneous tissue had been replaced by a robust pink lining that extended the entire length of the incision and filled in much of the wound, leaving a crater perhaps half the original depth. None of the dirty brown fluid that had collected in the bottom of the wound remained, although the gauze he removed was saturated with a thin pink liquid. No longer did the pungent odor fill his nostrils when the dressing was removed. A smaller amount of loose white material rested on the surface of the wound—"fibrinous exudate," as it had been referred to in the chapter on wound healing. He easily wiped it away with a piece of fresh gauze.

"I think we've got some healing here," he said.

"Don't hurt no more when you rub it," replied Luanne.

He focused on the wound, looking at each portion with great care as he scrubbed away the surface debris, intent on understanding the process he was witnessing. For a few moments Luanne simply watched his facial expression until she broke his concentration.

"Where you came from?" she asked.

Adam looked up. "I'm from the Midwest. Illinois, little farm town."

"You always goin' be a doctor?"

"Pretty much always wanted to be…except when I wanted to be a cowboy or a major league pitcher."

"You played ball?"

"Not well enough. And the Lone Ranger didn't need another partner."

"Never been to no baseball game… No team in New Orleans. We just got football, but I don't care for it."

"You're not missing much… You got that good quarterback from Ole Miss, but your team isn't winning very often… Fact is some people refer to them as 'the Ain'ts.'"

"I heared that but I don't pay it no mind… You married?"

"No." Adam hadn't expected her to ask about his personal life.

"Got a girlfriend?"

Adam couldn't remember any lectures on how to handle personal questions. He knew that doctors should maintain a professional distance from their patients. Her question seemed innocuous enough, but still he hesitated.

"None at present."

"You're nice," she said. "She be a lucky one when she find you."

Adam was a bit uncomfortable. He appreciated the compliment, but it felt sad and awkward to linger too much on what he was missing due to the demands of medical school.

"You've got what we call granulation tissue here... New blood vessels growing into the tissue... Dressings in place. I'll see you in the morning."

∽

The following morning, Adam found the residents huddled together with Shrevi and Barnett at the end of the ward. They were somber, wearing neckties and suits or sport coats instead of scrubs. He almost didn't recognize Kochenko. His hair was cut short, almost military style. He wore a double-breasted dark suit and had replaced his tinted aviator glasses with black horn rims that looked like they had been borrowed from Kittamura.

"What's going on?" asked Adam.

"M&M today," answered Kochenko.

"What's that?" said Adam.

"Morbidity and Mortality conference. Once a month all the services meet and review cases. All deaths and complications are discussed, and we have to explain or justify all decisions. The attending surgeons take us to task on everything."

"Do they ask any questions of the students?" Shrevi asked.

"Too brutal," said Kochenko. "They don't even allow you to attend."

When the residents filed out of the ward and headed for the conference, the three students looked at each other with the same uncertainty of their first day. Not one to waste downtime,

Shrevi, the master of the catnap, snuck off to the treatment room. Adam and Barnett stood for a moment. Adam watched Jen as she passed from one bed to another, taken by her graceful movements as she dispensed medications and wrote notes on the patients' charts. When she spoke to the patients, they seemed reassured and comfortable. He felt a powerful attraction to the way she went about her work. He longed to have that self-assurance and would have liked to compliment her on it, but he was afraid he would sound like he was making an awkward pass at her.

Adam suddenly realized he had more to do.

"I forgot to see the girl with the voodoo curse on the Medicine floor this morning. I'm going to run down there and check on her while we're waiting."

Battiste was standing at the foot of the bed, studying her chart and gazing at her with a dismayed look on his face as Adam approached.

"Hi. I'm here to check her dialysis shunt."

"Shunt's doing better than she is—almost arrested during dialysis… Developed a bradycardia and dropped her pressure when her heart rate slowed. Still running a low pressure. I just checked her shunt…didn't clot off when the pressure dropped… I don't get it… She just keeps getting worse."

Adam looked at the shunt in her forearm, which was wrapped with white surgical gauze. He listened with his stethoscope. The loud murmur confirmed Battiste's opinion that blood continued to flow through the shunt. He borrowed her chart and wrote a quick progress note: "General Surgery Service: Case reviewed with Internal Medicine. Shunt OK. Good bruit."

He handed the chart back to Battiste, who continued flipping the pages, looking for answers that weren't there.

Adam returned to find Shrevi had awakened and rejoined Barnett. Both held their notebooks open but were simply staring at the lecture notes without the focus to study.

"They're not back yet?" asked Adam.

"Not yet," said Barnett.

"If they do rounds we'll be here until nine tonight," said Shrevi.

The three students stood in mind-numbing silence until the residents returned to the ward just before 5 p.m. Their neckties were askew, their suits rumpled, and they looked as they would after a long night of ER call.

The more senior residents were uniformly somber; Turk stared at the floor as though the weight of the world had just come crashing down on his shoulders. Wantz looked like he wanted to scream at someone, and Kochenko was unusually reserved as he placed his hand on Turk's shoulder.

"The guy is a prick," he said. "Everybody knows it. No one wants to rotate on Brewster's service. It was obvious that he has it in for you… He was blaming you for things you weren't even involved in."

Turk nodded and stepped away, leaving Adam the opportunity to speak to Kochenko.

"What happened?"

"We got reamed, blamed for everything… Patient had a post-op urinary infection and they made it seem we did something wrong… Every little thing. That asshole Brewster went completely ballistic when he heard about the guy with the low potassium who died. The one big mistake of the past six months. He went apeshit yelling at Turk even though he didn't have anything to do with taking that guy to surgery… Everybody knows Brewster's the guy blackballing Turk from the program."

"That's so unreasonable," said Adam.

"Well, you know," reflected Kochenko. "Sometimes it's like a game…but a very serious one. They create these unreasonable expectations for us to be perfect, and we strive for it even though it's unobtainable. I guess surgeons think they have to be hard on their trainees so that we'll be ready to rise to the occasion when we're really challenged by something unexpected or unfamiliar. Generations have been trained that way, so it continues. They even made it sound like it was our fault the guy with the appendix had a pulmonary embolus. Maybe someday somebody will figure out a way to prevent them, but there's nothing now. You listen to guys like Brewster and he goes on and on about what bad doctors we are. Turk's a little slow and deliberate in the operating room and Brewster views that as a liability… Hell, we all learn at different rates. His patients do OK, but Brewster thinks it's a weakness and a reason to throw him out of the program. Last year when Bennett was on his service, Brewster really rode him hard. Destroyed Bennett's self-confidence. Without confidence there's no courage. Every field of medicine requires courage, especially surgery, if you're gonna accept the responsibility for someone's health. People's lives are at stake."

Barnett and Shrevi had drawn in closer to Adam to listen to Kochenko. The three students remained quiet. Adam wondered what perfection felt like to a surgeon. All three students were expecting a late night when Holiday stepped towards them and spoke in almost a whisper: "We're done for today. Y'all go home. See you tomorrow."

CHAPTER 47

RONALD WAS CLEARLY recovering. The last of his abdominal drains had been removed, and the holes they had left were sealing with scab formation as they closed. The nurses had recorded a low-grade fever of 99.3 degrees. Adam examined him closely. There were no abnormal sounds in his lungs, no heart murmurs. His incision was clean and dry. The urine in his catheter bag was a clear yellow. Adam wrote an order on the chart to send a sample of the urine for culture, but he doubted there was any source of active infection. Still, he resolved to ask Turk or Kochenko about the temperature.

Adam paused, thinking about whether there was any possible source of infection that he might have missed and noting the difference in Ronald's appearance from his arrival in the Emergency Room. Ronald was breathing slowly and unrestricted without the aid of a machine. His face was scrubbed clean and his hair combed. The particulate matter that had stuck to his matted hair and bruised extremities—the mixture of dirt, asphalt, and dried blood that the nurses called "road rash"—had been washed away. As he thought about how critically injured Ronald had been, Adam felt a sense of accomplishment, feeling that he had participated in something heroic and lifesaving, even though he had only pulled on a retractor while listening to a discussion about football.

∽

The lecture that morning was Part 1 of the section on the colon and rectum. Adam focused all his attention on the speaker since he was afraid he might not get the reading done anytime soon. The morning lecturer, Dr. Levin, from Service 3, methodically presented the material with such an incessant drone and lack of enthusiasm that he was able to turn an important and essential topic into pure boredom.

"That's more than another fifty pages added to what we've got to read," said Shrevi as they sat down at the cafeteria table.

"I've never been this far behind in my reading for any class," said Adam.

Barnett sighed. "Try concentrating on the book when you're swaying with a crying baby on your shoulder."

"You know," said Shrevi, "I'm great at taking tests and remembering stuff, but that's not good enough if you are really trying to understand the material. For example, remember the lecture on cardiac trauma when they were talking about pericardial tamponade and pulsus paradoxus… I mean, how the heck does that work?"

"Well," said Adam, "in some cases, like a stab wound, when fluid collects in the pericardial sac and compresses the heart, it causes pulsus paradoxus. Normally the systemic blood pressure drops with inspiration, but in pulsus paradoxus it drops more than 10 millimeters of mercury and the heart can't pump blood to the rest of the body."

"Yeah, that's what they told us…but that's what I mean… Why? I mean, how does that happen?"

"I think," said Barnett, "that it's partly due to pressure changes and filling of the ventricles with blood. With inspiration the pressure in the chest decreases, and that exaggerates the gradient from the systemic vascular pressure so more blood fills the right heart."

"So?" asked Shrevi.

"Well," explained Barnett, "when the right ventricle fills with blood, it probably pushes on the interventricular septum and that makes less volume for blood to fill the left side of the heart, so less blood is pumped out and the measured blood pressure drops… So in tamponade, like blood in the pericardial sac or if the sac is too tight, the right ventricle can't expand as it fills, but the septum between the heart's chambers can be pushed over more by the right ventricular blood and therefore there is even less volume for blood entering the left ventricle to be pumped to the rest of the body, so the pressure drops even more."

Shrevi and Adam looked at each other as they absorbed Barnett's logical explanation.

"Jesus, you really are an engineer," said Shrevi.

And the smartest guy I've ever met, Adam thought to himself.

Only Holiday, Doyle, and Kittamura seemed in any way relaxed when the members of Service 1 gathered on the male ward for afternoon rounds. Adam noticed the junior residents all looked uneasy waiting to face Dr. Theodorakis for the first time after the M&M conference.

At exactly two o'clock, the hall filled with the sound of an approaching crowd and Dr. Theodorakis appeared, accompanied by the throng of students and residents from the other services. His somber expression added to the tension in the room. He began rounds by quizzing Barnett about the patient with diverticulitis. Barnett struggled to retain his composure but answered most questions. Theodorakis then directed his questions towards the residents.

"Please summarize the salient points from the recent review article published in 'Annals of Surgery,'" he said.

Kochenko, Turk, and Wantz exchanged blank stares and remained silent.

"The article from the group at Vanderbilt stressed performing a temporary colostomy over primary anastomosis," began Rogers.

"I was addressing the junior residents," Theodorakis cut him off. "I expect that at this point of your training all of you will make the effort to stay current on the important literature."

The chief's displeasure set the tone for the rest of afternoon rounds. An interminably long time was spent on each patient, with Theodorakis thoroughly questioning each student and junior resident, peppering them with progressively more difficult questions until they couldn't answer. Shrevi was so nervous presenting his first patient that Adam took a step closer so that he could catch him if he fainted again. Turk answered all his questions correctly but was especially hesitant and nervous, even though his fate in the program had apparently already been sealed. Even Wantz's aggressive nature was subdued. By the time Dr. Theodorakis had finished grilling them, each student was humbled and humiliated and each resident rebuffed for their lack of knowledge or expertise.

"That was rough," said Shrevi. "How can we ever remember all this stuff like lab values and the textbook when we've got no time to study?"

Adam and Barnett shared the sentiment but had no solution.

Adam rode the elevator to make his last two stops before going home. Luanne's talkative nature lifted his mood, and he performed her dressing change while enjoying her childhood story of Saturday crawfish boils. He finished securing the dressing, said his goodnight, and made his way to the Medicine ward, only to find a vacant bed where the Voodoo Lady had been. As he walked back to the chart rack, Battiste entered the room.

"Where is she?" Adam asked, nodding towards her bed.

"Gone. Arrested during dialysis. Couldn't get her back."

"But she was so young."

"Yeah, never seen kidney disease progress that rapidly... Always thought nephrotic syndrome might take years to lead to complete renal failure."

Adam walked home through the Quarter, struggling to understand why they couldn't have done more for someone who had been so healthy such a short time before her admission. He was so lost in thought that he didn't realize he had passed Felix's until he was about four blocks beyond it. But it didn't matter. He wasn't much in the mood for oyster stew anyway.

CHAPTER 48

THE NEXT MORNING, the students were intent on making up for their failures on rounds the day before. The experience seemed completely foreign to Adam. If you prepared for a chemistry test, you basically knew what material would be on the exam. Surgery and Medicine just seemed to require endless knowledge. Yesterday, for every question they answered, a more difficult one followed. The lack of time to read and study was so frustrating to Adam. Throwing himself into their morning routine was the only recourse.

Jen was sitting at her desk with her head down. When Adam greeted her, she turned away and brought her right hand up towards her cheek. Stepping to the other side of the desk, Adam could see that she had been crying and that she held a crumpled tissue in her right hand.

"Are you OK?" he asked.

She straightened and stood up. "Yes, everything's OK."

At first she didn't make eye contact with Adam, but after a moment she said softly, "Actually, it's not OK… It's my husband. He works for a bank downtown but…he's an alcoholic. Last night I had to drive to Napoleon Avenue to pick him up when the conductor put him off the St. Charles streetcar." She paused and let out a long breath. "I try to help him, but…he seems to just get worse."

Adam's first instinct was to wrap his arms around her and comfort her with a hug. Instead, he gently reached out and touched her forearm.

"I'm so sorry to hear that. Please let me know if there is anything I can do to help," he said, knowing there was nothing he could do.

CHAPTER 49

THE STUDENTS FINISHED rounds with plenty of time to spare before the morning lecture. Barnett and Shrevi headed for the cafeteria. Adam picked up his book bag and the gym bag that contained his toiletries and clean underwear and shirt. He could easily stop on the Gyne floor and change Luanne's dressing before lecture.

He was standing at the side of her bed, marveling at how the wound seemed cleaner and smaller than even yesterday, when he became aware that someone was standing at the foot of the bed. He looked over and was surprised to see one of the LPNs cradling a supply of dressings in her arms.

"I seen you here twice a day, every day," she said.

"Yes, ma'am, my resident said there would be a better chance of her healing if we could redress it twice a day."

"How is it?"

"Well, it's clearly better, although I don't know how completely it will heal or how long it will take."

"It's good," she said, offering Adam the dressings.

"Thanks," he said as he took the gauze pads he needed and placed the rest on the small table near Luanne's bed.

"It's good," she repeated as she left him to finish and disappeared into the treatment room.

The morning lecture continued the series on cancer management with a discussion of breast cancer. Dr. Brewster reviewed the history of treatment for the disease dating back to Halsted's original description of the radical mastectomy. His slides summarized the survival statistics before and after the operation was introduced. He continued by displaying Patey's 1959 data indicating that in most cases the marked chest deformity could be avoided by preserving the pectoralis muscle without worsening the survival rate, the modified radical mastectomy. Adam's friend Melissa raised her hand and asked if Dr. Brewster could comment on the studies being done involving only removing the tumor and treating the breast with radiation.

"Experimental!" he glared at her. "Probably insufficient treatment... Don't be misled by these early provocateurs... Remember, to cut is to cure!"

Melissa remained silent and directed her gaze towards her notebook.

He completed his lecture by playing a film strip of a modified radical mastectomy, pointing out the underlying anatomy and emphasizing the careful dissection and preservation of the long thoracic and thoracodorsal nerves.

"As you can see," he finished while directing his gaze specifically towards Melissa, "a properly performed mastectomy and axillary dissection is an elegant, anatomic surgical procedure."

They sat clustered around the cafeteria table, mostly staring into their coffee until Shrevi broke the silence. "Seems like a pretty bloody procedure."

"Nothing elegant about that," added Adam.

"It's more like an amputation," said Barnett.

"They're not always that bloody," said Melissa.

"How do you know?" asked Barnett.

"I watched my daddy do some back home," she said. "He says if you get into the right area, there's a tissue plane and the skin peels away with very little bleeding."

"Brewster must have missed the flight on that plane," said Shrevi.

"You know," said Melissa, "I thought that idea about doing a lesser operation was really fascinating when I read the textbook. I mean, most of those patients don't die from disease in the breast or on the chest; they die from disease that has spread to other parts of the body. We know hormones affect the growth of cancer cells, like when the ovaries are removed to treat metastases…"

"Wouldn't it be great if there was a hormone that would stop tumor growth and spread?" said Barnett, picking up her line of thought.

"Exactly," said Melissa. "I read about a drug that they are going to start using in England to hormonally treat metastatic disease. It's called Tamoxifen."

$\sim$

Before returning to the hospital, Adam stopped in the bookstore and purchased a combination lock so that he could claim an empty locker in the call room on their nights on duty for the ER. He set his birthday as the combination and closed the lock on one of the gym bag's handles. Then he remembered that before leaving the bookstore he should look again for a bandage scissors. It was a futile attempt. The rack remained empty.

Adam arrived in the Emergency Department amid a flurry of activity. Holiday, Rogers, and all three of the junior residents were in one of the trauma rooms. Another resuscitation from circulatory shock was taking place. An older White male lay on the gurney in the center of the room. Kochenko, Turk, Wantz, and the nurses were working quickly, removing the man's suit and tie and cutting away his underwear while starting two IVs, drawing blood, and inserting a Foley bladder catheter and nasogastric tube.

Adam dropped his gym bag in the corner of the room and approached the cart. He couldn't read the name tag stuck to the pocket of the man's crumpled suit coat.

"Conventioneer from the Fairmount," said Kochenko. "Complained of back pain this a.m. and collapsed… Hypotensive at the scene. Check the X-ray on the view box."

Adam recognized that the film was a lateral view of the abdomen.

"See those white flecks bulging out in front of the spine?" asked Kochenko. "Calcium in the wall of a ruptured aortic aneurysm. Pretty diagnostic." Adam tried to step closer to examine the patient, but the crowd attending the patient blocked him from the cart.

"Pressure's up to 80," said the nurse on the opposite side of the cart.

"Let's go," ordered Holiday. "OR should be ready."

They pushed the patient's cart into the hallway, but Rogers paused and broke out in a wide grin as a thin, white-haired gentleman in a dark brown polyester sport coat walked down the hallway towards them, peering over his spectacles.

"Hey, Dad," he said, "a little busy at the moment."

It took a moment for Adam to recognize that the woman accompanying their visitor was Judy, the ER nurse, now out of uniform. She was wearing a black cocktail dress and heels. The bun that usually kept her hair out of the way had been undone, and now her long blonde hair hung down to her shoulders and highlighted how attractive her facial features were, even with little make-up.

"Welcome to New Orleans," said Rogers as he shook his father's hand and gave him a brief hug. "Looks like I'm not going to be able to join you for lunch. Y'all go on without me."

Judy, the accomplished ER nurse, who was not fazed by any patient no matter how badly they were injured or how severely they were bleeding, wrinkled her forehead, looking hesitant and nervous.

Rogers continued. "Lunch at Galatoire's is Daddy's favorite. It'll give you a chance to get acquainted."

With that, the group continued to move towards the elevators while the senior Dr. Rogers responded, "Looks like you fellas got your hands full. We'll see you after lunch."

Chapter 50

It was past five o'clock when Adam emerged from surgery and realized he had once again lost track of time while watching Holiday calmly operate on the ruptured aneurysm. He returned to the Emergency Room to recover his gym bag, but it was nowhere to be found. He remembered he had placed it aside in the trauma room. It was no longer there, nor was it in any of the other trauma rooms or at the nurses' triage desk or in the X-ray room. Carlos and the nurses on duty didn't remember seeing it. He felt stupid since he had been warned not to leave things unattended in Charity.

"Where's the other one?" Wantz demanded. "You know, Shreddy, the Indian kid."

"Haven't seen him," said Adam, not correcting Wantz's pronunciation.

"Me neither," said Barnett.

"Dammit. I sent him over to Peds to see a kid with a bad bellyache. I get there later: he's nowhere to be found. The patient turns out to be a nine-month-old who looks like he's got an acute abdomen—rigid, tender, won't stop crying. C'mon, take a look with me. I don't know what he's got but it's some kinda abdominal disaster that needs an exploratory."

∽

The child did indeed appear very sick.

"This belly looks just like some of those adults with peritonitis," said Barnett. "Could it be appendicitis?"

"Must be ruptured if it is," added Adam.

"He's a bit young for that, but I'm going to set him up for the OR," said Wantz.

"He doesn't need an operation," another voice chimed in from the doorway.

Shrevi stood there waving a lab slip. "I took his blood to the lab and ran the slide myself. He's got sickle cell anemia."

"Must be his first crisis," said Wantz.

"How'd you figure out to do that?" asked Barnett.

"Just asked. When I took the history from Mom, I asked her if there was any history of sickle cell in the family and she told me that her brother is a sickler and the baby's daddy has an uncle with the trait. Made sense that we needed the blood smear right away."

"That's the ticket... You two pay attention," said Wantz, waving a chubby finger at the other two students. "Good thing I had you do all those histories and physicals on the floor so's you'd learn to do them correctly. Let's let the Peds resident know."

CHAPTER 51

ADAM FOUND TERRY Rogers in the hallway of the ER and was waiting for the resident to give him instructions when the senior Dr. Rogers returned.

"We had a wonderful time," Rogers' father drawled. "Nothin' like a long lunch at Galatoire's… Shrimp remoulade, turtle soup with sherry, and oysters en brochette—finished with the prime ribeye and Marchand de vin sauce… Charmin' girl."

He lowered his voice, speaking softly to his son. "Your mother, God rest her soul, would have loved her. I'm sure she's a fine nurse, just like your mama. You should marry her…"

Rogers leaned towards his father. Adam was close enough to hear him whisper, "I intend to."

Judy stepped back into the doorway. She was radiant. Maybe it was relief from the nervousness of meeting the elder Dr. Rogers, or maybe it was the effect of the several Kir Royales that Dr. Rogers had introduced her to over their lunch, but Adam thought she positively glowed. Her deep blue eyes danced, her cheeks were flushed, and her broad smile presented a beauty and happiness that replaced the serious demeanor Adam associated with her care for patients in the ER.

Adam imagined a satisfying future for his resident and Judy—working together, providing care to their community, raising a family, and enjoying the simple pleasures of life in Rogers' small hometown. Adam couldn't help but feel a little envious of Terry Rogers, especially when he thought of himself in his lonely French Quarter apartment.

Shrevi arrived in the hallway just as Barnett stepped out of the treatment room and stood next to Judy. "I'm not sure you should drive yourself home," he offered, speaking loud enough that both Drs. Rogers could hear.

"Neither should you, Daddy," smiled Rogers.

"I can take them to the front of the hospital and call a cab," Shrevi volunteered.

"That's OK," the younger Dr. Rogers replied, "I'll take them. You guys head for the dining room and catch a bite of dinner. I expect the rest of the service is down there. Better eat now... We may have a busy night... I'll catch up in a few minutes."

Adam stood for a moment and watched them start towards the main entrance. Terry Rogers and Judy walked arm in arm as they followed the senior Dr. Rogers down the long hallway.

CHAPTER 52

HOLIDAY SAT ON the wooden bench at the end of one of the long dining tables, his back leaning against the wall. His eyelids hung heavy, and the perpetual bags under his eyes made him look like he'd already finished his call night, even though it had barely begun. The other residents were still in line at the steam table when everyone's beepers started going off.

Barnett was told to leave with Kochenko and Kittamura—motor vehicle accident. Shrevi accompanied Doyle and the returning Rogers in responding to a call for a gunshot wound. Turk headed to see an urgent consult in the MICU.

Holiday took another spoonful of gumbo while Wantz and Adam surveyed the remaining selection at the steam table. They had just picked up their plates when Wantz and Holiday's beepers went off nearly simultaneously. Wantz picked up the phone mounted on the wall near the door and took the message.

"Another gunshot wound… Trauma Room 3."

Holiday stood up, shoved the plastic spoon into the unfinished gumbo, and tossed the cup into the receptacle at the end of the room. He was the picture of calm as he led the way towards the ER with Wantz walking beside him and Adam, feeling his heart racing once more, a step behind.

The two police officers, Beaudry and Guidry, stood outside the trauma room. Guidry was agitated and disheveled. His shirt was only partially tucked in, with the shirttail on his right completely exposed and hanging over his protuberant belly. His eyes darted back and forth as he rapidly spoke to his partner. Beaudry placed his left hand on Guidry's right shoulder and guided his partner to a seat on the bench across from the next trauma room down the hall.

Guidry's voice carried in the hallway. "I was sure he had a gun… He had a gun, you saw it, didn't you? He had a gun, didn't he?"

Adam stepped into the trauma room with Holiday and Wantz. The room was eerily silent. There was no noisy ventilator, no respiratory therapist, and no nurses rushing to start IVs. Only Carlos remained, quietly straightening up and replacing supplies in the cabinets.

On the gurney in the middle of the room was a Black male, probably in his mid-teens, lying motionless. Nothing indicated that anyone had tried to insert an endotracheal tube or conduct a resuscitation.

Wantz stood at the head of the bed, feeling the young man's neck. "No pulse, no pressure…fixed and dilated pupils," he said, placing his penlight back in his pocket.

Holiday examined the three holes in the center of the boy's chest. "Powder burns...close range," he explained to Adam. "All three probably in the heart."

"Any family?" Holiday asked Carlos.

"I'll find them."

Adam stepped into the hallway with Holiday. Beaudry was still trying to calm his partner, who looked towards Holiday.

"He had a gun, you know?"

He turned his gaze back to Beaudry and beseeched, "He had a gun, right?"

Beaudry looked at Holiday. "I think we'd better go to the precinct. We've got a report to file. That OK, Doc?"

"Yeah," Holiday said softly.

Beaudry escorted his partner down the hallway.

Adam hung back and reentered the trauma room with Holiday. The chief resident surveyed the whole room, including the pile of the young man's belongings. He inspected the young man's body and remained silent even as Carlos reappeared and told them that he had the family in the waiting area.

Without uttering a word to Adam, Holiday trudged towards the waiting room. Adam stood back, but he was still close enough to witness the grief Holiday's words brought to the boy's mother and the relatives and neighbors who accompanied her.

Adam walked back towards the trauma rooms. A young girl in shorts and a white blouse stood across from the doorway. Her cheeks were stained with tears, but as she leaned against the wall her straight back created the illusion that her composure was intact.

"Can I help you?" asked Adam.

"I'm waiting for his things."

A nurse stepped out of the trauma room and handed the girl a small paper bag. The girl opened the bag and pulled out a gold chain with a crucifix on it. She looked back at Adam as she clutched the chain.

"My brother didn't have no gun," she said. "He was a good boy. Went to church every Sunday with our grandmother… He was drinking with his friends. First time he ever had alcohol."

"I'm sorry for your loss," stammered Adam, awkwardly searching for more words until he watched the young girl walk down the hallway. She passed Holiday as he returned, and Adam wondered if the senior resident felt the same hollowness that he did.

CHAPTER 53

ADAM ACCOMPANIED HOLIDAY when they left the ER. They took the elevator and walked together to the MICU, where they found Turk talking to a nurse at the foot of an elderly man's bed. The man was intubated. Adam was now accustomed to the rhythmic sound of the ventilator. The patient's wrinkled skin was discolored, as though he had been polished with an old floor wax that had turned a dull yellow. The liquid draining from his catheter into the urine bag was as dark as Coca-Cola.

"Eighty-two years old," said Turk. "Pretty good until night before last. Family says he initially complained of a bellyache and chills. Last night, became unresponsive, had a fever of 103 when he arrived here. Not the usual Charity patient. He worked as a fireman before he retired, and even though they live uptown, his family says he always told them to bring him to Charity if he ever got really sick. Blood pressure was only 80, but it improved when I added a little dopamine to his fluids. Look at this…"

He took two steps towards the head of the bed and placed the palm of his hand under the patient's rib cage on the right. As he pressed down, the unconscious man winced and tried to pull away from Turk's hand.

Holiday nodded. "How high is his bilirubin level?"

"Eight," said Turk, confirming to Adam that the patient was indeed deeply jaundiced.

"Do you know what the syndrome of jaundice, fever, and right upper quadrant pain is called?" Holiday asked Adam.

Even though he had read the lecture notes and textbook chapter on gallbladder disease, Adam was drawing a blank as he stared at the sick old man.

"It's Charcot's triad," explained Holiday, "and when you combine it with shock and mental status changes, it's called Reynold's pentad... Pretty characteristic for cholangitis, a very severe infection in the bile duct. We may have to operate on him tomorrow even though it's Saturday. Try to get him stabilized. Do you have an ultrasound yet?"

"Ordered but not done yet... Didn't want to move him until his blood pressure was better. White blood cell count is 21,000; alkaline phosphatase is high too—over 400. His family is in the lounge. I spoke to them briefly and told them he will probably need his gallbladder out and his bile duct drained."

"Adam, you can bunk in my call room tonight, but interview this guy's family first and write up a history and physical for the chart," said Holiday.

Adam picked up a pad of yellow progress sheets from the nurses' station, silently berating himself that he hadn't recalled either Charcot's triad or Reynold's pentad.

He tried to show confidence when he sat down next to the patient's daughter and teenaged grandson. They explained that he'd been nauseated after eating for a few weeks prior to coming to the hospital. The grandson reported that he had thought the old man's eyes were yellow when they sat down to breakfast in the morning. Despite the patient's age, the family reported no signs of mental deterioration or dementia. Adam listened intently, writing notes on the yellow pad about allergies, medications, possible familial illnesses. He reassured himself that he had covered all the important details.

"How long was he a fireman?"

"Thirty-seven years," answered the daughter. "He's lived with us the past fourteen years, since shortly after my mother died. They were married for fifty-three years. He still goes to the firehouse, plays checkers with the young guys, sometimes rides along on the truck."

"My dad left when I was a baby, so my grandpa and I do a lot of stuff together. We go fishing a lot… Built our own boat," said the grandson. "I still have the miniature fireman's outfit that he had made for me for Mardi Gras when I was about three."

"He's a big Saints fan… We like to get tickets and take him to a game a couple of times each season. He helps a lot around the house, and every Monday he makes a big pot of red beans and rice…walks all the way to Langenstein's by himself just to get the andouille sausage…swears they've got the best in town."

Adam looked at the yellow sheets he had filled out. He had followed the proper format and taken a complete history and physical, but despite his thorough questioning, he realized he hadn't known anything about Sam Elder until just now.

"I'm finished with my exam," Adam said. "Thank you."

"Dr. Turk said he may have to be operated on tomorrow," said the daughter. "Will you be there?"

"Yes, ma'am," Adam responded, thinking that anyone could pull on a retractor.

He walked to the elevator wondering if all doctors started out saying "thank you" to their patients. He wondered if he'd ever feel that he deserved the thanks.

CHAPTER 54

B**EFORE JOINING** H**OLIDAY** in the call room, Adam decided to check the ER once more. As he stepped off the elevator, he heard room number three alive with activity. The screams and yelling sounded like a familiar voice, but he couldn't place it until he opened the door and saw the large bloodstain on the familiar Hawaiian shirt.

Teddy's screams turned to complete hysteria when he saw Adam enter the trauma room. "Adam! Adam!" he yelled. "The bitch stabbed me and took my wallet! I was just flirting!"

Adam went straight to the head of the bed, ignoring the hectic atmosphere as Teddy's clothes were cut away, his blood drawn, and his IVs started.

"I don't deserve this! I'm not a bad person! I don't want to die like this!'

Adam leaned down. "Take it easy, Teddy, we'll take good care of you."

"He's got a single stab wound to the belly," stated Rogers, standing opposite Adam and gesturing towards the bloody opening just below and to the left of Teddy's belly button. "We have to explore him, but his vital signs have been good since he arrived, 120 over 80."

"Stay calm, Teddy," said Adam. "Best place will be in the operating room, and we'll get you there quickly."

The ER nurses proceeded efficiently, and soon Adam was helping to push the cart into the hallways and towards the elevators.

Another voice behind him spoke. "Friend of yours?"

Adam turned to see Doyle with a sardonic grin on his face.

"He's my neighbor...and my friend," Adam answered. He reached down and grasped Teddy's hand as the cart moved quickly along. He was still holding it when they transferred Teddy to the operating table and Anesthesia put the anxious patient to sleep.

Chapter 55

"**That's one lucky** faggot," drawled Doyle as he looked over Rogers' shoulder into the incision.

The knife had penetrated Teddy's abdominal wall, but the thick blanket of fat covering his intestines had prevented it from damaging any organs. There was only a laceration of a small omental vein that Rogers had been able to control with a single stitch.

The entire operation had taken only an hour, but after helping to move Teddy to the Recovery Room and taking the time to write a history and physical for the chart, Adam was surprised to find that it was nearly 2 a.m.

"We'll leave him on the ventilator tonight," said Rogers. "Sedation should be worn off so we can extubate him in the morning."

Adam found his way to Holiday's call room, where fortunately Holiday had left the door unlocked for him. The senior resident was asleep on the cot along the wall. Adam quietly kicked off his shoes and lay down on the cot across the room. He fell asleep nearly as soon as his head hit the pillow.

Adam wasn't sure how long he had been asleep, but he knew it hadn't been long enough when he was awakened by the sound of someone moving and breathing heavily from across the room.

When his eyes became accustomed to the darkness, he could see Holiday sitting on the edge of the bed in his underwear. Even in the faint moonlight, the beads of sweat on his forehead were visible as he wiped his face with a towel.

"Tom, are you OK?" asked Adam.

"I'm fine…" He paused. "I'm fine… Just a bad dream."

The room was silent as he calmed himself and wiped more of the glistening sweat from his shoulders and brow. The receding hairline, the big arms where fat had replaced what was once muscle, the knee-high black stretch socks, light blue boxer shorts, and white tank T-shirt combined to make him seem much older than he actually was.

"Just a dream…" he said. "I'm back on the ship off the coast of Nam. The helicopter brings in a kid from the field, about nineteen, originally from Indiana. He's shocky and scared but still mentally with it… I tell him everything will be OK… When we get him on the table and remove the blanket that was covering him, his legs are gone and his lower body mangled. I open him… Big expanding hematoma in his pelvis… He starts bleeding profusely… No matter what I did I couldn't stop it… I tried but I couldn't stop it…"

He took a long, deep breath. "He comes back to visit me every now and then…"

"I'm sure you did your best," managed Adam. He didn't know what else to say.

"You only remember the ones you wish you could have done better. Better try to get a little rest," Holiday said, lying back on his cot.

Adam lay down and closed his eyes. As tired as he had been, he was still awake, thinking about shrapnel, when the first rays of the sunrise found their way through the big window above him.

Wantz arrived in the Surgical ICU shortly after Adam and Barnett had begun morning rounds. He grabbed the bedside clipboard from Barnett's hands and watched closely as Adam examined Mr. Swenson, the aneurysm patient. He reviewed the vital signs and intake and output records, scribbled some fluid orders, and tossed the chart back to Barnett.

"Looks good," he said, "a real keeper. Write the chart note and be sure you have his morning labs by the time we all round together."

After he left, Barnett continued to look through Mr. Swenson's chart.

"I was reading the textbook about ruptured aneurysms. Do you realize how close this guy came to dying? It's amazing that Holiday was so calm. I mean, you know, operating on a guy under that kind of pressure."

"Ice in his veins," replied Adam.

CHAPTER 56

TEDDY WAS LYING comfortably, still on his cart on the other side of the unit from the nurses' station, the ventilator still cycling regularly paced breaths through his endotracheal tube. The nurse approached Adam while he was studying Teddy's clipboard.

"He's still sedated," she said, "but he's been stable all night since he got here from Recovery. Should be no problem extubating him when the sedation wears off. That tall blond student who saw that other patient was here early, left this at the nurses' desk."

She handed Adam a slip of paper on which Barnett had written the date, noted 5:13 a.m. as the time, and had scribbled, "T. Lemieux, stab wound to belly. Hematocrit 33."

"Thanks," Adam said.

He turned and noticed that Holiday had arrived and was reviewing Mr. Swenson's clipboard.

"He looks good," said Adam as he returned to the aneurysm patient's bedside.

"Yeah," Holiday answered, "great urine output and blood pressure. Good signs. Let's go check on the old man in the Medical ICU."

The MICU was quiet at that hour. A few nurses were delivering bedside care or simply charting notes. Turk stood at the old man's bedside, watching the EKG monitor. His rumpled scrub suit and the dark circles under his eyes made it obvious he had been up all night.

"His pulse is holding. Urine output is improved but still not adequate. His blood pressure is still dependent on the pressors. Got him on both dopamine and levophed, been adjusting them quite a bit. I think he was quite dehydrated when he came in, so I'm giving him saline, but going slow to make sure his heart can tolerate the fluid infusion. Hopefully can turn down the pressor drips a bit when he's hydrated, but I think he'll still need some pressor support because he's septic. I did get the ultrasound... Shows stones in the gallbladder and a dilated common bile duct."

"That's consistent with his picture of cholangitis," Holiday told Adam.

He turned back towards Turk. "How soon do you think we can operate?"

"I already called the OR," said Turk. "Their schedule is really full, probably could fit him in at five or six tonight. I could use a little more time to get him in better shape for an operation."

"I don't want to do it late in the day or at night when we might be understaffed or we're tired," said Holiday. "Do you think he'll be OK if we schedule him for tomorrow? Even though it's Saturday, we could probably miss Grand Rounds."

"I'll set it up," said Turk. "Like most cholangitis patients, he's improving with the fluids, antibiotics, and pressors. We should be fine as long as his condition doesn't deteriorate later."

"Sinclair," said Holiday, "you follow this patient and plan to scrub with us tomorrow. Check back here later to see how he's doing."

Adam and Holiday entered the elevator together. Holiday planned to stop by the wards, and Adam pushed the button for Luanne's floor.

"Will that guy really be OK waiting on surgery like this?" he asked.

"Most of these patients really can be temporarily stabilized like Bennett said," replied Holiday. "He does a great job with the really sick patients."

"How come he's being pyramided out? If you don't mind my asking."

"Usually anybody can be sent to the lab if they're blackballed by one attending. Last year Brewster came down hard on him when he was on Service 4. Turk's a little slow with his hands but he's careful and knowledgeable. It's not fair, but that's how all these programs work."

Jen was working when Adam reached the male ward. She was busy at the med cart. Adam wanted nothing more than to chat with her, but he felt pushed to get rounds done.

Fortunately, his patients were doing well. He noted that there would be no problem finding a bed for Teddy when he was ready to be transferred. Ronald was still unable to respond appropriately when spoken to, but his eyes seemed to track Adam's movements as he changed the dressings.

Danny Frer's intravenous line was still functioning, so Adam only had to change the wound dressing and write a note on the chart.

The first-grade scissors that Adam had purchased were no match for the thick bandage around Danny's thigh, even attempting one layer at a time. Just as Jen approached him, the blade on the scissors broke and he was left holding two useless pieces of metal.

"Nice instrument," she smiled, handing Adam her bandage scissors. "Try these."

He removed the dressing and inspected Danny's thigh. Adam judged it was healing well—a much smaller version of Luanne's open wound, now very shallow and filling in with the same type of healthy pink tissue. He handed Jen her scissors. She walked back to her desk. Wantz approached and looked at the wound.

"Much better," Wantz said. "Can probably cut his pain meds... Put him on oral stuff."

He walked to the end of the ward while Adam redressed Danny's leg and observed the worried look in Danny's eyes.

Wantz was standing near Jen's desk, writing on the chart, when Adam finished the dressing and approached the nurses' station.

"Doesn't he still need something stronger?" he asked.

"I'm just going to give him Darvocet," said Wantz. "No point feeding a junkie's habit. Don't you have to go to lecture?"

CHAPTER 57

MORNING ROUNDS WERE almost completed by dawn on Saturday. Most of the patients seemed to be doing well. Danny Frer, however, appeared anxious and in pain. Adam made his way up to the Surgical ICU. He wondered if an oral pain medication was enough to relieve Danny's back pain. He didn't have the opportunity to ask when Kochenko arrived on the unit.

"I wrote orders to transfer both the aneurysm and the stab wound to the floor," said the resident. "Just need their dressings changed."

Before leaving, Adam looked to Teddy's bed. The breathing tube had been removed and Teddy was lying with his eyes closed with a humidified oxygen mask hanging around his neck.

"Teddy, are you doing OK?"

He opened his eyes and stared at Adam with a sense of urgency. "Am I dying? You can tell me straight. How long do I have?"

"Teddy, you've got nothing to worry about. The knife blade barely penetrated your abdomen. It cut a little vein that was very easy to tie. You had no damage to any internal organs."

"So it was really bad?"

"No, Teddy, you're going to be fine. You'll have a full recovery. You are going to be fine."

"So you mean it's 50-50?"

"Better… Just rest. I'll keep checking on you."

"I'll try to hold on."

"You do just that."

Adam wrote a progress note on Teddy's chart. He walked to return it to the chart rack near the nurses' desk. Turk appeared in the doorway.

"You'll have to miss Grand Rounds and Bullpen today. Need you to scrub on the cholangitis case. Come on with me to the MICU and help me move him to the OR."

CHAPTER 58

ADAM STOOD NEXT to Holiday at the row of scrub sinks. They lathered their hands and arms while Turk and a petite nurse anesthetist student were positioning the patient on the operating room table, centering him and straightening out all the intravenous lines and medications.

The senior Anesthesia resident appeared at the sinks. He ignored Adam and spoke to Holiday.

"This guy is sick as shit; his blood pressure is barely holding. We need to get in and get him off the table as quick as possible. You should do this case instead of the guy in the room. We need some speed here. I heard that guy is leaving the program next year. You do the case."

Holiday's normally soft-spoken voice was replaced with authority. "Dr. Turk, my junior resident, is going to do this case. He has given this man excellent care since admission. This is his patient."

Holiday's response reinforced for Adam why he garnered so much respect from the other residents. They finished scrubbing, entered the room, gowned and gloved, and then painted the patient's belly with antiseptic and placed the surgical drapes while Turk scrubbed at the sinks. While they waited for him, Holiday stood close to the table by the patient's left side so that it was clear that the operating surgeon's position on the patient's right was reserved for Turk when he entered the room.

Once the incision was made, Adam was surprised that the gallbladder didn't appear much different from the other chronically inflamed ones he had seen. The normal robin's egg blue of its wall was instead replaced by a dull greenish gray. When the bile duct was exposed, a quick glimpse demonstrated that it was so packed with stones it was about three times wider than a normal duct.

While holding a retractor, Adam peered into the operative field and watched as Turk methodically performed every step of the operation. He was fascinated when Turk opened the duct and a rush of foul liquid, gravel, and bigger stones poured out.

With Holiday's assistance, Turk cleaned out the bile duct and placed a T-shaped drainage tube into the duct. A machine was brought to the operating room so an X-ray could be obtained. The flow of injected contrast on the film confirmed all stones had been removed. Another drain was placed near the liver and both drains were brought through openings in the skin and sutured to the abdominal wall before the incision was closed.

As they were closing, Holiday asked, "How's he doing?"

Adam's eyes were heavy and his legs and muscles ached, but the response awakened him.

"Great," said the voice behind the anesthesia drape at the head of the table. "I turned off the levophed and am coming down on the dopamine. Should be able to stop it in Recovery. His blood pressure is fine."

"Helps to get the pus out," Holiday said softly, and Turk nodded in agreement.

After the report that the patient could now maintain his blood pressure without medications, Adam realized how quiet and intense the operating room had been while dealing with such a critically ill patient. He hadn't been aware of the tension until he felt it dissipate.

Adam helped Turk place dressings on the incision and around the tube. He pulled the front of the cart as they started towards the Recovery Room. They hadn't gotten far when the elevator doors opened and Rogers and Kittamura pushed another patient's cart into the hallway. Adam recognized the girl he had admitted from clinic with the thyroid nodule.

"Thought we'd get this case done while there's an open operating room," said Rogers. "Besides, my daddy has never seen me operate. You saw her in clinic, right? After you get your patient to Recovery, come help us."

Once they arrived in Recovery, Adam was stuck. Despite how tired he was, there was no way to refuse Rogers' request. Students had probably flunked the block for less. And he felt a deep sense of responsibility as the admitting student. Adam looked at the clock. It was now a quarter to two in the afternoon and he hadn't eaten.

Before making his way back to the operating room, Adam stepped into the nurses' storage room. A round glass coffee pot, sitting on an electric warmer, was still half full. He poured some into a Styrofoam cup. There was no milk or cream in the small refrigerator. There weren't even any packets of that awful powder that companies tried to pass off as coffee creamer. *Better drink it black*, he thought. *Maybe that will make the caffeine more effective.* He had never seen a thyroid operation, and he did not want to experience the same fatigue that momentarily overcame him during the previous surgery.

He found a box of doughnuts next to the coffee brewer. Its contents had been well picked over, and the plastic knife that rested on the corner was covered with crumbs. No doughnuts remained intact, but he picked up the leftover third of a glazed, hoping a burst of sugar with the caffeine would be enough to get him through one more case.

The pot had been on the warmer but the coffee was only lukewarm. As Adam washed down the stale doughnut, he wondered if the coffee had been brewed on this shift, on the eleven to seven, or even earlier yesterday.

CHAPTER 59

ROGERS AND KITTAMURA had already started the case when Adam scrubbed in. They positioned him next to Rogers, near the head of the table so that he could hold the tissue retractors. A few moments later the senior Dr. Rogers entered the room. The scrub suit that he wore emphasized what a slight man he was, without any excess body fat. The muscles in his sinewy arms tightened as he bent down and picked up a square metal platform and placed it on the floor behind Kittamura. He stood on the platform and peered over Kittamura's shoulder into the incision.

Perhaps the caffeine kicked in or maybe it was the sound of the elder Dr. Rogers' voice as he commented on the case, but Adam suddenly revived and focused on the operation.

"Y'all will probably find it easier if you dissect the upper pole first and then pull the gland upwards and medially," offered the senior physician.

The younger Dr. Rogers said nothing but switched his dissection to the upper aspect of the right side of the gland.

Adam watched intently, trying to remember what he had learned about thyroid surgery. He recalled there were two unique aspects—identifying the parathyroid glands was the first. Finding the small structures adjacent to the thyroid that released a hormone controlling the body's calcium level could be difficult. Adam remembered that he hadn't been able to find any of the four glands in his cadaver. Watching intently, he recalled that the glands were first identified in the 1850s by a zoologist in London who was dissecting an Indian rhinoceros, a fact he could not forget but was sure he would never be asked to recall on a formal examination.

He remembered the second unique feature of thyroid surgery when Rogers pointed to a little wire-like structure he had dissected as it lay next to the trachea and asked, "What's this?"

"Recurrent laryngeal nerve." Adam felt pleased that he could answer that question with certainty.

"What happens if it is injured?"

"Vocal cord paralysis and hoarseness," Adam answered.

"What if the nerves are injured on both sides of the trachea?"

Adam paused in silence as he contemplated the effect of bilateral vocal cord paralysis.

"Permanent tracheostomy," said Rogers.

He finished removing half the gland and Kittamura began the identical dissection of the left side.

"Superior parathyroid," he pointed with the dissecting scissors.

Adam strained to see but couldn't distinguish exactly what Kittamura was pointing at from simple fatty tissue or a lymph node. Kittamura worked quickly with no wasted motion. Dr.

Rogers watched over his shoulder as intently as he had when his son had been operating.

⁓

Adam felt fatigued again by the time they brought the patient to the Recovery Room. He poured half a cup of coffee from the fresh pot and lightened it with a little skim milk from the waxed pint container someone had left open by the hot plate. Drs. Rogers and Kittamura stood nearby, sipping coffee and tea. Adam couldn't help but overhear their conversation as the younger Dr. Rogers explained Kittamura's situation.

"Kitty's wife and kids still live abroad. He's actually living in his call room so he can save money to send home and to help him prepare to bring them here after he serves his fifth year of residency next year."

"A man should have his family closer," said the senior Rogers.

He was momentarily quiet as he stroked his chin while considering something before he spoke. "I've got enough work in my practice for two, maybe three surgeons, and I ain't getting any younger… Been lookin' forward to you joining me and gradually taking over, but that's going to take at least another two years. What would you fellas think about working together? I could have Dr. Kittamura join me when he finishes, and then the following year, Terry, you could come onboard."

"That would be fine with me," Terry Rogers answered. "Kitty and I work well together, and quite honestly, when I start raising my own family I don't want to miss as many of my kids' activities as you had to."

His father answered, "I guess we both still remember the time you hit the two-run homer, won the Little League championship, and I didn't even find out about it 'til the next morning. You know, Dr. Kittamura, if that sounds like a good plan to you, I could also have my lawyer look into what it would take to bring your family here. I've got some apartments and we could move them in there. Still a distance from New Orleans, but a far sight closer than where they are now." He smiled. "What would you think of that arrangement?"

Adam detected a slight tremble of uncharacteristic emotion in Kittamura when the resident answered, "Very good. Very kind." He straightened and gave a respectful bow towards the two doctors.

"Well, it's settled," said the older surgeon. "I'll get working on it soon as I get home. That would be very good. I been looking forward to a time when I can just go fishing again."

Adam looked at the clock before walking to the elevators. 4:20 p.m.… He had been in the hospital all day Thursday, most of Friday, and now most of Saturday. He thought back to Dave, his high school buddy from home. He had probably spent his Saturday taking his little boy out for hot dogs and then watching college football on TV together. Adam couldn't help but be a bit envious. He didn't even have a TV, let alone a family of his own, and he wasn't even able to go home yet as he still had to finish his patient care.

Luanne, though, was glad to see him when he arrived at her bedside. He had perfected her dressing changes so that he felt like a master of efficiency as his well-organized series of quick moves allowed him to finish her dressing change in under ten minutes. As he was applying the last gauze, she became serious.

"After Momma died was when things got bad for me," she said. "Couldn't finish school, couldn't afford the house, and couldn't find no permanent man. There were men in my life, but they didn't treat me right and only wanted one thing… I regret now that I was pretty quick to give that to 'em. After a while I realized they'd pay me… I fell so low but I was so lonely… So lonely… It wasn't just for the money."

Adam listened carefully as she recounted one abusive relationship after another. She described a life which with he was so unfamiliar.

"I had a pimp for a long while, but he beat me… That was when I started to get so fat. I was always big, but now I think for a while I just wanted to be unattractive… Guess I done that because I had less and less tricks to turn. Roy got madder and madder but no matter how he beat me I just got myself fatter. Finally, he cut me loose, said I should come back when I lost weight. After that I'd still work some, but I got to keep all the money at least."

Adam looked up at the clock on the wall. It was nearly 6 p.m.

"Well, an illness like this makes you lose weight, and your incision is healing beautifully. Can't tell, but you know, when this is all over and you're all healed up you may find yourself foxy again. I'll be back in the morning. See you then."

"Foxy," she smiled.

CHAPTER 60

THE SUN WAS slipping away to the west when Adam stepped out of the hospital. He quickly walked down Canal Street towards the Quarter as a growing sense of hunger competed with his fatigue. He couldn't think straight trying to prioritize his evening. He was way behind in the assigned reading and hadn't reviewed the lecture notes in any detail. Staying late for the extra case and spending time with Luanne had interrupted his plans to use the afternoon to get back to his disciplined study habits.

Hunger won out by the time he crossed Canal Street and started down Chartres. He envisioned a large muffaletta in his hands. A dinner-plate-sized Sicilian sesame loaf, spread with olive salad and piled high with salami, mortadella, ham, mozzarella, and provolone. He hurried past the Cabildo, turned right on St. Ann's, and then left on Decatur Street. The tourists seemed to be moving in slow motion as he passed them and headed for the little red grocery store with the dangling sign that read "Founded in 1906," but his heart sank when he reached the double doors and saw the darkened store and the simple "Closed" sign hanging against the glass. He backtracked on Decatur and picked up an order of beignets at the Café Du Monde before slowly making his way home.

He entered his apartment and took a moment to place his notebook, markers, pens, and textbook on the coffee table so that everything would be in place for him to begin his studying. He finished the first beignet and stepped into his bedroom to put his head down for ten minutes before beginning his work.

Week Four

CHAPTER 61

ADAM AWOKE WITH his arms hugging his pillow and his face tightly pressed against it. In the living room, the light was still on and his textbook remained open on the used, chipped coffee table with its pages unturned. Two beignets remained in the bag near his books. They were stale, but the powdered sugar made them palatable. He took a relaxed shower and dressed before stopping for a fresh café au lait on his way to the hospital. It was not yet too warm, so the walk in the sunlight was particularly welcome, as he was accustomed to being on the street before daylight.

On the ward, Danny Frer's bed was empty and his chart was missing from the rack.

"Where's Danny?" he asked the LPN who was carrying a few bedsheets further down the row of beds.

"He gone," she said. "Left in the middle of the night."

Adam couldn't hide his surprise. "But he's got an infection in his back and needs antibiotics."

The LPN shrugged. "Musta felt he needed to see his dealer more. No keepin' 'em here when they wants they drugs."

She didn't seem to feel this was anything unusual, but Adam couldn't understand how someone they were helping with a serious medical problem could just leave. He was disheartened and concerned for the patient's welfare.

Barnett walked onto the ward. He looked disheveled, as if he had dressed in a hurry. His face was pale and drawn, with noticeable dark circles under his eyes.

"Sorry I'm late," he said. "Went home yesterday intending to study and get some sleep. Conked out with the book open and then the baby started fussing… Crying every thirty minutes or so… Hard to study when you're up all night with a crying baby."

Now that the patients had been transferred from upstairs, the ward was crowded. The man with the ruptured aneurysm was in the first bed closest to the nurses' desk, and Teddy was in the furthest bed across the aisle near the wall at the end of the ward. He lay motionless with a moist cloth covering his forehead and his eyes. Ronald was in the same row but three beds closer. He was sitting in his bed, propped up by pillows, aimlessly staring about the room. The young boy Barnett was following was in the next bed. Despite the tire track across his chest, he was smiling as he buttered the toast on the breakfast tray in front of him. Sam Elder was in the first bed on the right directly across from Mr. Swenson. He was resting comfortably.

A large humidified oxygen mask held in place with a green elastic strap lay on his chest, just under his chin. A single IV bottle was dripping dextrose and saline into his left arm, and apart from the empty antibiotic bag still attached to the tubing there were no additional bags of pressor agents to support his blood pressure. Before changing the dressing, Adam leaned over the bed and spoke. "Mr. Elder?"

The old man opened his eyes, looked at Adam, and whispered, "I want to go home."

The response from a man who had been unresponsive in a coma and shock twelve hours before startled Adam.

"Sorry, sir… Couple of days… You've been very sick."

Barnett had interrupted the young boy's breakfast and had his stethoscope pressed against his back. Adam came over after he had finished with Mr. Elder.

"I'll run all the hematocrits," he said. "Just get your dressings changed and notes written so you can get out of here and get some sleep as soon as we're done rounding with the residents."

Barnett looked at him with the appreciation of someone who had just won a Vegas jackpot. Shrevi was writing chart notes while Barnett completed his duties on the male ward. Adam finished the hematocrits just in time to greet the residents as they arrived to begin rounds. They began with the aneurysm patient in the first bed. The discussion about his care was so matter of fact that Adam wondered if anyone remembered how close he had been to dying.

They moved along the beds on that side of the room. Holiday and Doyle asked a few questions of the students or other residents, but there was no conversation with the patients until they reached Teddy in the bed across from Barnett's diverticulitis patient with the wound infection.

As the group crowded at the foot of his bed, Teddy lifted the washrag from his eyes and peeked at them. Adam reported his hematocrit and vital signs. Before there was any further discussion, Teddy spoke in the nasal twang that came from having a nasogastric tube in one nostril.

"Through some miracle I have survived the night," he announced. "I shall now try to endeavor along the long road to rehabilitation."

"Y'all gittin' enough pain medication?" Doyle asked.

"Yes, I believe I am," answered Teddy, "although I am trying to continue to survive in the face of any torment."

"Good," said Doyle. "Y'all gonna be fine."

When the service moved on to the next bed, Teddy replaced the washcloth on his eyes and leaned back with his lips pursed in a look of determination.

They continued down the row of beds, finishing at Mr. Elder's, where Turk spoke softly to the old man, moistened his throat with a few ice chips, and propped up his pillow while Adam gave a formal report.

As they made their way towards the female ward, Adam walked next to Kochenko and asked what would happen to Danny Frer.

"Well," he said, "he probably will have more bone destruction and pain, might turn up in the ER again, might continue to self-medicate with narcotics, might overdose. Don't fool yourself that he's going to have a sudden epiphany and stop using."

"But that's so sad."

"I know," said Kochenko, "but we can only do so much."

∾

Rounds had changed dramatically after Leticia Powell had survived the shotgun blast and been placed on the ward with the other patients. The constant stream of complaints and profanity coming from her disrupted not only the residents' rounds but also the routine care on the ward. Teaching discussions and presentations were cut short because no one wanted to talk over her. The nursing staff found her continued patter to be a nuisance, and consequently the bedside charting was not done in a timely fashion, causing information to be missing when the students came to do the dressing changes and write the notes recording their post-op exams.

Adam had hoped that they would fully discuss the patient with the thyroid nodule that morning. He knew that whatever the residents would explain would reinforce the material from lecture or the textbook when he finally got around to reading it. He was disappointed when the constant noise from Leticia was so annoying that the entire report on the thyroid patient was Rogers stating, "She's OK."

Rather than gather around Leticia's bed, the residents stopped four beds away, and Doyle told Barnett to report on his "private patient."

"I think she's doing pretty well," said Barnett, "but she's still got some pink fluid coming from the drain near her pancreas, and her blood sugars are running high."

"She may not be healing the anastomosis to her pancreas well," said Rogers. "Put a colostomy bag around the drain so we can measure the output and send a little of the fluid for an amylase level to see if it's leakage from the pancreas itself. Those high sugars could be from the pancreatic injury, or maybe she was an undiagnosed diabetic, or maybe there is just too much glucose in her IV fluids. Let's take the sugar out of her fluids and see what happens when she only gets saline in her IVs. We need to keep a close eye on that drainage. Healing the pancreas is tricky, and it's dangerous to feed her and further stimulate the gland before it's healed… May take weeks. We're stuck with her here for a while."

CHAPTER 62

THE CLOCK WAS a few minutes from striking noon when Barnett hung up the phone and smiled. Shrevi and Adam had placed all the charts in order on the rack and were preparing to leave the ward.

"My wife thought that since we're getting out of here early, you guys might want to come by our house for dinner tonight," said Barnett. "She said she'd like to meet the friends I've been talking about."

"Sure," said Shrevi.

"That's really nice," agreed Adam.

"Great," said Barnett. He pulled a page from his pocket notebook and scribbled on it. "Here's the address. We're on Napoleon about a block down from Baptist Hospital, on the other side of the street... Between 5:30 and 6:00. OK?"

"Perfect," said Adam as Barnett turned and left. "I guess I'll just read in the med school library for a couple of hours and change the dressing on the lady on Gyne before I catch the streetcar up to Napoleon… Although I guess I should get a bottle of wine or something to take to Barnett's."

"It's a bit of a hike from St. Charles on Napoleon," said Shrevi. "I might as well study here and give you a ride to Barnett's later. Let's get out of here before Wantz comes back with something for us to do."

"Kochenko says Wantz is just uptight because he's the only intern on the service. There's supposed to be two but the program lost one, so he's on his own."

∿

The medical school library was old, but Adam found it comfortable. The only wall not lined by bookshelves was painted the same shade of light green as the hallways in Charity, but the paint was not nearly as faded. Wood paneling and shelving lent a warmth to the big room. Adam preferred to study at one of the tables at the rear of the room since the high row of small-paned windows on the back wall filled the area with natural light.

They sat at a table and studied for two hours until Shrevi put his head down to nap. Adam left his textbook and lecture notes open when he took a break to change Luanne's dressing.

∿

When Adam returned to the hospital, he was surprised to find Bennett Turk standing over Luanne's bed when he arrived. The dressings were off. Turk had obviously been inspecting the wound. He grinned sheepishly at Adam, although Luanne greeted him with a huge smile.

"He says I am healing beautifully," she said, "and it don't hurt no more."

"Sorry," said Turk, "I'm not checking up on you. Just curious to see how her wound is doing… It looks great, by the way."

Together, they replaced the dressing and left the ward. Adam didn't feel offended that Turk had been on the Gynecology ward. In fact, the simple comment that the wound looked "great" was actually the most encouragement he had received the entire rotation.

Shrevi's shiny Camaro still had a new car smell to the upholstery. Adam slid into the bucket seat on the passenger side. As they pulled out of the school lot, a bright yellow Dodge Charger passed in front of them.

"Hey, that's Doyle," said Shrevi.

"I guess he gets to leave the hospital and go home sometimes too," remarked Adam.

They remained a few cars back on Claiborne Avenue. Doyle's car stood out ahead of them as they traveled uptown. Shrevi already had his blinker on to turn left onto Louisiana when they noticed Doyle's car make the same turn ahead of them.

"Where's he going?" Shrevi asked. "I wonder where he lives."

Before the students could answer that question, Doyle pulled over to the curb next to the Magnolia Street Housing Project.

"He sure doesn't live in Central City," said Shrevi. "What the hell is he doing?"

Still out of Doyle's sight, Shrevi pulled over along the curb. They watched in silence as Doyle sat in his car for a moment until a tall Black man and two teenaged boys approached.

"Jesus, is he buying drugs?" asked Shrevi.

"No, not that," said Adam.

Doyle got out of the car and reached back in to pull out a familiar-looking box of Unna boot bandages before he followed Rosalie Patton's son into the projects while leaving the two young boys to watch over his car.

"Is he crazy going in there?" Shrevi raised his voice in concern.

"Don't worry," said Adam, "I'm sure he'll be OK. He's just making a house call."

∽

They drove along Freret Street until they reached a liquor store nestled in the middle of an enclave of trendy boutiques and shops. Adam selected a bottle of chardonnay from the cooler. He thought it must be a pretty good wine since it had an attractive label in French. By the time he reached the counter, the clerk had already rung up Shrevi's purchase, a six-pack of Jax beer.

Adam noted the sharp contrast in the neighborhood when they turned off Freret onto Napoleon. He was accustomed to the buildings in the Quarter, crowded next to each other, often in disrepair with faded, cracked, and peeling paint or crumbling bricks and failed tuckpointing. The cobblestone streets of the

Quarter often weren't wide enough for two-way automobile traffic. Napoleon Avenue was a spacious boulevard divided by broad landscaped medians and lined by structures that ranged from large classical homes with elegant columns and expansive porches to small, neatly kept shotgun-style houses like the one Barnett was renting.

They parked directly in front of Barnett's home, a small, white clapboard structure featuring a walk-up front porch accentuated with carved wooden supports and railings. An old-fashioned swing was suspended by chains near the end of the porch, and two long windows flanked by dark shutters extended to the floor line. To the left a mailbox was mounted between the window and the leaded glass-paneled door.

Adam rang the bell and was surprised when the usually formal Barnett answered the door barefoot, wearing Bermuda shorts and a Saints jersey while cradling a bubbly baby in his arm.

"Hi, guys, c'mon in. Jane is anxious to meet you. This is my daughter, Mary."

The front room was quite a bit different from Adam's apartment. The furniture was nicely arranged on a slightly faded Oriental rug. Against the rear wall stood a dark bookcase filled with the same editions of textbooks that littered Adam's floor. Next to the bookcase sat a small desk and chair. Barnett's notebook and surgical text were neatly stacked next to the desk lamp. A playpen overlapped the rug near the front of the room, and in the far corner a large pine box was filled to overflowing with children's toys—colored balls, bright plastic blocks, and a big-eyed teddy bear.

"C'mon, meet my wife," said Barnett.

He led them through the rooms towards the rear of the house. Adam noted that, as the name implied, you could probably fire a shotgun at the front door and the bullet would exit through the back door without hitting anything. At the rear of the house was the kitchen, bright and airy with high windows on three walls. The appliances were old but spotless. In the center of the room, a shiny metal cart with a butcher block top provided extra counter space.

"Hi, I'm Jane," smiled Barnett's wife as she tossed a salad in an orange plastic bowl on the cart.

Barnett gestured towards each of their guests. "This is Adam…and Shrevi."

"I've heard a lot about both of you," she answered. "Only good things."

Adam thought Jane was pretty, but she wore a high-waisted floral skirt and a sleeveless white linen top, unlike the girls he had known in college who dressed in sandals, jeans, and tie-dye tops. Her hair was styled in a flip and remained perfectly in place. Her old-fashioned apron reminded him of Betty Crocker.

"I hope you all like wine," Adam said as he placed the bottle next to the salad bowl.

"I brought some beer if you don't care for the wine," said Shrevi, setting the six-pack down and pulling a can from the plastic ring.

"That was very sweet of you both," Jane said. "I think I'll try the wine."

She placed the salad utensils in the bowl and took the baby from Barnett. "Why don't you get some glasses down and open the wine—three? Or four?" She glanced at Shrevi.

"I'm fine," answered Shrevi, popping the top on his can of beer.

After Barnett had poured the wine, they reentered the dining room, where the table had been set with fine china, cloth napkins, beautiful silverware, and elegant long-stemmed water glasses. A tray of carrots, celery, and radishes sat with a bowl of spinach dip on the edge of the table.

Jane stepped into the room and handed the baby back to Barnett. "Why don't you start with the appetizers? I'll have dinner ready in just a bit."

They sat at the table and Barnett gently bounced the smiling baby up and down.

"This is really nice," Adam said before dipping a crunchy carrot into the spinach dip.

"Yeah, what a relief from the wards," said Shrevi. "None of that asshole Wantz."

He grimaced when he realized that Jane was serving plates of salad and had overheard him. "Sorry for the bad language," he said.

"I've heard all about him," she smiled. "Don't worry, the baby doesn't understand curse words."

Shrevi almost had the first forkful of salad in his mouth and Adam had speared a piece of lettuce when Jane sat down and said, "Barnett, would you like to say grace?"

They both lowered their forks and folded their hands. Barnett closed his eyes and put his head down.

"Lord, we thank you for the meal we are about to share and for all the blessings you have given us. We thank you for the fellowship and friendship at our table tonight. Amen."

Jane picked up the conversation immediately. "Are you guys having as difficult a time keeping up as Barnett?"

"Between the textbook, the lectures, and the wards, nobody can keep up," Adam groaned. "I even had to miss Grand Rounds and Bullpen to go to the operating room."

"Grand Rounds was pretty interesting," said Barnett. "Rogers' father was the guest speaker, talking about how communities respond to disaster. He had slides from Hurricane Camille."

"I liked when he told us about the woman who came out of nowhere and organized the efforts to rescue people, put down sandbags, and pull the downed trees off the road," said Shrevi. "Dr. Rogers said the City Council wanted to give her an award, but everyone said they didn't know her. Turned out they did. She'd run the gambling and prostitution concession outside of town for thirty years. The mayor even played poker there every Friday night."

While the students discussed the challenge of surgical training, Jane served a delicious meal—a chicken dish swimming in a tasty sauce containing dates and olives, dirty rice on the side, and large stalks of buttered broccoli.

As the evening was ending, after the chocolate cake and vanilla ice cream had been served, they all laughed as Adam recounted the story of how he had to have Danny Frer start his own IV.

After helping to clear the table and thanking their hosts profusely, Adam and Shrevi stepped outside into the humid night air.

"I can give you a ride down to the Quarter," said Shrevi.

"Just to St. Charles would be fine. I'll catch the streetcar. Won't take you out of your way."

Adam stood under the streetlight by the tracks in the median, thinking about how much he had enjoyed the evening and how lucky Barnett was to have such a supportive homelife. He only waited for ten minutes before he spotted the approaching headlight and heard the clacking of the tracks as the rickety streetcar approached. That late at night, there was only one other passenger. He got off when they reached the next stop at Louisiana, and Adam rode the rest of the way to the end of the line at Canal Street alone.

CHAPTER 63

THERE WAS NO breeze off the river that morning. Decatur Street remained quiet as Adam made his way in the dark to the Café Du Monde and then on to the bus stop on Canal. He'd slept well after Sunday night dinner but had feelings of guilt about not using any of the preceding evening for studying.

He was now efficient at making rounds, and he was not surprised or feeling rushed when Teddy questioned him during the dressing change.

"How am I handling the complications, Adam? Are they severe?"

"I don't think there are any complications. Everything looks fine."

"There's always complications… But be not afraid, I intend to persevere no matter how life-threatening."

"Good," said Adam, "I think that will help."

Sam Elder sat propped up by pillows and smiling as he spoke to the night nurse, who was offering him a cup of orange juice.

"I want to go home, Doc," said Mr. Elder when Adam approached. "How long, Doc? How long?"

"Soon, I'm pretty sure, soon." Adam remained amazed that an old man who had been on Death's doorstep could be making such a dramatic recovery.

He wanted to wait on the ward to greet Jen but joined Barnett and Shrevi in the cafeteria for a little more coffee before lecture.

"Thanks again for last night's dinner," said Adam. "I haven't slept this well since we started the rotation."

"I got a good night's sleep too," said Shrevi.

"Well, having you guys over must've brought good luck. The baby slept through the night, so I got about six hours."

Adam wasn't sure if it was because he was so well rested or if Dr. Fossett from Service 2 was just that good a speaker, but the morning's lecture on gastric cancer seemed so clear and thorough that he was able to take good notes. He left the lecture hall with the satisfaction that he hadn't missed any detail and that he would retain a full grasp of the topic just by reviewing his notebook before the exam without struggling through the textbook reading.

Clinic wasn't scheduled to start until the afternoon, but after lecture Adam was anxious to return to the hospital. He planned to stop by the male ward, ostensibly to finish his chart notes but secretly hoping for a chance to talk to Jen.

He stepped off the elevator and approached the entrance to the ward. He was almost knocked over by a tiny figure, dressed in black, who scurried past him. He bumped against the door jamb and looked down the hall and watched as the dark figure disappeared into another ward. Though she was running as fast as she could, Adam caught a glimpse of her dress and realized that the legends were true and he had actually seen one of the remaining Sisters of Charity.

Adam surveyed the ward. Nothing seemed out of place. The room was quiet. All the patients were resting in their beds except Ronald, who had been placed in a metal chair at the foot of his bed. He was prevented from falling out of his seat by a rolled white sheet that had been tied around his waist and looped through the vertical metal rods in the footboard of his bed. He was moving his head back and forth and swaying as he tried to focus his rolling, upward gaze on the ceiling.

"What's so funny?" Adam asked Jen as he stopped at the nurses' desk. She was holding her sides and laughing, leaning back in her chair with her legs stretched onto the top of the desk. She tried to stop laughing but had to pause several times before she spoke.

"Sister Wilhelmina was here. We had just gotten Ronald out of bed for the first time and put him in the chair. She went down the aisle sprinkling holy water on each of the patients' foreheads and blessing them. When she got to Ronald he lifted up his gown, grabbed his penis, and waved it at her!"

She began to laugh again while Adam stood dumbfounded, staring at Ronald.

"Well, you know," she said, "in a brain injury it's always the primitive reflexes that come back first."

CHAPTER 64

BARNETT AND ADAM began the afternoon in the female clinic,
working with Kochenko and Turk. Compared to the male side,
there was a lighter volume of patients to be seen, enabling
the flow of patients in and out of the exam rooms to proceed
quite smoothly. Each student admitted a gallbladder patient.
Adam finished a post-op exam of a patient one month after an
incisional hernia repair.

The last patient for Adam to see was a nicely dressed older
Black lady. Feeling confident, Adam flashed a smile while
assuming his most professional demeanor.

"I'm Dr. Sinclair. What brought you in to see us today?"

"There's something wrong with my titty," she said.

Not wanting to waste any time, Adam helped her up onto
the exam table and turned his back while she removed her
blouse and covered herself with a sheet.

Despite trying to appear professional, Adam was not at all
ready for what he saw when he gently pulled the sheet down.

Her left breast was unrecognizable, having been replaced by what appeared to be a gigantic moist scab. A gauze pad soaked with yellowish fluid remained stuck to just below the nipple until she peeled it off. Her nipple itself was barely identifiable. What remained resembled an island of skin, displaced further to the left and flattened against her chest wall. In her armpit Adam felt firm masses the size of walnuts.

"I'm going to have another doctor examine you too," Adam said, stepping out of the cubicle and waving at Turk to join him.

Inside, Turk examined her and pointed out to Adam that he could feel additional lymph nodes just above the clavicle.

"Supraclavicular nodes," the resident said. "Ma'am, we're going to put you in the hospital, but before you go upstairs Dr. Sinclair will take you for a chest X-ray."

"Probably metastatic in the lung," he whispered to Adam after he had turned away from the patient.

She dressed and Adam escorted her to the X-ray Department. Turk rejoined Adam while he was waiting by the film developer. When the completed film dropped onto the tray, they immediately placed it on the view box. Her normally dark lung fields were filled with rounded white shadows.

"Cannon balls," said Turk. "Pretty extensive spread."

"How long did it take to get like this?" asked Adam.

"Probably years," Turk replied.

"But how could she let it progress like this?"

"Denial," Turk said, "is not just a river in Egypt."

❦

The afternoon light was fading when Barnett and Adam returned to the male Surgery Clinic to join the rest of the service. Shrevi was writing a chart note and discussing a patient with Wantz and Rogers. Kittamura and Holiday had already left. Doyle was standing at the back wall, watching the students' arrival.

One more patient entered the clinic: an emaciated old man in a wheelchair accompanied by a teenaged boy. The old man's skin was yellowed and his belly was swollen while the muscles of his arms and legs had withered away to loose skin and bones. He sat in the chair wearing a dark blue stocking cap and a sweater that appeared several sizes too big and had lost its whiteness with age but had not yet become as deeply yellow as his skin. A folded blanket rested across his lap. Although his eyes were sunken and his face hollow, there was a familiarity to his features that Adam just couldn't place.

When Doyle saw him, he immediately headed towards him. Just as he reached the wheelchair and began speaking to the man and his young escort, Adam noticed Miss Viola walk into the room, in her distinctive prim blue dress and string of pearls. She gave the young boy a quick hug and took his place behind the wheelchair while she spoke with Doyle.

Rogers stood beside Adam and whispered, "Poor Bunkie… He's more cachetic and the ascites in his belly is worse. He's approaching the end of the line."

"Is that Bunkie Smith?" Adam asked, noting that the frail old man's facial features still resembled the famous trumpet player whose image graced posters and record album covers throughout the city. He was the central figure in the ubiquitous Preservation Hall photo. Every shop in the Quarter sold the postcard with the picture of Bunkie seated on a simple wooden chair between the trombone player and the clarinetist. The bell of his trumpet rested on his knee while he smiled and listened to the other musicians.

"Bunkie is Miss Viola's uncle," said Rogers. "Theodorakis operated on him about a year and a half ago for a locally advanced colon cancer. He did pretty well for a while, but then about six months ago he presented with a bowel obstruction while Theodorakis was speaking at a conference in New York. Doyle operated and found spread to his liver and an extensive recurrence of tumor in his pelvis that had trapped the small intestine. Doyle was able to bypass the obstruction so that his bowels opened up. Bunkie refused any more chemotherapy, and he's gradually been fading since that time. It's a shame to see him like this."

Adam looked carefully at the old man across the room and saw all the features that had been described in their lecture about the nutritional effects of advanced cancer: muscle wasting, weight loss, diminished strength and mobility, excess abdominal fluid. Just like the slides in lecture, except here they were features in an actual patient who just happened to be one of New Orleans' most famous musicians.

Doyle motioned for Adam to join them. Adam hurried across the room. Miss Viola nodded in recognition as he approached.

"Take Mr. Smith up to the ward. I'll do all the admitting paperwork with Miss Viola before she comes up to join you."

"I'll make sure he's comfortable upstairs," promised Adam.

"Thank you, Dr. Sinclair," responded Miss Viola.

The bed near the end of the ward next to Teddy was empty, and Adam helped the old man move slowly to it. Bunkie was easily fatigued.

Adam began his physical examination. Bunkie's tongue was dry and furrowed, his eyes yellow like his skin, and his belly was made huge by the abnormal collection of fluid it contained. Adam could not hear air moving in and out of the lower portion of Bunkie's lungs. He carefully centered his left hand on the man's back, middle finger between the ribs, and tapped his middle finger with his right hand so that he could appreciate the deep, clear sound produced by tapping over the air-filled lung in the upper part of the chest, while a dull thud indicated the extent of the fluid surrounding the lower lung.

Bunkie lay back as Adam was trying to remember how a similar technique, combined with turning the patient on his side, could outline the shifting of fluid within the abdomen.

Adam asked all the appropriate questions, but Bunkie couldn't remember the details of his past history at all. He didn't know his medicines or allergies. When asked if he smoked, he responded, "Used ta," but couldn't recall how much, how long, or when he quit. In addition to the incisions on his belly from the cancer surgery, there were two scars suggesting that he had undergone bilateral hernia operations, but he neglected to mention those.

"He's your uncle," Adam said when he approached Miss Viola in the hall.

"Yes," she said. "My daddy was Bunkie's brother... When Daddy died I was nine. Bunkie became more like a father to me and my brother."

She sat on the wooden bench outside the ward and removed a delicate handkerchief from her purse as tears welled up while she spoke.

"Uncle Bunkie pretty much raised us. He paid Momma's rent, and after I started working here in Housekeeping he gave me the money so I could go to school part-time and get a degree. He paid for my brother's schooling too."

"Where's your brother now?" asked Adam.

"He's a literature professor at a university in St. Louis. Has a PhD from Princeton. He'll be coming here in a day or two."

"Bunkie's pretty famous," said Adam.

"Oh yes, been all around the world, got all kinds of awards… Has seven Grammys lined up on the mantelpiece at home."

She gave a faint smile before turning serious again. "We knew this was coming, but, you know, you just can't own up to it sometimes."

"I know, it must be very difficult."

"I thought he would be gone six months ago, but Dr. Doyle took real good care of him."

"He's a great surgeon," Adam agreed, barely giving any thought to the fact that a world-famous musician had been operated by someone who was actually still in a training program.

He did, however, find himself asking, "Bunkie could afford to be cared for in one of the nicer hospitals uptown. Did he just come to Charity because you work in the Surgery office?"

"Oh no, he could afford one of those fancy places but he wouldn't be as comfortable. Charity has always been our hospital. My daddy and Bunkie were both born here. So were their parents and both my brother and me. We've always been treated well, even with care from the students and residents. Bunkie's wife was born here and died here after her stroke. When Hurricane Betsy came through, Uncle Bunkie brought us here and we slept in the lobby. This hospital has just always been here for us."

"You can go back to be with him now," said Adam. "I saw that Dr. Doyle wrote some admission orders, but if there is anything you need just let me know."

It was only after the elevator doors had closed that Adam realized he had neglected to ask Miss Viola anything that would answer the additional questions he still had about her uncle's past medical history.

Adam was still thinking about Miss Viola and Bunkie Smith while he walked home. Not only had Bunkie been one of the artists who brought New Orleans culture to the rest of the world, but Miss Viola's description of him as a loving and supportive uncle gave a more personal sense of what his loss would mean.

Adam opted for the route down Bourbon Street. He paused outside one of the clubs, more to listen to the traditional band onstage than to peer in and try to catch a glimpse of the near-naked pole dancers on the bar. He resolved that he would turn onto St. Peter Street later and look for Bunkie's image in the old photos on display at Preservation Hall. For now, though, he would take the time to stop for dinner at Felix's, where the waitress would undoubtedly recommend the oyster stew.

CHAPTER 65

AFTER LECTURE THERE was time to stop in the cafeteria before one o'clock rounds with Dr. Theodorakis, but neither Barnett, Shrevi, nor Adam went through the food line. Barnett leaned back in his chair, calmly thumbing through his index cards. Shrevi had his cards spread out on the table. He sat hunched, as though trying to memorize everything about his patients all at once. Adam pulled out a fresh card and wrote at the top "Bunkie Smith," thinking he would have to record the lab work from the chart on the ward. He took another blank card as he pictured the image of the lady with the advanced breast cancer. Although he would never forget the image of her chest wall, he was dismayed that he couldn't remember her name—Valerie? Victoria? Vivian?

Dr. Theodorakis was twenty minutes late, so Adam had time to check the patient's charts and update his index cards. He added Bunkie Smith's lab work and proceeded to the female ward. He wrote "Vivian Hall" on the new card he had created for the lady with the breast cancer and quickly summarized some of her lab work.

Returning to the male ward, Adam found the air filled with tension and anticipation as he joined the rest of Service 1 and the residents and students from the other services who were beginning to congregate in the ward and outside in the hallway.

Theodorakis arrived with a stern look on his face. The sea of white coats parted until he reached the first patient's bed. His questions were slow, deliberate, and demanding. He focused on the junior residents. Questions on operative technique were interspersed with requests to refer to current journal articles. Kochenko, Turk, and Wantz were all chastised if one of their answers was not exact or detailed enough or if one of them was not up to date in their journal reading.

Barnett stood rigid, lips pursed. Adam shuddered and gripped his index cards tighter. Shrevi was the first to suffer.

"Describe for me the pre-operative testing to be done for a gunshot wound to the abdomen," Theodorakis asked as he stood at the head of Shrevi's patient's bed.

"CBC, blood chemistries, amylase, type, and crossmatch should be done...urinalysis..." Shrevi paused in thought, grasping for additional answers. "X-rays," he said.

"Which X-rays?" asked Theodorakis. "And don't you think it appropriate to check coagulation studies on someone going into surgery? And which tests would that be?"

Shrevi stared at the floor. The stress of being questioned had rattled him so that he couldn't answer a question so basic that everyone should know the answer.

"Anyone?" said Theodorakis.

"Prothrombin time and partial thromboplastin time… PT and PTT," came a voice from the crowd of white coats.

Theodorakis turned back to Shrevi. "How do you assess whether the patient is bleeding significantly?"

Simple answer, thought Adam, remembering that if there was no visible external bleeding, then an assessment of pulse and blood pressure would be the first step in evaluating the patient.

Shrevi looked up, too flustered to think clearly. "You could tap his belly to see if there is any blood present."

Kochenko and Turk winced as they waited for the hammer to fall.

"Do you really think in this patient that would be necessary?" asked Theodorakis. "Are you confusing a perforating injury with blunt trauma? A bullet wound absolutely mandates an exploratory surgery, so tapping the patient is not needed. Haven't the residents taught you the difference in how to manage each type of injury or explained how changes in blood pressure and pulse can reflect the volume loss of bleeding?"

Shrevi looked as though he had just flunked the block. Kochenko and Turk had seen it coming since they knew the chief was still unhappy with the recent Morbidity and Mortality conference. Wantz seethed silently and stared at Shrevi.

Barnett's turn came next; no one expected any surprises with his diverticulitis patient. Everyone thought the drained wound infection of his patient had seemed to be healing cleanly since it had been opened and that his recovery was progressing well.

Barnett reiterated the patient's history and then added, "Although the wound seems to be healing well, the patient's white blood cell count has gone up from normal to 13,000 yesterday and to 14,500 today. Last night he began to run a fever again, up to 101."

While Barnett was removing the abdominal dressings, Dr. Theodorakis stepped closer to the bed.

"Are you having any pain?" he asked.

"Just the soreness in my jaw."

The swelling of the man's left cheek was clear when Theodorakis asked him to turn his head towards Barnett. The patient withdrew in pain as the chief gently touched the area.

"It's very fluctuant… What do you think this is?" the chief asked Barnett.

Theodorakis didn't let Barnett's silence linger for long. "It's an abscess of the parotid gland," he explained, turning towards Wantz. "Tell us about this."

"An abscess of a salivary gland such as the parotid may be precipitated by obstruction of the draining duct, as with a calculous, or it may occur spontaneously such as in a post-operative patient who has poor oral hygiene or may be dehydrated or without adequate oral intake to stimulate secretions from the gland."

"I think you had better drain this today." Theodorakis directed his suggestion to Wantz.

Barnett was crestfallen, feeling guilty that he had not recognized the abscess.

The group turned to face the beds on the other side of the ward, and Adam had to swallow the lump in his throat when he realized that his patients occupied four of the six remaining beds. He didn't expect to escape the next round of questioning unscathed. Even though he knew the histories of Teddy, Bunkie Smith, Ronald Candy, and Sam Elder, there was always something that could be asked on rounds that a third-year student would not know.

He was saved by Teddy. Before Adam could present the history, Teddy sat up, adjusted the purple, gold, and green Mardi Gras scarf that he had around his neck, and interrupted, "Y'all should be very proud of the way your young doctors saved my life! I was stabbed and hanging on by a slim thread when the police brought me to your doorstep and these fine young men swung into action to treat my nearly lethal wounds. Literally pulled me back from the jaws of death. Their care has been exemplary, reflecting the finest ideals of Hippocrates himself. Their surgical skills reversed my fatal course and made my recovery nothing less than miraculous."

Teddy's comments lightened the mood and immediately relieved the tension, particularly after Theodorakis looked quizzically at Rogers, who shrugged and explained, "Single laceration to a small vein in the omentum... Not much associated blood loss... Very stable on presentation."

Dr. Theodorakis approached Bunkie Smith in the next bed with a quiet respect and a sense of sadness that was apparent to all present. Kochenko and Turk, on either side of the bed, folded the pillow and helped prop Bunkie into a sitting position. Despite his frailty, his grin still expressed the charm and personality that had filled stages around the world for audiences who were eager to hear his music.

The chief leaned close and spoke with Bunkie for a few moments, so softly that most of the assembled residents and students couldn't hear the conversation. Straining to hear, Adam was able to catch Dr. Theodorakis' promise to keep him comfortable and an expression of gratitude from Bunkie.

Adam reported on Ronald's gradual neurologic improvement, but didn't mention that signs of his recuperation included waving his member at a nun.

The next bed was Barnett's patient, the boy who had been run over by a car. Barnett stood up straight, muscles tense as he presented the young man's history. Not wishing to be caught off guard again, Barnett described every intricate aspect of the young man's presentation with great care. He described the boy's position in his front yard, the direction he was facing when the car jumped the curb, the angle at which the car traveled across the yard, and its speed. Kochenko, Rogers, and Turk suppressed a laugh as Barnett added, "The tread mark left an impression across the patient's chest extending from the right upper quadrant of the abdomen to the left clavicle… I believe they were Goodyear wide-track radials."

Dr. Theodorakis asked, "Do you think it's possible that he could sustain significant trauma without any serious internal injury?"

"We have observed him for several days. Serial blood counts, physical exam, and vital signs have remained stable with no evidence of injury…so I believe it's possible."

"Young people have a more pliable chest wall so that an applied compressive force may not be as damaging as it would be to an older person." Theodorakis looked towards the residents. "If he is eating well and you are satisfied he is stable, I think it would be safe to discharge him."

Sam Elder's bed was the last on the ward. Adam steeled himself to answer any questions about cholangitis and shock, but as soon as he presented the elderly gentleman's history and treatment, Sam spoke up.

"When can I go home? I just want to get back to the fire station so's I can play checkers with the young fellas between calls."

"What station were you out of?" asked Dr. Theodorakis... and that was the last question asked on the male ward, as everyone listened while Sam spent ten minutes recounting his years with the New Orleans Fire Department.

⁓

"Run ahead and get the lady with the breast cancer into a treatment room," Turk advised Adam as the group shifted to escort the chairman to the female ward.

Adam rushed ahead and waited with Miss Hall seated on the exam table covered by her loose gown, untied at the back. Even with the doors to the exam room closed, it was easy to tell when the entourage entered the ward. Leticia Powell stopped her screaming and once again became silent in Dr. Theodorakis' presence.

Rounds went quickly without any trying moments for the students or residents. For the final patient, the members of Service 1 crowded into the small treatment room while everyone else remained in the ward. Adam presented his patient's history and assisted her in dropping her gown towards her lap.

Shrevi's eyes bulged and Barnett couldn't hide his being startled by the appearance of her chest. Dr. Theodorakis never altered his demeanor as he carefully examined her, inspecting her chest wall from different angles and feeling her enlarged lymph nodes before addressing the group.

"I'm sure you would expect that there is a high likelihood of metastatic disease with this presentation. Do we have any evidence of metastatic spread yet?"

Turk spoke up. "A bone scan has been ordered, but we have a chest X-ray."

He placed it on the wall-mounted view box near the supply cabinet and turned on the box's light source, illuminating the film so that the multiple lesions in her lungs were easy to see.

Dr. Theodorakis nodded and began speaking. "Obviously, surgery alone would not be helpful in this circumstance, so we have to approach this patient with some form of systemic treatment. In addition to chemotherapy, there is a growing awareness that the growth of many of these tumors is stimulated by the presence of estrogen. An ablative procedure such as bilateral oophorectomy, that is, removal of both ovaries, may reduce estrogen stimulation enough to slow the tumor's progression, perhaps inducing a remission and maybe even prolonging her survival."

After rounds, Wantz dragged Barnett back to the male ward in order to drain the parotid abscess, still expressing displeasure as though it was Barnett's fault that the infection had developed.

Adam helped Miss Hall with her gown and escorted her back to her bed.

"I didn't understand all of what the older doctor was talking about, but you know, when he looked at me and talked to you all he gave me hope."

"Yes, ma'am," Adam answered, letting the discussion sink in, "there is always hope."

Chapter 66

Teddy was sitting upright in his bed, a tray of liquid nourishment in front of him. The orange plastic tray that rested on the bedside table covering his knees contained plastic utensils and Styrofoam dishes—a bowl filled with unadorned chicken broth, a smaller bowl of red Jello, a cup of hot water, a single tea bag, and an orange popsicle.

"How on earth do they expect me to eat this? I simply cannot dine on such unappealing sick people food! When will they correct my diet?"

"If you tolerate liquids," Adam responded, "they usually advance you to solid food pretty quickly."

"I should hope so," he stated. "Certainly no one can gain enough sustenance to fend off disease from this unsavory drivel."

In the next bed, Bunkie was so weak and shaky that he couldn't manage to bring a spoonful of broth to his lips without spilling it. Adam picked up the Styrofoam container and brought it to Bunkie's mouth while he used his left hand to steady the old man's head. Bunkie sipped a little and then raised his hand to indicate he had had enough.

Adam passed Ronald's bed and stopped at the foot of the run-over boy's bed, where Barnett was reviewing the chart.

"Kid still doing OK?" he asked.

Before Barnett could answer, the doors to the treatment room opened and Jen and Sister Wilhelmina walked out. Jen's eyes were reddened and her cheeks moist. The nun patted her arm. Jen looked at the students, but before Adam could take a step towards her, she turned away, grabbed her bag, quickly said something to the night nurse, and disappeared into the hallway.

Sister Wilhelmina approached the two boys and paused between them.

"Husband still drinking?" asked Adam.

"Alcoholism is a terrible disease. You boys go about your business."

"I can't believe this boy had his chest run over by a car and has no significant injuries. I just went over all his tests again and re-examined him… I guess he really is ready to go home," said Barnett.

Sister Wilhelmina looked down at the chart he held in his hands and then looked up directly at both students.

"This is Charity Hospital," she said, "where the unusual occurs and miracles happen."

Chapter 67

ADAM AND BARNETT were facing the elevators when Kochenko came down the hall.

"Glad you guys are still here. C'mon with me. I want to teach you something important."

He was waving a long strip of paper, which he rolled up as the three of them boarded the elevator. "Know what this is?" he asked as he placed the roll into the pocket of his lab coat.

"It's the rhythm strip from an electrocardiogram," answered Barnett.

"Oh, it's so much more," stated Kochenko. "It is a ticket to peace and quiet. Do you know who Feldstein is? He's one of the chief residents in Internal Medicine... Kind of a nervous type... Doesn't like surgeons, always orders every possible test just for 'completeness.' He's the guy on call tonight, and that's perfect for us because he is going to rescue a patient from the incompetent surgical service. I'm told he's down in the ER, so let's look there."

Neither of the students understood, but they obediently followed the resident.

The Emergency Room was noisy and congested as usual, but Dr. Feldstein was easy to spot near the nurses' station in the Internal Medicine corridor. He was a small, thin, tremulous fellow who held his spectacles on his nose as he waved a chart over his head and barked orders at the nurses.

He wasn't happy to see them but calmed down when he heard Kochenko's warm greeting.

"Hi, Arnold. I was wondering if you could help us out a bit?"

Dr. Feldstein paused. "What do you need?"

"We've got this patient upstairs who's having a difficult post-op course. Her belly is OK after being hit with a shotgun blast. Had injuries to everything…bowel, liver, pancreas… All that's healing OK…"

"What's the problem that you need Medicine for?"

"We've been trying to figure out this complicated cardiac rhythm and we're wondering if you could help us out?"

Kochenko pulled the EKG strip from his pocket and unraveled it on the desk in front of Arnold Feldstein. The name "Powell, Leticia" had been written in black ink on the tracing.

"So we were wondering if this was ventricular tachycardia and how we should treat it."

A wide-eyed Feldstein grabbed the strip of paper and ran it through his fingers.

"It's only sinus tachycardia. No treatment needed…but if you want this patient properly monitored and managed, I will take her in transfer to the Medical Service. We will be more attuned to watching her heart. Write the transfer orders and include for them to page me when she reaches the Medicine ward. I've just got to finish with a patient down here."

"'Course, we'll do her wound care and follow her belly, but thanks, Arnold," responded Kochenko. "You're more a lifesaver than you know."

They left the ER with Kochenko grinning widely.

"You all take off," he said. "I'll write the transfer orders. Think how quiet the female ward will be now. Works every time... Just gotta find the right Medicine resident and ask him if it's a serious arrhythmia while you're looking at the EKG upside down."

CHAPTER 68

TEDDY'S DIET HAD been advanced on Wednesday morning. Adam finished Luanne's dressing change and arrived on the men's ward just after the breakfast trays had been placed in front of the patients. Teddy was sitting up with his tray on the table that stretched over his knees. He took a mouthful of coffee and violently spat it out, leaving his soft scrambled eggs and already soggy bacon swimming in brown liquid.

"This is swill!" he shouted. "I simply cannot sustain myself with this poor excuse for coffee! How on earth can I be expected to recover if my nutritional needs cannot be met in a passable fashion?"

Next to Teddy's bed, Bunkie Smith held his coffee cup in a shaky hand. Even in his weakened state, he was able to bring the cup to his lips and take a small sip. He closed his eyes and a faint smile appeared as he swished the warm liquid around in his mouth before he swallowed.

Barnett and Shrevi had finished their notes and left to see their patients on the female ward. Adam finished writing his notes after his patients' dressings had been changed. He looked at the clock and realized he'd need to return after lecture to finish on the female ward, so maybe he could use a few minutes now to talk with Jen.

He found her in the treatment room, stocking the medication cart.

"Hi," he said. "How are you?"

She continued her task, not making any eye contact, and answered, "I'm OK."

"Did you have a good night?" Adam asked, hoping for more conversation.

"Not too bad," she said, turning her head towards him. "My husband did his drinking at home last night and quietly fell asleep on the couch about 8:30."

There was sadness in her eyes. Adam couldn't find words of comfort.

"Well, I was just heading to lecture. See you later."

"See you later," she responded.

Adam hoped he wasn't being too intrusive. He wanted to be her friend, but he feared he might seem like he was just another guy hitting on her.

The morning lecture on head and neck cancers was an interesting topic to Adam, but he found it distracting and petty when Dr. Brewster, instead of throwing out questions to the general audience, directed every question to Melissa. She handled herself well under pressure, but there was always a limit to a third-year student's knowledge, and Brewster continually pushed her to that point.

Chapter 69

"**Storm's comin'**," said Luanne after Adam changed her dressing.

"What?"

"You live in New Orleans long enough, you can just feel it. Storm's comin'."

Adam decided to swing by the male ward on the off chance that Jen may have stayed late that day. She was gone, but at the opposite end of the ward Teddy had visitors, and a linen tablecloth had been placed across the tray table that straddled his legs. A closer look and Adam recognized the short physique of Teddy's friend from Antoine's, the waiter Laurance. He didn't recognize the other visitor—a tall, thin man with shortly clipped blond hair and a small mustache that made him look like a French gendarme. Adam assumed that he must be Laurance's lover.

At the foot of the bed was an enclosed metal cart that looked like the type used by Room Service to keep food warm in fancy hotels. Adam took a few steps towards them, and as he approached he could read the stenciling on the back of the wheeled cabinet: "Property of the Royal Orleans Hotel."

"Dr. Adam! How nice to see you!" Teddy waved him on while his visitors arranged a place setting of fine silverware on the linen tablecloth.

"My friends have decided to rescue me from the gastronomic assault of the hospital kitchen and to provide me with true sustenance… Particularly important in the face of the impending storm in the Gulf!"

Adam watched as Laurance placed a silver dish in front of Teddy and lifted the cover.

"Our finest oysters Rockefeller," he offered.

Teddy grabbed a tiny fork, but as he held it aloft in preparation to spear his first oyster, he hesitated and looked around the ward. Each patient had an orange plastic tray before them with whatever had been deemed their appropriate diet, but all eyes were on Teddy. He paused and startled the room when he addressed the other patients.

"You really should try these. They are a true delicacy."

He waved the offering away with a flick of his wrist and pointed so that Laurance and his friend could begin going from bed to bed serving an oyster to each patient, none of whom could have ever afforded anything from that renowned kitchen.

While his partner completed serving the incredulous patients, Laurance returned to the cart before Teddy's bed.

"Chef made his turtle soup especially for you."

He pulled a tureen from the cart, but before he could set it in front of Teddy, he was handed back the silver soup spoon from

Teddy's place setting. Teddy gestured towards the emaciated figure in the bed next to him.

"Laurance," he said, "this is none other than Bunkie Smith."

"The famous trumpeter?"

"I assure you, none other," stated Teddy. "As you can see, Mr. Smith is a bit under the weather."

He looked at Bunkie. "I am sure, sir, that you would benefit more than I from this delicious soup. I would be happy to trade for your broth."

The Styrofoam bowl was placed before Teddy while Laurance's friend lifted the heavy spoon to assist Bunkie with the turtle soup. Bunkie's eyes brightened with the first taste. He didn't speak but smiled with each spoonful.

Teddy picked up the Styrofoam container with both hands and sipped from it before addressing his friends.

"They serve an excellent broth here, you know... Very hearty chicken stock."

"I did not know which entree you would prefer," said Laurance, "so I brought both the Filet de Boeuf Nature and the Pompano Pontchartrain."

Laurance placed both dishes on Teddy's tray and lifted the silver covers off the plates.

"I also brought a variety of side dishes: the pommes de terre au gratin, the asperges au beurre, and, of course, your favorite, the épinards sauce crème."

Teddy leaned forward and, with an expansive gesture, waved his arm over the ward.

"Please," he said, "in my weakened condition I am afraid the capacity of my stomach has shrunk. We should allow this feast to be distributed among my fellow invalids."

Adam breathed deeply, noting the antiseptic odor of the ward had been replaced by the smells of a gourmet kitchen. He watched in amusement as the cart borrowed from the city's leading luxury hotel was emptied of one delicacy after another.

He waved at Teddy and said, "See you tomorrow."

Swinging his book bag over his shoulder, Adam started for the door but hesitated for a moment to watch as Laurance pushed the serving cart from bed to bed, dividing the gourmet meal so that each of the laborers, urban and rural poor, pimps, drug dealers, and the unemployed—both Black and White— could equally have a taste. Even those who were supposed to be taking liquids only had at least a small portion placed on their plastic trays. The patients stared at the treat with big, grateful eyes, including the world-famous musician Bunkie Smith, who had lived in New Orleans his entire life but had never set foot in Antoine's.

Chapter 70

Adam paid his bill for the bowl of Felix's oyster stew and carried his glass of Dixie to the bar so he could hear the TV suspended above the rows of bottles. He recognized Rob Swelter, the popular local newscaster, sitting in front of a map of the Gulf filled with circles and arrows pointing to the coastline. Adam placed his book bag on the floor.

"What's goin' on?" he asked the bartender.

"Storm brewing in the Gulf. May hit us pretty hard. You should get ready."

"What does get ready mean?"

"You know, masking tape on the windows, fill the bathtub with fresh water in case you need it for drinking, get flashlights and a battery-operated radio."

Adam finished his beer and stepped out into the Quarter, still thinking about the bartender's instructions. He could tell a light rain had fallen by the wet cobblestones on the street and the drops that glistened on the nearby iron balconies. The air was still, no breeze coming off the river, but the usual heat was tempered by the gray clouds that filled the darkened sky. He could feel it too.

Luanne was right.

CHAPTER 71

IT RAINED DURING the night but stopped early Thursday morning. By the time Adam had finished morning rounds and crossed the street towards the medical school, the sun had risen in an overcast sky heavy with dark gray clouds. A light rain was again falling when he crossed the street after class to return to the wards.

He had a few notes to write and a couple of dressings left to change when he reentered the male ward. He paused by Teddy's bed.

"Is it true discharge is being considered for a man in my state?"

"You're doing very well, and I heard the residents mention the possibility."

"I guess I should start making arrangements for private duty nursing at home, since I will surely face a long and arduous recovery."

Barnett and Shrevi finished their work on the other units and joined Adam to await afternoon rounds with the residents. They brought two rickety folding chairs out from the treatment room, and Shrevi commandeered Jen's chair so that the three of them could sit around the nurses' desk with open textbooks. Barnett pulled his baby's picture from his wallet and sat smiling at it while Shrevi wasted no time in closing his eyes and putting his head down on arms folded over his textbook. Adam couldn't focus on his textbook. He watched Jen as she worked on the ward, gracefully moving from bed to bed while supervising the LPNs, passing meds, and taking care of the patients' drains and catheters.

Forty-five minutes later, when Terry Rogers entered the ward, the three students were all awake, staring at their open textbooks, although Barnett was the only one doing any actual reading.

"No rounds with Holiday and Doyle this afternoon," said Rogers. "The news is saying the storm in the Gulf is going to reach hurricane proportions before heading north, may end up coming towards us. Go on home and get ready, fill your bathtubs, tape the windows. Start here early tomorrow. Remember we've got ER call."

Once the resident had left, the students picked up their books, packed them away in their bags, and headed for the elevators.

"My wife is going to call her relatives in Jackson. She and the baby will probably go there if the storm looks bad," said Barnett.

"My folks have been through this before," said Shrevi. "I'm just going to call them and see if they need anything."

∽

Before leaving the hospital Adam made his afternoon visit to Luanne's bedside. When he arrived on the ward, she was sitting up in bed, eating a small cup of sherbet with a tiny wooden spoon. Her face broke into a broad smile when Adam entered. She placed the cup of sherbet on her bedside table and leaned back on her pillow, pulling away the sheet that covered her abdominal dressings.

"You're a little early…but I been waitin' on you," she said. "How's it looking?"

"Your sherbet's gonna melt."

"That's OK, you're pretty quick now. There'll be some left. How am I doing?"

He removed the dressings and marveled at the improvement in the once frightening wound. The deep chasm across her lower abdomen had been replaced by a shallow trough of healthy pink tissue. The dark fluid at the base was gone, replaced with a few thin whitish-gray strands of dead cells that painlessly wiped off with a moist sponge.

"Probably looks like raw hamburger to you," said Adam, "but this pink stuff is really healthy tissue."

He set a new dressing into place and handed her the sherbet cup.

"Pretty melted," he said. "Want me to try to get you another one?"

"No, that's OK, Doctor. The nurse can send for one."
"Well, you're healing pretty well. I'll be back in the morning."
"Lord, I'll still be sleeping at that hour."
"Yeah, I know," said Adam, and they both laughed.

CHAPTER 72

ONLY A LIGHT rain was falling and a warm breeze blowing from the south when Adam made his morning stop at the Café Du Monde. Since the early dismissal on Thursday, he'd been able to read two full textbook chapters, review all his lecture notes to date, and even managed to get a good night's sleep.

After lecture, Shrevi and Adam dawdled a bit, talking with students on the other services. When they stopped in the cafeteria before going to the hospital, they found Barnett sitting alone at one of the tables. He had emptied the contents of his book bag onto the table. The large surgical text and his notebook were open, as was the small pocket notebook in which he wrote down their assignments. He scribbled on a larger notepad. As they approached, he ran his fingers through his usually neat blond hair, obscuring the part and leaving his appearance uncharacteristically mussed. He wrote more furiously and was wide-eyed with concern as his friends approached.

"We should be heading to the hospital," said Shrevi. "What are you doing? We've got ER call."

"Trying to organize my studying," said Barnett. "Lookin' at the schedule. You know we've got ER call the night before the exam? There's no way I can do all this reading in time, and there haven't been any quizzes or a midterm. Everything is riding on that one exam."

"Hell," Shrevi said, "calm down. Don't get all bent out of shape. You don't want to have a mental breakdown like the guy who was supposed to be the second intern on Service 1."

"What?" said Adam.

"Remember a couple months ago there was a murder in an uptown bar and a doctor was arrested? That was the other intern. In addition to the stress of the Surgery program, the guy's girlfriend had broken up with him. He freaked out, walked into the bar, and shot the first date she had after the breakup."

"I didn't realize that guy was part of this program," said Adam.

"First off, nobody is going to get all the reading done… Impossible," continued Shrevi. "Secondly, we showed up, we're doing all the work and reading as much as possible… We musta picked up something. And, you know, the damn test is multiple choice. Those kinda tests are bullshit. Don't have to know a lot of detail for that. You can always pick out one or two choices that you know are just wrong. When I was in high school, one of my buddies had joined the Marines before we took our SATs. He didn't read any of the questions, just blackened the dots… Still scored higher than the national average in math and English. Our only problem is going to be staying awake after being up all night."

Adam wasn't completely reassured, but Barnett must have been. He calmly packed up his book bag, brushed his palm across his head, and joined the other two as they left for the hospital.

The students found Rogers in the ER. As soon as they stepped into the waiting area, the entry doors swung open and Officers Beaudry and Guidry entered, struggling with a big Black man. The man's wrists were in handcuffs. He wore torn work slacks and an army fatigue coat. His hair was in dreadlocks matted on the right side of his scalp, where a large laceration had profusely bled onto the right shoulder of his jacket, leaving dried blood covering his swollen right eye, the bridge of his nose, his bruised cheek, and into his unkempt beard. He was wild-eyed as he kicked, screamed, and spat while Beaudry and Guidry tried to push him towards the triage desk. The more they tried to move him along, the more he fought. When he kicked a lady's purse from under her seat and sent its contents scattering across the floor, Beaudry took his billy club with both hands and forced it under the right side of the man's chin, pushing him away from the waiting patients and slamming his head against the tiled wall across from the seating area.

The prisoner was stunned for a moment, which allowed Guidry to lift the man's right ankle and place a shackle around it. Beaudry held tight to his nightstick and pushed towards the wall and upwards so that he almost lifted the man off his feet.

Adam watched a young man leave his seat and stand facing the officers. He had a large Afro and wore a brightly colored dashiki in yellow, black, and orange tones. He waved a pair of dark-rimmed sunglasses as he pointed to the officers.

"You don't have to beat him. Is this how you treat all Black people?"

Another young man joined him. "Why don't you cops just shoot him?"

More people stood and shouted. "You wouldn't be beatin' him if he was White!"

Beaudry and Guidry tried to ignore them while they continued to subdue their prisoner, but the taunts continued and the ER erupted into pandemonium.

Flashing red and blue lights shone through the glass doors as they opened and admitted a third police officer—with sergeant's stripes on the sleeve of his leather jacket. He pushed his way through the crowd with an air of authority.

He stopped near the prisoner and lifted the man's right leg backward, pulling up just enough so that an adequate length of chain remained for the struggling Guidry to place the remaining cuff around the prisoner's left ankle.

Although the man could no longer kick, he still spat at the newly arrived officer, hitting a spot near the officer's feet. Beaudry pushed harder, again lifting the man further up on his toes.

The sergeant ignored it and stepped towards the nurses' desk.

"Sergeant Landry," he introduced himself to Adam over the disorder in the waiting room. "I don't think this will calm down if we wait for stitches. We'd better take him directly to the parish jail. Do you have any dressings?"

Adam quickly turned to run for the supplies and almost bumped into Doyle and Rogers as they approached.

"Y'all get him some," instructed Doyle.

Adam skirted around them and into the closest treatment room, where he grabbed gauze pads, rolled gauze, an Ace bandage, and tape.

Rogers and Doyle stood near Sergeant Landry with their hands raised, trying to quiet the crowd, while Beaudry and Guidry hustled the man through the doors and into one of the squad cars and drove away from the door.

Once the prisoner was gone, the crowd began to settle down, and Sergeant Landry approached Adam to retrieve the dressings. Adam's head filled with images of police encounters from his college days. He remembered the grainy black-and-white TV images of police beating demonstrators at the 1968 Democratic Convention in Chicago and the Vietnam War protest on his own college campus a few months later, interrupted by the appearance of the city's police department in full riot gear.

"Did you have to be so rough on him?" Adam asked the officer, surprising himself with his own boldness. Sergeant Landry looked back as though he couldn't believe the medical student's naiveté.

"Look, Doc," he said, "when you find a guy hopped up on PCPs on a street corner, beating a pregnant woman with a baseball bat, sometimes you gotta use a little force."

CHAPTER 73

"**JESUS CHRIST!**" **SAID** Shrevi. "I was with Wantz and Kittamura when they got an emergency call to the OB triage. The ambulance drivers dropped off a girl about eight months pregnant. Severely beaten…distorted face, eyes swollen with big purple eyelids, facial bone fractures, and a depressed skull fracture. Neuro took her right to surgery. What's going on down here?"

The three students huddled together as Kochenko and Rogers made their way down the corridor. The two residents surveyed the empty exam rooms. Each was spotless, with gurneys made ready with clean sheets and equipment laid out to be available for the arrival of the next injured patient.

After they saw that there was nothing demanding immediate attention, they started past the students to leave the area.

"Anything we need to do now?" asked Adam.

Kochenko and Rogers paused.

"It's pretty quiet," said Rogers. "The rain has picked up, probably keeping most people inside. I don't know where everybody else is. I suspect most of them are in their call rooms."

"Turk was on the ward, reviewing charts I think," said Kochenko.

"He works hard. It seems unfair that he's leaving the program," said Adam before realizing that perhaps he was speaking out of turn.

"Yeah, he's a good guy," said Kochenko. "Brewster had it in for him when he was on Service 4 last year. Thought he was too slow in the operating room."

"My daddy says you can't judge a surgeon until he's been out about five years," said Rogers. "Most of the slow technicians catch up, and some of the guys with more technical ability turn out to have bad judgment or don't manage their patients well."

"No worry about how Turk manages pre- and post-operative care," said Kochenko.

"No kidding," added Rogers. "It seems like whenever we get a bad patient, Holiday asks Turk to look after the IV and medication orders. Remember the guy with the injured pancreas everybody thought was going to die? Turk handled that patient's drains and fluids... Had a post-op fistula that closed with no evidence of infection or other complications. Anyway, you guys can look for him on the floors if you want, but I'd recommend you rest up. You never know when all hell will break loose down here. We're all gonna try to meet in the dining area about five o'clock."

After the residents left, the students found spots in one of the trauma rooms where they could sit with their textbooks and read. They had enjoyed forty-five minutes of relative quiet when three sets of flashing lights pulled up the entrance ramp. One after another in rapid succession, the ambulance drivers hurried in with patients on carts.

"Mother and her kids," one of the drivers breathlessly reported to Judy as she directed each to a different trauma room. "Driving her kids home from school in the rain, tire blew out on the slick pavement, and she hit a retaining wall. Little guy was in the back seat of the station wagon, lying down with his seat belt on. He's pretty bad off."

Both the mother and teenaged daughter were conscious and crying. They both had bruises on their foreheads, and the young girl was cradling her swollen right forearm in a way that suggested a fracture. On the third stretcher was a pale young boy, about ten or eleven, lying still with his eyes closed. Judy directed them into the closest trauma room. Carlos and a nurse followed while Judy directed another two nurses to attend to the mother and daughter. All three medical students were drawn into the room with the injured boy.

"He's breathing but has a very weak pulse," Judy announced as she began an IV in the boy's right arm. Carlos used a bandage scissors to cut off the boy's clothing, and the students could see, even from the back of the room, that his belly was distended. Despite the child's dark skin, Adam could see the bruise from the seat belt across his upper abdomen.

The X-ray tech stood just inside the door, waiting for the child to be moved across the hall for films, but Judy checked the child's blood pressure after she had started the IV fluids.

"Only about 50 systolic," she said.

"Don't move him," Doyle commanded as he entered.

A second IV was started in the opposite arm.

"Get some universal donor from the Blood Bank," he instructed Carlos, who was out the door in a flash.

Doyle examined the child.

"Lungs are clear but probably a lot of blood in the belly. What's his pressure now?"

"Still only hear something about 50," Judy answered.

"Shit," Doyle spoke. "Call the OR and tell 'em I'm comin'." He turned to Shrevi. "Find Kittamura and get Carlos to bring the blood to the OR. Have 'em type and cross six more…and some plasma."

Doyle began pushing the cart; Adam and Barnett grabbed on to help him steer. Rogers suddenly appeared as they entered the hallway and Doyle ordered, "Head for the elevators."

Rogers and Adam continued to guide the cart when Doyle turned and looked into the other trauma room.

"Your son is critically injured. I'm taking him to surgery," was all he said to the mother before running to catch up to the cart.

The doors to the elevator were open, but the Orthopedic service occupied the compartment with a patient of their own on the cart.

"I need this elevator," yelled Doyle as the doors started to close on the startled occupants.

"Aw, shit!" he screamed and kicked his leg between the doors, forcing them to automatically open as he scooped the young boy off the cart and into his arms.

"Grab the IVs!" he instructed Barnett, who pulled the bottles of fluid off their poles and stepped into the elevator behind him. Two of the junior Orthopedic residents stepped off the elevator, allowing Rogers and Adam to jump in. Adam pressed against Barnett and drew in his breath as the doors closed behind him.

"Keep those IV bags up high so they're runnin'," Doyle told Barnett.

"They're holding Room 5 for us. You'd better take it," offered the senior Orthopedic resident.

The elevator made its way upwards in a slow, jerky movement. The doors opened and the Orthopedic service remained inside, one of the junior residents pushing the button on the wall panel to keep the doors apart while the general surgeons spilled into the hallway. The Orthopedic scrub nurse, anesthesiologist, and a nurse anesthetist stood in the doorway of Room 5 while Cookie, the usual general surgery scrub nurse, adjusted her mask and ran down the hall towards them. Carlos appeared from around the corner carrying four bags of blood. Doyle rushed into the operating room and placed the child on the operating table. The sheet that covered him was removed. Barnett placed the IV bottles on poles on either side of the table.

"Get me a mask," Doyle said to Barnett. "You and Sinclair too. No need to waste a lot of time scrubbing."

Barnett and Adam put on masks and briefly rinsed their hands at the scrub sink. Barnett grabbed an extra mask for Doyle, who tied it around his floral scrub cap. Cookie poured brown antiseptic fluid onto the child's belly and chest. The last bit she poured onto Doyle's hands before he slipped on a gown and gloves. After putting on his mask, Rogers gowned and gloved in time to help cover the child with sterile drapes.

Adam stood next to Rogers, across from Barnett and Doyle. Shrevi stood on a metal platform behind Doyle. The chief resident looked to the head of the table. "Ready?"

"I intubated him awake," said the anesthesiologist, "and I'll get an N/G down momentarily, but right now I've got electrical activity on his EKG but no blood pressure. Starting blood now."

When Adam looked up, he noticed Carlos assisting with hanging the blood. Somehow he had managed to fit himself with a scrub cap, mask, and shoe covers.

"Two suctions up," ordered Doyle. Barnett and Adam were each handed a suction catheter.

As soon as Doyle made an opening into the abdomen, blood rushed out and covered the surface of the belly. Rogers wiped some away with a lap pad and placed the tips of Adam and Barnett's suctions into the depth of the incision. Doyle stayed focused, continuing the incision the length of the abdomen.

The two medical students pushed the suction tips frantically around the open body cavity. The drainage tubing jumped and pulsated as Adam watched the steady stream of red be pulled into the suction canister. Even so, he had trouble seeing the operative field because the blood collected quicker than both the suction tips could remove it.

"Spleen's ruptured," said Doyle, "but, shit, the kid's liver is almost split in half!"

"I got no pressure," said the anesthesiologist.

"Keep sucking!" Doyle stated. "Give me some lap pads!"

He took the large cloth pads from the nurse and immediately stuffed several into the left upper portion of the abdomen against the spleen.

Kittamura joined the table opposite him, forcing Rogers and Adam to each take one step to their left. "Got a ruptured spleen packed off, but there's a bad liver injury here. Sinclair, get your suction back in here and use your other hand to hold this."

A metal retractor was placed along the edge of the incision and Adam pushed the catheter tip further into the belly.

"Move the Mayo blade up a bit and pull harder… Now everybody listen up, here's what we're gonna do. I'm going to compress the liver." He already had lap pads down and was pushing the cracked edges together. "We're not going to do anything else until we've got a pressure back."

"Second unit is in… Hanging the third blood," said the anesthesiologist.

Doyle calmly held the child's liver together. Kittamura made sure there was no bleeding around the pads over the spleen. Carlos helped the anesthesiologist and nurse anesthetist with the blood as they worked feverishly at the head of the table.

The footsteps of the Blood Bank tech could be heard in the hallway as he brought more blood and plasma to the door.

The anesthesiologist announced, "Blood pressure's up to between 90 and 100. Do what you gotta, I've got more blood and plasma ready."

Doyle took a moment to survey the belly, allowing Adam to notice that Kittamura's left hand was deep in the boy's belly just beneath the lower edge of the liver.

That's the Pringle maneuver they talked about in Anatomy class, thought Adam, recognizing that Kittamura's immobile grip was compressing the blood vessels that fed into the liver and reducing the amount of bleeding from the damaged organ.

"Kitty, this boy's gonna have to lose the whole right side of his liver." Doyle placed more gauze pads in the incision before addressing Anesthesia at the head of the table. "Gallbladder is in the way and has to come out before we do the resection… Keep the blood coming."

In the hands of the junior residents like Turk, Wantz, or Kochenko, Adam had observed that removing a gallbladder was a big operation unto itself, but in this instance Doyle dissected, isolated, tied off, and divided the important structures, peeled the gallbladder off the bottom edge of the liver, and deposited it in the metal basin offered by Cookie in about three minutes.

"Pressure's still holding," Anesthesia reported.

Doyle grabbed Barnett's suction, poked it along the liver's outline, removed much of the dark blood that had continued to accumulate, handed the suction back to Barnett, and announced, "Okay, everybody, here goes."

He used his index finger to bluntly divide the bridge of remaining tissue connecting the right lobe of the liver to the left side. Adam and Barnett stared as he lifted half the liver out of the abdomen and dropped it into the basin offered by Cookie. They watched transfixed as he and Kittamura worked simultaneously to stitch and cauterize the little vessels and bile ducts on the raw surface of the remaining liver. Doyle placed more lap pads to absorb the dark blood that had oozed into the operative field.

Doyle then began to remove the other lap pads he had packed around and under the damaged organ. Dark blood continued to accumulate from somewhere behind the liver.

"This little fella probably tore a hepatic vein from where it drains into the cava," Rogers finally spoke from his position between Adam and Kittamura.

"'Spect so," said Doyle.

"Very bad injury," agreed Kittamura as he completed oversewing one of the larger veins coursing through the torn liver.

Barnett and Adam continued to direct their suctions to the dark blood filling the area.

"Pressure's dropped to 60," said Anesthesia.

"I don't have good exposure, but I'm sure he has torn at least the right hepatic vein," said Doyle.

Adam remembered the difficult exposure of Leticia Powell's injury and the challenge of identifying the tiny hepatic veins in Anatomy lab.

Doyle wasn't hesitating. He removed Barnett's retractor from the right rib cage and Cookie handed him another scalpel.

"I'm going to open the chest and split part of the diaphragm. Better to risk a paralyzed diaphragm than to have a dead kid."

Although antiseptic iodine had been poured over both the chest and abdomen, in their haste the residents had placed the sterile towels and drapes so that they covered the lower rib cage as though only an abdominal procedure was about to take place.

Doyle angled his blade off the midline abdominal incision and didn't pause as he cut through the drapes, towels, and right lower rib cage, including the cartilage that connected the lower ribs to the breastbone. He used a scissors to partially cut through the diaphragm muscle so that when he asked for the "Finichetto," he was able to place the rib retractor without difficulty and create a much larger operative field.

Barnett leaned in and Adam stood on his tiptoes and craned his neck to see into the incision. The vena cava, the largest vein in the abdomen, was laid out so that all the anatomy was much easier to see than it had been in the students' cadavers. Even the tiny torn right hepatic vein could be seen where it connected to the cava's surface, dark blood still oozing from the torn end.

"Middle and left veins are still intact." Doyle sounded relieved. "Give me a small Satinsky clamp and get a double armed Four O Prolene ready."

He placed the angled vascular clamp on the torn vein and had Barnett hold the clamp. "Pull up and tear it and you flunk the rotation," he cautioned.

Barnett never took his eyes off the clamp. He remained so immobile that even his breathing was imperceptible while Doyle stitched the blue Prolene suture around the vein and carefully tied it under the clamp.

"OK," he said, "open the clamp but don't remove it."

Barnett released the clamp and remained motionless until Doyle lifted the clamp from his hand and announced, "No bleeding."

Rogers' beeper went off.

"Why don't you take off. We'll get the spleen out and make sure there's no other injuries. Gonna need chest tubes and a bunch of drains when we close," said Doyle.

Rogers stepped away while Doyle readjusted his exposure to begin removing the spleen.

Doyle moved quickly and, after dissection and tying, plopped the spleen into a metal basin. He spent a long time examining the rest of the abdomen, making sure there were no other injuries. Pancreas, stomach, kidneys, bladder, and small and large bowel were all intact and free of damage. He began the process of placing drains and closing the incision.

"Did you give any antibiotic?" Doyle asked Anesthesia.

"Yeah, Bobby, we hung some Keflin when you started. Pressure's up and holding. He's making some urine too."

Adam shared the sense of relief in the room and watched attentively as the residents worked together to close all the layers of the big incision. He and Barnett were allowed to place some of the sutures for the final layer of skin. When the dressings were applied, they stepped back and removed their gowns and gloves. Adam looked at the boy on the operating table, still alive despite the severe trauma. A wave of exultation suddenly overcame him, accompanied by the sense that he had been part of something so dramatic it seemed miraculous.

He knew Barnett felt the same way when he said, "That was amazing… Really something."

Hearing him, Doyle looked at both students. "Yeah," he said, "really something… I know who is going to get the SNOW award this week."

CHAPTER 74

TURK WAS WAITING for the liver injury in Recovery. Doyle and Kittamura described the operative findings to him while the three students huddled over the chart at the nurses' desk. Barnett pulled a spiral-bound manual of surgical care from his coat pocket and opened to the section on post-operative orders. Adam held an order sheet and a pen in his hand while Shrevi pulled up chairs so that they could collaborate on the orders.

Turk looked over their shoulders.

"This kid has lost a significant portion of his liver and with it a big part of where his body stores glucose. His blood sugars could drop, so we should change his IV fluids to 10 percent dextrose rather than 5 percent, and we should measure his blood sugar every six hours for a while."

"Like the way we monitor a diabetic?" asked Shrevi.

"Yeah, pretty similar."

"That's sure not in this manual's outline of post-op orders," said Barnett.

"Pretty specific to liver resections," explained Turk.

Together, the students worked on the post-op orders. They discussed each entry before Adam transcribed the specific order. Turk stood by, patiently watching and explaining every order's rationale. He discussed the possible complications that could accompany such an involved operation and described how they would monitor the young boy and, hopefully, guide him to an uncomplicated recovery.

When the order sheet was completed, Turk left the unit and the students spent a moment reviewing the orders they had written.

"I feel like I just took a whole course in liver resections," said Shrevi.

"That was like reading the textbook," agreed Barnett.

"Easier to remember, I hope," added Adam.

❧

When they returned, the Emergency Room was quite busy. There was an unwritten rule that as darkness approached, more and more patients would descend on the ER, some under their own power while others arrived by ambulance or were helped by neighbors, friends, or relatives.

Wantz had been insistent that students stay with him. Shrevi and Barnett were recruited to stay close, handle any tasks the resident assigned them, and be available to accompany him to surgery.

Adam found Kochenko and Turk, in a moment of calm, sitting on a cart in the hallway across from one of the trauma rooms. He joined their rather lighthearted conversation. They discussed what bands were scheduled to play the Warehouse and bemoaned the fact that neither of them would be able to attend any of the shows. Kochenko mentioned the latest scandal swirling about the governor, as the Times-Picayune had reported that another bribery investigation was opening. They discussed the approaching storm.

Kochenko spoke in more serious tones when he quietly asked Turk, "Do you know what you're going to do next year?"

That was the first time Adam had heard anyone speak to Turk about the fact that he was being sent to the lab as a preliminary to losing his place in the training program.

Turk didn't make eye contact and spoke in a soft voice. "I just plan to do a successful lab project and hopefully there will be a spot for me when I finish."

Before Kochenko could respond, one of the nurses approached them.

"Lady with abdominal pain in Medicine Triage," she said.

Turk jumped down from the cart. "I'll go."

Adam hung back, waiting for Kochenko to comment on his friend's fate.

When Turk was out of earshot, the resident spoke.

"Denial. Nobody wants to accept that they're going to be forced out of the program. Guys like Brewster only judge people by how technically aggressive and fast they are... It doesn't mean you can't learn the necessary skills. Too bad. He's a good guy... It'll be hard for him to find another program. Let's go see that patient with Turk."

They found Turk standing outside the triage cubicle next to Battiste.

"Terrible pain," Turk said, "but after I did a rectal exam she went into the washroom and had a bowel movement. Pain's gone."

"Probably what Doyle calls 'a deep fart arrest,'" said Kochenko.

"Comme ci, comme ca," added Battiste. "Aren't you the student who was seeing that young girl with the voodoo curse?"

"Yeah," said Adam.

"Remember the old lady they found saying the curse over her?"

"Sure, I couldn't forget that story."

"Turns out the girl had been raped. It was the old lady's grandson who was going to go on trial for the rape. Trial date was approaching," said Battiste.

"But you don't think the curse did anything?" said Adam.

"I'm still at a loss to explain why her kidneys failed so quickly. No victim, no trial. Not everything is in the textbook, you know?" shrugged Battiste.

"Told you, strong juju," said Kochenko.

Thinking of that bizarre curse while walking down the hallway was still giving Adam chills when a patient was suddenly pushed past him and wheeled into a nearby trauma room.

Officers Beaudry and Guidry guided the cart towards the room. Holiday, Kittamura, Rogers, Wantz, and Shrevi turned the corner from an adjacent hallway and quickened their pace towards the room.

"Drug deal went bad," Beaudry said to Holiday. "This guy was shot in the belly, and then, when he was down on the ground, a guy held a pistol to his face and fired. Can't believe it, point blank and the guy is still conscious."

"This we gotta see," said Kochenko, motioning for Adam to follow him into the trauma room.

Rogers was already examining the patient as he was helping to lift him off the ambulance stretcher and onto the ER cart. The patient was spitting blood and swearing as Rogers examined him.

"Lucky," he announced. "Small caliber entered the maxillary sinus by the nose and angled out through the cheek, nothing deeper… Gonna have to explore his belly, though."

Adam stood near the back of the room and watched the nurse move the patient's belongings off the stretcher. He immediately recognized Admiral Franklin's yachting cap and jacket as they were piled into the corner, but then she surprised him by tossing a dark blue, tattered and worn gym bag onto the pile. Adam recognized his lock still attached to one of the handles. The bag looked like it had been through a war since he had last seen it. He couldn't help but reach for it and started to enter the combination of the lock.

"What're you doin'?" demanded Officer Guidry.

"This is my bag," answered Adam. "It was stolen when I left it down here."

"It's loaded with pills, weed, and some white powder. Leave it alone; it's evidence now."

He dropped the bag onto the pile of clothing. *You really do have to watch your stuff around here. Good thing my textbook wasn't in it.*

Chapter 75

THE TWO AND a half hours of sleep between 2:30 and 5:00 a.m. left Adam feeling refreshed when he arrived to begin rounds in the Recovery Room. Shrevi had not been so fortunate. His hair was disheveled, his scrub suit rumpled, and there were dark circles under his eyes. Wantz had kept him up all night, directing him on which patients and lab results to check, tasks that easily could have waited until morning.

"How's the gunshot wound?" asked Shrevi.

"Not awake enough yet for them to take him off the ventilator," Adam answered.

Admiral Franklin remained motionless and intubated, with a large, eccentric dressing wrapped around his head to incorporate the bullet wound in his cheek.

"Had one small caliber shot to the belly... Hit the left colon. They just pulled up the intestine and brought it out as a colostomy, cleaned up the facial wound and packed it with iodine gauze."

Adam turned his attention to the boy with the liver injury. Like Admiral Franklin, he too remained on the ventilator; his blood pressure and pulse remained stable. A greenish stain on the dressings marked the sites of the underlying drains, but it appeared to Adam that it was not a significant leakage of bile. He listened to the boy's chest with his stethoscope, drew and spun his hematocrit, and wrote a chart note before he headed for the elevator to take him to the wards. Watching the elevator doors quietly close brought to mind the image from yesterday of Doyle kicking open the door while cradling the dying child. By all consideration, Doyle's care of this child was heroic. Adam recognized the contradictions in Doyle's seemingly racist comments. Life in the South was not always black and white.

Rogers and Kochenko were standing near the nurses' desk, surveying the ward, when Adam arrived. Since they had finished the night on call, not only were all the beds occupied but three additional patients remained on ER carts that had been crowded in between the regular beds. At the far end of the ward, Bunkie Smith and Teddy were still sleeping. Bunkie was in such a weakened state that while he lay back on his pillow with his eyes closed, Adam had to watch closely for a long time just to be sure he was still breathing. Teddy was snoring while wearing a black mask and earplugs with an ice pack propped across his forehead.

"With the storm coming, we need to clear out the wards as much as possible," said Rogers. "Gotta get these patients off the carts and into beds so they can have the carts back in the ER."

"That guy with the diaphragm hernia has been scheduled to go to a nursing home today. He'll benefit from the occupational and physical therapy," said Kochenko.

Adam was surprised that Ronald would be discharged in his present state. When he thought about it, however, he realized that perhaps Ronald wouldn't completely recover. Given that he was now more awake and could actually use a spoon to shakily feed himself, there actually might be a significant benefit to placing him where therapy was available.

"The old guy with cholangitis can go back with his daughter and grandson," said Rogers. "He'll probably prefer to ride out the storm at home with them."

Adam knew that was correct. Sam Elder had been asking to go home since he woke up after surgery.

"And Teddy could have gone home yesterday," added Kochenko. "He's fine. We may have a couple more who can go home, and I'm sure there's some on the female side... Couple of gallbladders, a hernia, and a breast biopsy."

Adam didn't understand why, but for some reason it struck him that in the whole discussion Teddy was the only patient the residents referred to by name.

CHAPTER 76

"**THEODORAKIS FLEW TO** Boston," said Barnett. "He's the keynote speaker at the Mass. General surgical meeting. Brewster is in charge of Grand Rounds and Bullpen."

Adam looked down at the dour little man standing at the lectern. Bald-headed with a humorless military bearing, Brewster was known to delight in intimidating residents and students alike. Adam took his seat reluctantly, recalling Melissa's comments about how she was being treated on Service 4 and Brewster's display towards her during the breast cancer lecture.

The first Bullpen case presented was a forty-six-year-old man who presented to clinic with complaints of weight loss, right flank pain, and dark urine. The student recited his history and physical exam. During the presentation, the man looked up and acknowledged the audience of students, smiling occasionally at the young doctors.

"His abdominal exam revealed a firm 8-by-11-centimeter mass on the right with some tenderness on flank palpation."

The student finished his presentation, feigning an air of confidence, but when Brewster began pacing in front of him, he became visibly weak in the knees.

"What X-ray would you order on this patient?" asked Brewster.

"I would order a lower GI," the student answered meekly.

"You would order a test that would fill this patient's bowels with contrast that would obscure the findings of any necessary additional radiographic studies and might hinder making an accurate diagnosis?"

The trembling student closed his eyes and leaned on the lectern as he slumped forward. Wantz sprang from the nearby bench, dropping the patient's X-ray folder but catching the student by the right arm before he could hit the floor. Kochenko rose from his seat and rushed around the front of the lectern, grabbing the student's left arm. The residents supported the pale young man, who opened his eyes and shook his head as he regained consciousness.

"Get him some orange juice," Brewster instructed the two residents as they escorted the student from the amphitheater. Brewster wasted no time in retrieving the X-ray folder from the floor and turning back towards the audience.

"Since our regular participant is indisposed, I will direct my questions elsewhere. Miss Engstrom," he said, looking up at Melissa, "perhaps you can tell us what would be the appropriate first X-ray for this patient?"

Adam watched Melissa's shoulders rise and the back of her neck stiffen. Amidst a few scattered gasps from the crowd, Shrevi leaned towards his friends and whispered, "Holy shit, I've never seen them put anybody in the audience on the spot."

Melissa's head was down when she softly answered.

"I can't hear you," said Brewster. "Why don't you stand up so your voice projects?"

Although she was tall, Melissa stood with a posture that implied she wanted to be as small as possible.

"That's better," said Brewster. "Now, what was your answer?"

"I'd get a kidney X-ray."

"And what's that called?"

"An IVP."

"No, what's the proper full name?"

"An intravenous pyelogram."

Dr. Brewster pulled films from the patient's folder and held them up towards the ceiling light while he selected which films to mount on the X-ray view box. He finally selected one that, when illuminated on the view box, showed contrast giving a normal appearance to the left kidney while on the patient's right side the contrast material was wildly distorted into an image that in no way resembled the normal organ.

"Read this, please," he directed Melissa.

"That's not fair," whispered Shrevi. "We haven't studied any of that kidney stuff… That's Urology."

"I think the abnormal appearance represents a kidney tumor, possibly a cancer," answered Melissa.

"Yes, but I asked you to *read* the film, not give me your diagnosis. Read it like a radiologist."

"There is a normal appearance to the left kidney. The contrast in the right kidney reveals distortion of the normal anatomy."

Brewster paused. He seemed to be waiting for more. Finally he spoke with an air of disgust. "I suppose that will have to suffice… Now, what can you tell me about this patient's treatment?"

"It should be removed."

"And what's that called—a kidney removal?"

"A nephrectomy."

"OK, now suppose you operate on this patient to perform a nephrectomy and you find the patient has a nodule of metastatic cancer in his liver. How should that be treated?"

Barnett frowned. "We don't know that… That's for residents."

Melissa was quiet, thinking for a moment before she looked at the floor and whispered, "I don't know."

Brewster pounced like a tiger. "I can't believe you are not familiar with the important paper by Straus and Scanlon from the 1956 *Archives of Surgery*, in which they reported a case of five-year survival after a metastatic renal tumor in the liver was removed."

Melissa hung her head. Shrevi turned towards Adam and Barnett and whispered, "Damn, how are we supposed to know that? We don't even have time to read the assigned textbook."

Melissa stood silently while Brewster addressed the gathering.

"I can see there is no point in continuing this discourse. However, before you are dismissed, I have an announcement to make. As you know by now, there is a storm gaining strength in the Gulf. It is moving towards the city and is expected to make landfall some time tomorrow. The hospital will be preparing for emergency status and therefore all non-essential personnel will be excused. Medical students will not be required in the hospital but will be expected to return to their clerkships after the storm has passed. Please take emergency precautions."

The students stood to leave. Melissa was the first one out the door. Adam tried to follow her, but by the time he reached the elevators, the doors were closed, and she was gone.

He waited for the next elevator with Barnett and Shrevi.

"My wife has been packing the car, but I guess now I can drive her and the baby to her aunt's in Jackson," said Barnett.

"This will give me time to go help my parents get ready for the storm," added Shrevi.

"I've never been through anything like this. What did Brewster mean by 'emergency precautions'?" said Adam.

"Oh, you know," said Shrevi, "buy a flashlight, a transistor radio, extra batteries, canned foods like fruits and stuff you don't need to cook, tape the glass in your windows…and fill your bathtub with water in case there isn't any drinking water for a few days."

Shrevi had repeated almost exactly the instructions Adam had received from the bartender.

"Where can I get that stuff?" asked Adam. "There's a little grocery in the Quarter, but I don't know where to get that other stuff."

"LaFollette Brothers Hardware…on Magazine Street near Constantinople. Everybody goes there," said Shrevi.

"Big storm's comin'," said Luanne when Adam arrived to change her dressing.

She pointed to the window. "Sky is not so bad now, but just wait… I spent a whole day during Betsy hiding in my bathroom. You be careful outside."

"They told all of us medical students to leave and come back after the storm."

"Who's going to change my dressing?" asked Luanne.

Adam smiled when he recognized that at least one person didn't feel he was "non-essential."

"Don't worry," he said. "I'm sure your wound will be OK."

He silently wondered if it would be OK to miss a few dressing changes or if her open wound would again turn into a sloppy mess.

"I'll get back as soon as I can," he assured her. "I'll plan to do a bit more reading on how to care for your incision."

He had studied the chapter on wound care and the remaining untouched reading assignments were daunting, but even though he didn't have time to do the reading, he would be anxious to get back on the ward after the storm.. The time spent with patients was both instructive and enjoyable.

With three of his patients being discharged in the face of the oncoming storm, Adam was drawn back to the male ward. Ronald had already been transferred to the nursing facility and Sam Elder's daughter and grandson had taken him home. The ward seemed quiet and relatively empty, with the exception of the activity around Teddy's bed. Laurance and his boyfriend stood at the foot. They could have easily taken Teddy downstairs in a borrowed wheelchair or, like most patients, Teddy could have walked out of the ward under his own power.

Teddy had, however, hired a private ambulance to take him home. The attendants helped him transfer onto the gurney after they had waited while he combed his hair and goatee and put on the silk robe that Laurance had brought from his apartment. He took a few moments to say goodbye to Bunkie Smith and reached out to shake his hand before they wheeled him into the aisle. Teddy sat upright as they slowly made their way towards the door with Laurance and his paramour in tow, each carrying a bag of Teddy's belongings. Teddy smiled and waved to each of the patients as they passed the other beds. They stopped at the nurses' desk where Adam stood.

"Merci, mon cher Docteur, Merci," said Teddy. "I must get home to prepare for the storm, although Laurance has already wrapped and crated my Steuben crystal... Who would have known when we enjoyed our first café au lait together that I would someday be indebted to you for saving my life? Merci beaucoup, mon Docteur!"

They wheeled Teddy into the hallway towards the elevator, where he waved to a group of housekeepers like Rex, the King of Mardi Gras, waving from the lead float in the annual parade.

CHAPTER 77

LaFollette's Hardware was a two-story brick building that opened onto Magazine Street. Its tall double doors were flanked on either side by large windows, positioned under sturdy brick arches. Iron bars on the windows, both inside and outside the building, protected against intruders but still allowed natural light to fill the building's main floor.

Once inside, Adam noticed the original intricate tin ceiling and the dark wooden floor planks worn down by years of traffic. To the right of the counter, a well-used stairway extended to a mezzanine where the store's office space was located. An old Victorian frame hung in the middle of the mezzanine's railing with a nicely embroidered message: "If we don't got it, you don't need it!" To Adam's left, a man sat on a blue cushion on top of a barrel that was dwarfed by the man's size. He was quite a sight, wearing work boots with leather laces and dingy socks that had lost both their whiteness and stretch. He had colorful shorts embellished with images of crawfish, red suspenders, and a tan, almost military-style short-sleeved shirt with epaulettes. His head was topped with a beat-up derby hat from which a pheasant feather drooped.

"What's your story?" he asked Adam.

"What?" said Adam.

"Your story," said the man. "It's hurricane season. Everybody in New Orleans has got a hurricane story."

"I don't have a story," said Adam. "I'm a medical student and my friend said this is where I need to come to prepare for the storm."

"You gonna need lotsa things," said the man. He reached for the rope dangling from the large iron bell that rested on the end of the counter and clanged the clapper.

From somewhere among the rows of tools, a skinny little old man appeared. He had thinning, short white hair and skin that looked like he had seen too much sunlight or smoked too many cigarettes or both.

"Lamar," drawled the fat man, "we got a newbie! First time he been in the path of a hurricane… I see you brought your own bag."

Adam offered them the canvas book bag that he had emptied before leaving his apartment.

"Get him a flashlight… Give him that medium-sized one… not the big one. Smaller one throws more light and is cheaper… But you're gonna need a lantern too… Got a nice red one. Don't take the same badrees, but we'll give you extras of both kinds… Can't have too many badrees if the lights stay out for a few days. You'll need window tape too. They say you should use masking tape, but truth is it don't hold well; duct tape is better. Harder to peel off after the storm but lots better to prevent them flying shards or big chunks of broken glass. Give him that big roll… Got a portable radio?"

"No, sir," answered Adam.

"Gonna need one… We got a real nice Panasonic. Lamar, get him one of those, and don't forget the badrees… Always need those badrees… Best give him extra. Well, that's a start. You got food—I don't mean none of them perishables?"

"Yessir. I've got a bunch of canned goods—fruits and stuff."

"Well, if the power fails, don't let that fruit juice go to waste… We got a little camp stove runs on a small tank of propane gas if you need it… Got a kayak too if it floods."

"Thanks," said Adam, "but I think I'll pass on the stove… and the kayak."

"All right, then," said the man. He grabbed Adam's canvas bag and tossed it to Lamar. "You know what to do."

"Be right back, Charlie," Lamar said as he scurried away and disappeared down one of the aisles.

He wasn't gone long. Adam stood at the counter as Lamar rang up the order and carefully repacked the canvas bag while Adam placed his payment on the counter.

"You want a Dixie?" asked Charlie, opening the big cooler next to him.

"No, thanks," said Adam.

"Well, you best take one of these, then." Charlie slid a can of root beer along the counter. "Gotta drink plenty of fluid when that hurricane's bearing down."

"Thanks." Adam placed the can in his bag and was almost out the door when Charlie yelled after him.

"And don't forget to fill your bathtub with water."

The seven-block walk while carrying his bag of purchases to the streetcar on St. Charles Avenue built up Adam's appetite and reminded him that he had nothing to eat at home unless he wanted to open the provisions he had purchased for the storm.

Across St. Charles he noticed a small po-boy shop nestled in between a record store and a laundromat. Adam crossed the street and stopped to look in the window of the record store. Next to the recent releases by Jethro Tull, Quicksilver Messenger Service, and the Grateful Dead were the covers of albums by Clifton Chenier, the Meters, and Dr. John, and a piece of cardboard on which had been written, "Visit our Collection of Local New Orleans Artists." Adam stepped into the dimly lit shop and went directly to the bins labeled New Orleans Music. There were seven or eight Bunkie Smith albums, but the one he liked best had a picture on the cover of a much younger, smiling Bunkie surrounded by White musicians in colorful, widely striped sport coats, crisp slacks, and white shoes. The title "Bunkie and the Dukes of Dixieland" figured prominently above the picture. Adam purchased the album and slid it into his canvas bag before going into the sandwich shop next door.

When his sandwich was ready, Adam stuffed it into his bag and crossed to the center of St. Charles, where he waited on the grass next to the tracks. Looking up the street, he could just make out in the distance the headlight of an approaching streetcar. He looked at the clouds, so closely joined together that their undersurface created a dark gray ceiling. As the tightly packed clouds drifted, the white patches above the gray occasionally opened to reveal a glimpse of remaining blue sky. Despite the motion of the clouds, Adam could feel no breeze, and the leaves of the nearby trees did not move at all.

Week Five

CHAPTER 78

ADAM TURNED ON the lamp in his living room, but the apartment remained dark. Behind the duct tape crisscrossing the windows, the charcoal sky and sheets of rain blocked the light.

He'd been sitting on his couch since the sound of the arriving storm had awakened him. He spent a considerable amount of time staring at the walls before he decided that even with all his preparation, this was not where he wanted to ride out the storm. Remembering Miss Viola's story from her childhood, Adam decided that he wanted to be at Charity. Not only would the building provide safety, but he could probably share one of the remaining residents' call rooms, and if things got really bad, maybe he could be of some help to the residents.

Pulling the dry cleaner's protective plastic off the sport coat in his closet and spreading it out on the floor, he placed his lecture notes and textbook on the plastic along with two pairs of clean underwear and a clean shirt. He folded and stuffed his white coat into the bottom of his book bag, along with his stethoscope. Then he carefully folded the plastic and placed the wrapped contents into the bag. Almost as an afterthought, he dropped in his toothbrush and a tube of Crest. There was no room for any of the provisions from the grocery store. He hoped the residents' dining room would remain in operation.

As he had no raincoat, he slipped on an old blue nylon windbreaker from college. Before leaving his apartment, he grabbed the bag of potato chips and zipped them into his jacket.

Standing under the balcony in front of his apartment, Adam paused as the storm blew rain against his face. There was no one else on the street. Down the block, the awnings flapped on the closed-up shops. The pelting rain filled the spaces between the cobblestones, creating currents that flowed like miniature rapids.

He was starting to have second thoughts about trying to brave the weather when he saw the approaching headlights. A lone taxicab was still on the streets. He waved down the cab and stepped into the rain to approach the driver's side. The driver cracked the window.

"You crazy to be out here," he said.

"You still workin'?" asked Adam.

"Going home."

"Could you do one more fare?"

"Where you goin'?"

"Charity."

"You a doctor?"

"Yeah."

"Get in."

Adam included a big tip with the fare but felt that no amount could express his gratitude for the ride. "Be safe," he advised the cab driver as he ran towards the front of the hospital. The massive building blocked the wind, and Adam arrived in the foyer relatively dry.

⌒⌢

Luanne was clearly surprised when he appeared at her bedside and placed his bag on the floor before readying her new dressing supplies.

"What you doin' here?" she asked.

"I missed you…and your belly," he said, giving her a wink. "You're healing too well to miss a dressing change. Besides, I was in the neighborhood."

The hallway was dark and the rain slammed against the windows with much more force than it had carried on the lower floors. The doors to the residents' call rooms were closed. For a moment Adam wasn't certain he would find anyone, but suddenly Turk appeared carrying several bottles of soda.

"What are you doing here?" he asked.

"Didn't seem my apartment was the place to be."

"We're hanging out in Kittamura's room. He's got a TV. C'mon."

They entered Kittamura's call room, a small space made larger by having one bed removed and replaced with a bookcase made of pine boards supported by cinder blocks. The top board held an electric teapot, a hot plate, and a kitchen rack containing a few pots and pans as well as silverware, plates and cups, and a small portable TV. Natural light came through the tall windows above the bookcase. A small Oriental carpet sat in the middle of the room with a low veneered coffee table surrounded by flat pillows for seating. Against the opposite wall was a bed. A wheeled clothes rack sat adjacent to the call room lockers in the corner, bracketed by a standard issue dresser on the far wall with a tiny refrigerator filling the corner on the right.

Holiday was sitting on the foot of the bed. Wantz sat forward on the other end. Kochenko sat cross-legged on one of the mats at the low coffee table, sipping a cup of hot tea. Kittamura stood near the windowsill, adjusting the rabbit ears on a small Sony TV.

"See what the storm blew in," said Turk, placing the bottles of soda on the table. Adam set the bag of potato chips down.

"Didn't have any better place to be, so I thought maybe I could be of help if things got bad."

"We're not even the scheduled backup for the ER," said Holiday, "so we'll only get called if things get really nasty down there…but we might be a little short-handed. Rogers is at Judy's and Doyle's moving his wife and kids further inland."

Adam paused. He hadn't even known Doyle was married.

"Have a seat," said Kochenko.

"You want tea?" offered Kittamura. "Good tea."

Kittamura had corrected the reception on his TV, and they sat in silence, watching the familiar visage of Rob Swelter with his dignified tie and sport coat, not a well-gelled hair on his head out of place.

"The Army Corps of Engineers has assured us that it is highly unlikely that any storm would breach the levees." He looked directly into the camera. "Residents are advised, nevertheless, to take all necessary precautions."

Someone handed him a slip of paper, and he read it twice through before looking up into the camera again.

"The U.S. Weather Bureau has just issued a statement that the storm has shifted and will not make landfall in New Orleans...will NOT make landfall in the city of New Orleans."

His eyes brightened and he straightened in his chair. "Landfall will not, I repeat, NOT be in the city. We are spared... The city is SAVED!"

He hung on the last word, sounding like an old school tent revivalist whipping into a religious frenzy. He looked up to the ceiling and raised his hands.

"The city is saved... We are SAVED... Praise the Lord, we are saved! THANK YOU, GOD JESUS, WE ARE SAVED!"

A somber Rob suddenly lowered his arms and looked back into the camera. "Of course, that is rather bad news for our viewers to the west in Thibodeaux..."

CHAPTER 79

ADAM DRAGGED HIMSELF off the extra cot in Holiday's call room. He made his way to the door in the dark so as not to disturb the senior resident who'd been sleeping across from him. By quarter to five he'd started rounds on the female ward, and even though he was only following the breast cancer patient, he felt he should see Barnett and Shrevi's patients in case their return was delayed by the storm.

He completed rounds quickly because most of the patients on this unit had been admitted through the clinic for elective surgery—no complicated injuries or gunshot wounds. He changed the dressings and wrote notes on the breast biopsies, incisional hernias, colon resection, and gallbladder patients with an efficiency he'd lacked just four weeks ago. He spun the hematocrits and recorded the values in his pocket notebook.

Moving to the male ward, he stood at the foot of Bunkie Smith's bed reading the chart when Shrevi approached him just as the first rays of the sun were finding their way past the drawn window shades.

"My parents are OK," said Shrevi. "No problem riding the storm out across the river, and my mom spent two days cooking in advance, so I've had my fill of Indian food for the month. What's going on here?"

"I came back to stay here with the residents," said Adam. "Slept in Holiday's call room, so I got an early start. Finished work rounds on the female side... Saw all the patients since I wasn't sure when you'd be back. Let's divide up Barnett's patients and finish here, then get ICU done before lecture."

Both students moved with equal speed, soon meeting up in the treatment room, where they spun the patients' hematocrits and recorded them in Adam's notebook.

"We've still got to see the boy with the liver injury in ICU," said Adam, "and I've got a dressing to change on the Gyne floor."

"Go ahead and do that," said Shrevi. "Meet you in ICU."

By the time Adam arrived in ICU, Shrevi was listening to the young boy's chest with his stethoscope. The boy remained on the ventilator, but review of his blood pressures and pulse rate indicated that he was very stable. A small greenish stain remained on the dressings covering the drains in his belly.

"I don't think that's any significant bile leakage," said Adam, indicating the spot on the dressings. "Not enough to measure. Maybe we should just leave the dressing unchanged so the residents can see for themselves."

"OK by me," answered Shrevi. "Gives us plenty of time to kill before lecture. Cafeteria's open now. I could go for some scrambled eggs and toast before class."

Adam was tempted to return to the male ward in hopes that Jen would have arrived to start her shift. He thought better of that idea, though, considering that he was unshaven, unshowered, and hadn't even bothered to brush his teeth yet that morning. His uncombed hair and the wrinkled scrub suit he had slept in would not make a good impression either. Besides, after a dinner that had consisted of only potato chips and the cup of warm noodles in broth that Kittamura had prepared for him, a plate of sausage, eggs, grits, and biscuits would be most welcome.

Towards the end of the morning's lecture about the anatomy and indications for removal of the spleen, Barnett sneaked into the lecture hall through the side door at the rear of the room and took a seat in the last row. After lecture, Adam and Shrevi joined him at the back of the hall.

"We got rounds done this morning," said Adam. "I've got all your patients' hematocrits in my notebook."

"Thanks," said Barnett. "I drove back in record time. Not a lot of people on the roads yet. My wife and the baby are going to stay at her aunt's for a few more days."

They made their way downstairs, but when they were ready to cross the street to the hospital they found a crowd of angry demonstrators blocking the entrance. People were shouting and carrying placards with a variety of messages: "Stop Beating Black People!", "End Police Brutality!", "Charity Doesn't Care!"

Adam didn't understand what was going on until the three of them made their way to the corner. Not only was there a crowd gathered at the ER entrance at the side of the building, but another crowd with similar signs blocked access at the front entrance to the hospital. A voice boomed through a hand-held megaphone, urging on the demonstrators. Adam recognized the man holding the megaphone as the young man in the bright dashiki and sunglasses who had confronted Officers Beaudry and Guidry when they had struggled with the unruly patient in custody three days ago.

"Shit," said Shrevi, "we can't get in this way. Follow me."

He turned and the others followed, hugging the wall of the medical school to keep a safe distance from the demonstrators across the street. At the corner they turned onto Gravier Street and crossed uninterrupted. Approaching the loading dock at the rear of the hospital, they caught a glimpse of a figure in a white lab coat disappearing through the doors.

"Was that Kochenko?" asked Barnett.

"We can get in here too," said Shrevi, scrambling up the wooden stairs by the dock and leading the others through the stockroom and maintenance areas until they reached familiar hallways and made their way to the Emergency Room, where Kochenko was standing and watching the tumult on the ambulance ramp beyond the double doors.

"Glad I remembered the back door," he said. "Went home last night to check on my landlady... Didn't expect all this excitement. Nobody out there probably has any idea why the cops had to be rough with that guy the other day."

Just then more motion shook the shadows in front of the frosted glass doors of the ER entrance. The clamor increased when the doors slid open and a red-faced Doyle forcibly pushed his way into the ER waiting room. He was wearing a faded blue T-shirt and cut-off white Levi shorts and carried a rolled-up scrub suit. Despite his not wearing a scrub suit, the black cloth scrub cap embroidered with the small wooden shoes of a Dutch boy didn't seem out of place on his head.

"Motherfuckers!" he muttered as he approached. "MOTH-ERRRFUCKERS! Those people beat each other, stab each other, shoot each other… They drink too much or use drugs, ignore stuff like heart disease, diabetes, and blood pressure un-til it's an emergency, and then they expect us to fix them! They don't get it that regular hospitals don't want to care for them! We're all they got and they're out there squawkin'… I'm going up to change. Meet you on the ward for rounds."

He added some odiously colorful racial slurs to the profanity, sputtering and stomping past Kochenko and the wide-eyed students who were silently left in his wake.

After they caught their breath, Kochenko spoke in a soft, calm voice. "It's a question of balance. Places like Charity exist to take care of people who live in areas prone to violence, poverty, and a whole raft of social problems we can't correct. Basically, we exist to help these folks, and in return they let us learn and master our skills. We do the best we can with inadequate funding. I'm sure they don't know that guy the police beat up was on drugs, hitting a pregnant girl with a baseball bat. I can see how they pissed Doyle off. Let's go make rounds."

Despite the interruption caused by the storm, Barnett, Shrevi, and Adam were up to date on the patients on Service 1. Perhaps because the storm had bypassed the city, or maybe because the slackening storm had slowed Charity's pace that day, the senior residents didn't seem to mind answering the students' questions, and they even took the time to review some of the textbook material that applied to specific patients.

Admiral Franklin had been transferred to the floor and sat upright with an expression on his face that suggested he was looking for a fight. Upstairs, he had pulled out his breathing tube before he had been evaluated to ensure it was safe to remove. He followed that almost immediately by pulling the nasogastric tube from his nose.

"Which one of you mofos is the guy who put this bag on me? I can't live leaking shit onto my belly, and why is this tube in my dick? I wasn't shot there. I oughta kill the guy who put this bag on me…"

There was silence from the residents. Adam didn't take the Admiral's threat lightly. He wondered if doctors at private hospitals ever heard that sort of thing.

Without altering his typically detached demeanor, Holiday stepped forward and pushed the palm of his hand into the Admiral's chest with so much force that he caused the Admiral to fall back against his pillow. Holiday stepped closer and stared him in the eye.

"Let's get the rules straight here. When you fly to Florida to pick up a load of drugs or visit your aunt Bertha, you don't walk into the cockpit and start asking the pilot what all the dials and flashing lights are for, and you sure as hell don't threaten him if there's a little turbulence on the journey… So you just shut up and let us fly this plane, and when the time comes in a couple of months we'll bring you back and close your colostomy… understand?"

None of the residents had ever heard Holiday speak that way to a patient. Adam noted Rogers' smug grin when the Admiral lay back, closed his eyes, and whispered, "Yessir."

The last stop was the ICU, where the only Service 1 patient remaining was the little boy with the liver injury. He lay in bed, the flashing monitors and EKG tracing revealing a steady, regular heartbeat. Clear urine drained into his catheter bag, and he breathed normally as he slept. Adam recognized the boy's mother sitting in the chair on the left side of the bed and holding an ice pack against her son's forehead. On the opposite side of the bed sat a thin, wiry man who Adam guessed was the boy's father. When the group reached the foot of the bed, the man stood up, hat tightly gripped in his hands.

Adam reported the child's lab work and vital signs and Shrevi demonstrated the bile stain on the boy's abdominal dressing. Both were reassured when Rogers confirmed that it was probably not a significant amount of drainage.

The group headed for the door, but the boy's father stepped into the aisle and stood, his eyes welled with tears. Only Adam and Doyle noticed and paused, waiting for him to speak. Words failed him, and he stood staring after the doctors.

Adam watched Doyle step back and walk towards the man. He stood close, putting his left hand on the man's right shoulder. Doyle spoke so softly that Adam couldn't hear what was being said, but he could see the man nod in affirmation. And as Doyle stepped away, Adam could hear him say, "That's one tough boy you've got there… Don't worry, he'll be OK."

Moments later, as Adam stood waiting for the elevator doors to open, Doyle remarked, "That kid's doing so well I may have to give the SNOW award to somebody else."

CHAPTER 80

EARLY THE NEXT morning, all of Service 1 met in ICU and returned to the injured boy's bedside since the chief had indicated he wanted to see the child with the liver injury.

Dr. Theodorakis entered quietly, unaccompanied by the usual throng of students and residents. He went straight to the boy's bedside and stood between Holiday and Rogers, facing Doyle and Kittamura across the bed.

"Who can present?" he asked.

Without any hesitation, Doyle was the first to answer. "Twelve-year-old boy lying on the back seat with his seatbelt on, mother lost control of the car when a tire blew out and they hit a retaining wall... Arrived in the ER in extremis with physical exam demonstrating signs of intra-abdominal hemorrhage. Taken immediately to the OR for resuscitation and exploration..."

Doyle's presentation made the case sound routine, but the image of Doyle lifting the boy off the cart and running to the elevator flashed into Adam's head. Rushing for the closing elevator was anything but routine.

"Findings at surgery included a significant liver injury, nearly an auto-amputation of the right lobe of the liver with a torn right hepatic vein and ruptured spleen. A thoraco-abdominal incision was required for exposure. Along with the right hepatectomy, a splenectomy was performed, during which it was noted that accessory splenic tissue was present."

"What resuscitation fluid was given?" asked the chief.

"Eight units of packed cells, three plasma, and five liters of crystalloid."

Dr. Theodorakis looked at the patient and the monitoring equipment. He examined the boy's hand and felt his pulse. "I assume from the color of his palm and the character of his pulse that his blood count is adequate."

"Yes, sir," Adam was surprised to find himself answering. "Hematocrit was 28 this morning."

Theodorakis nodded and looked from the monitor to Doyle. "Nice case."

And then he was gone as silently as he had entered, leaving the residents gathered at the bedside.

No one spoke. Adam sensed that, although Doyle and Kittamura had been the operating surgeons, everyone shared in the satisfaction of a compliment from the chief.

As the residents began to leave, Adam asked Kochenko, "Is that all he wanted to see on rounds?"

"Yep," he said, "the chairman knows everything going on with this service and sometimes just wants to see what's most important."

CHAPTER 81

THE LECTURES THAT week dealt with all the surgical subspecialities. For convenience, the topics had been piggybacked together, which did not leave time to cover any subject in depth on a given day and doubled the amount of assigned reading.

Adam, Barnett, and Shrevi sat in the cafeteria after the morning lecture, worrying that the lecture material might not provide sufficient explanation for questions that might appear on the test.

"That cardiac lecture went by so fast I could barely keep up with my note-taking," said Adam. "Tamponade and pulsus paradoxus still confuse me. I wish these lecturers would start with the basics. It always helps to know the physiology or a little historical background."

"Open heart surgery has a short history," said Barnett. "Most of the guys who pioneered it are still alive."

"The textbook mentions Gibbon, Blaylock, and DeBakey," said Adam. "It says that for many years, opening the chest wasn't done…but it doesn't say who did it first."

"I did a report once on the history of heart surgery," said Barnett. "The first one on a human in the U.S. was performed in Chicago in 1893 to close a stab wound."

"That long ago? I had no idea," said Adam. "I wonder why that's not mentioned in the textbook?"

"Maybe because he was a Negro," said Barnett.

"What difference does it make if the patient was a Negro?" asked Adam.

"Not the patient," said Barnett, "the surgeon."

The female ward was quiet. Several beds remained empty, having not been filled by any clinic or ER admissions. Sally, the RN, stepped out of the treatment room and handed Adam some packages of gauze dressings, including a large abdominal pad, a roll of gauze, and an Ace wrap.

"You may want to put a bigger dressing on the breast cancer patient," she said. "Miss Hall has already soaked through the dressing you placed this morning."

"How is she doing?" asked Adam.

"As good as can be expected," said Sally.

"Have you ever seen anything like that before?" asked Adam.

"Hon, we see lots of tumors like that."

There was a touch of sadness in her voice as she continued. "Lots of these poor women don't come in until it's advanced. They don't have general practitioners or any access for occasional general health exams, so they let things go... Just gotta accept it and do the best you can. Here, I'll help you with that dressing."

Sally accompanied Adam to Miss Hall's bed and put on a pair of gloves after handing him a similar pair.

She removed the soaked pads and discarded them in a nearby waste basket. She opened two pieces of Vaseline-coated gauze that were in the supplies she had brought over.

"These won't stick to her chest," she said before stacking dry 4x4 pads over the Vaseline gauze and covering the whole area with the larger abdominal pads.

"Put your hand here, Doctor, then hold this against the chest, please."

While Adam pushed the pile of dressings against the chest wall, Sally unwrapped a gauze roll and began wrapping it around the whole circumference of Vivian Hall's chest. Adam shifted hands so his fingers wouldn't be caught under the dressings. She then completed the wrapping with a less porous Ace wrap that stretched snugly around the chest. When she had secured the Ace bandage with two little clips and adhesive tape, she smiled at Adam.

"That should keep it drier." And she returned to her desk at the end of the room.

Adam watched the dressing for a moment until he was convinced that there was indeed no seepage through the new bandages.

"I haven't heard from the residents yet if they have found a spot in the operating schedule so they can remove your ovaries," said Adam. "Do you have any questions regarding the upcoming surgery?"

"No, not really," Miss Hall said. "I have faith that the Lord will guide my doctors."

"Do you go to church regularly?" Adam surprised himself that the question seemed so natural to ask. "Which one?"

"Mount Olive Baptist Church... Been part of the Ladies Auxiliary for years."

"I hope we can get you back to services very soon. I know that's important."

"Oh, I've got my own service right here," she said. She reached for the drawer of her bedside table, opened it, and pulled out a tattered Bible. "I read it every night."

"Are you scared about the surgery?"

"Doctor," she replied, "there will be a time when we all have to stand before the Lord. I've lived a righteous life and been kind to others. I know when it's my time, I'll be ready."

"Yes," Adam agreed. *The world might be a better place if everyone felt that way*, he thought.

He walked to the nurses' desk and said softly to Sally, "I wish there were more we could do."

"Hon," she said, "there's always gonna be cases make you feel that way. Fact is, all patients die... So do all nurses and doctors. You just gotta do your best every time."

"You've been a nurse for a long time, haven't you?"

"Long time, hon... Long time."

"Don't you ever get discouraged?"

"Oh, I did... Had real problems with it, but I learned you got to accept the bad with the good. Had a patient like Miss Hall some time back. First time I ever had a patient like that to have her ovaries out. Tumor shrunk so much they eventually brought her back and removed the breast tumor... Pulled the skin of her belly up to cover her chest. She had tumors in her lungs too, but they shrunk for a while too… She lived comfortably for about three years."

"Wish we knew more about how those hormones work," said Adam.

"Someday, someday," said Sally. "Progress is slow sometimes, but it happens."

"Thanks for showing me about the dressings," said Adam. "See you later."

"Sure thing, hon… You have a good day now."

Jen was on her break when Adam arrived on the male ward, but Miss Viola was there and had brought a new visitor. He was a well-dressed man who appeared to be in his late thirties or early forties. His light sport coat, delicately patterned tie, button-down blue shirt, and perfectly tailored slacks were right out of the Brooks Brothers catalog. An expensive gold watch adorned his left wrist.

"Dr. Sinclair," Miss Viola called, motioning for him to come closer. "Come meet my brother."

"I'm Jonathan," he said as he shook Adam's hand. "Thanks for taking care of my uncle."

"My little brother just came in from St. Louis," Miss Viola said. "He's a professor in literature."

"I've been very fortunate," he said. "Bunkie paid for me to go to Princeton and to get my PhD in Boston. We owe everything to our uncle."

The old man in the bed smiled weakly, reached out a withered hand, and gently patted his nephew's wrist.

"I'll be available if there's anything you need or if there's anything I can do to make Bunkie more comfortable."

For the second time in twenty minutes, Adam felt powerless against an advancing disease. As he left the ward, he couldn't shake the aching disappointment that he couldn't do more.

CHAPTER 82

TUESDAY NIGHT HAD been productive. Adam found plenty of time to stop at Felix's for oyster stew and a salad before settling into studying in his apartment. His eagerness to get caught up had resulted in a surge of energy. He'd completed two full chapters and the notes from the accompanying lectures. A major accomplishment in his mind, although it actually meant that he was now only about eleven chapters behind in his assigned reading.

Wednesday afternoon found Adam on the male ward with Turk. Barnett and Shrevi were still in the operating rooms, where the other residents were completing the day's elective surgery schedule. Adam noticed that Jen must have had the day off since another RN was running the ward.

They were standing at the bedside and reviewing the chart of a patient with pancreatitis. Adam was paying close attention as Turk explained the causes of the condition, both common and uncommon.

They were interrupted by the entrance of a familiar figure. Dressed in his tuxedo, Teddy's friend Laurance looked like he was on his way to work. He smiled as he approached.

"You're Adam, right?" he asked. "Just the person I am looking for."

"Yes, I'm Adam. You're Teddy's friend from Antoine's. What's up?"

"Teddy asked if I could stop by and find you. His incision is itching terribly and he's concerned that perhaps his stitches should be removed."

"They probably are ready to be removed," said Turk.

"He lives just around the corner from me," explained Adam. "If it's OK, I could stop by and remove them."

"Sure," said Turk, "take a disposable suture removal set from the treatment room."

"That's nice of you," said Laurance. "Should I tell him when to expect you?"

"I can probably stop by on my way home when we're done here."

"Tell him the itching is part of the healing and just getting the sutures out may not relieve it," said Turk, "and make sure he knows that we should still see him back in clinic."

The sun was moving to the west, but some daylight remained. Holiday was still scrubbed with Rogers, Wantz, and Barnett when Doyle returned to the ward and dismissed Adam and Shrevi, stating that they wouldn't do group rounds that afternoon since half the team was still in the operating room.

The suture removal set, pre-packaged with small scissors, pickup tweezers, and a gauze pad, all neatly arranged in a plastic tray, bumped against the roll of adhesive tape in the pocket of his white coat as Adam walked through Jackson Square and continued on Chartres until he crossed Esplanade.

The light from the setting sun highlighted the elegance of Teddy's old frame apartment building, a few doors in from the intersection with Decatur Street, kitty-corner from the Old Mint. The wide porch of the first-floor apartment with its ornately carved railings, classical white columns, and antique hanging light fixture was matched by the expanse of balcony on the second floor. Adam stepped onto the porch and rang the bell. Soon a familiar voice rang out.

"Who's there?"

Adam stepped back off the porch and looked up to see Teddy standing on the upper balcony wearing a Japanese kimono, his head wrapped in a silk turban.

"Adam, my friend," he said. "Here to make a house call in the grand tradition of Asclepius, Hippocrates, and Maimonides. I'll buzz you up."

Adam climbed the stairwell to the apartment door only to be surprised when he entered Teddy's living room. Leaning against an antique umbrella stand was a familiar bag, the corner of a book barely visible near the top.

Jen stepped into the room from the kitchen and smiled.

"I believe you know my private duty nurse," Teddy said. "Mother insisted I have help during my recovery, and so I was very fortunate that Miss Jen arranged for herself and enlisted some of her friends to attend my needs as I convalesce. Just like the old gospel hymn, 'Never Alone, Never Alone.'"

"Hi," Adam addressed Jen, hoping she didn't have the wrong idea. "I was asked to come by to take out his sutures."

Together, they escorted Teddy into his bedroom and helped him to lie down on the antique mahogany double bed.

"This was my great grandparents' bed upriver on the old family plantation," Teddy said.

He then pulled his kimono wide open, baring more than his incision. Having been embarrassed by what Jen might think when he arrived, Adam was now grateful that she could be a professional chaperone while he removed the sutures.

She brought a white towel and placed it over Teddy. Adam was glad that she was there to maintain a semblance of modesty even if Teddy didn't care. She was so professional in her demeanor that Adam could tell she had probably had experience in covering other purposely exposed men, and not necessarily all gay ones.

Adam opened the suture set and used the scissors and pickups to carefully remove each stitch. When finished, he gently closed the edges of the kimono over Teddy, who remained with his eyes closed and his head resting comfortably on a ruffled, deep burgundy satin pillowcase.

"I swear," said Teddy, "I am most exhausted. I need to rest, and I would suggest you take advantage of the breeze on the balcony while I refresh myself."

"Call if you need anything," said Jen.

"Of course," answered Teddy.

Together, Adam and Jen passed through the living and dining rooms, admiring the perfectly positioned and polished antiques from upriver.

The setting sun wasn't visible from the porch, but the sky over the French Quarter was filled with beautiful colors that filtered through the low-lying clouds. White wicker furniture gave the porch a plantation-like atmosphere. They sat together in the big chairs facing a suspended porch swing.

There was a moment of awkward silence before Adam spoke. "I didn't know you also worked as a private duty nurse."

"I don't, but Teddy is such a sweetheart—and he pays very generously. Teddy doesn't really need any nursing, but it gets me out of the house. Away from my husband's drinking."

"I'm sorry that you have to deal with that. Can't you get him some help?"

"I've tried," she said, "but he resists. I got him to see someone, but he went back to drinking as soon as he went back to work."

"Was he always a drinker?"

"No..." She had a far-away look. "He was my high school boyfriend. We got married after he finished college. I did two years and then we moved here for me to start nursing school. He didn't start drinking heavily until after he started working at a bank here."

"In our Psychiatry lectures last year they talked about alcoholism as a disease, you know, like an addiction that some people are more readily attracted to—maybe even genetic."

"His father was a heavy drinker."

"Our professor said that the environment may play a role. If he's around a lot of friends who drink, it may reinforce his behavior."

She nodded as though contemplating that idea before switching the subject.

"Are you enjoying the surgery rotation?"

"It's hard," he said. "I'm used to classroom work where everything you have to learn is well-defined. Now there's too much to learn and no time to study. It's kinda upsetting when your studying has always been well-organized."

"Where'd you go to college?" she asked.

Adam did not usually like to talk about himself, but her smile and attentiveness made him open up. He told her about his education, his hometown, his family. After he had talked for several minutes, he became self-conscious. He didn't want her to think that because he lived in the neighborhood and had come to Teddy's, he was gay.

He fumbled for more words, only to be saved by Teddy, who appeared on the porch carrying a silver tray outfitted with delicate china cups, saucers, a matching teapot, and two hefty slices of bourbon-flavored pecan pie baked on a layer of dark chocolate.

"You two are probably in need of refreshment," he said as he put the tray on the table between their two chairs. "I made this last night as part of my rehabilitation program. It is my favorite recipe, uses the finest Swiss chocolate from my friend at the French patisserie on Royal Street."

"I thought you were supposed to be resting," said Jen.

"I assure you I feel quite rejuvenated, but perhaps you are correct and I would benefit from a longer respite. I shall return to my room."

Adam poured the tea and they sat, enjoying the pie and talking about nothing in particular that seemed like everything to Adam.

The sun had almost completed its circuit across the sky when the buzzer rang. Adam looked down from the porch to see one of the LPNs from the hospital.

"That's my relief," said Jen.

After Jen gave her replacement her nursing report, "He's fine," Adam walked her to her car parked on Frenchman Street. They talked for a while longer about their families, music, and Jen's love of literature. She laughed when Adam said, "My histology book was definitely not written by Ernest Hemingway."

Darkness had crept in when they said goodnight. Adam opened the car door for her. She unexpectedly reached for his hand and squeezed it. They stood for a moment with their eyes locked together. Adam leaned closer, fighting the desire to kiss her.

She took her seat behind the wheel and smiled up at him. "Thanks for the good chat."

Adam blushed and stood watching her drive out of sight, still feeling the warmth of her touch before he turned and headed back to his apartment.

CHAPTER 83

THURSDAY MORNING'S LECTURES covered organ transplantation and orthopedics. The unusual pairing of topics meant only one thing.

"Hundred and fifty-three," Shrevi said, slamming his textbook shut on the cafeteria table.

"Huh?"

"Hundred and fifty-three more pages for today's lectures. How on earth do they expect us to get this reading done, be on the wards or in the OR, and be ready for tomorrow's lectures? I'm so frigging behind in the reading… No way I'll catch up."

"I know what you mean," said Adam. "They expect us to read it once and remember everything. Even if I could get the reading done, I'd need time to study afterwards before it would stick in my memory."

Barnett was already on the ward making rounds with the residents when Adam and Shrevi joined the group. All of the beds on the male ward were filled and all the patients doing well. The wound was clean and healing nicely in Barnett's diverticulitis patient. Admiral Franklin was behaving better. He wore his yachting cap while he sat in bed drinking fruit juice through a soda straw. The young boy with the liver injury was very stable, sucking down ice chips from a Styrofoam cup. Bunkie Smith was growing weaker but never complained of any pain and appeared comfortable and content when his family kept vigil at his bedside.

Before the students could leave for the female ward, Rogers and Kochenko approached Adam, pulling him aside, and spoke quietly.

"Your lady with the breast cancer is on the OR schedule to have her ovaries out in about twenty minutes," said Kochenko. "You can leave rounds with us if you want to scrub. Miss Viola called and said Theodorakis is not going to make rounds until tomorrow, so everybody's going to Tillie's after we're done. You guys are all invited… See you in the OR."

"What's Tillie's?" Adam asked Barnett.

"Beats me."

Wantz overheard them and stepped closer. "Tillie's is a little bar a couple of blocks up Airline Highway. We'll be going over there about 4:30. All of you are expected to be there… It's an honor for students to be invited."

"Are the nurses invited?" asked Adam.

"You can ask them… Sometimes the ER or OR nurses come… That Jen turns guys down all the time… Good luck with that."

There was time to finish rounds on the female ward before going to the operating room. When he finished, Adam noticed Sally, the older RN, still working in the treatment room.

He stopped in the doorway.

"We're going to meet at Tillie's about 4:30. Want to join us?"

She stopped stocking the dressings cabinet and looked at Adam with surprise.

"Tillie's? That's really sweet of you, hon…but I've been sober now for eleven years. I don't think that's a good place for me, but I sure appreciate the offer."

On his way to the elevator, Adam passed the entrance to the male ward. Jen was sitting at her desk just inside the doorway, writing on a patient's chart.

"Hey," he said, "we're going to Tillie's about 4:30. Wanna join us?"

He steeled himself for the rejection, but she paused for a moment and then gave him a smile. "Yeah, I probably have time for one drink. I'll see you there."

Adam grinned as he rode the elevator up to the operating room, imagining the look on Wantz's face when Jen arrived at the bar escorted by lowly medical students.

In contrast to the urgency that gunshots or trauma brought to the operating room, the elective removal of Vivian Hall's ovaries was relaxed, straightforward, and almost simple.

Through a small incision, Kochenko brought up and removed the ovaries, irregular white structures no bigger than an olive.

"Post-menopausal ovary is atrophic as expected," said Rogers.

The operation was completed in no time. Before they closed the incision, Adam peered in and reviewed the anatomy of the female pelvis. He appreciated how much more meaningful being in the operating room was than looking at pictures in a textbook, particularly when Rogers named all the structures while pointing with a forceps.

Adam stopped to change Luanne's dressing before heading up the street to Tillie's. Luanne was in good spirits. He realized how shallow the wound had become, filling with healthy pink granulation tissue while the skin edges grew closer together than they had been the previous week.

"When am I going home?" she asked. "How much longer I gotta be here?"

"I don't know," Adam answered. "I promise I'll ask my residents."

It wasn't until he stepped off the elevator into the foyer that he realized that Luanne's question must have indicated how much better she was actually feeling.

Tillie's was a simple building with white clapboard sides and a shingled roof, easy to miss if you were driving down Airline Highway towards Charity. The building was raised by brick supports about two feet off the ground, and a couple of weathered and unfinished wooden planks provided the steps up to the door. The only identifying characteristics were the neon beer signs in the windows on either side of the door—one read Jax and the other Dixie. The only indicator of the bar's name was a wooden sign nailed above the door, which displayed a crude fleur-de-lis followed by the name "TILLIE'S" painted in irregular purple letters that looked as though someone had used paint left over from a Mardi Gras float.

Jen was standing by the steps when Adam arrived. He was glad she didn't have second thoughts about joining them.

"Hi," he said. "Hope I didn't keep you waiting long."

"I just got here," she said, placing her right foot on the first step.

Inside, the light was poor and the paneling was dark. The well-worn black and white checkerboard tiles on the floor were grimy and pitted, and more than a few had chunks missing after years of use. The ceiling fan pushed the smell of beer through the room while Fats Domino played on the jukebox.

The entire back wall of the room was occupied by an ornately carved antique bar that seemed out of place with the array of wood and metal tables and chairs that could have been randomly plucked from a Goodwill store. On the right of the bar was an oblong table and a long, curved banquette, its red vinyl seating patched with duct tape. Barnett and Turk were seated on the banquette, each with a bottle of Dixie beer. Kochenko, Wantz, Shrevi, and Kittamura stood near the table. If Wantz was surprised to see Jen, he gave no indication.

"Y'all have a seat. I'll be right with you," instructed the skinny waitress in a maroon tank top and faded jeans as she lifted a tray full of drinks from the bar and scurried towards the occupied tables across the room.

Barnett and Turk slid over to make more room for Kittamura and Kochenko. Jen sat on the open end of the booth and slid across the red vinyl seating towards Barnett. Before Adam could sit next to her, Shrevi plopped down and moved in. He sat close, with a huge grin on his face as he draped his right arm across the banquette behind her. Adam wished he could push Shrevi out of that seat but tried to mask his disappointment with an air of no concern. Wantz crowded in next, leaving Adam on one of the old chairs that hugged the table but seemed miles from where he wanted to sit.

Kittamura sat on the banquette next to Turk. He was wide-eyed and smiling, enjoying the change of surroundings from the tiny call room where he lived.

Before sitting on the banquette next to Kittamura, Kochenko met the waitress when she returned to the bar and spoke to her out of earshot. After he took his seat, she came to the table.

"What can I get y'all?" she asked.

"Could I please have a glass of white wine? Chardonnay, Chablis, or Sauvignon Blanc would be fine," said Jen.

Barnett and Turk indicated they were fine with their beer.

"Don't worry, Kitty." Kochenko patted Kittamura on the shoulder. "I ordered for us."

"I'll have a Jax," grinned Shrevi.

"A double Manhattan," said Wantz.

"I'll have a Dixie, please," requested Adam.

The waitress headed back to the bar as Rogers and Judy entered, smiling, and took seats at an adjacent small table for two. Holiday and Doyle entered and took the last seats at the big table.

Doyle looked at Jen. "Nice to have you finally join us. You certainly are the person who makes our ward run so smoothly."

Jen seemed a little embarrassed acknowledging the compliment, and a little more so when Kochenko added, "Yeah, Theodorakis seems really happy with the care on the ward. I heard that he once had an RN transferred because he felt she wasn't keeping the medication schedule on time."

"That's true," said Holiday, "but he's even more demanding of the resident staff. I've seen junior residents come and go over the years. Although I have to say, if you prove yourself worthwhile he'll go out of his way to teach you and treat you as a colleague."

"I'd agree with that," said Doyle as the waitress returned. "I'll have a bourbon if you've got a good one and a scotch on the rocks for my friend," he said, indicating Holiday.

The waitress served the first of the drinks. She placed six shot glasses in front of Kittamura and Kochenko and set two saucers, one covered in bar salt and the other filled with lime wedges, between them.

Rogers and Judy angled their chairs towards the big table and ordered two glasses of red wine.

"Y'all go ahead, don't wait for us," said Doyle.

Everyone raised their glass except Kittamura, who stared at the shot glasses with a quizzical look on his face.

"C'mon, Kitty," Kochenko said. "Sake. In America we take a little salt first and then a bite of citrus after...like this."

Kochenko dipped his finger into the salt and sucked the granules off before lifting one of the small glasses.

"Banzai!" he declared before downing the first shot and following with a bite of lime wedge.

Kittamura followed suit but made a sour face and asked, "Sake?"

"Yes indeed," explained Kochenko. "The finest in America... Jose Cuervo Sake." He handed Kittamura a lime wedge.

Wantz ordered a second double Manhattan, and Kochenko and Kittamura kept downing shots. Rogers and Judy finished their wine and excused themselves.

Kochenko began telling stories about having been on call in the ER last year for Mardi Gras and treating the parade of people in costume who had suffered minor mishaps during their revelries.

"One guy fell off a float in a tomato costume and cut his forearm. Smashed the heck out of the right side of his costume. With the blood on his arm, he looked like a tomato somebody had tried to make ketchup out of."

Everyone enjoyed the conversation, laughing as the waitress brought more shots and the silent Wantz downed his third double Manhattan and ordered a fourth.

Finally, Holiday and Doyle stood up to leave. Jen indicated that it was time for her to go as well.

Wantz sat quietly with a glassy stare. Before he stood up to let Jen slide across the vinyl seating, he looked up with an air of seriousness.

"I just want to say," he said, "I just want to say... This is the besht! This is the besht service I've ever been on!"

He raised his glass and downed his fourth, or maybe his fifth, Manhattan before sitting back in his seat and emitting a loud belch.

"Banzai!" applauded Kochenko and Kittamura as they each downed another shot.

~

Adam walked Jen to her car and opened the door for her.

"Can I give you a ride home?" she asked.

He paused, imagining more before responding, "No, thanks, it's a beautiful evening and I'll enjoy the walk through the Quarter. Besides, the traffic would be horrible and it would be really out of your way."

He watched her car pull away towards Claiborne Avenue, still wishing Shrevi hadn't grabbed the seat next to her and feeling regret at not taking her offer of a ride home.

CHAPTER 84

NOT ALL OF Service 1 was available to start rounds with Dr. Theodorakis. Barnett, Holiday, Kochenko, and Turk were in the operating room. Adam and Shrevi waited on the ward along with Doyle and Rogers.

The other services' residents and medical students crowded into the ward. Jen interrupted her routine to bring the chart cart close enough to the group for her to hear the patient presentations and discussions.

Just before they were to begin, Kittamura appeared in the doorway. His white coat was unbuttoned, his necktie imperfectly knotted. His normally perfectly combed hair revealed an uncontrolled cowlick, and his horn-rimmed glasses had been replaced by sunglasses in the same style frame. He struggled to take his place at the foot of the bed, where he stood, weaving a bit and grabbing hold of the bed frame to steady himself.

Wantz was next to arrive and stood next to Kittamura. He moved slowly—like a turtle in pain. His face was puffy, and he had made no effort to hide his bloodshot eyes. He took his place at the bedside in silence, grabbing the frame since he too had to check his wavering balance.

A momentary hush passed as the group waited for Dr. Theodorakis to begin his formal teaching rounds. He posed the first question to Doyle.

"Tell me, Bobby, do they still keep a bottle of Maker's Mark for special customers hidden behind the bar at Tillie's?"

CHAPTER 85

WORD GOT AROUND quickly Saturday morning. Grand Rounds and Bullpen were cancelled.

Adam found Barnett and Shrevi in the student lounge at the medical school. A crowd of students had gathered near the old black-and-white TV that sat on a table in the corner.

"What's going on?" asked Adam.

"Shots fired down the street at a motel," answered Barnett, moving over to allow Adam to see the screen. "Fire on the top floor."

The newscaster spoke: "To recap what we know so far, a half hour ago, members of the police and fire departments responded to the report of a fire on the upper floors of the NOLA Motor Lodge. Shortly after their arrival, shots were fired from the motel. Initial reports state that several of the responders were hit by gunfire. We have no information on the status of guests in the hotel itself. The wounded officers and firefighters are reportedly being taken to Charity Hospital."

"We'd better go," said Barnett.

Two squad cars and an ambulance were already parked at the ER entrance. Inside, the hallway to the trauma room was packed with people. Nurses, lab techs, radiology techs, and pharmacists hurried to the individual rooms.

The students paused at Room 1. A body covered by a sheet was on a gurney, the bottom sheet near the head of the cart soaked with blood. Two technicians were preparing to move the cart. Adam recognized one of them from the day last semester when his Pathology class observed an autopsy in the morgue.

"Assistant fire chief, shot in the head." Carlos hurried by, carrying two units of blood. "Got two policemen, one shot in the shoulder and one in the leg, and a fireman shot in the belly in Rooms 2, 3, and 4."

He disappeared into one of the other trauma rooms while the students stepped aside so the cart from Room 1 could be pushed past them. Before they could move further down the hallway, a flurry of activity and shouts of alarm began at the entrance to the Emergency Room. Barnett, Shrevi, and Adam all stepped back and focused on the waiting area, where both doors were suddenly flung wide open.

To their right was Officer Guidry, red-faced, shirt rumpled and untucked, his hat gone. On the left was a firefighter in dark, heavy boots, his long coat open and flapping. In between them slumped Officer Beaudry. They half-carried, half-dragged him with his outstretched arms across their shoulders. His head hung down to his chest but did not obscure how ashen his face appeared. He moved his pale lips as if trying to speak. A large bloodstain filled the right side of his shirt.

"Get a cart!" Shrevi screamed even as Carlos pushed a gurney past him.

Barnett and Adam helped the others load the fallen officer onto the cart.

"Room 1 is open," said Adam. "Let's get him in there!"

Barnett and the fireman pushed the cart as Adam pulled the other end forward with the panting Guidry beside him.

"Didn't see it coming!" he gasped. "Went up the stairwell to the top floor when we heard there was a fire. Opened the door and as soon as we stepped into the hallway he was hit. I carried him down all eighteen floors."

"Sit out here while we work on him," said Adam.

Guidry took a deep breath, pulled a kerchief from his pocket, wiped the sweat from his face, and plopped down on the wooden bench in the hallway.

"We been partners eight years…"

There was no hiding the fear in his eyes.

Adam rushed into the trauma room. He caught a glimpse of Rogers and Judy leaving one of the other rooms and hurrying towards them. They wheeled the gurney into the center of the room. The supplies were untouched since the previous patient had been declared dead on arrival. Two IV poles were on either side of the cart with bottles and tubing ready.

Carlos moved quickly, giving a quick tug to pop the buttons on the officer's shirt and using a large bandage scissors to cut open the bloody T-shirt and divide the long sleeves of his uniform.

Barnett and Adam grabbed tourniquets and intravenous catheters. Adam caught a glimpse of the single gunshot wound in the right chest, above and lateral to the nipple, just before Shrevi covered the bullet hole with a pad of Vaseline-soaked gauze. Rogers stood at the head of the table, watching Beaudry's breathing and adjusting a high-flow oxygen mask.

Barnett and Adam each steadied an outstretched arm, placed tourniquets, wiped the skin with alcohol pads, and, in unison, threaded intravenous catheters into veins of both arms. Carlos handed Adam tape to secure the catheter and helped attach the IV tubing and bag of fluid.

On the other side of the cart, Judy handed Barnett a large syringe, which he filled with blood from the catheter and handed to her before he attached the IV bag and secured the catheter. She filled multiple test tubes from the syringe before sticking labels on the tubes.

"We're going to need a chest tube," announced Rogers.

Carlos handed him the tray that he had already pulled from the storage cabinet.

"After I've got the tube in, we'll turn him to see the exit wound," Rogers said. "How's his blood pressure?"

"I can feel a thready pulse," said Adam.

Barnett had a blood pressure cuff on the other arm and held a stethoscope against the skin as he pumped the cuff.

"About 70," he said.

Carlos finished opening the chest tube tray for Rogers and took the blood-filled test tubes and requisition slips from Judy.

"Get three units of universal donor and cross-match him for six packed cells and three fresh frozen plasma," instructed Rogers.

"The other tubes go to the lab," said Judy.

Rogers poured iodine solution on the officer's chest, donned a pair of sterile gloves, and created a field by placing sterile towels around a portion of the chest. He used a small syringe of local anesthetic to infiltrate a spot between two ribs. Taking the scalpel off the tray, he created a one-inch incision and pushed his finger between the ribs and into the chest. Before much blood could escape, he removed his finger, grasped the end of the chest tube with a clamp, and forcibly pushed the clamp over the upper edge of a rib, threading the tube into the chest. A rush of blood covered his shoes and stained the lower legs of his scrubs before Judy could attach the tube to the rubber hose leading to the suction chamber that had been placed on the floor. Bubbles passed through the water in the vacuum chamber once it was attached to the suction machine, and the lung expanded.

Officer Beaudry opened his eyes, took a deeper breath, and coughed up a little bloody material that settled on his bare chest until Adam wiped it with the corner of the bedsheet. Rogers secured the tube with a heavy suture and dressing while Judy rechecked the policeman's blood pressure.

"Up to 80," she said.

"Put the head of the cart up a little more," said Rogers.

Barnett turned the crank at the foot of the bed while Shrevi and Adam helped the officer lean forward so that Rogers could seal the exit wound with another piece of Vaseline gauze and a tight dressing.

Carlos appeared carrying the units of blood, and only then did Adam notice Holiday, Kochenko, and Turk standing in the doorway.

"Theodorakis is coming in," stated Holiday. "Doyle and Kittamura are taking the fireman shot in the belly upstairs—one of you students should join them in the OR."

He pointed to Barnett, who nodded and was joined by Turk as he headed for the elevators.

"What do you have here?" Holiday asked.

"Single gunshot wound to the chest…exit in back. Tube is in, 1,000 cc's drained out but still dripping down the tube," said Rogers.

Judy finished hanging a unit of blood. She spoke as she moved with a second unit towards the IV on the other side of the cart. "Pulse is 130. Blood pressure came up to 80 with the IV fluid alone."

"He's breathing better with the chest tube in place, so I didn't intubate him," said Rogers.

Holiday studied the blood collecting in the drainage chamber.

"Let's get him ready for the OR. Can intubate him there. Gonna need to empty his stomach and place a Foley in his bladder."

Carlos handed Adam a nasogastric tube, a cup of ice, lubricant, and a large syringe resting in an emesis basin. Adam pulled on gloves and, without hesitation, lubricated the tube and slid it through Beaudry's nostril while the officer swallowed a few ice chips. He verified the tube's placement by injecting air over the stomach, hearing the whoosh with his stethoscope, and watching the gastric liquid collect in the suction canister he had attached the tube to after securing it with tape to the policeman's nose.

Adam stepped back to allow Judy access to the IV and noticed Shrevi standing on the other side of the table. He was wearing sterile gloves and had prepped Beaudry's penis with antiseptic. He straightened the shaft with a gentle pull and, despite wincing, deftly inserted a lubricated Foley catheter into the officer's bladder. It was a skill Adam didn't know his classmate had mastered.

Holiday turned to Adam. "Gonna need a couple more units from the Blood Bank… Go get it…and bring back some plasma too."

Adam arrived at the front desk of the Blood Bank. Through the windows in the double doors that opened into the lab, he could see techs hurrying back and forth.

"I'm here for the blood for the policeman in the ER," he said, "and they might need some more."

He handed the requisition to the receptionist.

"I know just what you need," said the thin Black lady in the long white coat who was standing behind the receptionist. "The type and cross should be ready in just a moment. Wait on this side of the counter, and when the blood is ready I'll go back to the ER with you and make sure they have enough."

Adam stepped behind the counter and was distracted by the sound and appearance of a large group approaching down the hallway.

He was shorter than he appeared on TV or in the newspapers, but there was no mistaking Governor Hubert Herveault. He strode down the hallway, leading a crowd of aides and reporters with notepads, cameras, klieg lights, and even the three new mini-cams that the local TV networks had recently acquired.

The entourage stopped about twenty feet from the Blood Bank's front desk. The notepads were poised for writing, the mini-cams were aimed from the operators' shoulders, the flash cameras popped, and the klieg lights bathed the whole area in blinding light. The aides motioned for the reporters to stay back while the governor approached the desk alone.

"Ah'm here to give some blood fo' the officer in surgery," he drawled.

A nurse approached and ushered him back to a smaller desk near Adam. Before she could speak, the governor turned around, smiled, and waved to the cameras.

"It's very kind of you, Governor," the nurse spoke as she motioned for him to take a seat on the small chair next to the desk. "There is some routine paperwork that must be done. I'll try to expedite the process for you."

She placed a few forms and a pen in front of her and pulled a blood pressure cuff from the desk drawer as she sat down.

"First we need to take your blood pressure…"

The governor turned his chair to face the press, smiled again, and then used his right hand to dramatically push up his white shirt's already short sleeve. The hallway was illuminated with bright light and popping flash bulbs. Adam watched the scene unfold, only interested in returning to the ER.

The nurse wrapped the cuff on the governor's arm and recorded his blood pressure. She removed the cuff from his arm, picked up her pen, and straightened the pile of forms in front of her.

"Now, Governor, just a few questions and we'll be done. Have you ever had hepatitis?"

The governor sat back, relaxed, and smiled. "Oh shucks, I grew up in Louisiana eating oysters and crawfish. Everybody Ah know has had hepatitis."

"Including you?"

"Well, sure."

The nurse looked at him directly and said, "Governor, I can't take your blood."

A worried look came over the governor's face as he glanced over his right shoulder at the eager reporters. He leaned forward and whispered so softly that only the nurse and Adam could hear, "Cain't y'all just take a little bit and throw it away?"

∾

The Blood Bank technician grabbed another requisition and left the trauma room. Adam passed the blood bags to Shrevi and Carlos and watched as they helped Judy hang the blood.

"Better put them on pumps," said Rogers. "Last pressure was down to 70."

He looked at the chest tube canister. "Sixteen hundred and fifty cc's—still bleeding."

"How soon can we get him in the OR?" uttered the calm, even voice of Dr. Theodorakis as he entered the room.

"They should be ready for us," answered Holiday.

"Get the blood in and his pressure up a bit before we transport him."

Theodorakis stepped to the head of the bed and watched as the units were started. Shrevi and Carlos squeezed the rubber bulbs on the canvas wraps around the blood bags. The canvas inflated, increasing the pressure on the bags and creating a faster infusion.

Shrevi pumped so furiously that he didn't notice when the canvas wrap slipped and a corner of the plastic blood bag became exposed. There was an audible "pop" when the bag burst. Blood splattered over Dr. Theodorakis, covering his patterned sport jacket, crisp white shirt, tie, slacks, and shoes. His face and forehead were dotted and smeared with red.

The room was frozen in silence. No one moved or spoke while they waited for the second explosion with all eyes on the chief. He pulled a handkerchief from his pocket, wiped his forehead and cheek, and softly said, "I think we need another unit of blood."

The operating room was packed. Holiday and Rogers assisted Dr. Theodorakis while Kochenko filled the fourth position at the table. Even standing on a metal step, Adam couldn't see into the operative field. The crowding was made worse when the rest of Service 1 arrived after Doyle and Kittamura had finished operating on the fireman who had been shot in the belly.

The chairman had chosen to make a large transverse incision, beginning near the entrance wound and extending across the chest. He cut the sternum with a saw and continued with a scalpel across the left chest.

"That'll open him like a clamshell," whispered Wantz as he pushed his way onto Adam's step, trying to get a better view. "Great exposure."

Dr. Theodorakis moved quickly, each motion exact, without hesitation. He called for two 3-0 silk sutures and after placing the stitches spoke to those who could not see into the operative field. "The bullet did not traverse the mediastinum, so there is no injury to the heart or major vessels. There is a single wound through the parenchyma of the lung which is not bleeding. Upon exiting the chest, the bullet hit one of the ribs along the posterior of the chest wall. The rib was shattered and its accompanying intercostal artery and vein were torn. This was the site of his bleeding. The small vessels were easily controlled by suture ligature."

"I am maintaining a pressure of about 100, and there is urine in the bag," added the anesthesiologist.

Dr. Theodorakis stepped back, removed his gown and gloves, and left the operating room. Holiday called for chest tubes, and he, Rogers, and Kochenko began to close the incision.

By the time they finished closing and Adam left to return downstairs, the drama at the motel was over. Sergeant Landry was in the ER with Officer Guidry.

"Sharpshooters got him when he ran out on the roof," said the sergeant. "At least two hundred bullets in him."

CHAPTER 86

THE EVENTS OF the morning paralyzed the city, but by late afternoon Charity returned to its normal state of crowding and confusion. The city's indigent population still sought medical care. An initial trickle of patients began to enter the ER, and soon the waiting area was full.

The only indication of what had happened in the morning was the increased police presence in the hospital. The officer who had been shot in the thigh had been initially seen and later rechecked by Turk and Kittamura. The femoral blood vessels were intact, but the bullet had broken the femur as it passed through the back of his thigh. The Orthopedic service had taken him to the OR to clean the wound and he was returned to the Orthopedic ward, where two police officers sat in the hallway near the entrance while another two officers remained in the ward, one seated by the nurses' desk and the other near the wounded officer's bed. Officer Beaudry and the wounded fireman remained in ICU with a similar complement of officers.

The policeman with the shoulder wound had been transferred to the General Surgery ward, again receiving the same number of guards.

Around four o'clock, the surgical side of the ER suddenly became very busy. A patient with appendicitis, one with an incarcerated hernia, and three people injured in a motor vehicle accident all arrived within twenty minutes of each other.

The students followed the residents as they dispersed to care for the new arrivals. Shrevi joined Turk and Rogers to take the patient with appendicitis to the operating room while Barnett, Wantz, and Kittamura brought up the incarcerated hernia. Kochenko entered the trauma room to assess a patient from the motor vehicle accident. Holiday and Doyle had been watching from the hallway. Doyle stepped up to check on the extent of the two motor vehicle injuries. Adam followed Kochenko into a room to see a lady from another auto accident. The nurses had already started two IVs and waited for orders from the residents about how rapidly the fluids should be given.

"Back seat passenger, no seat belt, hit her head on the back of the driver's seat, obvious black eye and hematoma, front of the scalp on the left, no complaints of belly or chest pain," Carlos related as he passed by carrying the test tubes of blood destined for the lab.

"That kind of facial trauma may have caused a blowout fracture of the orbit," said Kochenko. "I'll examine her with you and you record the history and physical."

Adam checked the name on the chart—Belinda Malveaux.

"I'm Dr. Sinclair, Miss Malveaux," he said. "This is Dr. Kochenko. What happened to you?"

"I don't know," she said, pressing a large ice pack against the left side of her head, covering her cheek, eye, and forehead. "One moment we're driving along, talkin' and laughin', and then suddenly bang, and we're up on the sidewalk with police and ambulance there."

Adam began to ask the standard history and physical questions without referring to any outline.

"Feel here," said Kochenko, pressing his thumb along the bony surface under the left eye.

Although the area was swollen and bruised, Adam could feel the underlying bone grind under his touch.

"Crepitus," said Kochenko. "Our X-rays will confirm the zygoma fracture."

Adam's questions and the maneuvers of the remainder of the physical exam were automatic and natural. When the patient was able to move across the hall to X-ray, he began writing on a yellow tablet.

He sat on the bench outside the trauma room and wrote down every detail of the patient's history and physical exam without once referring to the format outline in his pocket notebook. He signed, "Adam Sinclair, M3" at the bottom of the page and leaned back in his seat, satisfied that what had begun as rapid questions was now a coherent story.

When the surgeries were finished, Barnett and Shrevi returned to the Emergency Room. Both Barnett and Adam were allowed to close lacerations while Shrevi accompanied Wantz to evaluate a patient with abdominal pain whose findings turned out not to require any surgery. Barnett removed a piece of broken glass from a patient's forearm and closed the wound while Adam cleaned and sutured a nasty gash on a patient's forehead. The students shared in evaluating several other patients with the residents, but none required emergency surgery or even admission. The pace had slowed down, so Adam found time to break away and change Luanne's dressing before meeting Turk, who had suggested they check on the fireman and police officers.

In the male ward, the officer with the shoulder wound was resting comfortably. Further down the row of beds, members of Bunkie Smith's family remained gathered around him. Miss Viola and her brother were absent, but two other adults and a teenaged boy and girl crowded around the bed, holding his hand, fluffing his pillows, and soothing him with their words.

In the ICU, the fireman and Officer Beaudry were being visited by an easily recognizable well-dressed man with neatly combed, wavy silver-gray hair, a double-breasted suit and bright tie, and wire-rimmed glasses. Unlike with the governor, there were no bright lights, reporters, or TV cameras.

Adam overheard the mayor having a conversation with Officer Guidry, still wearing his untucked, blood-stained shirt as he sat near the head of his partner's bed.

"We've been partners for ten years," he said. "Brought him down the stairs myself... Don't feel I should leave him."

"Officer," the mayor replied, "you've done more than your share today. You need to go home, get cleaned up, and get some rest."

"You can come back tomorrow," Turk interjected. "It'll be more important for Beaudry to know you are here when he wakes up and we get him off the ventilator."

Officer Guidry stood up, straightened himself, and tucked in his shirt. The mayor rested his hand on Guidry's shoulder.

"C'mon," he said, "my driver and I will drop you at home."

The mayor looked directly at Turk and Adam. "Thank you, fellas. The city appreciates what you did today."

∾

Adam was sitting on one of the carts in the hallway near the trauma rooms, waiting for the other students, when Carlos walked past.

"How'd you learn so much?" Adam asked him. "Seems like you're always ready and understand exactly what the residents need."

"I've worked here five years," Carlos answered. "Learned on the job."

"But you know so much," said Adam. "Did you ever think about going to medical school?"

"Yes," said Carlos. "Took a chemistry class in junior college. Didn't do so well."

"Couldn't you get a tutor or something to help you?" asked Adam.

"Can't afford that," replied Carlos. "Work a lot of double shifts. Sleep on my cousin's couch. Send most of my money to my mother and sisters in Mexico."

"I think you'd make a good doctor," said Adam.

Carlos gave a faint smile and shrugged, "Thanks."

Watching Carlos enter one of the trauma rooms gave Adam a moment to reflect on his own good fortune in having the opportunity to follow his dreams.

"I'm starved. Let's head to the residents' dining room," Adam suggested when he, Barnett, and Shrevi finally met in the ER hallway.

"Too late," said Barnett looking at his watch. "Closed twenty minutes ago."

An hour later, Adam was still fighting off hunger pangs while sitting outside one of the trauma rooms with Barnett. Shrevi came down the hall and rejoined them.

"Saw a girl with a bellyache with Wantz. Probably a ruptured ovarian cyst. They admitted her to the Gyne service," he said.

Before he could provide any more details, the double doors of the Emergency Room swung open. The ambulance crew rushed past. A young man with a small Afro was lying on the cart with his eyes closed in a frozen grimace. In the trauma room, controlled chaos again erupted, and the students helped as the young man's clothes were cut off, intravenous lines were inserted, and tubes of blood drawn.

"Drug deal went bad. Single shot to the belly. That's all we know," the ambulance crew said in leaving the trauma room and passing Kochenko and Rogers as they entered.

"Single small caliber wound entered above the umbilicus." Rogers inspected the hole above the belly button. "Probably a .22."

"Blood pressure only about 60," Judy announced while making sure the intravenous fluids were running as fast as they could.

Kochenko stood at the head of the table. With Carlos' help, he intubated the patient, first inserting an endotracheal tube into his airway and then threading a nasogastric tube into the stomach. Rogers watched as Barnett cleaned the young man's penis with antiseptic and carefully inserted a Foley catheter into the patient's bladder.

"No blood in the urine," said Rogers. "Hopefully missed the bladder."

"Blood pressure 70," said Judy.

Doyle stepped in and surveyed the scene from the foot of the bed. Kochenko handed Carlos the amber bag forcing oxygen into the patient's lungs. He watched Carlos squeeze the bag and then took one step towards Doyle.

"Low caliber single gunshot to the belly, probably angled down to the pelvis, hypotensive… Not much response to initial fluid bolus."

"We need to go," declared Doyle. He turned towards Adam. "Get the blood to the operating room."

Judy handed Adam requisitions for an immediate four units with more blood and plasma to be typed and crossed for later. Adam clutched the requisitions tightly as he ran to the Blood Bank. This time there was little waiting. He was given the four units and hurried to the elevators.

They were placing the drapes when Adam handed the blood to the circulating nurse. Rogers, Doyle, and Shrevi were dressed in their gowns and gloves.

"Go ahead and scrub," Rogers instructed Adam. "Kochenko is seeing another patient downstairs. Your buddy Styles is with him. Holiday, Kittamura, Turk, and Wantz are down the hall with a GI bleeder."

Adam scrubbed quickly and joined them at the table.

Doyle had opened the belly with a long midline incision. The small intestine had been pulled out of the abdomen, the bullet holes controlled with Babcock clamps, and the bowel wrapped in moist towels.

They placed Adam next to Rogers and across from Shrevi and Doyle. A retractor was placed in his hand, and Rogers handed him a plastic suction. Shrevi already held a suction into the field, but despite the addition of the pull of Adam's second suction, the pelvis remained filled with dark blood. Adam repositioned his suction deeper into the pelvis, but it had little effect in reducing the volume of blood there, even though the continuous flow of dark crimson liquid through the attached tubing indicated that both suctions were working properly.

"Fuck," Doyle muttered as he and Rogers packed the pelvis with lap pads. "Can't see the site of injury. Too much bleeding."

Doyle continued to work quickly as the students tried to suction the pelvis enough to show where the blood was welling up from.. He clamped the external iliac artery leading to the leg and tied a thick silk suture around the internal iliac where it split from the external and dived into the adjacent muscle to supply the deeper pelvis.

"Send for more blood and plasma," Doyle advised the anesthesiologist and circulating nurse. "I don't see the injury to the vein," he said as he applied clamps to the external iliac vein. None of his maneuvers to decrease the inflow of blood seemed to affect the continuing collection in the pelvis. Despite Shrevi and Adam's struggle to suction away the blood the rate of pooling was such that even with the two suctions they barely had any effect.

Rogers held pressure with the cloth pads against the side of the pelvis and gradually peeled them back, hoping to allow Doyle to see the bleeding site. Each time he tried this, he would reach a point where the blood welled up and obscured their vision before any vessel was visible.

While the blood was being transfused and Doyle kept working, the other members of Service 1 finished what they had been doing and gravitated into the room. Wantz and Turk stood on metal steps near Anesthesia and peered over the drapes. Barnett stood beside them.

"Candidate for the SNOW award?" said Shrevi.

No one laughed. Desperate silence filled the room.

Holiday and Kittamura went to the scrub sinks, washed their hands, and reentered the room, crowding Shrevi and Adam at the table.

No one spoke as the four most experienced surgeons on the service continued trying to control the bleeding for another twenty-five minutes.

"His pressure is tanking around 50," announced Anesthesia, "and he's bleeding from the endotracheal and N/G tubes. I think we've lost his clotting factors."

"Shit, shit, shit!" Doyle said under his breath before announcing, "Let's pack him and close. If the pressure slows things down and we can get his clotting factors normalized, we can bring him back from Recovery."

They filled the pelvis tightly with lap pads and thick rolls of gauze. Doyle quickly closed the incision, running a single long suture along the abdominal fascia and then asking for a lot of towel clips. He placed the small, pointed clamps, normally used to hold sterile towels in place around the operative field, in a row along the skin so that the edges of the incision were pinched together. Heavy padded dressings were secured over the belly. The patient was lifted onto a cart and the group sprinted down the hall to Recovery.

They hung more blood and drew samples for coagulation studies, but within fifteen minutes there was no longer any recordable blood pressure, and soon the electrocardiogram monitor showed deterioration into an irregular rhythm. When the tracing became a straight line, Doyle instructed the students and junior residents to begin chest compressions and inject epinephrine. After twenty minutes, Doyle quietly stopped them.

"Damn it, he's gone," he said.

Adam, Barnett, and Shrevi stood back while the nurses began their routine. They removed the tubes, IVs, and Foley catheter. Rogers removed the towel clips and replaced them with a few big sutures as the nurses washed the dried blood from the young man's skin. When they finished, his head was placed on a clean pillow and he was covered with fresh sheets.

Doyle left the unit without saying anything else.

The circulating nurse from the OR approached the remaining group.

"I know some of you didn't get to eat," she said. "We've been keeping some plates of jambalaya and French bread in the sterilizer so it's warm. There's plastic forks in the nurses' lounge if you're hungry."

The group sat in the bare room on straight-backed wooden chairs or on the vinyl-covered couches with tarnished metal armrests and legs. Holiday, Rogers, and Kittamura had left, but Kochenko, Turk, and Wantz sat with their plates and discussed the difficulty in getting control of bleeding in pelvic injuries.

"There's so many vessels mixed up down there, he couldn't have done more," Wantz said. "That bleeding was deep in the pelvis."

"He tied off the arterial inflow," said Kochenko, "but even that didn't slow the blood loss."

Adam tried listening to their analysis of the case, but his hunger forced him to focus on the paper plate on his lap. The steam pressure of the autoclave had kept the jambalaya warm, but when the sterilizer had switched to the drying mode, the moisture had disappeared from the bottom layer of white rice and the top layer of sauce had developed into a thin crust. Nevertheless, when Adam tried the first crispy mouthful, he found it delicious. He could tell Barnett and Shrevi were savoring each bite as much as he was.

When Adam finished his last forkful, one of the nurses said, "There's one plate left. Do you know if any of the other residents might want it?"

"I don't know where Doyle went," said Kochenko, "but the other guys have eaten. We'll ask him if we see him."

"If you guys are finished, you should go check the ER and see if there's anything else going on for us," Wantz said, wiping a piece of French bread through the sauce on his plate.

"I'll go," said Adam.

He left the lounge and took the elevator down to the first floor. He walked down the hallway and found all the trauma rooms were empty. He stepped into the triage area and surveyed the waiting room. A few people were waiting to be seen, but, even at that late hour, it was surprisingly empty. He walked towards the front of the room and peered into the adjoining tiled room that opened into the larger area. Straight ahead, a large group of Black people surrounded a dark wooden bench on the far wall. Their heads hung down, and some were crying or softly moaning. In the center of the bench sat a large woman in a faded dress and a thin, worn dark sweater. She held a handkerchief in her left hand, but her tears fell onto the shoulder of the man in the scrub suit sitting next to her. Bobby Doyle hugged her tightly, red-faced, tears rolling down his cheeks, holding onto his bright purple scrub cap with its embroidered giraffes.

Week Six

CHAPTER 87

ADAM WAS STILL sleepy when he began work rounds early
Sunday morning. He was surprised to find Luanne awake when
he arrived. She was sitting up with her huge legs dangling off
the side of the bed. She smiled when she saw him and lay back
against her pillows. She pulled the sheet over her knees, lifting
her gown to expose her abdominal dressing.

"You're an early riser this morning," observed Adam.

"Ah'm feeling a whole lot better today... Nurses helped
me walk to the bathroom last night. Ah am definitely gettin'
stronger."

"I can see you are moving better," he said, although he
wondered just how well someone her size could actually move.
Despite her illness, it didn't seem to Adam that she had lost
any weight.

He removed her old dressing and studied the wound. The
bright pink granulation tissue was only about three-quarters
of an inch lower than the skin, and the skin edges were much

closer together than they had been previously. Despite her dark complexion, there was a clearly visible quarter-inch rim of a purplish hue that ringed the entire border of the wound. Adam had noted the color change before, but now he understood what it represented.

"See that color?" he said. "I think that's the new skin growing in to close the wound."

"How long will that be?"

"I don't know…but it seems like it's progressing pretty quick."

"When can I go home?"

"I don't know… Not up to me."

He spread a thin layer of streptokinase on the wound and replaced the dressings. "It's nice to see you awake this morning, and I'm glad you're feeling stronger."

"Well, Ah ain't planning to wake up this early again," she answered. "You know I still gotta wait two hours for them to bring breakfast."

None of the residents wanted to spend a lot of time on their rounds once the students had completed the early morning work. Most were eager to leave the hospital after the night on call, and so, by 11 a.m., Adam was on his way back to his apartment. He dawdled on the way home, stopping by the drugstore on Canal Street, making yet another futile attempt to find a bandage scissors. While he strolled along Royal Street his thoughts were on organizing his studies for the evening.

He stopped at the corner grocery and picked up a shrimp po-boy and a can of cream soda to take home for his evening meal. Walking through Jackson Square, he thought of doing as much reading that evening as possible, even though he knew it would not make a dent in the remaining assignments, and the upcoming week's lectures would add a few hundred more pages to the reading list.

CHAPTER 88

MONDAY MORNING'S LECTURES added yet another hundred pages to the subspecialty readings. As they walked back to the hospital, Barnett and Shrevi again discussed the upcoming exam.

"You know," Barnett said, "if everybody can't do all the reading, it won't matter much. They've got to grade us on a curve."

"Some curve," said Shrevi. "Could be the highest grade is like 25 percent and the lowest is 23."

"How do you curve that?" said Adam. "I wonder if they give a lot of weight to the residents' evaluations."

"I don't know," said Shrevi. "Fact is, I always seem to do pretty well on exams. For this, don't worry about being at the top of the class. I mean, we showed up, did as much as possible. We ought to have learned enough to pass."

"I hope so," said Adam.

Rounds with the residents were relaxed and brief, as had been the habit on clinic days.

As the afternoon began, Shrevi went to the female clinic with Wantz and Kittamura. In the male clinic, Barnett and Adam eagerly joined Kochenko and Turk in seeing as many of the post-op and new patients as possible. Adam thought that if they worked efficiently, they might finish in time to study that night.

When the waiting area became crowded, Rogers would grab a few charts and help thin the crowd while Holiday and Doyle, sipping coffee, remained available to check the students' work. Mostly, though, they stood near the exam rooms discussing college football unless there was a post-op patient they wanted to check on or they were specifically requested by one of the junior members of Service 1.

At first, Adam didn't recognize the tall, well-groomed old man when he stood up in the middle of the crowded waiting area. Only when Sam Elder's grandson stood up next to him did Adam recognize their recent patient. When Sam began slow, steady strides towards the long table near the exam rooms, his grandson fell in step behind him.

"Hi, Doc," the old man said when he recognized Adam standing at the table. Adam marveled at Sam's height, realizing when Sam had been sick in bed or hunched over in the wheelchair, he had no idea how tall the ex-firefighter actually was. More important, it was hard to believe that this was the same elderly man who had been so close to death.

Turk joined them in the treatment cubicle. Sam pulled up his shirt to reveal the long incision under his rib cage and the brown tube draining green bile into the plastic bag that was taped to his side.

"Looks like you're doing pretty well," Turk said. He disconnected the drainage bag from the brown rubber tube, folded the tube on itself, and sealed it by crisscrossing a rubber band around it. "We'll leave the tube clamped for another couple weeks and X-ray your bile duct before we remove it—just a precaution to make sure there's no more stone fragments in the bile duct."

Turk covered the exposed portion of the tube with a piece of gauze and taped the gauze down.

"Sooner it's out, the better," Sam said. "At least the damn bag's gone."

"In the meantime, you come right back if there's any pain, fever, or green drainage around the tube."

Sam nodded in understanding, but his grandson spoke up. "Grandpa's not being a good patient. He walked six blocks the other day to the fire station. My mom kinda freaked out when she realized he was gone."

"It's a little too warm to be out walking that much," said Turk.

"Well, I wanted to see the boys and help them polish the equipment."

"See, he's difficult," said the grandson. "Doctor, what do you recommend we do?"

Turk turned to Adam. "What do you think they should do?"

"Drive him to the station instead of letting him walk," said Adam.

Nodding in agreement Turk added, "We'll see him back here next week."

By mid-afternoon the waiting area had thinned out considerably, although quite a few patients remained to be seen. Teddy suddenly appeared in the doorway, paused, and surveyed the clinic as everyone stopped to stare at him.

He looked like an Alpine hiker. He was wearing heavy tan boots with red laces, white stockings that extended to his knees, a short-sleeved pink oxford cloth shirt, and lederhosen. A small fedora with a colorful feather displayed prominently in the hat band completed his outfit. His right hand held an elaborate cane, which he leaned on as he began a slow approach to the nurses' desk. As he moved up the aisle, he took his time and stopped to greet the other waiting patients. The closer he came, the more the details of his cane became visible. The handle was ivory carved in the shape of a rearing bull with a penis enlarged beyond normal proportions. The handle rested on an ebony shaft that was adorned with inlaid silver bands and stars.

The intake nurse at the table was taken by his appearance while he registered.

"I'll try to get someone to see you right away, Mr. Lemieux," she said.

Teddy countered, raising his left palm, "Oh, no, nothing special. I will take my place in the waiting area and await my turn with the other patients."

The pace of the clinic returned to normal, and the flow of patients into the exam rooms resumed. Teddy seated himself in the middle of the waiting area and pleasantly conversed with all around him. He clearly enjoyed talking with everyone and hearing their stories, no matter how indigent, uneducated, or unwashed they might be.

Adam and Kochenko ushered Teddy into an exam cubicle. Holiday, Doyle, and Rogers all left their spots along the back wall to crowd into the small space.

"It's nice to receive the ministrations of so many of my benefactors," said Teddy.

He unbuttoned his suspenders and opened his shirt, revealing a huge stack of large gauze pads taped to his skin. Adam peeled the dressings away, exposing a perfectly healing incision.

"That looks great," said Kochenko. "That scar is going to be a very thin line someday."

"I don't think you need to cover it with so many dressings," said Rogers.

"One can never be too careful," said Teddy.

The senior residents excused themselves and left Adam to replace the gauze over Teddy's incision. He neatly secured a much smaller gauze over the wound and waited while Teddy buttoned his shirt and fastened his suspenders. Once he felt he was presentable, Teddy picked up his cane and slowly hobbled towards the canvas covering the entrance to the exam station. Adam noted that the hobble in his gait had been absent when Teddy had entered the clinic and walked down the aisle.

"What's with the cane?" he asked.

"I find it essential to my convalescence."

"Did you injure your leg or ankle?"

"No, but I find when one is recuperating from a close brush with death, everything helps."

Clinic was winding down; the waiting area was nearly empty. Kochenko offered advice for the next day.

"Be sure you're up to date on your patients and the consults on other wards. Dr. Theodorakis likes to make thorough rounds on everybody on the service before you take your final exam."

CHAPTER 89

THE NEXT AFTERNOON, Dr. Theodorakis arrived on the ward with his entourage. He waited for his residents and students to take their places close to the bedside while the other services crowded around behind them. Everyone remained paused for a moment before he asked, "Who is ready to present the first patient?"

The first patient was Barnett's. He sailed through the presentation. Dr. Theodorakis set the tone for the afternoon. When he discussed the patients, he asked questions, but not in a way that would embarrass anyone. If someone didn't know an answer, he provided a concise explanation. Over the course of the afternoon, he went into detail about each patient. The entire group listened carefully as he reiterated the important points regarding each case. He expanded on the topics familiar to the students from their textbooks or lectures, pointed out journal articles that brought new insights into each case, and discussed practical aspects of surgical techniques and patient management primarily for the benefit of the resident staff.

When the group approached the last patient in ICU, Officer Guidry was again at his partner's bedside. He stood, hat in hand, and listened intently as Theodorakis reviewed his fellow officer's case. The policeman didn't understand all of the discussion about pulmonary trauma, the distinction between simple pneumothorax and a "tension pneumo," the approach to stabilization and evaluation, or concern for other accompanying thoracic injuries. What he did understand—bringing a smile to his face—was the conclusion that Officer Beaudry was quite stable and expected to recover fully.

As the other residents and students began to leave, Guidry addressed Dr. Theodorakis. "Thank you, sir, for saving his life. You know, we've been partners for fourteen years."

Later, in the hallway, Barnett remarked to his buddies, "Guidry keeps adding to the time they've been partners. If he doesn't get his math straight, pretty soon he'll be saying that they were partners since they were twins in utero."

"Let's continue to the consults on other floors," said Theodorakis once he had dismissed the others and only Service 1 remained.

On the female medical ward, Barnett presented Leticia Powell. Her wounds were healing well, and she was noticeably calmer and less argumentative, probably due to the psychiatric medication that Battiste had begun slipping into her morning oatmeal starting soon after his senior resident had accepted her in transfer.

On the Gynecology floor, Adam presented Luanne's history as he removed the dressings from her incision. He looked up to see approval in Holiday and Doyle's faces before he focused on Dr. Theodorakis.

"Nice and clean," Dr. Theodorakis said as he examined the site. "This wound should soon be ready for you to take her back to the OR and close the skin over a Hemovac drain. Leave her on antibiotics for a couple of days before you pull the drain and discharge her."

Luanne's smile indicated to Adam that her questions about discharge had been answered. Adam returned a smile that reflected pride in his accomplishment. The same LPN who kept dressings at the bedside was on duty. She came to the bedside and began replacing the dressings so that Adam could leave the ward with the rest of the group.

They followed Theodorakis and the senior residents towards the elevators. Before they stopped, Kochenko whispered in Adam's ear, "You see, it takes patience to care for patients. Really is a virtue…especially when combined with a rigorous regimen of wound care."

<h1 style="text-align:center">CHAPTER 90</h1>

ADAM AND BARNETT missed lecture the next morning, as both were required to attend the elective surgical procedures being performed on patients who had been admitted through the Surgery Clinic. Both hoped that Shrevi would take clear notes in lecture and that there wouldn't be too many more pages added to the assigned reading.

Adam was holding retractors while Doyle and Kittamura helped Kochenko repair a hernia in a patient's previous C-section incision. Barnett was in another room, poking a suction into a patient's anus made bloody when Wantz's clamp slipped off the hemorrhoid he was removing. Rogers and Holiday sat outside the room, chatting over their morning coffee.

By noon, five cases had been completed. Barnett went to find Shrevi and his lecture notes while Adam returned to the male ward to finish the chart notes from that morning. Jen smiled at him when he entered the ward. She sat at her desk

~ 418 ~

and rummaged through her bag while he carried two charts to the foot of a patient's bed and began to write the first of his notes. Jen put down her bag and joined him, carrying a small white box with a red ribbon around it.

"I know it's your last week," she said. "I'm going to be taking a few days off, and I wanted to give you a gift to thank you for the advice."

"That's nice of you…but I'm not sure what advice I…uh…"

She handed him the little box. "What you said about enablers when we were at Teddy's… It struck a chord with me. I looked at the people around my husband…his friends at work… They don't realize it, but they encourage his drinking. It's not a problem for them to drink, but it is for him. So I decided I need to get him away from that. I'm taking a few days to take him across the lake to Mandeville. He's actually agreed to enter the alcohol rehab center there."

"Oh," said Adam, still not understanding how simple conversation from him could be considered sage advice from a medical professional. "Can I open the box now, or should I wait?"

"Go ahead," she said. "I noticed you needed it."

He gently removed the ribbon and opened the box. Lying on a bed of cotton was a bandage scissors, but not the usual silver of stainless steel. This scissors was tinted gold.

"Everybody always loses their scissors," she said. "I thought this one might be easier to keep track of."

"It's gold," he said, "like an award."

"Well, I see new students come through here every six weeks, and I thought you did a good job."

Adam was taken by the smile in her eyes.

"Use a safety pin to hold it in the pocket of your lab coat," she said.

"Thanks." He paused, then added, "Maybe we'll get to work together again sometime."

"That would be nice," she said, looking back over her shoulder as she walked towards her desk.

Adam kept glancing at the scissors he had placed on the corner of his desk while he studied that night. He read through the copy of Shrevi's morning lecture notes that Barnett had made for him on the machine in the library. He copied them into his own notebook, referring to the textbook whenever something wasn't clear or when he couldn't decipher Shrevi's handwriting.

He worked until well after midnight, refreshing himself when necessary with a short walk around his apartment or a moment of standing and stretching. He focused on each lecture or textbook chapter to retain as much as he could, doing his best to not be distracted or overwhelmed by how much more there was to read and commit to memory before the exam.

CHAPTER 91

THURSDAY MORNING WAS Adam's turn to attend the morning lecture and take notes while Shrevi and Barnett joined the residents in the operating rooms. He carefully wrote his notes in complete sentences and paragraphs and made them as legible as he could. He ignored the frustration of having more textbook pages added to the list of things he wouldn't have time to read before the exam. He stopped in the library and made photocopies of the lecture notes for his friends before returning to the wards.

He waited on the ward for the rest of the service to return. Jen was gone; the nurse filling in for her was another young RN. She was friendly when Adam introduced himself. Like Jen, she carried herself with a sense of confidence and professionalism.

Miss Viola had called Holiday to inform him that Dr. Theodorakis would not be making rounds that afternoon. Instead, the students made rounds with the residents. All three knew their patients' illnesses and their surgical procedures, but that brought no satisfaction when rounds ended and they gathered on the male ward to pick up their book bags before leaving.

"Too bad the exam doesn't just cover the patients we've been following," said Barnett.

"No kiddin'," agreed Shrevi. "I don't even know how much of that book I haven't read."

"It's so different from other coursework we've done. I don't think I've ever gone into a test with so many loose ends," said Adam. "I've always felt I knew everything before a test, but this…"

"Sorry to butt in," said Kochenko, "but we told you not to expect to learn everything in six weeks."

Turk and Wantz stood behind him. They were eavesdropping too.

"Treatment room will do. Pull up some chairs," said Kochenko. "Maybe we can help you prepare for the exam a bit. It shouldn't seem like facing an execution."

They moved into the treatment room, cleared some floor space, and placed folding chairs in a circle. Turk and Kochenko took their seats, but Wantz left the ward.

"This is a different kind of learning than you are used to," said Kochenko. "Nobody remembers it all. I've heard it said that the whole point of medical training is to learn how to function in the face of ignorance. It all changes anyway. Just when you think you do know it all, some research or some new idea comes along and upends everything. In surgical training there's another dimension. We learn surgical technique and try to master it even though at some point we're going to have to use it to treat something we've never seen or done before. I mean, think about it. If you owned a dynamite company and had to send an order to the mines in West Virginia, who would you want to deliver it? Some guy who had memorized all the roads in West Virginia but had never driven an eighteen-wheeler, or some guy who had never been to West Virginia but knew how to drive the friggin' truck?"

Turk smiled weakly in agreement. Adam worried that Turk looked like someone who lacked confidence in his ability to face unexpected situations.

"Is there anything specific you guys want to go over—from your lectures or the textbook or what you've seen on the rotation?" asked Kochenko.

All three students were thinking about a response when the double doors to the treatment room opened. Wantz stood there, his stocky frame threatening, short legs apart, hands on his hips. Clutched in his left hand was a large paperback book filled with multiple choice questions as thick as the New York City phonebook. Big block letters were printed on the cover: *SURGICAL REVIEW*.

"OK, children," he said, "nobody on MY service does poorly… Time to teach you about tests. I have always loved a challenge. Nobody beats me!"

He handed Kochenko the book while he found a folding chair and opened it. Kochenko passed the book around so the students could thumb through it. Adam noted it was divided into sections not unlike the regular textbook's table of contents.

The book was handed back to Kochenko.

"Any specific questions?" he asked. He passed the book back to Wantz.

"I didn't understand the physiology of congenital heart defects," said Shrevi. "Pretty much all of them were listed without much explanation."

"Right," said Adam. "How do you keep straight which ones cause blue babies and which ones get enough oxygen to keep them pink?"

"Hell, you don't have to know that much detail," said Wantz. "Mostly in a test for junior students they'll only ask you the four components of the Tetralogy of Fallot."

He looked to Kochenko for agreement while he thumbed through the pages on congenital heart disease.

"I think that's usually true," agreed Kochenko. "If you remember the pressures in the chambers of the heart, you can figure out the direction of blood flow, but I doubt they'd ask more."

"Next topic," Wantz announced.

No one volunteered a topic, so Wantz thumbed through the book until he found a suitable page.

"Hernias," he said. "Here's a good question. 'The use of Cooper's ligament to support an inguinal hernia repair is integral to which type of repair: a) Bassini repair; b) Davidson repair; c) Smith repair; d) Martin repair; or, e) McVay repair.'"

"It's e," said Barnett.

"I don't even remember what the Davidson, Smith, or Martin repairs are," fretted Shrevi.

"Ha," laughed Kochenko. "They don't even exist. The only other real hernia repair is the Bassini. Do you remember which anatomic structure it uses to do the repair in place of Cooper's ligament?"

"Inguinal ligament," said Adam.

"Correct," said Kochenko.

"Next question," said Wantz. The gleam in his eye seemed less sadistic than usual.

They continued until well after 8 p.m. Wantz, Kochenko, and Turk took turns reading the questions. Anything missed they discussed in detail as they proceeded through several sections of the big book. They promised to do more the next day if there was time to be had in the afternoon.

During his walk home, Adam found himself rushing with enthusiasm. He foraged through his kitchen cabinet, pulling out a can of condensed vegetable soup. While the soup was heating on the stove, he began to read his lecture notes. Before he knew it, the soup boiled over, leaving the bottom of the pan scorched. He poured it into a bowl and casually took spoonfuls while he continued reading. His studying continued until just after midnight when he crawled into bed, still thinking about the McVay repair...

CHAPTER 92

BUNKIE SMITH PASSED sometime during the evening. When Adam had left the night before, a curtain on a metal frame had been rolled around his bed, where Miss Viola sat holding Bunkie's hand while her brother and their relatives shared the vigil. In the morning, everyone was gone, the screen had been removed, and his empty bed was now freshly made.

Adam paused at the nurses' desk for a moment, staring at what had been Bunkie's bed. He imagined the widespread mourning for a musician whose fame extended well beyond New Orleans, but he knew the greatest loss would be felt by Bunkie's family.

No one else acknowledged the loss. The residents excused the three students from the morning surgeries so they could attend the last lecture, which covered the surgical pharmacology of the cardiovascular system and extracorporeal and assisted circulation, and added another hundred and twenty pages to the reading assignments. In closing, the lecturer advised them that Monday's exam would begin promptly at 10 a.m.

The promised review session that Kochenko, Wantz, and Turk conducted later in the afternoon continued well past sundown. Adam felt somewhat better about facing the exam on Monday, so he decided to take a slow walk home down Bourbon Street and stop at Felix's Oyster Bar, where he sat at a corner table reading his notes on extracorporeal circulation while awaiting his bowl of oyster stew.

CHAPTER 93

ROGERS AND KITTAMURA were on the wards early Saturday morning.

"No need to stick around for additional rounds after Bullpen," said Rogers. "Get your work done now and then you can take off to use the time to study for your exam. Remember, we've got ER call tomorrow, so expect we might be busy."

Rogers' statement sent a momentary wave of anxiety through Adam. He had always been one to cram before a test. He usually studied right up until the exam booklets were passed out. He first memorized his notes, then recited them over and over so that they would be imprinted in his memory. A day of ER call would distract him from that routine. He worried that it would affect his performance on the test, obsessing over the possibility that he might have to take the exam after a busy night of ER call with little or no sleep.

The morning's Grand Rounds focused on rectal cancer. The attending surgeons again tried to outdo each other by quoting arcane and obscure studies suggesting whether the use of radiation therapy was more beneficial pre- or post-operatively. Adam sat only half listening as he read through the textbook section on rectal cancers. Barnett appeared to listen, but Adam wasn't sure if he was paying attention or thinking about something that was more likely to be asked on their examination.

Shrevi had picked a seat behind the student in their class who had been an offensive lineman as an undergrad at Denison. The football player's broad shoulders shielded Shrevi, who sat for the entire Grand Rounds with his notebook open, reviewing his lecture notes for several topics, none of which involved rectal cancer.

When Grand Rounds ended, the students stood up to stretch and move towards the front seats. Adam was surprised to see Melissa stand up far to his right. After Brewster's treatment of her, he'd doubted she would attend another session. Instead, she moved deliberately to the center of the third row, where she sat straight up, her natural height making her plainly visible.

Shrevi was the first to move. He marched down the steps and took the seat directly in front of her. Barnett and Adam followed and slid into the seats on either side of her. They were followed by others until she was surrounded by male students, chivalrous as knights, eager to shield her from any further unwarranted attacks from a mean-spirited preceptor.

Their concern turned out to be unnecessary. There were no moments of embarrassment or humiliation in this week's Bullpen. Dr. Theodorakis conducted the session in the most relaxed manner anyone had seen. When the first student, who happened to be female, missed the important physical finding of a metastatic nodule in the liver of a patient with rectal cancer, he simply stood up and walked towards the patient. He then demonstrated how distracting a patient with conversation could cause him to relax his abdominal muscles and allow an easier examination. He took the student's hand and moved it back and forth across the patient's upper abdomen until her eyes brightened and she acknowledged that she could feel the irregular, hard mass.

"The spread of disease to the liver often makes the performance of a radical resection of little value…although local control of the rectal tumor may be difficult," he explained.

The second student elicited snickers from the audience when he mistakenly listed "tuberculosis" as the most likely cause of his patient's apparently benign breast mass. Dr. Theodorakis calmly pointed out that although TB could cause a breast lesion, it would be a very rare circumstance. He reviewed the absence of any other findings in this particular patient that might suggest the possibility of a tuberculous infection, including a review of her normal chest X-ray, which Wantz conveniently placed on the view box for all to see.

Dr. Theodorakis then simply walked the student's thinking back and helped him to construct a more realistic differential diagnosis of benign breast tumors, beginning with the frequently encountered fibroadenoma.

He completed the lesson with the careful admonition, "Remember, common things are common… When you hear hoofbeats look for horses, not zebras."

Adam walked to the elevator alongside Melissa after Bullpen had been dismissed.

"I didn't get to say anything to you, but I thought it was unfair that Brewster singled you out for all those questions last week. I guess he's still giving you a hard time on your rotation… Probably doesn't think women should have careers in medicine."

She stopped walking and looked Adam directly in the eye.

"I plan to be a surgeon just like my daddy…and no one, including that motherfucker, is going to stop me."

Adam relaxed as he walked home along Chartres Street. The sky was sunny and bright. A breeze off the river made the heat somewhat bearable as he navigated through the tourists that milled about Jackson Square. He crossed Decatur Street near the Café Du Monde and followed the sidewalk until he entered the colonnade of the French Market. He stopped at one of the food stands and purchased an oyster po-boy, a bag of chips, and a can of lemon-lime soda to take back to his apartment. He then leisurely walked the main aisle of the market past the carts selling souvenirs, scarves, pictures, leather goods, jewelry, and African statues and small drums.

Stopping at one table that held little sculptures of musicians made from twisted wire, he stood for a moment and watched as the proprietor, a heavyset Black man in a bright red T-shirt, nimbly worked on his latest creation.

Adam scanned the row of figures until he found one in a familiar pose. It was a trumpet player, sitting on a chair like the musicians who performed at Preservation Hall. He interrupted the sculptor long enough to give him two dollars, and they chatted as the sculptor wrapped the figure in tissue paper. Adam thanked the artist and slipped the figure into the pocket of his white coat before continuing to his apartment, where another long afternoon and evening of study awaited him.

CHAPTER 94

EVEN PREDAWN ON a Sunday morning, the newsstand on the corner of Royal and Canal Streets was open. Since the bus wasn't running that early on the weekend, Adam chose Royal Street to avoid encountering any of the hungover stragglers on Decatur or Bourbon. His morning bag of beignets rested in his book bag, and he carefully clutched the cup of café au lait in his left hand.

The man running the corner newsstand cut the string binding the most recently delivered papers, lifted the bundle, and stepped from behind his counter so that he could plop the stack of newspapers on the floor near the cash register. Adam read the little box in the lower corner of the front page of the *New York Times*: "Bunkie Smith, famed trumpeter, 76."

Adam bought a copy of the paper, rolled it up, placed it in his book bag, and did not open it until he was comfortably seated on a bench in the hospital's lobby. He placed the beignets next to him and took his first sip of coffee before opening the paper.

Bunkie's obituary took up half a page. Stretching all the way across the top was a reprinted photograph that Adam vaguely recalled seeing many years ago. On the right, the back of Bunkie's head and his left shoulder had been captured while he stood on stage. His left arm spread across the bottom of the picture until, near the edge of the frame, his outstretched arm held his trumpet with the mouthpiece pointing straight up. Over his arm was an audience extending as far as the eye could see, hemmed by the familiar spires and turrets of Red Square. The article mentioned Bunkie's groundbreaking tour of the Soviet Union in the late 1950s and also included a small insert reproducing the ubiquitous postcard with him sitting as part of the Preservation Hall Jazz Band.

Finishing the beignets and taking the last swig of his coffee, Adam folded the newspaper and slid it back into his book bag. His first stop was the Gynecology ward, where he changed Luanne's dressing without disturbing her slumber.

"Appendix and a trauma in the ER," Shrevi said, striding out of the male ward as Adam approached. "We gotta go."

Completing rounds would have to wait. Adam followed his classmate to the elevators. In the ER, Adam found Kochenko with the appendicitis patient, a young boy who appeared to be about ten years old. Shrevi went on to join Turk, Wantz, and Rogers in the trauma room.

"Go take a look at the trauma case," Kochenko instructed Adam, waving him down the hall, "but come back to go to Surgery with me."

Adam stood in the doorway and calmly watched the controlled chaos in the trauma room. A middle-aged woman lay on the cart with two IVs running in her arms and a Foley catheter and nasogastric tube in place. The nurses were adjusting the IV rate and labeling the blood tubes to be sent to the lab. Rogers was positioning an oxygen mask strapped around the patient's head.

"Seat-belted driver, T-boned on her way to church this morning. Guy who ran the red light probably going about 60," was Wantz's introduction.

Adam gazed around the room and filled in the rest of the story. A blunt-tipped Potter's needle lay among the crumpled paper drapes on a small metal tray table that had been pushed to the side. The band-aid on the right side of her belly further indicated that the diagnostic abdominal tap had been completed.

"Blood in the belly," Rogers said before Shrevi whispered to Adam, "No studying tonight."

Soon Shrevi, Wantz, and Rogers were headed for the OR with the trauma patient while Adam and Kochenko were joined by Kittamura to take the appendix to another operating room.

When they returned to the ER, they found Barnett grasping the edge of a waste can just outside the door to a commotion-filled room.

"Horrible burn," he said.

He took a few slow, deep breaths while leaning forward as though he was waiting for his breakfast to come up.

"You OK?" asked Adam.

"Yeah, I'm OK." Barnett pushed the can back against the wall and lingered while Adam and Kochenko moved towards the nearby room.

Holiday and Doyle were standing over a cart containing something that resembled a human form. The singed, charred body filled the room with a smoky odor. A ventilator pumped oxygen into the endotracheal tube. A Foley catheter and nasogastric tube were in place. Two IV lines were running wide open, allowing fluid to pour through the tubing into the patient's arms.

"Is it the worst you've ever seen?" Sergeant Landry was standing in the opposite corner of the room.

"I'd estimate 85 to 90 percent burned," Holiday answered.

"Gasoline explosion in the garage," Landry said. "Mighta been smoking." The policeman continued, "I'll check back with you later before I file my report. If you need me, I'll be upstairs visiting the fellas from the shooting."

Doyle was scribbling something on the chart in his hand. He held up a progress note covered in calculations. "Brooke Army formula for determining fluid replacement in badly burned patients. You boys better learn it for your exam."

Holiday had the nurse prepare some sterile saline-soaked gauze and watched attentively as Barnett and Adam donned sterile gloves and placed the gauze over the burned areas. Shrevi, Wantz, Rogers, Turk, and Kittamura stood just inside the room. Their patient from the auto accident was now resting comfortably in the Recovery Room following removal of her spleen.

"I can get a burn unit bed ready," said Rogers.

"If they've got one," said Holiday. "You guys do what you need to with any other patients. Larry and the students will stay here with me."

Holiday was quiet as he watched the EKG monitor. The heart rate slowed to 60, then 50. The EKG spikes became irregular and distorted and the waves widened when the rate slowed to 30.

Alarms buzzed first from the heart monitor and then from the ventilator. A moment later, another alarm sounded when the EKG tracing became a straight line.

"What do you want to do, doctors?" Holiday asked.

A nurse rolled a crash cart near the gurney.

Kochenko thumped his fist on the patient's chest and then placed one hand on the other and began rhythmic chest compressions.

The nurse opened the top drawer of the crash cart and stood by, waiting.

"What else?" asked Holiday.

Barnett pulled the spiral-bound *Guide to Surgical Therapy* from the pocket of his white coat, checked the table of contents, and then set it down on the foot of the bed so that he could share the open page with Shrevi.

Looking down, Shrevi blurted out, "Epinephrine! We should give him some epinephrine!"

The nurse who had brought the crash cart injected the contents of a small syringe into the patient's IV tubing.

"One amp given," she said.

Kochenko disconnected the ventilator and replaced it with a rubber bag attached to oxygen tubing. He twisted a dial on the attached oxygen tank and squeezed the bag twice before he gestured for Shrevi to take over.

The EKG monitor remained in an erratic pattern until Kochenko told Adam to stop the compressions and the monitor revealed a straight line interrupted by a few spikes.

Barnett was focused on the open book. "Bicarbonate," he said, "he needs sodium bicarbonate."

The nurse injected the contents of a much larger syringe.

"Another epinephrine," requested Barnett while Kochenko told Adam to resume the chest compressions.

After the injection, an EKG pattern appeared on the screen.

"Hold the compressions. Is there a pulse?" asked Kochenko.

Adam placed his hand into the patient's groin and pushed his fingertips against the femoral artery.

"I don't feel a pulse," he said.

"Don't get tired. You two switch." Holiday indicated it was time for Barnett to perform the chest compressions.

The students worked for another thirty minutes, changing positions, ordering medications, and hoping the patient would respond. The EKG pattern returned to the screen intermittently, usually with a slow rate, until only a straight flat line remained. Kochenko took the paddles from the defibrillator on the cart and placed them on the patient's chest. He had Adam take the paddles and cautioned, "Don't lean against the cart. Announce before you fire so everyone is back from the cart. Like this," he said. "Get back... Stand by... Fire!"

Adam pressed the buttons on the handles and the patient jumped as the jolt of electricity shot through him. Wide electrical complexes appeared momentarily on the screen and then disappeared.

"You," Holiday pointed so that Shrevi understood he was to take the defibrillator paddles from Adam.

"Clear," said Kochenko.

Everyone stood back from the cart.

"Ready," said Shrevi. "Fire!"

The patient jumped again as Shrevi sent another electrical charge coursing through him.

"Nothing on the monitor," Kochenko announced.

"One more," said Holiday.

Barnett took the paddles. "Clear… Fire!"

Nothing appeared on the screen but a straight green line.

"I'm calling it," said Holiday. "We're done."

Adam rode up in the elevator with Kochenko. He was planning to change Luanne's dressing again before the ER got too busy.

"I feel so bad we lost that guy," said Adam.

"Nobody survives who's that badly burned," Kochenko answered.

"But Holiday had us work so long on him…"

"Now you'll know how to do it for the next time when it may really matter."

CHAPTER 95

LUANNE WAS SITTING up in her bed, sucking the wooden spoon from another cup of sherbet. She smiled when Adam entered the ward.

"Didn't expect you'd come no more," she said. "They told me I get closed up tomorrow."

Adam smiled. "Didn't want to leave anything to chance. You know I'm finished with my surgical rotation tomorrow."

"You're not gonna be doing my operating?" she asked. "Who's gonna?"

"I'm just a third-year student," he reminded her. "One of the residents will close your wound. I've got to take an exam tomorrow."

He efficiently changed her dressing, squeezing the last bit of remaining streptokinase onto a tongue blade and smearing it across the wound surface before covering the area with gauze pads and securing the dressing.

"Looks good," he said. "Should heal beautifully when it's closed."

God, I hope it heals, he thought.

As Adam cleaned up the supplies and discarded the old dressing, Luanne was quiet. She searched for the right words.

"Doctor…" She hesitated. "I want you to know I appreciate what you done for me. Most of the men I've met never done good by me, but you've treated me real nice, like a real person. I knowed how bad my belly was. My nurses said they'd never seen anything like it, and I could see the scared look on the face of that doctor who done my surgery every time he and the others passed by my bed. You done real good, and I wanted to say thank you. I'll never forget you."

"Well, Luanne," Adam said, "I am sure I will never forget you."

As the elevator took him back to the first floor and the ER, Adam wondered how anybody could ever forget meeting a sweet, 400-pound prostitute who used to sing in the church choir.

∽

Sergeant Landry was speaking with Holiday and Doyle when Adam joined them in the ER.

"I got a report on my way here," said the officer. "Three dead bodies found in a warehouse along Tchoupitoulas Street… Gunshot victims… Something's going down. We've had reports of increasing drug activity over the past few days. This may mean a war between rival dealers. Just wanted to give y'all a heads up."

Holiday and Doyle thanked him, but after the officer left, they seemed to shrug it off.

"Oughta just let those fuckers kill each other," said Doyle. "And good riddance. We'll probably be busy enough tonight."

At quarter to five, Barnett was in the ER, sewing a laceration under Kochenko's watchful eye. Wantz had insisted that Shrevi accompany him to consult on a twenty-three-week pregnant woman with abdominal pain who had been admitted to Obstetrics earlier in the day. Adam followed Holiday and Doyle to the residents' dining room, where Turk, Rogers, and Kittamura were finishing plates of red beans and rice or jambalaya.

They helped themselves to dinner but had only taken a few bites when the residents' pagers began to beep, one after another, as if the ER might be turning into a battlefield hospital.

The first page, answered by Kochenko, involved a motor vehicle accident in which the driver, neglecting his seat belt, had been knocked unconscious. Moments later, Rogers answered another page.

"Two more patients—gunshot to the belly and a stab wound—both picked up in the warehouse district."

Adam shoveled three more forkfuls of red beans into his mouth before he joined the others in tossing their plates in the trash as they headed for the ER.

"Isolated head injury, probably just a concussion," said Kochenko, referring to the patient from the motor vehicle accident. "Belly, chest, and extremities are OK... I alerted the OR about the gunshot wound. Single shot, small caliber, mid to lower abdomen."

"Other guy with the stab wound to the belly needs to be explored too," said Wantz. "He was a little hypotensive at first, but his blood pressure has come up a little with fluids."

There was little opportunity for the students to evaluate the patients, as they were moved to Surgery quickly. Barnett accompanied Doyle, Kittamura, and Kochenko with the gunshot wound while Shrevi joined Wantz and Rogers with the stab wound.

Adam and Turk remained in the ER and Holiday calmly informed them, "This could turn out to be a very long night. I'm going to catch a snooze in my call room. Just let me know if I'm needed."

There were a few other patients to see in the Emergency Room, although none of the consults required a trip to the operating room. Turk did, however, give Adam the opportunity to close a small forehead laceration.

After about an hour and a half, Shrevi, Wantz, and Rogers were back.

"Two holes through and through in the small intestine and bleeding from vessels in the mesentery... They resected the piece of small bowel," Shrevi reported to Adam.

Another twenty minutes and the others returned.

"Bullet hit the small bowel and lodged in the back, just missed the aorta by about two inches... Lucky for him," said Barnett.

A short time later the ER doors swung open as two ambulances arrived simultaneously. When the first crew entered, they were accompanied by Sergeant Landry and two other patrolmen.

"Pretty sure it's a drug war," said Landry. "They're not confined to just the warehouse district. These two were shot on

Bourbon Street. We've got extra patrol cars all over the city, but this may just have to play itself out."

While the new patients were being prepared for surgery, another stab wound to the neck and belly arrived. Rogers paged Holiday, who soon appeared in the ER. All three of the patients had their clothing removed, blood drawn, tubes inserted, and IV lines started. Adam and Turk remained in the ER while the three cases were taken to the operating rooms with remarkable efficiency.

At 10:30, another stab wound arrived. The patient was bleeding profusely from a wound on the right side of his neck. Turk instructed Carlos to put on gloves and hold pressure with a piece of gauze against the neck in order to relieve the ambulance attendant who was pressing a blood-soaked pillowcase on the wound. When Turk popped open the buttons on the man's shirt, Adam counted at least five separate stab wounds on his torso.

Carlos pressed tightly on the man's neck while Adam and the nurses started the IVs, drew the tubes of blood, and began to resuscitate the patient with a rapid infusion of IV fluids.

Fortunately it wasn't too long before Doyle arrived with Shrevi. He had Carlos lift the gauze so that he could examine the wound quickly before the resumption of dark blood flow obscured the field.

"Probably jugular vein," he said. "You got blood ready?"

"Typed and crossed six and thawing two of fresh frozen plasma," answered Turk. "He seems to have an open airway, but I was just going to intubate him."

"Do it," said Doyle before instructing Shrevi to take Carlos' spot and sending Carlos running to the Blood Bank.

"Just bring it up to the OR," he instructed him.

A few minutes later the respiratory therapist taped the breathing tube in place and attached an Ambu bag and oxygen supply. Turk listened with his stethoscope as the therapist squeezed the bag and pushed oxygen into the man's lungs.

"Good breath sounds on both sides. I think the tube is in good position. Do you want a chest X-ray?"

"Later," said Doyle. "We'll do one upstairs... Need to get the bleeding under control."

Moments later, Adam watched as Doyle pulled the cart from the trauma room and headed towards the elevators with the respiratory therapist squeezing the oxygen bag, guiding the rear wheels while a wide-eyed Shrevi ran alongside, pushing on the patient's neck with both hands.

While the nurses straightened the room, Adam kicked his book bag into a corner in the trauma room before helping the nurse put sheets on the cart that had been brought in to replace the one taken to the OR.

Rogers returned to the area and spent a brief respite of ten minutes explaining to Turk and Adam the findings on the patients that had been taken to the operating rooms.

Sirens screamed outside and flashing lights announced the arrival of two more gunshots. Holiday and Kittamura appeared with Barnett in tow just as the patients were placed in separate trauma rooms, their airways secured, clothes cut off, IVs started, blood drawn, bladder catheters and nasogastric tubes inserted, and X-rays taken.

"Large caliber wound, right upper abdomen," reported Rogers.

Adam had finished taping the patient's endotracheal tube in place when Turk called from the hallway.

"This one is a large caliber too. Two entrance sites, left upper quadrant. One exit wound in the back. Lower wound looks like it exits in the right flank... Must have turned when he was hit by that one. He's intubated, pressure is about 60."

Holiday picked up the wall phone. "Two more gunshots, both hypotensive. Can you accommodate two more rooms?... Okay, on our way."

He turned to the others. "Wantz is scrubbed with Doyle. Kochenko will meet me in the OR. Kitty, you and Rogers take one guy. I'll take the guy with the right-sided wound."

He looked at Barnett. "Stick with me."

Carlos ran down the hall with blood for both patients, and transfusions were started before they were wheeled out of the trauma rooms. After Rogers and Kittamura moved their patient towards the elevator, Adam stepped into Turk's room. Turk finished placing a chest tube on the patient's left side and announced, "Ready to go."

Once the tube was secured, Barnett and Holiday swung the cart into the hall. Barnett looked at Adam as the cart began to move.

"I haven't had a chance to look at the textbook or my notes."

"We're fucked," agreed Adam, unsure if Barnett even heard him as the cart sped down the hall.

Adam wasn't sure if he should have followed one of the carts to the operating rooms. No one had given him any instructions. The trauma rooms were in disarray. Equipment wrappers, unused gauze, blood-soaked towels, and the patients' clothing littered the floors. Some of the discarded items even spilled out into the halls. He and Turk helped the nurses clean up so that at least two of the rooms were ready to receive patients again.

They had barely finished when the doors swung open and another ambulance cart rolled in and the attendants were directed to the closest clean trauma room. A young Hispanic man sat bolt upright on the gurney. His skin was ashen. He was gasping for each breath. His face reflected the anxiety that indicated he was not getting enough air despite his labored attempt at deep breathing.

The left side of his short-sleeved shirt was bloodstained, and when the shirt was unbuttoned and removed, a stab wound was visible next to the breastbone, between the fifth and sixth ribs on the left side of the patient's chest. Adam judged it was between an inch and an inch and a half in length when he sealed the hole by slapping a piece of Vaseline gauze over the wound.

The patient's shoes and pants had not yet been removed. He remained insistent upon sitting up while he struggled to breathe. One IV was inserted in his right arm and his blood drawn. An oxygen mask was placed over his nose and mouth. With the patient still upright, Turk prepped the left chest and inserted a chest tube far lateral to the actual stab wound.

For a moment the patient appeared to breathe easier.

"Blood pressure is up from 60 to 80 with the tube in," reported the nurse.

Turk secured the tube with sutures and attached it to the bubbling suction trap hanging on the side of the cart, making the patient comfortable enough to lie back, although the head of the cart was still elevated at a 45-degree angle.

"I need to intubate him," said Turk as the patient leaned back against the head of the cart, closed his eyes, and became unresponsive.

Carlos was ready with all the necessary supplies. With the table flat, Turk placed a lighted laryngoscope into the patient's mouth and inserted an endotracheal tube just as the respiratory therapist arrived in the room. Turk taped the tube in place and turned the crank on the cart, again elevating the head of the bed to 45 degrees.

"Blood pressure down again…60," said the nurse.

Turk looked closely at the patient's neck and then placed his stethoscope just above the gauze covering the stab wound. Adam looked at the patient's neck and mimicked Turk's moves with his stethoscope.

"Do you see it?" Turk said. "Neck veins are markedly distended… Full all the way up to the jaw… Can barely hear any heart sounds. He's got a pericardial tamponade."

Blood from the stab wound filling the pericardial sac, recalled Adam.

A few days earlier, the effects of tamponade had been a confusing abstraction described by the lecturer and in the pages of the textbook.

"His pressure is 60," said the nurse.

The patient momentarily opened his eyes. The terrified and anxious look returned to his face.

"Do I need to check for pulsus paradoxus?" asked Adam, remembering the textbook.

"You can if you want," said Turk, "but the diagnosis is pretty obvious… I need a big syringe, cardiac needle, and some bulldog clips on EKG wires."

Carlos readied the equipment while Turk flattened the head of the bed, again poured betadine antiseptic onto the patient's chest, and put on a pair of sterile gloves. He placed sterile towels around the lower chest and upper abdomen where he had spread the antiseptic.

"Call upstairs and see if anybody is available to get this patient to the OR," he said.

He took the large syringe from Carlos and attached a bulldog clip and its EKG lead to the long cardiac needle. He looked up at the monitor.

"Other leads in place?"

Turk's hand shook as he felt along the lower part of the patient's breastbone. Steadying his left hand on the sternum, he guided the long needle under the bone and pushed it into the chest. Adam watched him carefully and was looking at the EKG tracing when the T-wave jumped upwards.

"Through the pericardial sac, tickling the heart muscle," said Turk.

He slowly began to pull the needle back, aspirating the syringe. A sudden rush of blood filled all 50 cc's of space in the barrel of the syringe.

"Blood pressure?"

"Back to 90," said the nurse.

The patient opened his eyes and struggled a bit at the discomfort of having a tube down his trachea. The respiratory therapist used one hand to steady the endotracheal tube while his other hand continued to squeeze the bag that forced oxygen into the man's lungs.

Only when the patient opened his panicked eyes wider and tried to sit up did Adam realize that the nurses had strapped the man's arms down to the cart. His shoes had been removed. His pant legs and under shorts had been cut open but remained spread beneath him.

"What's the word from the OR?" Turk asked with urgency in his voice.

"They're all tied up, nothing available for a while. Everyone is scrubbed."

"Did they say how long?" Turk asked.

"No," said the nurse, "the circulator couldn't stay on the phone long, sounded pretty hectic up there."

Turk paused. Adam wondered if he was thinking about how to stabilize the patient until one of the senior residents could open the chest in the OR.

The patient continued to buck and pull against the restraints but then suddenly went limp, losing consciousness again.

The nurse responded quickly and called out, "BP down to 50."

"I need a thoracotomy tray," said Turk.

Adam turned to see Carlos already unwrapping the instruments on a nearby table.

"Gloves, gowns, and masks. No time to scrub," said Turk.

He emptied a bottle of betadine over the man's entire chest.

One of the nurses handed Adam a surgical mask. While he put the mask on, she opened a sterile gown and gloves. Adam slipped on the gown and gloves as he had been taught, careful to maintain their sterility.

Turk dressed as well. He placed sterile towels as a perimeter around the chest. He reached for the light blue paper sheet that Carlos had partly unwrapped and offered one edge to Adam so that they could unfold the drape and place it over the patient's lower body just as they would have done in the operating room. Turk turned to the instrument tray and slid the scalpel blade into its handle. He rearranged the other instruments on the tray so they were within easy reach.

"Keep bagging him," he instructed the respiratory therapist. "Somebody make sure we have vascular suture and pledgets. I'm going to need a rib spreader."

Carlos wheeled a spotlight over the field. Its curved metal reflector and central bulb looked like a smaller version of the overhead light in an operating room.

When Carlos plugged in the light, brightness filled the room. He adjusted the fixture so that its illumination was intensely focused on the patient's chest.

The rest of the room dropped away. As he stared at the stab wound, Adam's peripheral vision became a blur. He was aware of others in the room, but they were reduced to slow-moving, silent shadows. A sense of calmness from Turk was transferred to Adam, and time seemed suspended from the moment Turk's blade touched the patient's skin and moved in one long, deliberate motion between two ribs to create an incision in the patient's left chest just above the site of the stab wound.

Adam's focus sharpened on the operative field and he noted every detail. The incision that passed through the skin and intercostal muscles was well-defined, leaving intact only the thin layer of pleura that lined the interior of the chest cavity. Turk used the blade to create a small opening in the pleura and then inserted the blades of a scissors to slide along the thin membrane and reveal a glimpse of the pink surface of the lung, moving with each ventilating squeeze from the therapist.

"I'll need the rib spreader," said Turk.

Carlos unwrapped the Finochietto retractor and held the paper wrap while Turk lifted the instrument into the field. It consisted of a long, serrated stainless steel bar with two bladed arms. The blades were bent to fit snugly against the ribs.

"Help me with this," Turk said to Adam. "I'll steady the blades against the ribs, you turn the crank."

Adam grabbed the handle on one of the arms and began turning it after Turk had positioned the blades in the incision. Adam made circles with the lever. The blades caught the ribs and then spread them apart with each successive turn, giving a clearer view of the lungs and then exposing the patient's beating heart.

The pericardial sac around the heart was invested with yellow fat, but Adam could clearly see the dark line of the stab wound and the blue discoloration of what appeared to be a surrounding bruise.

Turk's hands moved methodically and without hesitation. He took a scissors and pick-ups from the tray. He pinched the yellow tissue around the heart, pulled up on it, and cut it, releasing a gush of blood. He cut further, peeling back the edges of the sac until Adam could clearly see the site of injury in the red-purple heart muscle, a one-inch slit with edges abutting each other. It looked almost insignificant, but with each beat a squirt of blood popped through the cut.

Turk placed a piece of moist gauze over the hole in the heart.

"Keep your fingers here with gentle pressure so the wound is sealed... Won't do well if air gets sucked into his bloodstream... Brain doesn't like bubbles."

Adam placed his fingers on the moist gauze. Turk loaded the blue strand of vascular suture onto his needle holder.

"Do we have pledgets?" he asked.

"None down here," said the nurse.

"Gotta have them on the suture or they tear right through the heart muscle," he said.

Carlos rummaged through the cabinet, pulling out a package containing a narrow white tube.

"How about this?" he said. "One of the other services left this dialysis graft down here the other day. It's still sealed and sterile."

"Open it and drop it on my tray. I'll cut the pledgets from it," said Turk.

Adam closed his eyes and felt the heart beat beneath his fingertips. Although the heart was beating rapidly, Adam held his breath as he waited and hoped to feel each next beat under his fingers.

Turk cut small pieces from the graft, squares of about a centimeter apiece. Adam opened his eyes to witness the single movement of Turk's wrist that smoothly pushed the needle through the piece of graft. The little square slid along the suture and remained suspended while the needle entered the heart muscle and exited on the other side of the laceration. Another flick of the wrist and a second piece of graft slipped along the suture. The needle holder was set down while the suture was tied, leaving the bolsters of graft snug against the heart muscle on each side of the laceration. Three more sutures were placed, each bringing the edges of the laceration together until no further spurt of blood occurred with each heartbeat.

"Another angled chest tube, please." He placed the bent tube over the diaphragm after creating an opening for it in the lower left chest. A third, smaller tube was placed through an incision that exited in the upper abdomen and was directed so it lay closer to the heart.

All the while, Adam watched the heart as it continued to fill with blood and empty in a strong, regular beat.

Still the room remained out of focus, and everyone moved in slow motion as the tubes were sutured in place and the rib spreading retractor removed.

"We don't close the pericardial sac," said Turk, "so no more fluid can collect around the heart."

Adam watched the heart continue to beat while Turk placed sutures on a wide needle around the ribs to pull them together. Adam's view of the heart disappeared when Turk tied the sutures and then closed the intercostal muscles between the ribs with a long absorbable suture placed over and over along the length and tied at the end.

Turk handed Adam a silk suture on a straight needle and opened one for himself.

"Let's get the skin closed as fast as we can," he said.

Adam stuck the skin to place his first stitch and was startled when the patient jumped in response. Adam stepped back and looked at him. His eyes were wide open.

"BP back up to 90," said the nurse.

"Better give us some local anesthetic for the skin," Turk said. "One or two percent xylocaine will do."

Adam was jolted back to reality when the patient began kicking frantically while the anesthetic was injected into his skin. The ER was again noisy.

"I got it!" announced Carlos, throwing his full weight across the patient's lower legs. The nurses each grabbed an arm to make sure the restraining straps held against the young man's attempts to forcibly flex his way out of them. The respiratory therapist pushed his forearm onto the patient's forehead and continued to pump oxygen into his lungs.

Adam moved along, placing each stitch in the skin with a speed and accuracy that he had not known before. He was placing his final skin stitch when he heard a familiar voice.

"You guys OK here?" Rogers asked from the doorway. "Whatcha got?"

"Stab wound to the right ventricle with tamponade," Turk answered. "We're OK here."

"I'll call for an ICU bed," said Rogers. "Wantz and Kochenko are checking out two other gunshot wounds. ER said they're in the extremities, so maybe no trip to the OR. Later."

Adam took a step back and watched Turk place dressings on the chest tubes and tape large gauze pads over the incision. He looked at the clock. It was 5:15 in the morning. He was left with only a couple of hours until the exam. His pulse was still racing when he stepped into the hall to look for Barnett and Shrevi.

Adam looked back into the trauma room as Turk plopped down onto the metal stool in the corner. He pushed his head back against the wall and used the sleeve of his gown to wipe the sweat from his face. He focused his eyes on the EKG monitor and watched the regular pattern of the heartbeat for a few moments before he took in a few slow, deep breaths and buried his face in his hands.

CHAPTER 96

BY TEN MINUTES to six o'clock, rays of sunlight were entering the Recovery Room through its tall windows. Adam returned from changing Luanne's dressing for the final time. She had slept through the change and therefore didn't notice the care with which he placed her new bandages so that they would be secure and satisfactory when the residents removed them in the operating room. As tired as he was, he could not tolerate any sloppiness.

The nursing staff was quite busy caring for all the arrivals from the night's work in the OR. Adam walked to the coffee pot in the nurses' station. The heating element had been turned off but there remained enough to fill about a third of a Styrofoam cup. He sipped the tepid, bitter brew as he met Barnett at the nurses' desk and wished that there was time to shower before their exam.

Barnett was exhausted and uncharacteristically ungroomed as well. The stubble of a beard covered his chin and a blond cowlick protruded upwards from the back of his head. Shrevi joined them. The bags under his eyes were so puffy that Adam wasn't sure where his friend's cheekbones began.

The students stood in silence for a moment and surveyed the unit. Holiday stood at the foot of the bed of the gunshot wound he had taken to the operating room. Rogers, Kittamura, and Doyle were crowded around him as they discussed the severity of a high caliber wound to the right lobe of the liver. Holiday always seemed older than the rest of those on service, but that morning he looked as though he had aged even more overnight. Doyle's face was drawn, his puffy eyes edged by dark circles. The homemade scrub cap, usually a spark of humor, was tucked into his back pocket. His brow was furrowed in concern as he and Holiday discussed the large amount of green drainage that soaked the patient's dressings.

Wantz was checking the patient two beds down from the liver wound. His uncombed hair stuck out like wings from the side of his head and the left leg of his scrub pants was splattered with blood up to his knee. Turk quietly watched the EKG monitor of the patient with the cardiac stab wound he had closed in the ER. The patient had been moved to Recovery since no ICU beds were available.

"By the time they get these patients transferred to ICU, there won't be room in that unit for any other services' patients," observed Barnett. "Really quite a night… Apart from the guy with the bad burn, it's amazing that nobody else died."

"Yeah," agreed Shrevi, "but that guy of Holiday's with all the bile drained on his dressing may not last. Top of the liver was really chewed up. He had bleeding from the vena cava behind the liver. Holiday controlled all the bleeding and debrided the liver, but the guy's got a huge raw surface that must be where the bile is coming from."

"Our exam starts in three hours," said Barnett. "Don't know if I have the strength to hold a pencil."

"I've never felt so poorly prepared for a test," said Adam, "particularly one this important… All the marbles for the block are riding on it."

Shrevi put things in perspective. "Relax, guys, we've just got to sharpen our pencils and say, 'What the fuck!' Only way to get through it. Look at the bright side. We'll be done by noon."

Kochenko walked over to them. "The chief is coming for rounds. Wants to see the patients from last night. He should be here in a few minutes."

"But we haven't even seen our patients on the wards yet," said Adam.

"Don't worry about that. Last day on the service. We'll make sure you get to your exam in time."

∿

Dr. Theodorakis soon arrived, looking composed and enviably well-rested but oddly unaccompanied by his usual entourage of residents and students.

"Before we begin, I want you all to know that Miss Viola has requested that we attend her uncle's funeral tomorrow. Students as well. There are armbands here that will serve to get you into the church."

He handed a large manila envelope to Kochenko, who opened it and pulled out a black armband decorated with a small plastic trumpet pin before he passed the envelope around so everyone could help themselves to an armband.

Rounds started with the patient in the first bed, and Theodorakis directed his questions to the residents, focusing on each patient's injury, what was done in the operating room, and how stable they were at present.

Adam found it hard to focus as they moved from bed to bed and the questions and reports droned on. By the time they stopped at the bed of Holiday's gunshot patient, Adam could barely stay awake while Theodorakis discussed how the bile leakage should seal and stop with proper management.

Finally, they arrived at the bed of the last patient. The stab wound to the heart had been extubated. He lay comfortably with his eyes closed, a misting high humidity oxygen mask hanging from his neck and resting on his upper chest in front of his nose and mouth.

The service crowded together and lined up around the bed. Holiday stood at the head of the bed on the patient's right. Turk stood next to him and Kochenko next to Turk. Doyle was on the patient's left across from Holiday, with Rogers and then Wantz standing next to him. Kittamura stepped to the side near the foot of the bed so that Dr. Theodorakis could approach. The three bedraggled medical students crowded behind Kochenko.

Holiday began to present the case.

"Stab wound, left lower chest… Hypotensive with findings of tamponade… Responded initially to needle pericardiocentesis but then re-tamponaded… Thoracotomy and repair of cardiac laceration were then performed in the Emergency Room."

Theodorakis listened intently to the presentation. Afterward, he studied the patient's cardiac monitor before turning his gaze to Holiday.

"Nice case, Tom," he said softly.

"Not mine, sir," responded Holiday.

The chief turned to Doyle. "Nice case, Bobby."

"Not mine, sir."

He looked at both Kittamura and Rogers, who shook their heads to indicate they weren't involved.

"Well, who did this case?" asked the chairman.

"I did, sir," Turk quietly responded.

Dr. Theodorakis paused. He looked at the monitor and then at the young man resting comfortably in the bed.

"Who assisted?" he asked, his eyes scanning each of the more senior residents as he waited for a response.

Adam heard the question, but it didn't register through the fog that clouded his brain and the fatigue that weakened his every muscle. He heard Theodorakis's voice again.

"Who assisted?"

The sharp stab of Barnett's elbow in his back awakened Adam's attention.

"I did, sir," he was able to answer.

Dr. Theodorakis looked at the student for a moment and then back to the EKG monitor. He surveyed the patient from head to toe, then pulled back the covers and exposed the patient's dressing. He lifted a corner of the dressing so that he could see the incision and then knelt by the bedside and examined the bubbling in the chamber attached to the patient's chest tubes.

When he stood up, he again stared at the patient's monitor. Everyone waited an eternity for him to speak. He only addressed one of them—Turk.

"It has come to my attention that the department will not be able to fund your research project next year. If you have no objection, you will have to move on to the third year of clinical rotations. Please stop by my office next week to have Miss Viola set up your schedule. Make sure she knows I want you to begin on Service 1."

"Thank you, Sir, I'd like that very much," the soft-spoken Turk replied.

No one moved or spoke. He looked back and forth from Turk to Adam and then back again. He nodded his head and stepped towards the doorway. He paused and looked back.

"Nice case," he said.

They stood in silence until Holiday placed his right hand on Turk's left shoulder. He leaned in and whispered in Turk's ear. "He wants you on his service so he can scrub with you and show you a few tips."

Doyle reached across the bed to shake Turk's hand. Wantz smiled and nodded affirmatively before turning to leave. Rogers followed Doyle in reaching over to shake Turk's hand before they both followed Wantz out of the ward. Kochenko lightly punched his friend's arm before he left with a thumbs up sign and a broad grin. Holiday finished whatever he was saying and left the ward with his arm around Turk's shoulder. And Kittamura stood at the foot of the bed and smiled.

Chapter 97

"**Rule of nines,**" said Shrevi. "Probably got to know it for the test."

He passed around his textbook, open to the page with the diagram that served as the guide to estimating the percentage of body surface involved in a burn.

"We need the Brooke formula for fluid replacement in burns too," said Barnett. "It's a couple of pages later in the chapter."

Adam thumbed through the textbook chapter and passed the book back to Shrevi. He had committed those formulas to memory but reviewed them anyway as they sat in the cafeteria drinking big cups of coffee before leaving for the exam. Other students who had been on the Surgery block were waiting in the cafeteria. Some of them appeared haggard and had probably been up most, if not all, of the night studying, but no one appeared as unkempt as the three students from Service 1.

"Time to go," said Barnett, the first to rise from his seat. He and Shrevi joined Adam in refilling their coffee cups before walking to the elevator. They rode in silence until the doors opened and they entered the lecture hall.

"We'll do OK if we can just stay awake," reiterated Shrevi before they took their seats.

They sat in silence after placing their book bags under their chairs, surrounded by a roomful of over-caffeinated, apprehensive classmates either tightly clutching their number two pencils or chewing the paint and erasers off the ends. The tension only dissipated when the exam booklets were distributed and the seals broken. A quiet shuffling of paper broke the stillness as they began the test.

Adam relaxed when the first question was exactly as Wantz and Kochenko had predicted:

1. The congenital defect Tetralogy of Fallot includes:
a) ventricular septal defect
b) pulmonary stenosis
c) right ventricular hypertrophy
d) overriding of the aorta
e) all of the above

He marked "e," took a breath, and moved on to the next question:

2. A patient involved in an industrial accident sustains severe burns to all of his back to his waistline, and the entire left arm. This would account for what percentage of his body surface?

Adam remembered the diagram of the rule of nines. He marked the answer: c) 27%.

The next question applied the Brooke formula to the fluid resuscitation of the same patient. *So far, so good... Just stay focused.* He continued:

4. In cases of cholangitis, the addition of which two features change the diagnostic features of Charcot's Triad to Reynold's Pentad?

He didn't have to read that question twice. A second wind like a strong gust across Lake Pontchartrain gave him a burst of energy better than any espresso or café au lait. He ignored thinking about his lecture notes or textbook. Instead, he visualized the image of Sam Elder on the day he was admitted—unresponsive with yellow eyes, fever, tenderness in the right upper abdomen—and Turk, standing at the bedside giving IV fluids and medicine to raise his blood pressure: d) altered mental status and hypotension.

Adam began to relax, smiling to himself as each question brought him back to a patient he had seen.

32. Venous leg ulcers are managed by:

b) elevation, control of infection, and compression wraps

39. Metastatic breast cancer may respond to eliminating the stimulating effect of which hormone?

c) estrogen

46. Allowing an open wound to close slowly represents healing by the process of:

b) secondary intention

Bless you, Luanne, he thought, smiling as he confidently answered the question that described the large wound to which he had devoted so much time.

They met in the hallway after the exam.

"Not as bad as I expected," said Barnett.

"I told you not to worry," said Shrevi. "I'm heading home to shower and get some sleep so I can go to the Maple Leaf tonight. What're you guys planning?"

"We're going out to the lake for lunch, probably going to take my wife and baby to Fitzgerald's. You guys are welcome to join us."

"After the past six weeks, I'm sure Jane would much prefer just your company to ours," said Adam.

"Definitely," agreed Shrevi. "We want to be welcomed to dinner again sometime. What are you going to do, Adam?"

"Sleep. But I'm going over to the hospital first. I want to see how my friend Luanne is doing. Want to see how she's looking after they closed her wound. Are you going to the funeral tomorrow? I heard they don't expect me to start Psychiatry until Wednesday."

"I got Peds starting Wednesday too," said Shrevi. "I think they gave us the extra day because everybody cuts out to see the second line. Heard they cancelled lecture for the first and second year classes 'cause nobody is going to show up on the day of a jazz funeral."

"I heard that too," said Barnett. "I start Internal Medicine on Wednesday."

"Woo," said Shrevi, "don't know if that's out of the frying pan and into the fire or out of the fire and into the frying pan. Either way, that's another tough rotation."

Barnett shrugged. "At least I've got a little time to rest and recuperate. See you at the church."

THE CAB DRIVER was forced to drop Adam off three blocks from the Mount Mercy First Christian Missionary Baptist Church because he couldn't get past the crowd of mourners filling the streets. Bunkie's neighborhood was overflowing with people whose behavior and dress was more suited to a Mardi Gras parade than a funeral. Some were dressed in bright colors, some carried decorated broomsticks or parasols. Many had cameras slung around their necks. They lined the street corners, waiting for the neighborhood bars to open, or spilled back onto the streets after finding a tavern that had opened early.

Adam walked through the neighborhood of modest but well-kept shotgun houses, most of which had trim painted in brilliant colors. He met Barnett and Shrevi outside the small frame church that glistened under a fresh coat of white paint.

Ushers in black suits and sunglasses stood on either side of the front door. When they saw the armbands, they allowed the students to enter the already crowded church. A section of well-maintained, shiny wooden pews on the left side had been reserved for them. Kochenko, Turk, and Rogers were already in their seats a few rows back from the front row, where Dr. Theodorakis, Holiday, and Doyle sat with Miss Viola, her brother, her children, and her cousins. The front pews on the right were filled with dignitaries. The mayor and a few city councilmen, a state senator, and the lieutenant governor stood and talked. The remaining seats in the front pew were occupied by Allen Toussaint, Professor Longhair, Alan Jaffe, Art Neville, and Dr. John, who had traded his usual outfit of glaring colors for a dark suit with a purple cravat that matched the hue of the feather in the brim of his black top hat. In the row behind them sat several of the musicians from Preservation Hall along with the other Neville brothers. Aaron wore a black velvet waistcoat and black shirt with a bolo tie, while the other brothers wore African prints in muted, dark colors. One wore a dark beret while the other added the colors of a traditional Kufi cap. Ellis Marsalis and his boys sat in the next row.

At the front of the sanctuary, Bunkie rested in a lavender casket framed by lilacs. His battered old trumpet was nestled in his arms. The entire altar was covered with floral arrangements that surrounded the pulpit and extended onto the floor.

The service began promptly at 9:30. A gospel choir sang hymns, and the pastor made his remarks before Miss Viola and her brother spoke about how Bunkie had been like a father to them. Bunkie's children spoke too, exhorting Gabriel to move over because Bunkie was now in Heaven. The most moving tribute came from Luther, an old man who had been Bunkie's childhood friend and touring drummer for many years.

"They's lots of people who plays the trumpet," he said. "Lots of talent and skill. But most times, that talent, that skill don't mean nothin' if you ain't got a good and pure heart. Me and Bunkie traveled the world together, and what made Bunkie stand out was that, whether we was in London, France, Russia, Ghana, New York City, the Philippines, or at home here in New Orleans, he put his heart and soul into that horn, and people saw it and it spoke to them no matter what their language. Bunkie's music let them know he cared, and they always got his best…"

He tried to say more. He paused, visibly shaken, seeking the words, but finally all he said was, "I'll miss you, brother."

The pastor took his arm and helped the old man towards the steps, where several musicians, including fellow drummer Zigaboo Modeliste, met him and helped him down the stairs to his seat.

Following the final notes sung by the choir, Bunkie's casket was closed and rolled on a cart to the center aisle of the church. Before the mourners could begin filing out, the doors opened and a dignified man stepped into the church. He was an older gentleman, bald with a rim of white hair at the back of his head and bushy white sideburns. He wore a black tuxedo with tails and polished black shoes that gleamed when their surface reflected the overhead lights. He carried a black top hat in his left hand and a long golden scepter in his right. A dark banner edged in purple was draped across his chest and his big belly. Amidst the silver decorations on his black sash, letters spelled out "GRAND MARSHAL."

On the street, the back of the white hearse had been opened. The members of a brass band in black trousers, white short-sleeved shirts, and white caps with black visors moved back and away from the open doors.. A little boy, dressed identically to the band members, stood with them. He appeared to be five or six years of age. He held a trombone scaled down to his size.

The Grand Marshal turned and slowly exited the church. Then the band members lined up behind him before the pallbearers began to move Bunkie's casket forward. Each pew emptied, and the mourners fell in line in an orderly fashion. Miss Viola carried Bunkie's spare trumpet close to her chest as she walked directly behind the casket.

When the students stepped out of the church, their eyes adjusted to the sunlight. The streets were filled with people as far as they could see. It seemed the whole city had turned out for Bunkie's send-off.

The ushers placed the students and residents in line behind the family. The Grand Marshal began the procession, stepping from one side of the street to the other and pausing between steps to set the pace while the band played "Just a Closer Walk with Thee."

The band continued to play spiritual dirges until the group reached the cemetery six blocks away. Police barricades were up to keep the crowds out, but the armbands allowed the members of Service 1 to enter the cemetery. The pastor led the crowd in reciting the Lord's Prayer, and Bunkie was interred in the family crypt that rose above ground like a small Roman temple.

As the procession left the cemetery, the barriers came down and the crowd mingled with the mourners while the band continued with a slow version of "How Sweet Thou Art" for another two blocks. When they finished, the Grand Marshal turned to face the marchers. Their pace slowed until he raised his arms and signaled the drummer to begin a spirited second line beat, and the band broke into "Oh Didn't He Ramble."

Parasols, scarves, white hankies, and colorful bandanas came out, and the crowd began to pulsate in all directions as they moved along the street and sidewalk. The infectious rhythm turned into dancing. Adam found himself moving in time and noticed the familiar faces of many students and faculty as they joined the crowd. Behind the band, Miss Viola lifted Bunkie's second trumpet and waved it high over her head as she swayed to the music. Adam looked to his right to see Shrevi grab two girls from the freshman class, still in their white coats, by the hands and dance them into the crowd.

By the time they returned to the church, the funeral parade had broken up. Crowds filled every street corner bar to avoid the heat from the blazing sun. Adam turned to see that Barnett had been joined on the sidewalk by his wife and baby. He was awkwardly adjusting the strap on a baby carrier that looked to Adam like some kind of backward harness for a papoose. When Adam approached, Jane handed him a cold can of Dixie and popped the top on another one for Barnett.

They stood watching the band disperse, most of the members congregating near two station wagons parked near the side of the church with beer coolers resting on the open backs. Adam watched them set down their instruments and pass out chilled cans. He again noticed the little boy with the mini trombone standing near the curb. Miss Viola walked over and knelt down by the child. They spoke for a moment and then she kissed his forehead and handed him Bunkie's trumpet. She stood and walked away, leaving the horn in the little boy's possession.

Kochenko appeared next to the students. He was wearing his aviator glasses with darkened lenses.

"That's the way it's done, you know," he said. "One generation masters it and then they teach the skill to the next to keep learning and improving on before they pass it on. Heck, that's why they call it going into practice. See you guys around the hospital."

He disappeared into the remaining crowd. Adam looked over as Barnett was adjusting his daughter's sunbonnet while she sat in the baby carrier on his chest. He looked back at Adam and asked, "Was he talking about music?"

CHAPTER 99

ADAM DIDN'T HAVE to report to his Psychiatry rotation until 10 a.m., so he was unusually well-rested when he rode the elevator up to the Department of Surgery office that morning. He opened the door to find Miss Viola seated at her desk.

"Hi, I'm…"

"Sinclair," she said. "The grades from the exam won't be posted until later today, but I heard your group did quite well if that's what you want to know… If not, what brings you by?"

"I picked this up at the newsstand and didn't know if you had a copy."

He handed her the obituary from the *New York Times*, and she spread it out on her desk.

"Thank you. I hadn't seen this… Got a copy of that picture at home somewhere."

He reached into the pocket of his white coat and placed the wire sculpture of the trumpeter on her desk. She picked it up and silently turned it over in her hands.

"I saw this in the French Market. I thought you might like it. Kinda reminded me of your uncle."

"Why, thank you. I've got the perfect spot for it right here on my desk."

She placed it next to the picture frame on the far-right corner. "It will go well with this," she said, turning the frame towards Adam.

The image was at once familiar and different. Adam thought it was obviously taken at the same photo session and angle as the well-known Preservation Hall postcard. In this picture, Bunkie was no longer seated. He stood in front of his chair, horn pointed towards the ceiling, the mouthpiece held against his puffed-out cheeks.

She turned the picture around and looked at it as she arranged the tiny sculpture next to it.

Adam started for the door but stopped and turned back towards her.

"Miss Viola, I've got a favor to ask... I want to sign up for Surgery as the first elective of my senior year. Could you make sure I get assigned to Service 1?"

She placed her arms on the desk in front of her, leaned forward, grinned, and winked.

"Dr. Sinclair, I'll see what I can do."

Charity Hospital
1736-2005